Essarai

Book 1 of the Drasana Series

DeeAnn and Zachary Fuchs

And so the first stone along the path has been set and a dream, however small, has in part become a reality. Thanks to our readers, Hannah, Kelsey, Josh, & Pat for their willingness to provide insight on our storyline and to Scott, Lauren & Nate for giving us productive feedback that helped keep the momentum going.

To my co-author and mother whose toil, passion, and patience made this book possible, I am forever in your debt. Zach

For my son and co-author Zach, whose imagination took us on this incredible journey. DeeAnn

RULE ONE
AN ESSENCE READER MAY ENTER THE ESSENCE OF
ANOTHER WHO IS NOT A READER. HE MAY ENTER
UNDETECTED AND READ THIS PERSONS ESSENCE. HE
CAN READ THEIR EMOTIONS, MEMORIES AND THOUGHTS.
HE CAN COMMUNICATE WITH THEM TELEPATHICALLY.

RULE TWO
WHEN AN ESSENCE READER IS INSIDE THE ESSENCE OF
A NON-READER HE MAY ALTER THE EMOTIONS, MEMORIES
AND THOUGHTS OF THE NON-READER'S ESSENCE. HE
MAY ALSO ENTER ANOTHER ESSENCE FORCEFULLY. THIS
WILL LET HIM CONTROL THEIR PHYSICAL BEING. AS SOON
AS HE RELEASES THE ESSENCE THEY WILL REGAIN
CONTROL OF THEIR BODY.

RULE THREE
EVERY ESSENCE-TOUCHED HAS THE ABILITY FROM BIRTH
TO TAKE A LOST ESSENCE BEFORE IT TRAVELS TO THE
SPIRIT REALM. HE CAN CAPTURE THIS ESSENCE AND USE
IT TO STRENGTHEN OR RESTORE HIS ESSENCE FOR A
PERIOD OF TIME. A LOST ESSENCE IS ALWAYS SEEKING
THE SPIRIT REALM AND IT DISSIPATES TO NOTHING IF IT IS
KEPT FROM THE REALM.

RULE FOUR
AN ESSENCE READER MUST NEVER TAKE THE ESSENCE
OF ANOTHER ESSENCE-TOUCHED BE HE HERETIC,
STUDENT OR READER FOR IT WILL DESTROY HIM. HE
MUST NEVER ATTEMPT TO ABSORB THE ESSENCE OF A
WITCH OR HE WILL MEET DEATH INSTANTLY.

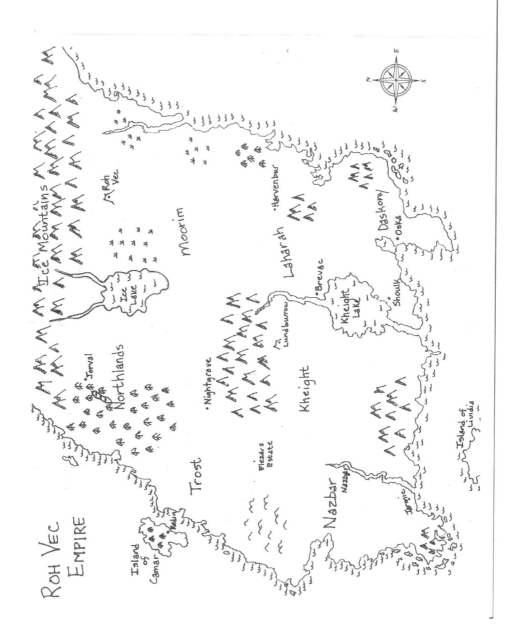

Essarai

Prologue

The tower room was cold, the stone walls damp with moisture. The air was stale and smelled of old blood, the feeling of fear so thick the man could almost taste it. Today was a pivotal day in his life and he was nervous, a feeling he wasn't used to. Weakness of any kind had to be purged from the body and he took a calming breath and forced his heartbeat to slow, his hands to stay still. He opened his mind and took in everything around him; the sounds of water dripping in the distance, a rats claws scrabbling against the rough stone floor, the other heartbeats that were present. His eyes had already adjusted to the dim light of the glowing red stones that gave off no smoke, just a blood red sheen that glimmered off the walls. Calmer now, he stood in the center of the room, waiting. His robe was the same deep red color as the stones, the hood shadowing his face. He stood motionless, power radiating from his body. Three men in black robes stood unmoving behind him, their power burning as strongly as his. They were essence readers, the elite of the Roh Vec Empire. Today he would earn his black robe and join them.

A side door opened out of the stone wall, and a single man entered carrying two oil lamps which he hung from small hooks on the ceiling increasing the light in the room slightly. Three more men entered following the first, walking carefully in the dim light. They wore fine leather armor and short swords; each led a bound woman. Two of the women were young, in their late teens, and the other was clearly their mother. They were pushed to their knees before the man in red and held in place by the guards. They stank of sweat, but far stronger to the man in red was their smell of fear. The guards were afraid of him as well, although they tried to hide it as they looked straight ahead, avoiding eye contact with him.

"*Are you ready?*" a voice asked him telepathically. It came from one of the black robed men behind him.

"*I am,*" he replied silently.

"*Begin.*"

He stepped forward to the youngest girl on the right. Her fear escalated, she could not look away and as he leaned close she began to shake uncontrollably. Suddenly recognition came to her eyes as she saw his face in the lamp light. Yes, she knew him, just as he knew her. She spoke a name, his name, a name he no longer recognized as his own.

He reached into her mind making sure to stay undetected. She was still afraid of him, but she was also hopeful that he might help her. He read these emotions no longer than he deemed necessary for the hooded men to understand that he was capable of doing it. Next he read her memories; at the moment they were of her playing with him as a boy. Finally he read her thoughts; *"Why are you here brother? Are you going to help us? Tevarian please speak to me!"*

He brought himself away from her mind and back fully into the physical world. He was still leaning over the kneeling girl who was looking at him with pleading eyes. He looked back at her with a face as cold as the stone walls. He drew a small iron dagger from within his robes and without hesitation, pierced it straight through her heart. One small jerk and it slid in easily; then he watched as her eyes looked into his with confusion as the life slowly drained from her. He withdrew the knife and her guard released his hold allowing her body to topple forward, her head hitting loudly on the ground, her blood already pooling out. He watched as her essence escaped from her body and floated toward the spirit realm. The mother cried out once, just once and then looked away. The other young woman screamed, first in fear, then in anger, but he ignored her. He turned and looked at the three men.

They nodded and said, *"Continue."*

He approached the next young woman, who was slightly older than the first. She spat at him and continued to scream, struggling against the guard's hold until the mother spoke to her. "Peace Elizabell, Tevarian is only doing what he must. Go with grace, I will be with you shortly, my daughter."

He leaned forward to the second girl, touched her defiant face and entered her mind undetected. Rather than simply reading her emotions as he had her sister, he altered them. One moment she was glaring at him in anger and the next, tears were coming down her face in sadness.

The memories were slightly more difficult. He had to reach in secretly and slip one of her memories away then change it and place it back in her mind. To alter the smaller memories was easy, but tampering with an important memory was often noticed.

Finally he took her mind by force and took control of her physical body. She struggled against him but though her will was strong she had no power to stop him. Overcoming her strength was simple, but he remained aware of her constant push as it slowly drained him.

Holding the dagger that was still sticky with her sister's blood he held it out to her; had her reach out and take it. He was the puppet master and she the puppet. Wasting no time he had her turn the dagger towards herself and thrust it into her own heart. She gave a quiet gasp then stiffened and he let her fall lifelessly into the pool of her sister's dark blood as her essence left her body. He stooped forward, retrieving the dagger, and once again turned, looking at the robed men.

Another slow nod, urging him to continue.

Now he stood before the mother, bloody dagger in hand .He held out the dagger and placed it to the mother's throat, leaned forward and looked her in the eye. She no longer smelt of fear as she did when she came in.

"Tevarian, my son," she whispered, tears in her eyes. "I know you will succeed and make us proud. I love you and I forgive you."

He drew the knife across her throat and blood came gushing out, spattering on the sleeve of his robe. A gurgling sound came from her throat as if she was trying to say something but she never looked away. Eventually her eyes rolled inwards and she too collapsed to the floor. He watched as the woman who had raised him to a boy of twelve years died; slain by his own hand. Her essence floated out of her like her daughters, but this time he reached out and stopped it from leaving.

He pulled in his mother's essence as if taking a deep breath of air. Immediately the fatigue that he felt from controlling the second girl washed away, and he felt stronger within, more powerful. He knew her essence would never travel to the spirit realm. She would never reunite with her daughters. She would never rest peacefully in the realm for the fallen. This was why people feared the essence readers above all else.

He turned to the three robed men behind him and waited. He remained empty. No emotion. No thought. No remorse for killing his own family. The other three essence readers had been in his mind throughout his ordeal, watching from within him. Now they left to confer amongst themselves, leaving him alone within himself. This

11

was the moment that they would decide his fate. After a short time, the three minds of the robed men reached out to him once again.

"*You have passed the three tests. You can perform three of the basic rules of the Book of Essence, and more importantly you have passed the test of loyalty. You are hereby granted the black robe of an essence reader*," they said simply.

He bowed before the three men and the middle one stepped forward carrying a black robe. He let his red robe fall to the floor, and the dim light revealed a pale young man in his early twenties. He was of average build, his body was well muscled. His face was clean shaven as was his head, hiding the dark brown hair that was similar to his mothers. He had multiple black tattoos covering his body, arms, and legs. They seemed to sway and shimmer in the blood red light of the glow rocks. They were artful symbols of different kinds; some flowed in circles while others were overlapping blocks. After he put on the black robe another of the readers came forward with a small bottle. Its content was a black liquid which the reader now rubbed on his forehead. Using his thumb he traced the shape of a triangle and when he had finished the young man felt a burning sensation where his thumb had been. Almost immediately a new tattoo appeared on his forehead, the first one anywhere on his shaved head. It was a simple triangle with a black book at its center, the symbol of an essence reader.

The three men stepped away and all bowed to him. "Welcome to the order, brother," each one said aloud. He placed his hood over his head and bowed in return.

He was an essence reader.

Chapter 1

Lily filled the last jar of honey and placed it on the table next to the herbs that she had already tied into bunches. Everything was nearly finished for market day tomorrow and she was ready for a much deserved rest. She stood by her table, a hot cup of tea in her hands and surveyed the small room, pleased with what she saw. The tall bottles of syrups and tinctures, the smaller jars of creams and ointments all filled and ready to be used in her healing were lined up neatly in the cupboard attached to the wall. Dried herbs and flowers hung from the rafters and would be used for making other herbal remedies when the cold weather brought on many ailments. The bright colors and scents also helped to remind her of the warmer days to come as she endured the wet, cold winter months.

She had been busy for weeks, rushing to harvest everything before the cooler weather hit. Tomorrow was the season's final market day in the nearby town of Redin and her last chance to trade for items that would have to last her over the winter. Although she kept much of the honey and herbs for her work, she had more than she needed and the extra she sold at the market. While in town she was also sometimes asked to help someone who was ill but most of the time she healed her friends and neighbors in the forest where she lived. She was drawn to it and seemed to have an innate ability to diagnose a problem and then choose the proper herbs to fix it.

She knew that her mother had been known for her healing abilities just like herself, because her father had told her as much. She also had been told that although her mother often used the herbs and simples that Lily herself used, her mother could also heal with just a touch. Lily discovered on her own, that she also had this power. It happened when she was twelve years old on the day that her brother Jon fell out of a tree and broke his leg.

She was working in the garden when she heard him scream. Dropping her tools she ran and found him lying at the base of the tall maple tree that grew near their house. Most girls her age would have turned away in horror at the shards of broken bone jutting through his skin and the blood that soaked his short pants. Lily, however, had run to him and tried to straighten his leg, carefully pushing the snapped bone down to meet with its other half. Jon had passed out and didn't witness his bone slowly growing back together, the torn skin closing over the once broken leg as Lily's hands touched it. She heard her father come up behind her and looked up to see him staring at her in dismay before she collapsed at his feet.

Later that evening her father told her about her mother's ability and in an angry voice that he rarely used, had made her promise not to ever tell anyone what she could do. He also made her promise not to use her power again, saying only that it wasn't safe. Jon had been so woozy from the fall that he didn't seem to remember much about the accident and neither she nor her father had told him how he had been healed. Her father never explained why she had to keep it a secret but he had left her feeling frightened by what she had done. Later, whenever she tried to bring the subject up he refused to say anything more, only reiterating that it wasn't safe. He died two years later and left her with all her unanswered questions. She continued to keep her promise to him but lately she had been wondering why, if she had such an ability, she should keep it a secret.

She sat down in the old rocker that had been in the house as long as she could remember and went over the list of items she wanted to trade for tomorrow. She didn't need a lot now that her brother was gone, but there were always a few things she couldn't make or grow herself.

Thinking of Jon always caused a well of mixed emotions in Lily. On the one hand she missed him badly, despite their far too frequent arguments. On the other hand, though, he hadn't liked farm work and spent too much time at the inn in town listening to stories of foreign places and drinking far too many pints of ale. He made friends with the wrong people and Lily had been afraid before he left that he would be spending time in jail if he didn't change his habits.

Even though they were only two years apart she had always felt much older than her brother. Their mother had died giving birth to Jon and their father had been too busy taking care of the farm and trying to keep them all fed to coddle his two young children. Their aunt Molly had helped but she had five children of her own and could only spare so much time for her niece and nephew. Lily had sometimes felt like she had had no childhood, only responsibilities.

14

She and Jon had been close as children but the years after her father died had been hard and their relationship had suffered as she tried to parent him and he resented it. She supposed it was inevitable since she was his sister not his mother but she really thought it was those stories of faraway places that finally prompted him to leave. He went off seeking adventures and she often wondered where he was now. Would he have left the island where they had both grown up? The Roh Vec Empire was a huge place and she hated to think of him wandering around it alone. He'd just turned seventeen when he left a year ago and although children grew up quickly on the island and shouldered responsibilities at a young age, she still worried about him. Despite their many quarrels she hoped he'd return one day, healthy and happier than when he left.

Jezebel the cat came winding around Lily's legs, interrupting her thoughts. "Are you hungry for your dinner, Jezzie? Aren't there enough mice in the shed to keep you full?" She gave the cat a small piece of cheese that she had saved from her earlier supper. Picking the ginger cat up she stroked her gently, glad for the company. What she wished for more than anything, though, was the company of her mother. She had few memories of her; the scent of lavender and soft hands tucking her into bed. What she wouldn't give to have a long conversation with her; to ask her all her unanswered questions.

Lily shook herself from her daydreaming as she heard someone calling her name.

"Lily, are you home?" came a woman's voice from just outside.

"I'm in the house Grandma Joan," Lily responded as she set the cat down and went to the door. Grandma Joan wasn't really her grandmother or anyone else's, for that matter, but everyone called her that. She had no family in the area and no one really knew much about her past. In the town she was known as a wise woman to some, others called her a seer because at times she had visions of the future or issued warnings to people. Lily, though, always thought of her as the grandmother she never had because she always seemed to be there when Lily needed help, a shoulder to lean on when times were hard. She was a tall woman with thick, white hair and often walked with a cane although Lily sometimes thought she did it more for appearances than need. She was always willing to help anyone and was a favorite with the local children although she could be harsh if anyone misbehaved. One swat from that cane on your backside was enough to stop even the most unruly child. Also Joan's weather predictions were legendary in their accuracy. The farmers wouldn't plant or harvest without first consulting with her.

"Are you still going to the market tomorrow Lily?" Joan asked as she entered the house, her cane held tightly in her hand and a scarf resting lightly on her hair to keep off the autumn chill.

"Yes," Lily replied. One of her chickens tried to follow Joan through the door and Lily gently pushed it out with her foot causing it to cluck loudly. "I'm leaving at first light. Did you want me to trade your wool for you?"

"No, dear, I'm keeping all my wool this year. It's going to be a cold winter," she said. "I was hoping we could sit and spin together like last year but..." the old woman's voice lowered and she muttered absentmindedly, "I guess that won't be possible."

Before Lily could ask her why, Joan walked briskly toward the fire Lily had burning, holding her hands out to warm them and spoke again. "I came by because I have something I must tell you. It's important that you remember it."

Lily suddenly felt chilled, as if a cold breeze had gone through the room. She tugged her sweater tighter around herself and rubbed her arms to warm them. "All right," she said hesitantly, "I'm listening."

Joan turned slowly toward her and the room seemed to darken. The late afternoon sunshine that had been shining in through the open doorway abruptly dimmed, as if a cloud had passed in front of the sun. Lily could see the fire burning brightly behind the old woman but her face was in shadow. She stood motionless and when she spoke her voice became deeper; her words slow and measured. She stared into Lily's eyes as she said, "You will find what you are seeking to the north, you must follow the black book."

For a moment it seemed that time stood still. The fire that had been burning brightly just moments before suddenly died down to a low flame. The noise of the chickens outside her door abruptly stopped and Jezebel the cat, who had been sitting contentedly in front of the fire, quickly darted under her bed. Lily looked at Joan and didn't recognize her in the dim light. Her features had changed giving her the appearance of an old man for a moment. Lily released the breath she didn't know she had been holding, rubbed her eyes and looked again at her oldest friend trying to comprehend what had happened. "I don't understand," Lily said hesitantly.

"You will when you need to," was Joan's terse reply. The room seemed lighter once again as the sun came out from behind the cloud and she saw that her fire was burning as brightly as before. Joan's voice was pleasant when she said, "Now, I must be off to tend my animals before it gets dark." She moved quickly toward the door.

"But Grandma Joan," Lily began, wanting to ask more about her cryptic words.

"Take care, Lily," Joan said cutting off her questions, "and make sure you get to the market early tomorrow." With that the old woman opened the door and left and Lily watched her walk quickly away. Lily shook her head wondering what Joan's message could possible mean. She had no plans to travel in any direction but she would remember it just the same as Joan had asked her to. No sense in borrowing trouble, as her father used to say, there was always plenty out there to be found.

The next day dawned bright and clear and Lily left home with her burdens to walk the hour into town. Despite the heavy pack she carried she didn't really mind the time it took because she loved to walk in the forest. The evergreens towered over her but the early sunlight filtered down making it light enough to see the path. There were small animals already going about their business and she heard the birds calling to each other from high in the trees. The forest was always so full of life. She had grown up here and knew it like the back of her hand. She knew where the huckleberries grew sheltered in a sunny thicket, where the stream widened a bit making a small pool the perfect place to catch fish and where the honeysuckle, that she used in syrups to help a cough, climbed the maple trees which were even now turning shades of orange and red. She couldn't imagine living away from the forest. It made her feel safe, almost like it was a living being protecting her. When she returned after being in town, she always felt like it welcomed her home.

The hour passed quickly and as she neared the edge of the trees she saw the dust rising from the road in the distance. She could see the farmers with their wagon loads of goods heading toward the walls of the town of Redin and many people going through the gates. She also saw that there were soldiers on the road marching into town which surprised her. It was unusual in a small town this size and she hadn't heard of any problems nearby but then she didn't come to town often to hear the local gossip. As the path merged with the road she met up with a farmer she had once treated for a bad cough.

"Good morning Patrick" she called to the older man riding in a wagon full of apples and pumpkins. "You must have had a good harvest this fall."

"Aye, Miss Lily, I did. How was your honey this year?"

"The bees cooperated very nicely, thank you. Perhaps we could trade for a few of those apples in your wagon. They're making me hungry just looking at them." She edged closer to his wagon and lowered her voice before asking, "I notice that there are soldiers about, do you know what's happened to bring them here?"

"I've heard that there's going to be a war with the Roh Vec Empire. They'll probably be conscripting the local young men to fight. I also heard that they're asking about healers. You might want to stay out of their notice today, we wouldn't want you to be sent to war."

"I don't know anything about treating war wounds and surely they wouldn't force anyone to go with them, would they?" Lily nervously asked. She was suddenly thankful that she had heeded her father's wishes and not revealed her powers to anyone. They all knew her as a simple healer that used teas and tinctures to heal and occasionally a bag of herbs to put under your pillow to help you sleep. She couldn't imagine the horrors of war.

"Oh, aye," Patrick responded, "they'll take anyone they think they can use. The king doesn't care if you agree or not. That's always the way with those in power."

"Well, thank you for the warning. I'll steer clear of any soldiers I see. Good trading today." The soldiers were getting thicker on the road and Lily had to move onto the grassy verge. Her conversation with Patrick ended when he had to pull ahead to get out of the way of another wagon. She kept her head low to avoid drawing attention to herself and tried to mix in with a group of women also carrying bundles on their backs similar to hers. The road was getting more crowded the closer she got to the town gates and she began to feel hemmed in and anxious. Crowds had always oppressed her and she could feel herself close to panic and tried again to push forward faster. The soldiers were mixed in with the common people, everyone almost at a standstill as the masses crowded together to squeeze through the gate.

The sweat was trickling down her back by the time she finally got through. She wondered again about the soldiers. She supposed that Patrick was right about the conscriptions. The Island of Camar was small and wouldn't have enough volunteers to form a large enough army to protect them from the Roh Vec Empire. She had heard that the Empire had been moving closer in recent years, conquering neighboring lands and it appeared that King Rubin was getting nervous. Lily didn't know why the Empire was interested in her island, but she was sure that she wouldn't like the reason. She had heard stories about their brutality and didn't want to find out if they were true. Some even said that the Empire was filled with slaves. Slavery was unheard of in Camar and she couldn't even imagine it.

Lily had been so preoccupied with her thoughts that it took her a moment to notice that one of the soldiers had been watching her. He looked young and was taller than most of the men around him which made it easy to see that he had a scar up one side of his face. She wondered if the scar was earned honestly as he served his king or picked up in a back alley while he was doing something he shouldn't have been. When she caught him staring she ducked behind a large man and hurried on even faster, losing herself amongst the growing number of sellers and buyers. The market was crowded but not like the crush at the gate and she quickly lost sight of the soldier. She walked swiftly past the booths selling everything from fruits and vegetables to great wheels of cheese that could be eaten by the slice. The booths were set side by side and all sported striped awnings that made the market very festive. She hoped that Bridgett had saved her a space next to her, as she usually did. Bridgett was a weaver and sold her cloth at the market, befriending Lily after her father died. They enjoyed chatting and often shared a meal at midday. Her husband Liam and two young sons often helped Lily set up her wares, sometimes helping themselves to a sample of her honey as well.

Bridgett was waiting as Lily hurried through the square. She was alone, which surprised Lily as Liam always helped with the selling of their cloth.

"Where are Liam and your boys?" Lily asked as she came closer to their space.

"Liam was here earlier and helped me bring our goods, but I sent him home with the boys. With the soldiers conscripting any man under forty years of age I didn't want him dragged off to war. I'm hoping that they don't go door to door searching for available men,"

Bridgett answered in a hushed tone. Lily was surprised to hear such fear in her friend's voice.

"I can't believe that it has come to this. It's unthinkable that the Empire would be interested in our little island. I only hope that it doesn't come to actual war," Lily said quietly, as if speaking it loudly could cause it to happen. "It frightens me."

The morning slipped away quickly and Lily had sold a good portion of her herbs and most of the honey when she realized that the apothecary hadn't been over to pick up the order of herbs he had requested the last time she had been in town.

"Have you seen Samuel the apothecary?" she asked Bridgett. "He usually comes first thing in the morning to pick up his order."

"No, not yet," replied her friend as she handed over one of her woven scarves to a waiting customer, "why don't you run it over to him. I've sold most of my cloth and I can easily watch your things for you. It won't take but a moment for you to run over and back".

"If you're sure you don't mind then I'll do that," said Lily as she found the herbs she needed to take. She picked up the parcel and left their space heading toward the apothecary shop which was several streets over. As she walked she looked at some of the other things for sale in the market. She was able to grow most of her food and she traded honey and beeswax candles with Bridgett for cloth to make her few dresses, but there were always some things she needed to buy or trade for. Salt was one of these and the salt merchant usually insisted on coins. Thankfully the apothecary always paid in coin for her herbs which was one reason she particularly needed to see him.

The streets were almost empty once she left the crowded marketplace and other than several small children playing on a tumbled down wall she saw no one else. As she walked she had an odd feeling that she was being followed but each time she turned her head, she saw no one. It made her heart beat faster and her steps quickened. She was nearing the apothecary shop when suddenly the unthinkable happened. One of the boys playing on the wall accidently slipped and fell off. Her heart came to her throat as she saw him hit the ground and heard something crack. She had stopped walking as she watched him fall and it was his screams following a second later that brought her to action. Lily hurried over to see if the child was all right. It wasn't too far of a fall but the ground in front of the wall was made up of broken rocks and the boy had landed on a particularly sharp one. He had hit his head and was bleeding badly, as she knew head wounds always did, and the other two boys looked terrified. Lily felt anxious as she knelt down to examine the boy and saw that not only was it a very bad cut but the boy was unconscious.

"You!" She said anxiously, pointing to the boys. "Do you know where this child's mother is?" They both nodded their heads. "Then run and fetch her and I'll take care of him. Hurry!" As soon as they were gone Lily turned his head gently to apply pressure to the badly bleeding wound. She used the scarf that she was wearing to try and stop the flow but the sharp point of the rock had gone in deeply and the blood continued to dampen her scarf unchecked. He was just a small boy and the amount of blood he was losing was alarming to her. She began to worry that he could possibly die from the wound and that thought brought back her memories of healing Jon. Was it possible that she could heal this child as she had her brother so many years ago? Perhaps this was her chance to see if she still had that power. Remembering her promise to her father, though, she looked around furtively to be sure that she was alone, not wanting anyone to see what she was going to attempt. She thought she saw movement on the side of the building next to the wall, but after watching for a moment decided that it was only a shadow. She didn't want to wait any longer to heal the boy, so sending up a quick prayer to the Maker, she placed both hands on him and thought "heal" in her mind. Not really understanding what she had done the first time with Jon she was terrified that it wouldn't work but amazingly the blood slowly stopped and the wound began to close up. Lily let out a sigh of relief. She removed her hands and gently placed his head in her lap as the boy started to come around. She was feeling very dizzy and sat quietly as he awoke. While she rested she saw a woman she assumed must be his mother and the other two boys coming down the street toward her.

"How is he?" the woman shouted, "how's my boy?"

"He's just starting to wake up and the bleeding has stopped," said Lily as the woman got closer." I think he'll be fine. It wasn't too bad of a cut." In fact the cut had already closed completely but thankfully there was plenty of dried blood so the woman wouldn't be able to tell that it had healed so quickly. The boy's mother thanked her and Lily stood up unsteadily but was still able to help the woman get her boy to his feet and watched as they walked down an alley toward their home. She leaned against the wall he had fallen from

21

wanting nothing more than to lie down and rest. She remembered how she had collapsed after healing Jon and assumed that the healing must have made her this tired. She looked nervously over her shoulder and set off walking the short distance to the apothecary's shop, still with the feeling that she was being watched.

As she entered the shop she saw immediately why Samuel hadn't come for his herbs when he hobbled in from the back room. The old man had his foot wrapped in a thick bandage and he was leaning heavily on a gnarled cane.

"Oh, Lily, bless you child for bringing them. I fell and twisted my foot and can't walk far. I was hoping you'd come." He paid her in coin for the herbs and sat down to have a little chat with her. He had been a good friend of Lily's mother and Lily had known him most of her life. Her mother had sold him herbs and when Lily first started growing and drying her herbs, he had shown her just what to do and how he liked them prepared. He also told her which should be harvested when the moon was full and where to find some of the wild ones that she didn't grow herself. He was much older than her, maybe even nearing sixty years. His white hair and friendly wrinkles were a familiar sight and he was one of the few people that Lily trusted. She had been thinking of questioning him about her abilities knowing how well he knew her mother, and now, after just using them, she felt more than ever that he might have some answers.

"Samuel, there's something I've been wanting to ask you for some time now," Lily began. She thought of her father's words and coughed nervously before she continued. Taking a shaky breath she looked directly into his eyes and said quietly "What do you know about healers with *special* abilities?"

Samuel looked around uneasily and also spoke in a quiet voice. "Would you be talking about those that can heal with a touch of their hands?"

Lily nodded at him, at a loss for words when she realized that he understood what she meant.

"Well, then, only that there are very few born anymore, and that although they are trusted in our country they mostly stay hidden. The Empire calls them witches and the Emperor of Roh Vec has killed all those that he's found, or so I've heard. 'It's not a safe subject to be discussing, I'm thinking, so why do you ask?"

Lily ignored his question and asked instead, "Why does the Emperor want them all killed?"

"That I don't know, child, but if you know of one, you make sure she stays hidden. In the old days most towns had at least one healer and they were revered as holy women. I don't know if they're all dead or in hiding, but if you know one and she ever needs help, she can find sanctuary with me. Do you understand?" Samuel asked and looked deeply into her eyes. Lily felt certain that he was trying to tell her that he knew more than he could say aloud. Could he have known what her mother could do and did he guess what she was also capable of? She heard the shop door open and someone come in and knew the conversation was over for now. More questions would have to wait for another time. She patted his wrinkled hand and stood to go.

"Thank you, I'd best be getting back to my space now. Bridgett will be wanting to get home to her family. Good day to you Samuel."

"Good day, Lily," the old man said and winked at her as she left.

The rest of the afternoon went by quickly. Bridgett left early to go check on Liam and the boys which gave Lily time to think on everything that Samuel had told her. She still couldn't understand why the Empire would want to harm healers. It worried her enough that as soon as she could, she bought her salt, traded the rest of her honey for some oats and left the town much earlier than usual. Her bundle was heavier now and she could not walk as quickly as she had this morning. She was glad when she entered the forest and felt its reassuring presence around her. Nothing would harm her now that she walked within its shelter and the tension she had been feeling left her as she headed for home.

Chapter 2

Gavin waited in the shadows until the woman he had been following entered the apothecary shop. He needed to get back to his sergeant and tell him what he had seen. There had been something about her that had caught his eye on the road into town. She was a pretty woman and her long blonde hair stood out amidst the brown hair of most of his countrymen, but there was something else, some kind of aura surrounding her. He could sense it, as he could always sense unusual things. His grandmother had said he had a sixth sense that most others didn't have. It had saved him a time or two, letting him know which men to avoid and which could be trusted. So he had followed the woman into town and watched her set up her space and when he saw that it was herbs she sold he wondered if he had found a healer. Now, after seeing what she did to that child, he was certain. He headed back to the marketplace, hoping that she would return to her space after she was done in the shop. He wanted to find out what the sergeant wanted him to do now.

He caught up with him at the town gates and hurried to his side. "Sergeant, I need to speak with you about a matter of some importance," Gavin said in a quiet voice trying not to be overheard. "I think I've found one, a healer."

"A witch? Are you sure Gavin?" his sergeant asked in disbelief.

"I'm telling you I saw her, you know I have a sixth sense about these things."

"But you know there haven't been witches seen on Camar in years."

"I'm positive, sergeant, trust me." Gavin reasserted his claim.

"All right, then, where is she?"

"She's in the apothecary's shop just now, but I know where she's been selling her herbs all day and I'm sure she'll head back there. She left her goods with her friend."

"Why do you think she's a healer, a witch?"

"I saw her heal a child. He fell and hit his head, there was blood everywhere and then she touched him and it stopped. I wasn't close enough to see the wound but I'm sure all she did was touch him and he healed. A few minutes later he got up and walked away with his mother. I tell you it was amazing." Gavin's eyes were excited as he revealed his news. He was certain he was right about this woman.

"Go back to the market and watch her. I want you to find out where she lives and then we'll take her to the commander. No one is to know. Do you understand? I want this kept quiet," the sergeant hissed. "After you find out where her home is you report back to me, and only me, and then we'll make a move."

"I understand," Gavin said, and hurried away to watch over the woman. He spent the rest of the afternoon hiding in the shadows of a nearby building staring at the herbalist until she finally packed up her goods and left the town. He stayed well behind her and stood at the town gate as she entered the woods. Hurrying now, he found the path she had followed and crept behind her, keeping enough distance between them that she wouldn't see him if she glanced back. The undergrowth was thick here and the path she took so narrow that it disappeared from time to time; the branches pushing him back and slapping him in the face as he went. He lost her more than once but his father had trained him in the art of tracking and she walked carelessly, not worrying about bending the occasional branch or erasing her footprints since she couldn't know she was being followed. He was tripped by logs that seemed to appear out of nowhere, scratches covered his hands and face and clouds of small insects seemed to hover around him but he wouldn't let this thrice blasted forest keep him from his task. Muttering all the curses he had learned since joining the army and making up a few new ones of his own, he finally saw her enter a small house. He watched the house for some time making sure that she did indeed live here. After he saw her secure her animals in their shed he decided it was time to head back to tell his sergeant what he had found. As he turned to go he saw an old woman with white hair waiting in the path he was about to take.

"Do you make it a habit to stalk young women to their homes, Gavin?" she asked.

"Have we met?" he asked cautiously, wondering how she knew his name and sensing that this harmless old woman was not what she appeared to be.

The old woman stared at him with such intensity as she spoke that he couldn't look away. *"Since you have an interest in my Lily, I lay this burden on you, help her find her purpose,"* she said, then watched him for a moment more before turning and disappearing into the forest.

Gavin knew without a doubt that whoever this woman was, she had power. He didn't understand the meaning of what she had said; was she talking about the witch? Was her name Lily? He headed down the trail, eager to talk to his sergeant and tell him what he had found out. For some reason he had no trouble on the way back with stray branches and mysterious logs. The forest seemed happy to let him leave. It took another hour of walking and a brief search before he found his sergeant sitting in a tavern near the town gate. He bought himself an ale and sat down at the table with him.

"Well, what did you find?" his sergeant asked.

"She has a house an hours walk through the woods. I didn't see anyone else so I'm pretty certain that she lives alone, although I met...that is, there was..." Strangely, Gavin found he couldn't tell him about the old woman.

"What? Does she live with someone or not?" his sergeant asked again impatiently.

"No, I'm sure she doesn't," Gavin finally said.

"Then go back and first chance you get, grab her and take her to the camp. I'm done here and will be heading back soon with the new recruits. I'll let Commander Versan know we think we've found a healer."

Gavin finished his ale and once again took the long walk back through the woods surprised at how easy it was this time. Once he'd found the path it seemed to take him straight to her door. Now he only needed to spend a cold night in the forest watching the witch's house, waiting for his chance to take her.

It had been dark for some time and Lily was just thinking of her bed, when she heard it. Someone was walking outside her window. She heard something snap and then silence, as if someone had stepped on a twig and then stopped so as not to be heard. Her heart beat erratically as she paused in her spinning and listened for another sound. Calm down, she told herself, it could be an animal, but that feeling of being watched from earlier in the day had never really left her and now she wondered if she really had been followed.

She looked around her house to see what she could use as a weapon. She had her eating knife, of course, but it was small and she would have to be very close to the intruder to do any damage. She wasn't sure she could stab someone anyway. She knew how to kill and skin animals but she had never harmed a person. She looked at her stack of firewood sitting near the hearth and chose a solid looking log small enough to hold in her hand.

The next few minutes passed very slowly for Lily. Her heartbeat had slowed but she was still on edge waiting for the next sound. The door was bolted but a determined man could probably beat it down. Her conversation with Samuel about the killing of healers had scared her. Suddenly she heard another sound, this time just outside the door. She jumped up, log in hand, and backed into the corner. The door handle turned and someone pushed against her door. Thankfully, the bolt held and the door stayed shut. One more jiggle of the handle and then nothing. Her heart was beating fast and hard again and Lily felt like the next few minutes lasted hours. She waited a bit longer and then sat down, her knife and the log on the table in front of her.

The morning light shining through the cracks in her shutters woke Lily. She hadn't gone to bed, being much to frightened to think of sleeping, but had sat at the table all night and dozed off and on. She felt horrible and desperately in need of sleep. As she made herself a cup of peppermint tea and toasted a piece of bread over the fire she decided to feed the goats and chickens and then lay down for several hours. There was nothing that needed her attention that badly and surely whoever had tried to get in last night would be gone by now.

She lifted the bolt and opened the door a crack, peering out into the farmyard. All appeared quiet and the chickens were making no noise, a good sign that all was well. She took a deep breath and quietly left the house, still frightened from lasts night's vigil. She crept through the yard, starting at every noise. Safely in the shed she cared for the animals and was heading back quickly when suddenly she was grabbed from behind. She struggled and kicked out managing to connect with something judging from the grunt her attacker made. As she continued to flail about, strong arms circled her, trapping her arms at her sides. A length of rope wrapped her hands tightly behind her and she was then lifted up and placed on a horse; her attacker climbing on behind her, arms encircling her to hold her steady. She continued to struggle and almost succeeded in falling off the horse.

"Keep still miss and no one will hurt you," said the stranger's voice gruffly in her ear as he clucked to the horse to get him moving.

"What do you want? Untie me and let me go at once," Lily demanded.

"I can't do that miss. The commander wants to speak with you and the ropes are for my protection. We don't know what a witch can do with her hands." Lily kept quiet as they moved off, frightened that she might be riding toward her death as she remembered Samuel telling her that only the Empire called healers witches.

They rode in silence for some time, even the sounds of the horse's hooves were muffled by the leaves that littered the forest floor. Lily finally decided that knowing the truth, even if she didn't like what she'd hear, was better than this uncertainty. "Why does your commander want to see me? Does he want to kill me? Are you with the Empire?" Her voice quavered as she asked the last question, but the need to know outweighed her fears.

The man spat on the ground. "The Empire? That accursed place? Not likely. I'm Camarian through and through. We'll be fighting those bastards soon enough, but the commander needs you first. He'll explain it when we see him. No more questions now. Just sit tight and no tricks and you won't get hurt."

The man, who she now knew must be a Camerian soldier, said no more for the rest of the ride. The forest, her forest, was reassuring as it surrounded her. Somehow she thought that if this man was going to hurt her it would have stopped him. It had a way of dropping branches on anyone who didn't belong here or who wandered through with violence in mind. She was still frightened but the soldier's words had calmed her somewhat. It didn't sound like she was heading for certain death, anyway, but what did they want with her? She was so tired from last night's vigil that she found herself leaning back against the man. She jerked forward, not wanting to touch him and tried to stay upright but last night's sleeplessness finally caught up with her and she gave in to sleep.

Gavin wasn't quite sure what to think. He was confused by this woman he was taking to his commander. After finding her door firmly locked, he had waited the night watching from the trees until she came out to take care of her animals. He hadn't wanted to hurt her but she was like a wildcat when he grabbed her. She had managed to kick him twice in the shins despite his much bigger size until he managed to tie her up. He knew he should be wary of her because who knew what a witch was capable of, but he couldn't sense any evil in her. There hadn't been any witches seen in such a long time and he, himself, had never met one in his life but as he looked at the woman leaning against him, she seemed harmless. He found himself inhaling her scent, she smelled of lavender and herbs, a clean smell. Her hair was beautiful and he rubbed it between his fingers just for a moment. His arm encircled her to keep her steady as she slept. She was thin, as if she never had quite enough to eat, but pleasantly shaped all the same. She was a woman he would like to take to his bed, maybe even be lucky enough to marry.

He stopped himself with a shake of his head. Not for the likes of a common soldier, this one. She had power, he was sure, and would find herself caught up with more important men than him. Then he remembered the old woman's words, was he meant to help her in some way? His simple life was suddenly becoming far too complicated. In the distance he heard the sounds of men and horses and knew he was nearing his destination. Hopefully, he could turn the witch over to his commander and be done with all of this.

As they came nearer to camp, he gently prodded the woman awake. "We're close now. You'll be in the commander's tent soon and he'll know what to do with you. I promise you that no harm will come to you if you cooperate."

Lily woke to the sight of a large meadow filled with what appeared to be several hundred soldiers. They were engaged in a number of activities, some currying horses, others gathering firewood and water, others tending several cooking fires. Their horses were tied to picket lines at one end of the clearing. A stream meandered along the edge of the meadow, providing water for the men and horses. It looked very much like a temporary camp, with no permanent structures to be seen. There was one large tent set at the edge of the forest and several smaller ones nearby. Lily and her captor were riding in behind the larger tent, possibly to go unnoticed. Perhaps he didn't want to call attention to a woman, especially one tied, in a camp full of soldiers, she thought. He jumped down from the horse, reached up and pulled her carefully into his arms keeping her back to him. He set her on her feet and guided her forward. She walked slowly so as not to trip but the soldier stayed behind her holding her in place carefully.

They ducked inside the large tent where Lily saw four men, one reclining on a cot. He seemed to be in command as he was dictating a letter to a young man sitting near him and the other men stood a respectful distance from them. The tent was just large enough so as not to feel crowded despite the number of people in it, but not so large that it couldn't be taken down quickly. The man she assumed was the commander looked up at her but continued dictating for several more minutes. When he stopped, the young man who was writing rolled the paper up and placed it in a leather pouch.

"Take that dispatch straight to Commander Terrin's camp. It's important that he know that the Empire's ships have been spotted just off the coast of Camar. Ride straight through and return with any information he has for me," the man said. The soldier nodded and took the dispatch as he headed out the tent's flap.

The man looked Lily over carefully before asking everyone to leave. "Gavin, you stay, please." He waited for them to go and then gave Gavin orders to remove the ropes that still tied Lily's hands. Her arms were numb and she rubbed them gratefully then started when she got a good look at Gavin for the first time. It was the soldier with the scar that she had seen on the road to town. He was not as young as she had thought, maybe five years older than her twenty years. He was much taller than she was and had a thick shock of brown hair with startling blue eyes. Why had he been watching for her? How could he have known that there was something different about her?

The commander then spoke to her. "According to my sergeant, my man Gavin seems to think that you're a witch. Gavin has a sense of these things, says he sees something special surrounding you. Are you a witch?"

Lily nervously licked her lips before answering. There was something about this man that projected power and authority despite the fact that he was lying on a cot. He appeared to be about forty years of age with dark red hair and a carefully trimmed beard and looked every inch the commander of an army. She knew he held her life in his hands and that she should answer him respectfully but she was tired and sore and wanted answers so she spoke more defiantly than she intended.

"Why should I answer you? I've been told that witches are killed by the Empire. If I answer yes why should I trust you not to do the same? And if I answer no, what then, you bundle me back up and take me home or do you kill me to keep me quiet? I need answers before I tell you anything."

"Have you been harmed in anyway yet? Has Gavin hurt you?" he asked her quietly and waited until she shook her head. "To tell you the truth, my sergeant and Gavin cooked this scheme up among themselves. They've been trying to find a way to cure me since this happened." He pointed to his legs. "I only just found out what they had planned a short time ago. I believe I would have done it differently, but I'm glad you're here and you're right to want answers. Let me give you some background and then I hope you'll feel comfortable to answer truthfully".

The commander looked at her as he spoke. He hadn't moved from the cot and she was beginning to wonder if indeed he could. "My name is Commander Versan. I come from the north end of Camar where witches used to be quite common I am told. My mother's mother was a witch but as you may know not all the women in a family inherit this ability. My mother did not. My grandmother was a kind woman and was often called out for a healing. She was greatly loved in the area and greatly missed when she disappeared one day. They never found out what happened exactly, but the story is a ship from the Empire was spotted around the time she disappeared. It was assumed that they kidnapped her and probably killed her. From that time on, the witches that lived in the north went into hiding. I'm sure others were taken and killed but no one really knows how many are left in our country, if any. When my sergeant told me that he thought he had found a witch that might be able to help me I was intrigued."

The commander paused for a moment in his story to take a sip of ale from a wooden cup that was setting near him. He appeared tired, more tired even than when she had entered the tent. "You see six months ago I fell from my horse. We were gathering the troops in preparation for the war that is coming. It's a job we don't much like. Some men come willingly, others do not. Dusk was fast approaching and I was hurrying as we crossed a farmer's field. My horse stepped into a rabbit hole and went down; I wasn't able to fall clear and my horse landed on my legs. They've been useless ever since. I'm still able to make decisions but what good is a commander that can't sit a horse and take command in the field? So you see, if indeed you are a witch it's the first hope I've had in six months to be a whole man

31

again. I have no desire to hurt you and in fact would give you anything you ask for your help."

Lily thought about what he had said for several moments before she replied. "I don't think you really need my answer as you obviously already believe I'm a healer. I would like to trust you, Commander, but I only just learned yesterday that healers are called witches and that the Empire has them killed. I do have a question for you, though, I'm curious as to why you use the term witch and I would like to know why you think that I am one?"

"My grandmother called herself a healer but the locals called her a witch. I suppose they were somewhat frightened of her power even though they appreciated it. I grew up with that term and never thought anything about it. As I told you, in the area where we lived, witches were revered. I assure you that I have the greatest respect for you and won't harm you, nor allow any harm to come to you. As to why I think you're a witch, Gavin's sergeant told me that Gavin saw you heal a boy yesterday in town. You'd know more about that than I do though."

Lily looked at Gavin as she said, "You must have been the shadow I saw." She felt like her world was turning upside down. She had kept this secret for so long and now in one short day it was out, leaving her feeling very exposed. She didn't completely trust these men but felt she had no choice but to go along with them for the moment. "All right, commander, I'll take you at your word," she said and walked over to the cot that Commander Versan lay on. His legs were covered with a wool blanket.

"My name is Lily and I do have some power to heal but I've kept it a secret all my life which is why I'm having trouble trusting you now. I've only healed by touch twice. Once eight years ago and once yesterday so I have no idea what I'm really capable of, but if you're willing to chance it, I'm willing to try." He nodded at her to continue. "May I remove the blanket so that I can touch your legs?" she asked him.

"Of course, whatever you need," he responded.

She gently took the blanket off and looked at him. His upper body was broad and well muscled like a man who was used to working hard. His hands were calloused from holding a sword. His legs, though, were thin and withered. It was obvious that he had not been able to walk for a long time. "I'm going to touch you now. I

32

don't know if you will feel pain or feel anything at all. I'm sorry I have so little experience with this."

"If you can do anything, I'll be grateful. Just do whatever you have to," the commander said.

Kneeling beside him, she reached out tentatively and touched his right leg. She felt nothing, no power coming from her. She pressed harder against him but still felt nothing. "I'm sorry but I can't feel a thing. This isn't the way it happened to me before. It could be the injury was too long ago."

"My mother used to tell me that when my grandmother did a healing she always touched skin to skin. Do you think if I removed my pants it could help?" the commander asked.

Lily felt herself turn bright red before she could respond. "I really don't know. If you think that my touching your bare skin will help, then it's worth a try. It'll be one more step in learning what I can do if it works."

Commander Versan motioned for Gavin to help him remove his pants. Lily turned her back on them as he did and when Gavin touched her on the shoulder to let her know it was done, she saw that he had covered the commander's legs with the blanket again. She decided she would leave it where it was and reach under to touch him. It would be easier for her and wouldn't embarrass him either, although since he was a soldier perhaps he didn't worry about such things.

Lily knelt in front of the cot to begin. When she touched the commander's legs under the blanket she knew immediately that he had been right about skin touching skin. She felt her power begin to build and closed her eyes as it left her fingertips and as it surged into his legs she heard the commander gasp. She had never felt it this strongly before and was amazed at it. She said the word "heal" silently as she had done with the boy in town yesterday. The commander was watching her in wonder when she opened her eyes. His skin was flushed and he was breathing hard. She kept her hands on his legs for a moment more until it felt like there was no more power for her to use. She took her hands away and tried to stand. Gavin caught her before she hit the ground and just before darkness took her she had a moment to wonder if it had worked.

Chapter 3

The essence reader opened his eyes to the same familiar red glow that he had woken up to for the last twelve years. He stared at the crude stone walls and vowed for the thousandth time that he would never sleep here again. He slid off his cot and out from underneath his scratchy wool blanket. He placed his bare feet on the cold floor and winced at the feeling. Using his power he tactically retreated within his own mind so that all his bodily needs were greatly muted. He slipped into his black robe, the only possession he could call his own; it would be the key to finally leaving this place.

He went to stand in the open door frame, for no student was ever allowed the privacy of his own door, and looked back into the room. It was completely bare, except for the cot and a small table containing an empty water bowl. Twelve long years he had lived here in the training compound, exactly half of his life. A memory surfaced of when he first arrived at the essence-touched compound. He was the oldest child ever to enter as a student at age twelve. Normally essence-touched children were taken as soon as their abilities became known, around the ages of five through eight. Children older than this were often times too difficult to train or their loyalties lay elsewhere than with the order of essence readers. These boys and all the essence-touched men who were not in the order were deemed heretics and killed on site. Only the male sex had the chance to be born essence-touched, females were never born with such abilities. He floated through his own memory for a moment, feeling how angry and emotional he was at the time; how the room seemed small to him even then compared to the wide open plains he had grown up on. His fury still burned deep within him but he had learned to hide it with years of training and patience. He brushed the memory aside and left the room for the last time.

The halls to the large compound were all the same, much as the rooms; cold stone walls, simple wooden floors, and red glow rocks called crystallus, that were set in small nooks in the walls gave the only illumination. He made a quick stop to the privy and then went to the kitchen for a simple breakfast roll. He walked out into the autumn sunrise which hadn't quite crept over the massive dark wall surrounding the compound for essence-touched students. The grounds were vast, consisting of only rough dirt and stone buildings, not a single weed grew in the poor soil. Every essence-touched person in the Roh Vec Empire was trained here and the fortress could house well over one-thousand students ranging from ages five to fifty. A student did not leave the compound unattended until he had earned the black robe of an essence reader.

Though he had arrived at almost twice the age of the other students, he had felt ready to become a reader when he was twenty but for some reason they had made him wait for an additional four years. Perhaps they were only teaching him patience but he suspected it was because they just didn't trust him. Every year it became more difficult to mask his growing frustration. He could easily pass any test they threw at him but still they held him back.

He looked about the grounds and noticed that several students had already started their morning Shai-Yi exercises. Shai-Yi was a martial art taught only to the readers. He stripped to his loins like the rest of the students revealing his tattoos and shaved head. He focused on his physical body and found that he was shivering from the early fall chill, especially his bare feet. He clenched his teeth against this pain and began performing a series of stretches and holding positions along with everyone else. Within minutes he felt his joints warming up, and after forty five minutes he was covered in sweat and his muscles had begun to ache.

Shai-Yi was very important to the readers and its purpose was twofold. First, all essence-touched students and readers alike were just as vulnerable to physical dangers as any other mortal man. A simple blade or even a stone could kill them, so they had to learn to defend themselves. The second purpose of Shai-Yi was to force the reader to feel his physical needs. By practicing this martial art each day, the students could check on the health of their physical body. In recent years he had found the daily exercise was his favorite part of the day because it was the only time he was able to release his frustrations through aggression.

At this point many other students and masters were awake and joining the main group. He was tempted to continue practicing but knew he had other places to be. He put his black robe on and walked across the vast grounds towards the only gate to the compound. The walls around the compound enclosed more than just the student fortress. There were the guard quarters, a small armory, stable, the slave housing, and even a small granary to store additional food. The entire complex was one of many walled areas within the capital city of Roh Vec.

As he approached the dark gate he noticed that there was another reader waiting along with the normal guardsmen. It was impossible to see who he was for every reader kept their hood up but he reached out tentatively with his mind over the long distance and instantly knew him to be the compound's headmaster and a sub-minister within the order.

He bowed to him as he approached. *"Headmaster,"* he communicated telepathically.

The headmaster bowed to him in return. *"It is incorrect for you to refer to me as headmaster, reader, for you are no longer a student. You may refer to me as sub-minister Tasitus, or simply brother Tasitus. I am not as rank conscious as some of our brothers as long as we are in this form of communication."*

"You honor me sub-minister," he replied bowing once again.

"Have you chosen a name for yourself now that you are a reader?"

"I have chosen Arius, sub-minister."

"Do you mind if I ask why you chose this name?"

"Atarius was my preferred teacher in the compound, sub-minister. I thought that by choosing a name in his likeness I would honor him," Brother Arius explained.

"I will tell him that, Brother Arius. I am sure he will be honored," and Arius bowed to the sub-minister for the third time.

It must have appeared strange to anyone watching to see two men continuously bowing to one another without saying a word. The guards however were quite familiar with the essence-touched communicating with one another telepathically and did their best to ignore the two readers. The head master now turned and signaled to one of the guards who brought forth two black horses.

"This horse and everything on it are now yours Brother Arius," he said taking the bridle from the guard and giving it to Arius. There was also a leather satchel bag attached to the saddle and Arius eyed it curiously.

"Go ahead, open it. Everything inside belongs to you as well," Tasitus said. Arius did so and found that his list of possessions was

growing greatly. He had lived the last twelve years knowing he owned nothing, not even a name.

Some of the objects in the bag were quite simple. There was a pair of leather strapped sandals, a rough woolen blanket similar to the one on his cot, a leather water pouch, and a few other minor camp essentials. There was also a large purse of coins which was of only minor importance because just about everyone in the Roh Vec Empire would give a reader whatever they wanted out of fear. Slightly more valuable to Arius was a set of five finely crafted daggers. Arius also noticed a short sword which was the standard weapon for the Empire's soldiers but, unlike the daggers, it was something that the students had rarely trained with. At the bottom of the bag he also found a crystallus and wondered why the sub minister would think it important enough to send a common glow stone with him.

"You look surprised by the crystallus Arius. Do you not realize its importance to a reader?"

When Arius shook his head, the sub-minister continued. *"Have you never realized that only readers can see the red glow that the crystallus gives off? To a common man or woman this is just a dull gray rock but to a reader it will give you light even in the darkest places without the need of a torch. In Roh Vec we have many of them, but in your travels you will rarely see them. Keep this one close; it will be hard to find another."*

Tevarian looked at the stone with more respect as he returned it to the bag.

"Come, I will go with you to see the high minister," the sub-minister said. Both men mounted the horses and rode out of the compound. Arius and the other students might travel out from the compound once or twice a year to go into the city for various training reasons, but this would be the first time he would travel into the city as an official essence reader.

The whole of the Roh Vec Empire was built on the back of slaves. It had a vast road network that stretched for thousands of miles, from the western sea to the northern ice lands, all built by slaves. There were over one hundred legions of soldiers who were fed from great estates with thousands of slaves bending their backs in the field. Whole fleets, great fortresses, and new cities all created with the power of slave labor. Yet of all the feats, none of them could equal the creation of the capital city of Roh Vec.

Arius and the other students had received an excellent education along with their essence training, and he had read the story of the city's founding many times. Almost three hundred years ago when the Empire was just blossoming and slave manpower was at its height, the Emperor suddenly left the capital city of Oska. He traveled with only a small group of advisors and generals far to the north. He stopped after leaving his furthest province, in a land simply called the Roh plains. It was a meager land only fit for the raising of cattle and selling of animal hides. In those plains stood a lone mountain called Vec just a few leagues before the great ice mountain range where nothing survived the winters and no man dwelled.

It was said that the Emperor stretched out his hand and pointed to the top of the mountain. He claimed that he would not move from where he stood until his palace was built on the highest peak. His advisors and generals begged him to reconsider and brought forth architects and engineers who tried to explain just how difficult this task would be but the Emperor would not be moved. He pitched his pavilion where he stood so that he could view the city's construction.

It took ninety-two years to complete the initial building of the city. True to his word the Emperor remained in his pavilion for all those years, surviving on whatever powerful magic he had which still sustained him today. While he remained in one spot, however, the rest of the Empire moved at his command.

Hundreds of thousands of slaves were brought to the mountain to build the city. During summers they would chip away the peak of Mt. Vec stone by stone, rock by rock. Sheer sweat and time brought the mountain down so that it was habitable. During winter when it was impossible to work on the snowy summit they would use the stones they had chipped away all summer to build the lower city walls and buildings. Through the years millions of slaves died on Mt. Vec earning it the subtle nickname, Death Mountain.

The cattle herders on the Roh plains could not even come close to supporting the working population. Supplies were needed to feed these slaves, as well as soldiers to keep them in line. The trade routes of the whole Empire were altered to provide for the new city. An entire make-shift town was built around the base of the mountain to house the workers. This still existed in Arius's time as the slums for the slave population.

The readers played an important role in the creation of the city as well. While governors and generals provided the supplies, soldiers, and labor necessary to physically build the city, the readers were the Emperor's eyes and ears. They could read the thoughts of these men and make sure they were loyal to the Emperor. The city could not survive long without supplies and a well planned rebellion could very well cut the crucial trade to the capital city. Thanks to the readers there hadn't been a successful uprising within the Empire for over four hundred years.

It was said that when the Emperor finally entered his palace at the top of the mountain, one of his generals had the tenacity to ask, "Why on top of this mountain your Imperial Majesty? Surely in your wisdom you can see that we have overstretched the Empire by building out this far." To which the Emperor simply responded, "because... I can."

Arius and Tasitus took the path to the stone paved street that led to the top of Roh Vec. There were few trees this high up the mountain or on the Roh Plains in general. Those that did exist were small, gnarled, and as tough as the stone used to build the walls of the city. The cold winds only favored small tundra shrubs which could be seen poking out between buildings or in the cracks of the street. During the summer they would bloom with small white flowers; when the petals were blown away it occasionally gave the impression that it was snowing in the summer.

There was only one main road up the mountain and typically the higher one went in Roh Vec, the more likely they would meet those of higher social class. The lower city was largely built around the southern portion of the mountain where the trade caravans approached. To walk from the furthest gate to the palace would take more than two days travel. Side to side the city was nearly a league wide, centered around the wide highway that went straight up the mountain.

Arius had traveled down into the poorer sections of the city several times and was always amazed to see how many different goods were brought into the city. It seemed as if the only thing that the city supplied on its own were the cold stones that held up every structure. He had never traveled up towards the palace as they were now. The head minister whom they were going to see had a palace of his own just below the Emperor's. Every section of the reader's order answered to this man, and he in turn answered only to the Emperor. If a heretic was discovered, a noble caught conspiring, or an essence reader killed, he would know of it sooner rather than later.

Though it was early the main road was already well packed with important messengers hurrying to their destinations. Arius was always a little caught off guard to see so many people moving around and speaking out loud. The noise itself was slightly distracting but far worse was the chilly autumn breeze carrying the smell of filth from the lower city up the mountain. For some reason Arius never seemed to smell it when he was with the other students. In many ways he felt free without other readers always brushing his mind, but in other ways this was an unfamiliar world that set him on edge.

A group of high level bureaucrats on horseback came slowly trotting down the road, and guards, messengers, and slaves alike all bowed quickly as they passed. When Arius and Tasitus passed any workers there were always varying reactions. Some would bow, others would shrink back in fear, and Arius had even seen some people flee in terror but nearly everyone kept their eyes diverted and well out of arms reach from the readers. When the bureaucrats passed Arius and Tasitus, both groups nodded to one another though the bureaucrats also kept their distance. Neither group was officially considered above the other; they performed completely different duties under the authority of the Emperor.

While on the busy street Arius followed his training and made sure to constantly reach out and briefly touch the thoughts of all those near him. It was impossible to reach everyone at once so he usually only read those closest to him. The most common form of death for every essence reader in the Empire was not from disease, assassins, nor even heretics; but from random individuals who attacked out of revenge or desperation. The readers were also trained to read emotions in large crowds. Anyone who radiated hatred or more simply who wasn't afraid of them could be a potential threat.

Arius was so focused on scanning the street that he almost missed Tasitus turning his horse off the main road. It was then that he noticed that they were already at the palace of the head minister, the beating heart for the order of essence readers. He looked down the hill and could make out the training compound far below them. On the outside, the palace of the order of essence readers was quite similar to the compound for essence- touched students. It was surrounded by the dark stone walls and had the same feeling of severity about it.

"Let us speak plainly brother, as non readers do," Tasitus suddenly said. His voice was quiet and patient, but time had given it a rough throaty edge as well. Arius was so surprised to hear the old man speak that he didn't even respond. He couldn't remember that last time he heard the headmaster speak. In fact he wasn't sure if he had ever heard the headmaster's actual voice in all his twelve years at the compound.

"You will find that your training will serve you well Arius, but there are experiences outside the compound that will take some time to get used to," Tasitus said as if he was giving a lecture. "For instance, common speech will become necessary. There will be times when you have to give orders or instructions and you won't be able to simply communicate telepathically."

"Yes headmast…" Arius started and then caught himself. "Yes Sub-minister. I will learn and adapt, for the glory of the Empire."

"Others can claim the glory of the Empire, Arius. We insure its survival, even if it means we must put down loyal subjects." Arius nodded his understanding.

As they approached the gate, Tasitus once again fell silent. A pair of guards took their horses from them and they entered the outer palace on foot. The courtyard looked much like the grounds in the compound; hard stone buildings and bare dirt. People moved around quickly with various activities. A vast majority seemed to be messengers who brought vital information to the order from all over the Empire. Arius also noted that there were many essence readers in their black robes. Some approached Tasitus to give their respects.

Arius wasn't sure exactly how old Tasitus was but he knew that he had been the headmaster for the last twenty years so many of those who approached him were simply former students. One particular reader stopped and had a long telepathic conversation with Tasitus. Arius waited patiently doing his best to show no emotion or discomfort at being delayed from his meeting with the head minister.

As he waited his eyes caught two readers who knelt fifty yards apart from each other at one end of the courtyard. They were each controlling the physical bodies of male slaves in a small circle centered directly between them. The slaves each held a dagger, each one attempting to kill the other.

Controlling another body at twenty five yards was not easy but Arius could certainly perform the task. What impressed him so much was the skill with which they controlled the two slaves. Their movements seemed natural as if they were moving by their own will power. Whenever Arius controlled another body, their movements were always jerky and awkward.

"Domination dueling," Tasitus said quietly, obviously finished with his conversation and noticing what Arius was looking at. "It is a test of skill and stamina. Readers who excel at this skill are called dominators."

"Sub-minister, we rarely practiced anything like this in the compound. Why not?"

"Slaves are at a premium these days," Tasitus explained. "Most students can't dominate bodies very well, so the death of the host slaves would be common. We used to allow the older students to try but it proved too expensive. Hopefully when the Empire captures the island of Camar, slaves will be cheaper."

They watched the two dominators control the slaves for several minutes, but both readers were very cautious with the beings they controlled and neither could kill the other. Eventually one of the slaves just collapsed and Arius realized it was because one particular reader was too exhausted to maintain his control over the host slave. The other slave was soon released as well and both were bound by guards and allowed to live another day. Both the dominators appeared to be exhausted and the loser was helped away by another reader. Arius knew that they could easily kill the two slaves and use the lost essences' to quickly replenish their own, but readers were taught not to do such things unless they had to. If they grew too familiar with using another's essence then they would never grow accustomed to their own natural strength and recovery time.

Arius and Tasitus left the courtyard and entered the central palace. The inside was not lit by crystallus but with simple oil lamps that gave off a strong scented odor. Knowing what he now did about the stones he suspected this was for the many messengers that came and went who would need the light in this dark building. They ascended a flight of stairs towards the main hall and half way up the steps they met what appeared to be a servant woman in black robes as she began to descend. Her belly was swollen with life and Tasitus hurried up the stairs towards her. "Let me help you sister," he said in his soft voice and proceeded to guide her down the dark stone steps.

Arius stared in stunned amazement. No one bothered to help slaves; not soldiers, not messengers, and most definitely not essence readers, the most feared men to walk the roads of the Roh Vec

Empire. He was not sure if it was proper for him to do so but he couldn't resist his own curiosity and he reached out tentatively with his mind to hers. He focused in on her emotions and thoughts. To his surprise he found that she had no fear of him or Tasitus and the majority of her thoughts were only on some certain type of smoked fish she was craving. When Tasitus came back up the stairs toward him he tried to act like what had happened was completely normal, but once again the sub-minister seemed to guess his thoughts.

"I can see you have forgotten lessons on the sisterhood, otherwise you being the younger man would have helped her and not I," Tasitus said, and though he was clearly scolding Arius he maintained a perfectly emotionless tone as readers were trained to.

Arius cursed himself for forgetting about the sisterhood, he bowed apologetically and responded flatly. "You are most correct sub-minister, please excuse my rudeness. I have not forgotten the sisterhood; I simply didn't recognize her robes. She is after all, the first sister I have seen that was not in a book," Arius reasoned.

"Of course, I know you were not deliberately being rude. While we are on the subject, I think it best to remind you to be mindful of mating with women," he stated nonchalantly as they once again began walking towards the main hall. Arius was taken aback by Tasitus's comment.

While being born with essence-touched abilities could certainly happen at random, it was a far more common appearance if the father or the grandfather had been essence-touched as well. The Empire could never have too many readers so it was their duty to find time to impregnate as many suitable women as possible. Like most things in the order, the task was looked at practically. There were houses built in most major cities where women that were deemed suitable by the order were kept and fed for the very purpose of having reader's children. These women were shared like other items owned by the order, and if they became pregnant they then became part of the sisterhood. These women would instantly be brought into the order and cared for. If the child was a boy and was essence-touched he would be taken to the compound. The woman would remain in the sisterhood and would live the rest of her life serving comfortably within the order. If her child was a girl or a boy who was not essence-touched, the child would be fostered out to a middle class family to become a craftsmen or merchant. This allowed a chance for the next generation to be born with essence-touched abilities.

"I know to only mate with women chosen by the order, Sub-minister," he said.

"I am more concerned with how you are mating with these women Arius." Unsure what Tasitus was getting at, Arius decided it was wisest to remain silent.

"Many students have asked me why there are no women within our compound. The answer is because even slave women will distract the students from their training. As you travel you will see slaves and governors alike becoming infatuated with women. Some will throw away everything they stand for to be with the one they love. Even we readers are not immune to the effects. When I was your age a fellow brother became a heretic by running away with a woman and her child; we were forced to hunt him down." Arius was surprised to hear a tone of sadness in Tasitus's voice.

"Remember," he continued, "always mute your physical body when you lay with a woman, just as when you eat food. We readers must not ignore our physical bodies but we should not indulge them either. A reader who becomes greedy or a glutton is no longer worthy of his black robes."

"I will remember Sub-minister. I will not become a slave to my body," Arius said. Tasitus nodded at his response and the two of them came before the great hall. There was a slight wait because of the many messengers coming to see the head minister but eventually they were let through. Just before the doors opened Tasitus gave him one more piece of advice.

"*Be truthful,*" he said telepathically so the guards wouldn't hear. "*The head minister is a very powerful reader.*"

Arius felt a pang of worry and anxiety within himself, but he quickly controlled it. He emptied his thoughts, worries, doubts, and fears, and became Brother Arius of the order of essence readers. Twelve years of waiting and this moment could very well decide the next twelve years. The doors opened and he walked calmly through to meet the head minister.

Chapter 4

The main hall was well lit with oil lamps but the dark walls still made the large room feel cramped and gloomy. Several scribes sat at desks near the back wall and messengers and guards stood silently at the walls ready to move at a moment's notice. The head minister himself sat in the center of the room. In most ways he resembled a simple reader but his hood was down revealing three tattoos on his aging face. One was on his forehead for being an essence reader; another was on his left jaw line for becoming a sub-minister, and the last was on his right jaw line for being the head minister.

Tasitus removed his hood to match his superior and Arius followed suit. Both the older men appeared quite similar physically. They both carried a number of wrinkles around the forehead and eyes but each obviously kept their bodies in good condition.

"Have you chosen a name brother?" the head minister asked. His voice was strong and hard, quite the opposite of Tasitus, Arius noted.

"Arius, head minister," he said, his voice sounding weak in the vast room.

"Let it be known that Brother Arius is the newest member of our order," the head minister said for all to hear and the scribes began writing furiously.

Arius felt the head minister's mind reach out to his own and he allowed him to enter. *Brother Arius, you may refer to me as head minister Vetrix, but in the common tongue only call me head minister.*

"Yes, head minister."

"Yesterday you became a member in the order, Brother Arius," he continued in the common tongue, "but today we will decide how you serve it. The sub-minister," he said acknowledging Tasitus, "has given me a recommendation based on your skill set, but ultimately the decision remains with me. However, if there is a certain task that you wish to pursue, speak now so that I can take it into consideration."

"If it pleases the order I would like to serve the core, head minister," Arius said. The room seemed to freeze completely. The scribes stopped writing, the guards held their breath, and even the oil lamps seemed to dim. The core was a select group of a dozen or so essence readers who answered to the Emperor alone. They were chosen because they were the strongest and smartest in the order. The head minister was also a part of the core.

"Are you still so eager to stand before his Imperial Highness?" the head minister said telepathically.

"I'm not sure I understand head minister," Arius said trying to portray confusion.

"Don't play coy with me Tevarian," the head minister said using his childhood name. *"Tasitus has told of your skill with memories, I know you can't have forgotten how you were brought here."* Arius was afraid that Vetrix would treat him differently because of his past and realized it was foolish for him to think otherwise. Vetrix brought forth his own memory from twelve years ago and let Arius view it. As was usual when looking at old memories, the vision appeared blurry and he found looking through Vetrix's eyes to be quite odd.

He watched the twelve year old boy Tevarian being drug into a dark stone room at the training compound. He was still wearing his stained leather clothes, and even in this old memory one could smell the dried horse shit on his pants. The room was filled with ten other black robed essence readers like Vetrix, though he was only a sub-minister at the time. The boy began to shout insults to keep from showing his fear before the silent readers.

"You black devils! I'll see you all rot in hell where you belong! Where are you keeping my mother and sisters? I demand you release them!" One of the guards cuffed him heavily and he fell silent, but he continued to glare at them. Arius knew this memory well, but he had never seen it from Vetrix's point of view so this time he could hear what the readers were saying to one another telepathically.

"He is too old to be trained, we should have killed him back on the steppes," said one voice. Since this was Vetrix's memory Arius couldn't feel the other essences, so he had no way of knowing which readers were actually speaking or who they were under the robes.

46

"*Surely an exception can be made? He is obviously incredibly gifted,*" countered another.

"*He is too much like his father.*"

"*His father was killed six years ago. The least we could do is try to teach him.*"

"*His mother has already turned him against us.*"

"*But after what he did on the plains…*"

"*All the more reason he should be killed.*"

"*But….*"

"*Enough, it would be far too difficult to train him. He should never have been brought here. He dies tonight.*"

Just then a side door opened and a single blacked robed man stepped into the room. All the readers dropped to one knee and the guards quickly did the same. They pulled Tevarian down with them and he threw an elbow in retaliation. He was cuffed so hard that he fell with a yelp to the ground. The black robed man watched this in silence and then spoke two words with his mind.

"*Teach him,*" he said, and then left the room.

One of the readers stepped forward whom Arius would later identify as the head minister preceding Vetrix. "You will be trained to become an essence reader. You will remain in this compound and learn to be the Emperor's subtle hand. Your kin will be held hostage to see that you cooperate. When your training is done, you will kill them to prove your loyalty to the Emperor," the head minister said.

The boy Tevarian glared back up from the floor in sheer hatred. "The first thing I am going to do when I escape from here is free my mother and sisters. And then I am going to kill the Emperor and all of you black monsters." The head minister simply nodded to the guards who drug Tevarian away.

At that point head minister Vetrix pulled his memory away, leaving Brother Arius with his head spinning. He had no idea that they had come so close to killing him right then. How did they know his father, he wondered? Did they know something about his death? And what had he done on the plains? All he could recall was being taken by the readers. Lastly, who was the man who came in from the side door? He had authority over the head minister, but there was only one person Arius knew who had that kind of power and that was the Emperor himself.

He would have liked to ponder these discoveries more but he knew that head minister Vetrix was waiting for an answer. He responded with his mind.

"My only wish is to serve to my highest potential head minister. If you believe me to be disloyal to the order you have but to ask and I will give my life."

"A statement often said but not always true," Vetrix countered. *"But I know you are loyal Brother Arius, you proved that yesterday by ridding yourself of your family. I only saw fit to remind you that you're a special case among the readers. We will be watching you closely, even though you will no longer be at the compound."*

Then the head minister spoke aloud so all the scribes could here. "While it is noble that you wish to serve in the core, you do not have enough experience in the field yet to perform such a task. Perhaps a seeker position would be more suitable." It did not seem to be a question and the scribes were already writing it down. Arius struggled to control his disappointment. A seeker was nothing more than a glorified watchdog. Whenever a report came in that a possible essence-touched boy was born it was their task to confirm the report and bring the child back to the compound. He knew he should accept the head minister's decision but he was desperate not to become a simple seeker.

"Forgive me head minister, but I feel that this task will be a waste of my talent thus making me less efficient for the order," he said a little too quickly. Again the room fell awkwardly silent and all eyes turned to the head minister.

"I will decide how you will be most efficient to the order," Vetrix said sharply but then he paused in consideration. "But, perhaps you're right Brother Arius. Your talents might be of better use elsewhere. I believe that you would best serve the order by joining the hunters."

Arius quickly bowed his head and the scribes began scribbling furiously. The hunters were the essence readers who hunted down heretics and witches. They were also usually responsible for the assassination of disloyal high ranking officials. Arius was quite pleased with the task, he was certain he would learn much needed skills and skilled hunters were sometimes selected to join the core.

"You will be assigned to sub-minister Falx in Trost province. Their compound is located in a town called Nightgrove," head minister Vetrix said. Arius felt his heart drop. Trost was at the other end of the Empire. It would take weeks of hard riding to get there and the land was sparse and unpopulated. He doubted he would be noticed enough to be allowed to join the core. Still he had waited twelve years and he had learned patience. He knew that he could wait another twelve years if he had to.

"You should leave as soon as possible before the weather gets any colder. The invasion of Camar is scheduled for today so I am sure that Falx will appreciate the extra help," Vetrix said. Both Arius and Tasitus bowed and made their way out of the room. When they entered the courtyard Tasitus reached out to Arius's mind.

"You did well brother, the hunters are one of the most respected groups within the order. Listen well to Falx; he has been the sub-minister at Trost for over a decade. Remember to always obtain knowledge and wisdom from whoever you meet, be they reader, slave, or even your enemy. I will return to the training compound now." Tasitus bowed and quickly left.

Even though he was still surrounded by essence readers Arius suddenly felt alone as he watched Tasitus leave.

On the shores of Camar, General Gavrus blew on his numb hands one more time. The common soldiers often called him General Tigris or The Tiger. He had earned the name as a spry recruit when he killed a tiger with a sword in front of his entire legion. He was over forty now, and couldn't help but wonder if this would be his final campaign for the Roh Vec Empire before retirement. His hair was salting and he awoke each morning with a stiffness in his joints. The two day rocking boat ride hadn't helped the situation either but at least he didn't suffer from sea sickness. A majority of the soldiers had spent most of the trip hanging over the rails with sick stomachs. He watched his army unpack the beached ships through his steamy breath. He had four legions under his command, a little over twenty thousand men. The activity was good for them he could see, or perhaps it was just being on dry land again.

"Damn it's cold," Jacobo, his second-in-command said as he approached. He was several inches taller than Gavrus and dark skinned with close cropped black hair. He had grown up near the southern lands and the cold had never set well with him Gavrus had noticed. He was popular with the soldiers, though, and brutally efficient in completing tasks. Best yet, he was fiercely loyal to Gavrus, and it had been an easy choice in selecting his second-in-command for the campaign.

"It's the damn sea breeze that makes it so bad," Jacobo continued. "I can't feel my fingers. Why the fuck aren't you wearing your winter coat?"

"The men aren't wearing winter clothing, so neither will I," Gavrus said gruffly.

"You won't be any good to the men if you catch cold."

"Thanks for the advice mum," he responded and blew on his hands one more time. Both men slowly broke into long familiar smiles and watched the legions bring the supplies ashore. They had served several military campaigns together and formed a strong trust and friendship.

"I suspect we'll get a scouting report shortly," Jacobo said eventually. The wind picked up and Jacobo swore. "The men will think that their commanding officer is crying," he said wiping his nose and wind struck eyes.

"Just tell them you're weeping for all the widows we will make at the end of the week," Gavrus said, but he too could feel his nose running and wiped it away on his sleeve.

"Why couldn't we have landed in spring again?" Jacobo asked, though he was only joking with Gavrus. Both men were always frustrated with how slow the bureaucracy could be when it came to easy decisions. It didn't take a genius to see that the Empire's economy was declining and the island of Camar was the obvious choice to find new slaves to stimulate it. Now when they finally received orders to make the attack, they came in mid-autumn rather than spring.

"How many men will die come winter because of this foolishness?" Gavrus asked the wind. "A hundred, a thousand, ten thousand? Do you think the governors actually care how many men we lose so long as we succeed?"

"They may not care about the men, but they do care about the honor of the Empire," Jacobo said, believing the question had been aimed at him.

"Honor," Gavrus snorted. "These islanders understand honor better than those politicians. Don't listen too close to those pretty speeches they give, Jacobo."

"Our cause is a necessary one though, wouldn't you agree?" Jacobo asked. "I mean the west doesn't have the infrastructure that the east does, and Roh Vec is always in need of slave labor. What we do here should help the Empire and in doing so it will help feed our men."

"Will it?" Gavrus asked, willing himself not to shiver as a gust of salty air blew by. "There are a total of eight legions under my command, four here and four back in Trost. When was the last time that they received a rest, when was the last time they had more than a few days to see their families? Sometimes I'm not sure who has the better life, the slave or the legionnaire," Gavrus said with a heavy sigh.

Jacobo shifted uneasily at his words. "Don't say such things, the readers may hear you."

A scout approached on horseback interrupting the two generals.

"Report, soldier," Jacobo said. "General Tigris Sir, we have made no contact with king Rubin's army, but several of the locals have led us to believe that he is gathering his army just three days east of here. There is also a minor town that they call Redin just over ten miles from here Sir."

Gavrus scowled to himself. He absolutely hated not knowing exactly where his enemy was. "Very good soldier, your priority remains the same. Find King Rubin's army and report back to me when it's located. Dismissed." The scout departed leaving Gavrus and Jacobo alone.

"Summon the legion commanders, Jacobo" Gavrus said. "I want the eighty-seventh legion to take that town tomorrow, its time they earned a name for themselves. The rest of the army needs to be ready to march in two hours."

"Do you think it wise, to split our forces?" Jacobo asked. "A full legion is a quarter of the army."

"I won't need all the legions to defeat these islanders," he said confidently. "Now make it happen, Jacobo. We have an island to conquer."

As Jacobo gathered the commanders, Gavrus walked across the beach to where twelve black robed readers stood. The legionnaires had given them a wide berth so that they stood out amongst the sea of red shields and leather. Most officers disliked and feared the readers but Gavrus had come to respect them. They were incredibly efficient at everything they did. They were practical, showed no fear, nor did they have a blood lust. On the other hand they were also a huge drain on morale, no soldier wanted to have his essence sucked out of him during a battle.

"Sub-minister Falx," he called out as he approached. One of the readers came over and both men bowed slightly to one another. Gavrus had worked with Falx on a few campaigns and knew that the man liked to be kept informed of most of his decisions.

"Sub-minister, I am sending the eighty-seventh legion to capture a small town nearby." Falx nodded beneath his hood and signaled one of the other readers to come forward. "This is brother Sylvius; he will accompany the commanders to this town," Falx said quietly.

"Do you suspect trouble?" Gavrus asked.

"No, this is only a precaution. Most likely any heretics or witches will be with King Rubin. We will stay with you so that we can seek them out during the battle."

Gavrus worried that sending just a single reader with a quarter of his army wouldn't be enough to protect his officers.

"Sylvius is my most experienced hunter, General," Falx said, reading Gavrus's thoughts. "If there is a heretic or witch at this town he will kill them, he has never failed an assignment."

Chapter 5

Lily woke to darkness. She felt a moment of panic, peering at her surroundings as she tried to determine where she was. Memory of the healing she did on the commander came back to her and she realized she was lying on a blanket in a small tent. She could hear someone breathing nearby and sat up slightly to see better. Her movement must have woken whoever it was because they stirred and a male voice asked "Are you awake then?"

A dark form rose from the ground in front of the tent flap. "Just let me get a light and see how you are," the man said. "You've slept through the day and the night." He stepped through the tent flap and was back in a moment with a lamp that he had lit from one of the cook fires. She saw now that it was the soldier called Gavin, the one who had taken her.

"Where am I? How did I get here?" she asked him sleepily.

"We're right next to the commander's tent. I carried you in after you collapsed from healing the commander. He asked me to bring you to him when you feel able. He wants to see you," Gavin answered.

"So he's all right then? Can he walk?"

"I'll just see if he's awake and you can see for yourself," Gavin answered as he stepped outside the tent, leaving the flap open. Lily saw that it was almost dawn and the sky was lightening in the east. She got to her knees and was trying to stand when Gavin came back inside.

"Here let me help you, you had a bad time of it after the healing," he said as he reached down and held her hand as she stood. She felt shaky but after a moment that passed and she stepped out of the tent. Gavin still had hold of her hand as she stood looking at the sunrise. He let go abruptly with an embarrassed look on his face. "He's just this way, Miss," he said as they headed toward the large tent.

"Please call me Lily," she said as Gavin moved the tent flap aside and she stepped in. The first thing she noticed was that the commander was sitting up on a stool. When he saw Lily he smiled and motioned her to another stool near him. "Please come in. Do you have any idea what you have done for me?" he asked excitedly. He grabbed a stout stick setting near him and said "watch this" as he stood up using the stick for balance. He slowly paced the length of the tent before turning back to sit on the stool. "I can't go very fast or very far yet, but I'm walking again after your healing. What you did was a miracle," he said emphatically." I can't thank you enough."

"I'm so pleased that it worked, what did you feel as I touched you?" she asked him curiously.

"Heat, I felt heat and for a moment pain, but just for a moment, then my legs felt like they had pins poking them. It was the same feeling you get when your foot goes to sleep. I could feel a difference in my legs so I didn't wait long before standing. I almost fell over but thankfully Gavin caught me. But you, what happened to you? I was afraid you'd hurt yourself, you slept so long."

"I don't know enough to answer that. I've only used this power twice. The first time I was young and I passed out, the second time was yesterday and it just made me very weary."

"I know you probably still don't trust me but I'm going to ask you something," the commander said. "We have other men in camp that have injuries. Could you heal them, like you healed me?"

Lily walked over to the camp stool opposite the commander and sat down. She stared at him as she thought about what he asked. Did she want to stay here with these men? They seemed sincere in not wanting to hurt her but they had abducted her even if it was done with good intentions. "I was rather hoping you would take me home now that I've done what you asked," she said, wanting to see what his reply would be.

The commander looked disappointed as he said "If that's what you want, then of course we'll take you home. I just hoped you might be willing to stay for just a day or two and see to some of the men."

Lily thought for a minute before replying. Truth be told she would like to try her hand at some more healing, but she felt nervous surrounded by all these men. "If I was to stay, where would I sleep? I don't feel entirely safe here in a camp full of unknown men."

"I assure you that you'll not be harmed in any way. You can have the tent you stayed in last night and Gavin will sleep across the threshold to make sure no one enters without your permission. I hope you trust him a bit already."

Although she was still uncertain, she made the decision to stay. After all, if need be, she could probably escape into the woods and find her own way back home. The forest would hide her. She hoped she was making the right choice when she said, "Alright then, I'll stay for a few days and try to heal your men."

"Excellent," the commander said with a grin. "Gavin, get Lily something to eat and then take her to see Campbell. I believe he broke his arm yesterday when his horse threw him. If she can fix my legs, I'm sure she can fix his arm and we'll see how tired it makes her. Lily, don't push yourself past what your body can handle. It'll do you no good to pass out every time you heal someone."

Gavin went out and brought back a bowl of stew for Lily to eat. She sat quietly on the stool eating while the commander read through reports. When she was done Gavin pushed the flap open and Lily followed him across camp to a man sitting beside one of the cook fires. He had his arm in a sling and was gingerly trying to eat without jostling it. He looked up as they reached the fire. "Hey Campbell, looks like that horse of yours really fixed up your arm," Gavin said. "How's it feeling?"

"It hurts like hell, begging your pardon Miss," Campbell said looking at Lily, "and I can't do much of anything one handed."

"This is Lily, the healer who helped the commander and she'd like to see if she can heal your arm. Will you let her try?" asked Gavin.

Campbell narrowed his eyes and looked closely at Lily. He was a big man as were most of the soldiers and somewhat intimidating. She found herself wishing that they could have tried this out on someone a little less frightening. After studying her for a moment though, he nodded. "If there's something you think would take away the pain and give me back the use of my arm, I'm willing to let you have a go at it. What would I need to do?" he asked.

Gavin motioned him toward the baggage wagon. "Why don't you just sit in the shade of the wagon and Lily will take a look at it."

"You won't have to do a thing, just stay still. I'm just going to touch you, alright? Try not to jerk," Lily said.

Campbell sat beside the wagon as Lily knelt down in front of him. She gently removed the sling and pushing up his sleeve, placed her hand on his broken arm. Once again, she thought "heal" as she touched him. She felt heat and something seemed to click into place in his arm. Campbell looked up at her; his eyes widened and he gently

55

straightened out his arm. "Son of a b.., oh sorry Miss, but it's healed!" he exclaimed. "The pain is completely gone; it feels as good as new. What did you do woman?" He grabbed Lily by the shoulders with both arms and hugged her tightly. She hadn't fainted but her head was buzzing and his squeezing was making it hard to breath. She moved out of his grasp but smiled as she did. She looked around and noticed that there were several soldiers watching them. It frightened her for a moment until she saw that they were all looking at her in wonder.

Gavin helped Lily get to her feet. She was still a little shaky and clutched his arm as she got her balance. "I think we should get you back to your tent until you regain your strength. I'll see if I can find another soldier who could use healing if you still want to try some more. You can see them in the tent," he told her.

"Thank you," Lily replied. Campbell went off, showing off his healed arm to everyone he saw, as Lily and Gavin walked back to the tent. She went inside to rest while Gavin wandered through the camp in search of sick soldiers.

Lily was able to heal a dozen more men over the next few days. She found that the sicker they were the more exhausted she felt, which didn't surprise her. If she let more time pass between healings that helped, but eventually she reached a point where she couldn't heal at all. She wished she knew if there was something she could do to regain her strength more quickly. As much as she wanted to return to her home she also was glad for this chance to try out her healing powers.

Gavin was always at her side and she found him to be an interesting companion. He knew a fair amount about plants as his father had been a farmer, and they spent some time discussing the uses of various herbs. He took her through the camp each day to see the soldiers that needed healing and when she was tired, he brought them to her tent. He slept outside the door of the tent until one night when it rained and she insisted he sleep inside. He looked a little embarrassed by this until she assured him that she felt safer with him there. Although most of the soldiers she met treated her kindly, there were others that looked at her suspiciously making her aware of her vulnerability in the camp.

Gavin walked through camp after seeing to his horse one morning several days after Lily's arrival. He was sure they would be moving on soon and always liked to check his gelding's feet for himself. His father had always told him to take responsibility for his horse himself and it wouldn't let you down when you needed it. He had been spending so much time with Lily that he hadn't been following his normal routine and felt a little unsettled, although he was enjoying the time he spent with her and was continually amazed at what she could do with just a touch of her hands. He'd always considered his sixth sense unusual, but what she could do was just plain amazing.

"Hey, Gavin," one of the soldiers called to him, "I haven't seen you around for our nightly dice game lately. Is your money all gone?"

Gavin walked over to the man as he squatted with friends beside a cook fire. "Commander asked me to help the healer while she's in camp. It's been keeping me busy."

"I've seen her; she's a looker, isn't she? How does she heal anyway?"

"She just touches you wherever your hurt and you're healed," Gavin explained.

The man laughed and stood. "She can touch me wherever she likes. Do you think she can cure a case of the clap with a touch," he said grabbing his groin with a lewd grin on his face. "Has she been touching you, Gavin, is that what's keeping you so busy?"

Gavin had hit him with a solid right fist before he even had time to think about what he was doing. Before the soldier could recover and take a swing of his own, Gavin grabbed him by the neck of his tunic and lifted him an inch off the ground. "This woman is not a whore, nor is she to be treated as one." He lifted him another inch higher and shook him roughly. "Do you understand?" he said as he looked him in the eye.

The man nodded and Gavin dropped him and pushed him away. He left without a backward glance, hoping he had gotten his point across.

Four days after she had first come to the camp Commander Versan sent a man to ask her to join him for a meal in his tent in the early evening. She had been resting but went gladly as she wanted to

57

find out what would happen now that she had healed most of the soldiers that needed healing. Would she be sent home, or would they expect her to join them as they marched toward potential battle to help with any injured men? She had seen a horse and rider come in earlier and suspected that he had news of the Empire. She stepped in to the commander's tent and was pleased to see that Gavin had also joined him as well as several other soldiers she didn't know. "How are you feeling Lily? I understand you healed more of my men this afternoon. I hope you didn't tire yourself out too much?" Commander Versan asked her.

"I was tired earlier but after a rest I feel almost like my usual self. How long do you think you'll be staying here? When I was in your tent yesterday, I overheard you say that the Empire has been sighted off the coast. Do you think they will invade Camar?" she asked anxiously.

"Yes, I'm afraid it's already happened. I heard from a courier earlier today that they've landed some way north of here. I don't have orders yet but I'm certain that we'll be sent to meet up with the King soon. I think there should be time yet to get you safely into Redin. Do you have friends in the town that you could stay with?"

"Yes, but do you really think that's necessary? I'd rather just go home," she said uneasily.

"I'll feel much better if you're protected within the town walls and it will be easy for us to pass by and leave you there on our way north," he answered. Just then they heard the sound of a horse being ridden hard coming nearer. Gavin opened the tent flap and they saw it stop abruptly just outside. A man jumped from the horse and entered the tent.

"Commander Versan, I've just come from the town of Redin," the man said breathlessly. "There's a large force of soldiers from the Empire seen heading our way. We don't stand a chance without you, you must help us!" The man leaned forward in an effort to catch his breath as he looked imploringly at the commander.

"Damn it, how did they get here so quickly?" Versan said as he turned to one of the soldiers in the tent. "Strike the camp and prepare to leave at once. The rest of you prepare yourselves." As soon as the tent was empty of everyone except Lily and Gavin he looked at Lily and said, "It seems that we have no choice in where you go. I can't send you alone in to the woods so you'll have to come with us for the time being." He turned then toward Gavin. "You'll be her guard. It's imperative that she does not fall into the hands of the Empire. I don't know if the Empire has some way of recognizing what she is, but you must keep her away from them. Hide her, disguise her, whatever you can, just keep her safe. Hopefully the enemy will wait for morning to attack and we can prevent them from taking the town. I don't think they'll send a large force for such a small town but I wish I knew their numbers. In the meantime, though, I'd like her safely hidden away somewhere within the walls." He turned then to Lily, "You said you have someone who can hide you?"

Lily thought at once of Samuel. "Yes, there's an apothecary shop just east of the town square where the markets are. The owner was a friend of my mothers and has known me since I was a child. The last time I spoke with him he told me to come to him if I ever needed a safe haven. I can go there."

"Good, then let's get this camp down and ride to the town's defense. I may not be walking far yet, but at least I'll be able to ride a horse thanks to you, Lily. I'll never be able to repay you for what you've done but I'll do my best to see you safe." Commander Versan surprised her by giving her a brief hug and then walked as quickly as he was able from the tent. Lily and Gavin followed.

The dark ride to the town of Redin was frightening for Lily. She didn't have the necessary horseman skills to ride at the fast pace they needed so she rode with Gavin on his horse, hanging on tightly. The moon was waxing toward full giving the soldiers plenty of light to ride by and they set their pace accordingly. Staying out of the forest they rode through open meadowland for several hours making good time. They were perhaps thirty minutes from town and had just topped a small rise when they saw the lights from the campfires of the Empire's soldiers spread across the lowlands to the east of Redin. The commander ordered a halt. He called to the man from town and several soldiers, Gavin included.

"Look at the numbers. We'll never get past their camp without being seen. There's too much open area and no cover. Dawn is coming soon. Ideas?" he asked.

The man from town replied, "They marched in from the east so you'll have to come to the west end of the town to avoid them. If you enter the forest over there," he pointed to the west, "you will eventually come out near the western gates. We have someone prepared to open them when we reach it. The darkness will hide your approach."

Lily waited while the men looked over the area and spoke quietly among themselves. They did a lot of head shaking and muttering. "The trail is too hard to find in the dark and we'll lose too much time trying to find it," one soldier said, looking nervously over his shoulder at the woods. "Besides I've heard strange things happen in that forest."

Lily wasn't sure if they would listen to a woman but she spoke up when she heard his comment. "Nonsense, I've grown up in those trees and I can lead you safely through. We would have to go single file but I promise you no harm will come to you with me in the lead if you just stay on the trail."

Commander Versan waited a moment to see if any other suggestions were put forth. When no one else spoke he said, "I see no other way to get inside the town before sun up. Gavin, you'll lead the way from here on out with Lily guiding you. Let's go, we have no time to lose and from this point on I want silence."

They entered the forest single file with Lily whispering directions to Gavin who skillfully guided the horse wherever she told him. The only sounds were the hoot of an owl, the rustlings of the small night creatures and the creaking of branches swaying in the wind. No tree limbs fell on anyone and nothing untoward happened but it seemed to Lily it took forever until they were coming to the edge of the trees on the same path she had taken on her way to market just three days ago. As much as she loved the forest, the ride in the dark had made her nervous. She and Gavin stayed just inside the tree line while they waited for the rest of the men to leave the woods. Lily noticed the relief on the faces of most of them as they left the trees.

The man from town rode over to speak quietly with Versan. "I hope to never do that ride again in the dark. I didn't want to say anything, but there's some in town who say that these woods are haunted and I'm thinking I agree."

"Nonsense, we made it through fine. Now, where is the west gate? We haven't much time and I think we'll have to ride straight in. Can you go ahead and make sure it's open for us?"

"Aye, that I will sir," he said. He rode off toward the town and Commander Versan addressed the soldiers.

"We'll give him five minutes and then follow. Go quickly but as quietly as you can. We'll need that gate shut the minute we're all

60

through. Hopefully the Empire won't have sentries on this side of town." The horses shifting their weight was the only sound Lily heard for several minutes until suddenly there came a cry of alarm and the sound of an arrow leaving a bow. "Ride! They're on to us, ride straight to the gate now!" the commander shouted as he spurred his horse forward, his men following in his wake.

Chapter 6

Gavin heard the sound of arrows hitting the wooden gate as it slammed shut behind the last soldier to enter. He wasn't sure that they had all made it in. The sun was just rising as the Empire began their attack and he knew if they had arrived any later they would have never made the gate. The sounds of soldiers shouting could be heard on the other side of the wall and arrows began raining down around them. He could see some with fire that even now were landing on the roofs of thatch on many of the buildings. The quiet town was in chaos. The soldiers with him had dismounted and were running up the stairs to the top of the walls to help the townspeople repel the ladders that were even now being set up, while others were firing their arrows back at the Empire. People were hurrying in every direction, one man was trying to save his horses from a burning byre as they snorted and stamped, their eyes rolling in terror. He managed to yank the door open and the horses ran through the crowd causing even more confusion. A few people were throwing water on some of the fires but there were too few people and not enough water and it was evident that the whole town would soon be up in flames.

Gavin could see that the situation was hopeless. He never imagined that the Empire would send so many soldiers to the town of Redin. He knew that Commander Versan needed every man to fight off the legionnaires but he had also told him to take care of Lily. The words of the old woman in the woods suddenly flashed through his mind *"I lay this burden on you, help her find her purpose."* He still wasn't sure what she meant but he was obviously supposed to keep her safe. If he hurried maybe he could get Lily to her friend's house and still have time to fight alongside his commander. "I have to get you away from the walls to safety. Where did you say your friend lived?" Gavin shouted, trying to be heard over the noise.

Lily yelled something that Gavin couldn't hear and pointed. Gavin turned his horse in that direction and headed down an alley that wasn't too crowded with people. He saw Lily look with terror at a home which was quickly becoming engulfed in flames. She slid off the back of his horse and was about to run inside when Gavin quickly dismounted and caught her by the arm. "Are you trying to get yourself killed?" he yelled angrily. "If anyone is in there, then they're already dead and if not then we'd do better to search outside. Is this where your friend lives?"

"No, this was the home of my friend Bridgett and I need to see if she's all right," she told him. He watched her looking about frantically, turning when she heard a woman's cry. She ran toward the woman who stood in the doorway of a nearby house and hugged her tightly. "Come quickly," he heard the other woman say. "Liam is hurt." He hurried over and followed the two women inside.

Lily was surprised when Gavin grabbed her and kept her from entering the burning house. She hadn't even realized that she was about to run inside until she heard him yell. The terror she felt when she saw her friend's house burning had apparently temporarily relieved her of her senses. She was thankful when she saw Bridgett calling her from a neighbor's house. She hugged her friend tightly and entered the home with her, as Gavin followed. The first thing she saw were her friend's two little boys, they appeared to be frightened but fine. They were staring with wide eyes at their father who was lying on the floor with an arrow in one thigh. "Can you help him?" Bridgett asked her.

Lily knelt beside him assessing his injury. There wasn't much blood, she was sure she could pull the arrow out and quickly heal him hopefully without weakening herself too much in the process.

"Yes, it doesn't look too bad. Gavin can you snap off the arrowhead for me and then hold him still while I pull the arrow out. Bridgett, do you have some strips of cloth to bind it?" Lily ordered them both about with a new found confidence. She was glad she now had some skill with her healing from the time spent in camp. She watched as Gavin broke off the head, causing Liam to moan when his leg was jostled, and Bridgett quickly ripped a piece off the bottom of her shift and gave it to Lily. "All right, now hold him still," Lily said as she jerked the shaft of the arrow out the front of his thigh. She put her hand over the wound to heal it and then took the cloth and bound the wound quickly hoping that Bridgett hadn't seen what she did. Bridgett didn't know of Lily's powers and Lily felt it would be better to keep her ignorant. With the Empire just the other side of the town walls, she would feel safer with less people knowing she was a witch, as the Empire called her. She was relieved when the healing didn't tire her too badly.

"Thank you, Lily, I feel better already," Liam said. He sat up and was preparing to stand when Bridgett pushed him down.

"You stay put for awhile, we'll be safer in here than out on the streets."

"No, I need to get you and the boys to your father's cellar and then get back on the walls and push these bastards back. None of us will be safe if we don't keep them out." He stood and picked up the smallest boy, took the other boy's hand and went out the door. Bridgett, Lily and Gavin followed him. Lily hugged Bridgett. "I'll come and find you if I can," she said. "I need to go to Samuel right now." She watched as they hurried down the alley hoping that she would see them again.

Gavin looked at Lily. "Which way?" he asked her. She pointed in the opposite direction her friends had just taken. As he took her hand to pull her down the street Lily felt a tingle when their hands met and the tiredness she felt after Liam's healing left her. She saw that Gavin swayed a little and they looked at each other in confusion for an instant, releasing each others hands. What had just happened, Lily wondered. There was no time to question, though, as another barrage of arrows flew over their heads landing on a nearby roof. The roof went up in flames and they ran, covering their heads as best they could from the falling sparks.

The apothecary shop wasn't far but it took them much longer than it should have because of the mass of people running in confusion. They had left Gavin's horse behind knowing that it wouldn't be possible to ride with the streets so full of people. As they approached the shop Lily was relieved to see that it, at least, was not on fire. They heard a loud cry of many voices coming from the town square. "The walls are breached, the walls are breached, they're in!" the voices shouted. She looked over her shoulder and could see a mass of red Roh Vec soldiers crawling over the walls in the distance. Hurrying even more quickly now, Gavin pushed open the heavy wood door of the apothecary shop, shutting it firmly behind them.

The quiet in the shop was palpable in contrast to the noise outside. Lily stood for a moment just listening but couldn't hear a thing. "Samuel?" she said quietly. She nervously repeated his name twice more while she waited for a response, walking slowly toward the back of the shop. She looked at Gavin and lifted her shoulders in a shrug as if to say "what now?" when they both heard a slight moan from behind the back curtain. Hurrying through the door she saw Samuel crumpled on the floor of his workroom.

"Samuel, what happened?" she said as she knelt down and slipped her arm under his head to raise him up slightly. His face was ashen and there was a gash on the side of his head that was bleeding slightly. She automatically reached up her hand to heal the wound, but he pushed it away weakly, saying "No, no, don't heal me. The Empire is bound to have at least one reader with them and he'll sense your presence if you heal me."

Gavin looked at Lily, a question on his face, as she said, "I don't know what you're talking about Samuel. And how do you know what I can do? I suspected you did when you offered me safe haven with you the last time we met, but why didn't you say anything?" It seemed to her that there was no point in trying to be secretive with him and no time left for it either.

"I suspected that you were but it wasn't until I watched you from my window on market day as you healed that boy that I was certain. I wasn't sure how to approach you about it. It was your secret and I hoped you would trust me with it one day. When I offered to help you I had no idea that the day would come so soon or that the Empire would be on our very doorstep. There are things that I must tell you quickly before they find us, but first who's this?" he said eyeing Gavin suspiciously. "He has the look of a soldier, can he be trusted?"

"This is Gavin; he's a soldier with Commander Versan's men. He's been helping me and yes I do trust him with anything you want to tell me."

Samuel looked at him, sizing him up, as Lily said, "But let's get you more comfortable. You didn't tell me what happened to you," she said as she and Gavin helped him sit up against the wall in a more comfortable position. She found a cloth and wet it, holding it to the wound on his head.

"I have a bad heart and had a dizzy spell while I was on a stool trying to reach something on the top shelf. I fell and hit my head on the edge of the table. It's of no consequence, though. We have very little time and there are things I must tell you. First, do you know what a reader is?"

Both Lily and Gavin shook their heads and he continued.
"They are evil men with the ability to read our minds. I don't know

what all they are capable of but I do know they're the reason the witches were killed all those years ago. They're the reason any witches that are alive today are in hiding, as you should be. I blame myself for not telling you this sooner so you could have left the area, but I thought it would be safer here with me watching over you than sending you off to the Northlands in search of a dream."

"The Northlands? Why would I want to go to the Northlands?" Lily asked.

"If there are any witches left alive, that's where they'll be," he answered. "It was the plan all those years ago when the witches went into hiding. A safe place for them to live in the hope that one day the Empire would be brought down and they could take their proper place in this world. I don't know what came of the plans or if anyone even survived. If your mother is still alive, she'll be there too."

"My mother?" Lily said in astonishment. "My mother died when my brother was born. What are you saying?"

"Shortly after your brother was born, we had word that the Empire was conducting another witch hunt. She didn't want to bring them down on your family and you two children were too young to travel so far, so she left you all to travel to the Northlands alone. The plan was that she would send word when she reached there and your father would join her, bringing you children with him. You were too young to understand, so when he never got word, he let you think that she had died. It seemed easier at the time and he thought he would tell you when you were old enough to understand. He died before he got the chance. I think he was afraid you would hate him for not telling you the truth."

Lily was stunned as she listened to Samuel. All these years she had thought her mother dead and now to find that she might possibly be alive. It left her speechless. She looked at Samuel and saw that he was even weaker than when they had found him. The talking had tired him and she resisted the urge to touch and heal him. He said it wasn't safe because of someone called a reader. There was still so much she didn't understand and she was afraid that time had run out for them.

Samuel looked at Gavin as he spoke again. "If you want to help Lily now, you must listen to me. The Empire's soldiers will be here soon and they're looking for people to round up as slaves. If you want to live you must not let them know you're a soldier. They'll separate you from Lily if they find out. Pretend to be her husband or brother and it's more likely that you'll be kept together, at least at first. Once they ship you across the water, as I suspect they will, I don't know what they'll do."

"How do you know so much about the Empire and what their plans are?" Gavin asked him.

"Another life time, young man, I wasn't always this old. We all have our secrets," he replied as he closed his eyes and leaned back against the wall. "I'm afraid there's no time to share them with you now."

Other than the sound of Samuel's harsh breathing, the shop was silent now that he stopped speaking, so silent that when the door was roughly shoved open and banged against the wall it sounded like thunder to Lily's ears. Roh Vec soldiers had entered the shop and in moments they would be caught in the back room. Gavin jumped in front of Lily as the curtain was pushed aside and a soldier from the Empire thrust himself in, his spear pointed directly at Gavin's chest. Lily's heart thumped painfully as she shouted at him, "Please don't kill my husband," and threw herself into Gavin's arms.

~

The hunter Sylvius sat on his horse and watched the assault of Redin. It was a pointless confrontation to him, not to mention extremely inefficient. True, the Empire had soldiers to waste, but the whole purpose of the invasion was obtaining slaves, not burning villages. If he had been in command he would have at least asked the town to surrender before storming in and killing the labor they needed. Yet he was not in command so he watched in silence. Through his eyes he could see hundreds of shimmering souls slowly departing the battle up towards the spirit realm. He wondered how many would make it there and how many would remain trapped forever, a ghost on this world.

It was at this moment that he felt a faint hum of power. He reached out quickly with his mind and tried to follow it. The feeling stopped before he could pinpoint its source but he knew enough to act. He dismounted and approached an officer near him.

"Send a message to sub-minister Falx immediately. I have made contact with a witch and I'm closing in for the kill." The man shrunk back from Sylvius in fear but rode off quickly to do as he asked. Sylvius turned to the small town and drew forth his twin

67

daggers. "Let the hunt begin," he thought, and walked towards the flames and screams of agony in the burning town.

Chapter 7

It only took two days to find King Rubin's army. General Gavrus had been watching them through the light fog since dawn. They were positioned a quarter mile away on a great open hill surrounded by pastures. Clearly he didn't wish to be taken by surprise but then again he couldn't hide his army very well either. He estimated that the King had gathered almost every able bodied man on the island, roughly twenty-five thousand men. General Gavrus had hoped he would do just that because it saved him from fighting more battles. Now he could claim the whole island in one solid victory.

"That's quite a hill to climb." Jacobo pointed out from behind him. The wind spread the smell of campfires and human waste across the fields.

"It's a small matter," he responded.

"Are you sure you don't want to send some skirmishers first? We could have some catapults built by tomorrow and…"

"Peace Jacobo. We're not here to slaughter them all, we want them alive."

"I still don't like it, what if they don't take the bait?"

"Just be ready to close the jaws of the tiger when I give the signal," Gavrus responded without looking. He sought out sub-minister Falx and gave him a nod, knowing the man would read his thoughts.

"The plan is sound, General, we will be ready," the dark robed man said eerily.

Gavrus called for his horse and rode before his army. Three full legions, fifteen thousand men, the seventeenth, twenty-second, and the veterans of the fifty-fourth. They were situated near small campfires to keep warm. Some talked but many were quiet as they checked then rechecked their equipment. Short swords were sharpened, straps to helmets and shields were closely inspected and comrades helped tie down breast plates. The veterans portrayed confidence which heartened the less experienced soldiers. The legions

69

rose and stood in formation when they saw him, forming a sheer wall of red shields and discipline. He almost felt sorry for the islanders.

"Legionnaires!" he yelled at the top of his voice. "It's damn cold! But I woke up this morning with a fire in my veins, because today, today we get to do what we do best. And what is it we do best legionnaires?"

"Kill!" Came the deafening roar of fifteen thousand men.

"What!" Gavrus said holding a hand to his ear.

"Kill!" The roar came back even louder this time.

"That's more like it, I was worried my army was still on the mainland!" he said grinning and the army began to laugh.

"We are outnumbered today and they have the high ground," he said seriously, "but I ask you, have I ever failed you? When have we lost a battle? We defeated the Tornes! We crushed the Altiats! We conquered the whole territory of Trost and we will conquer here!"

"Tigris, Tigris, Tigris," the men chanted.

He raised his hands to silence them and continued. "Discipline leads to victory and victory to glory." They smacked their swords against their shields once in perfect unison. Silence followed and he turned away from his army. It was a short speech he knew, but he often felt that the shorter the speech, the more focused the men would be. Slowly he pointed to the hill and his army marched across the open field.

It was natural for almost every army to wish to charge with a war cry and the sound of drums, but the Empire's legions marched to the eerie sound of a few flutes. It was their silence not their ferocity that unnerved their opponents. Gavrus dismounted and marched at the head of his army. Most generals led from the back of the army, making decisions that were to benefit the battle, but Gavrus found that leading from the front greatly inspired his troops. Any commander who shared the burdens of his men and placed his life in danger as they did would wield an army that would follow him on to any battlefield.

He was armed as his legions were with a tall rectangular shield and a thick short sword. He had only a small guard of twenty men, one who carried his solid gold standard of a small tiger. The seventeenth and twenty-second legions marched with him in perfect square formations. The veteran fifty-fourth legion marched with Jacobo one hundred yards behind the front force. As the lead legions approached the base of the hill the islanders began roaring taunts and battle cries but they made no move to charge down at the legionnaires.

"Arrows!" a legionnaire suddenly cried out and pointed to the sky. Each legion bunched together even tighter, all the soldiers lifting their large rectangular shields above their heads so that they overlapped one another. As a result each of the legions had a solid roof over their heads when thousands of whistling missiles came crashing down. The legions kept marching up the hill with cold efficiency, stepping to the eerie tune of the flutes.

At one hundred yards Gavrus felt the all too familiar fear of death descend upon him. The cold no longer bothered him and his shield seemed weightless. His stomach tightened up and he focused on just breathing in and out. He would never let his men see the fear in him but there were times that he envied the readers who always seemed so detached.

At fifty yards the islanders gave a great roar and charged. Immediately the legionnaires brought their shields down and widened their formations, closing the gaps between each legion. The soldiers of Camar charged straight into a wooden wall of red shields. Gavrus held his large shield before him and slashed out with his short sword. Heavy blows from Camarian spears and swords rained down, rattling his arm, but the strong wood held. A rather fearsome Camarian singled him out as a commander and charged him. His long sword stuck into Gavrus's shield and he took the opportunity to quickly slice up the man's groin to the belly. His face went white and he fell to the ground groaning. From experience Gavrus knew the man could live for a few minutes, but his death was sealed. Gavrus fought on until one of his guardsmen took his place. He rested briefly and surveyed the carnage.

The islanders had the height of the hill and weight in numbers and they were slowly pushing the Roh Vec legions back down the hill. The Camarians seemed to think that they were winning the fight for they pushed hard, trying to force the legions to break and flee. Gavrus smiled because that was exactly what he wanted the Camarians to think. Any skillful observer could see that far more Camarians had perished than the legions. Gavrus nodded to the nearest flute player who changed his dreary tune to a fast high pitched song. The other flute players were expecting the signal and likewise altered the tunes they were playing. To most the sound was drowned out by the dying screams and challenging roars but the legionnaires were hard trained to listen to the music of the flutes.

Immediately the legions began to retreat as was planned. The Camarians roared with victory and chased after them down the hill. Gavrus turned and ran with his men. He prayed silently because he knew this was when his slow moving soldiers were most vulnerable to being cut down from behind. Meanwhile the remaining fifty-fourth legion in reserve with Jacobo split and began to move to the left and right of the retreating force. When the pursuing Camarians reached the base of the hill Gavrus and his two legions turned to face them and Jacobo and the fifty-fourth attacked from the sides.

The Camarians realized the trap too late and suddenly found themselves nearly surrounded by legionnaires. Gavrus noticed King Rubin amongst his soldiers attempting to get them to move back up the hill, but the legionnaires were far more disciplined and quickly completed the choking ring of death. With no retreat, the Camarians fought back like a wounded animal. Gavrus admired them for their courage but knew the end was near. The Camarian long swords and axes were ideal for individual combat but the close pressed bodies made them hard to use without hitting your own comrades. The Legionnaires suffered no such fate. Their short swords and large protective shields allowed them to step forward so close that long swords were useless and they could slash at will. They aimed for the often exposed groin, armpits, or throat. For every legionnaire that died at least three islanders if not four died first.

Gavrus gave another signal and soldiers to the rear of the fighting drew forth heavy javelins and threw them into the surrounded islanders. Gavrus let the one-sided battle continue trying to judge when the Camarians would realize that their situation was hopeless. When he deemed the time was right he called for his horse. Mounting up he nodded to one of his guards who blew three long blasts on a horn he carried. The legions stopped their deadly advance and withdrew five paces, bringing the battle to a pause. Gavrus didn't waste the moment.

"Camarians!" He yelled at the top of his lungs. "Camarians! Listen to what I have to say!" He began to ride around the massive circle of bodies, making sure the eyes of his enemies followed him. "Today you have seen the might of the Empire. Today you have seen why the whole world is under our rule. Lay down your arms, surrender now and I promise you as high general of the west that I will spare your lives."

As soon as he finished speaking some islanders began to lay down their weapons but then another voice began to shout out over the crowds. It didn't take long for Gavrus to discover that it was King Rubin himself who was speaking. "And what would we do if we surrendered!" he shouted angrily. "It is well known that you make slaves of everyone you conquer including women and children. We are not as foolish as the mainlanders; we would rather die than lick the heels of your Imperial boots!" At this the islanders began to nod with grim determination.

Gavrus was unfazed by the King's words. His eyes sought out the black robed reader Falx and he gave him a curt nod before continuing. "Well spoken King Rubin. You Camarians are no fools, so I make this pledge to you. Surrender now and I will offer you each the chance to join our legions. Those that join will free their families from slavery as well." The partial lie flowed forth from him so easily that he almost believed it himself. He would take some of the islanders into his army if only to fill the places of the legionnaires who had died, but most would become slaves.

"Please King Rubin see reason, there is no need for you to destroy all of your subjects," Gavrus finished. At hearing his words the Camarians seemed unsure of what to do and many eyes turned back to the King. Rubin appeared about to speak but then he stiffened. In a dream-like state he dropped to his knees and laid his weapons down. The rest of the islanders followed suit with their heads held low. Gavrus couldn't help but smile; he had just vanquished the island's army, saved the lives of thousands of his men and captured almost twenty thousand capable slaves.

He wasn't sure who started it, but slowly the chant burst forth from his legions. "Tigris! Tigris! Tigris!" they shouted. He raised his sword high above him and let them praise his victory.

Chapter 8

Lily walked despondently next to Gavin and the rest of townspeople as they were marched from what had been the town of Redin. Nothing in her life had prepared her for how she, along with everyone else, was now being treated. She had known sadness in her life when her father had died, loneliness when her brother had left and fear when Gavin had first taken her to the camp, but she had never known such cruelty as the soldiers practiced upon them now. Their hands had been tied in front of them, their feet tied loose enough to walk but too tight to run. They were taken out of town and told to watch as the soldiers burned it to the ground, along with anyone who hadn't made it out. At least the dead had been burned along with the town, as was their custom and judging by the number of people around her, there had been plenty who died. She guessed that there were two thousand others with her, maybe half the town and surrounding area's normal population. They had slept on the ground last night surrounded by guards, given a bite of hard bread and water to break their fast and been told to march this morning. They were heading east to the coast and from there, no one knew.

She glanced at Gavin stumbling along beside her. She was still embarrassed when she remembered how she had thrown herself into his arms and proclaimed him to be her husband. She wasn't sorry that she had done it, though, because Samuel had been right. The soldiers had been herded together and taken somewhere separate from the rest of them. She shuddered with her last memory of Samuel. The Empire's soldiers had left him on the floor of his shop to burn along with it. Taking the role of her husband, Gavin had stayed beside her protectively as the soldiers had pushed them down the streets and out of town. He hadn't fought back as she knew he had wanted to. He had played the part of townsman and husband, not the soldier that he was. Later, when they had been herded together with the rest of the townsfolk, the soldiers circling the large group to stop any escapes, he had slept close beside her, protecting her. With winter coming soon she had appreciated his warmth as much as his protection since they hadn't been given any protection from the cold.

74

Time passed slowly as they walked giving Lily plenty of time to think. She knew Gavin must be wondering what had happened to the rest of his comrades and Commander Versan, just as she was worrying about Bridgett and Liam. She hadn't seen either of them since the morning she had healed Liam. She would like to think they were safely hidden somewhere but feared they were dead along with so many others.

When she thought of all Samuel had told her before the soldiers left him to die, she was incredulous. Readers, witches in the Northlands and her mother possibly alive, none of it seemed possible. It gave her hope that if she could survive this and whatever came after, maybe she could escape and try to find her way north. *You will find what you are seeking to the north, you must follow the black book,* Grandma Joan had told her. Is that what the old woman's words had meant? That she should go to the Northlands? The only black book she could think of was a holy book she had once seen that told the story of the Maker and how he had created their world but she couldn't understand how she was supposed to follow a book.

"What are you thinking about?" Gavin suddenly asked, causing her to jump.

"I was wondering what's happened to Bridgett and her family and to Commander Versan and the rest of the men," she told him, then said shyly, "I need to thank you for staying with me. I know you'd like to be with your commander right now. I'm sorry I got you into this."

Gavin gave her a look and then shook his head. "You didn't get me in to anything. My orders were to protect you, I only wish I'd managed it. I didn't expect the soldiers to get into the town so quickly, I thought I'd have time to hide you somewhere. Besides, even if the commander hadn't ordered me to stay with you, I feel responsible for you. I brought you into our camp and you're in this mess because of me."

"I don't know that I would have been any safer staying alone in the forest. The soldiers would have gotten there eventually. I'm glad you're with me, though, I'd be much more frightened alone."

Gavin winked at her. "You wouldn't expect me to leave my wife by herself, would you?"

Lily blushed. She was growing to like this man. "Of course not, my husband."

As the day wore on Lily grew more and more tired. They had taken a brief rest at midday and were given another piece of hard bread and more water. She had never been so hungry and sore in her life. The ropes chafed at her wrists and ankles and if you didn't walk slowly, it was easy to trip. The soldiers would then prod you with beating staves until you got up and if you weren't quick enough you might find yourself with a few new bruises. Of course, if you walked too slowly you would still be prodded with the stave so no matter what you did you couldn't win. The elderly seemed to have the most trouble and were often the butt of the soldier's cruel tricks.

She was watching the soldiers and trying to keep a safe distance from them when she stepped into a pothole, causing her to stumble. Gavin turned to help her up when he was pushed back by a soldier. "Oh no, you just keep walking, I'll help your pretty wife up," he said as he leered at Lily. Gavin lunged for him but the man shoved him and with his feet tied he fell heavily to the ground. As he rolled to get up another soldier appeared and pointed his sword at Gavin's throat.

"If you want to live you'll get up and stay where you are," he told him. He backed the sword up a few inches and waited while Gavin got slowly to his feet. The soldier grabbed his arm and held him. When he once again started toward Lily, she shook her head at him and mouthed the word "go" as she tried to get up. The first soldier grabbed her arm and helped her to her feet.

"Now how about a kiss since I helped you up," he said roughly as he grabbed her hair with one hand and pulled her face to his. She tried to turn her head away but he pulled harder on her hair and kissed her on the mouth. With his other hand he fondled her breasts. She used her tied arms to try and push him away but he easily held her in place and laughed as he kissed her again. Gavin had stood watching but now lunged forward until he was stopped by another soldier grabbing his other arm. They laughed as a third punched him in the stomach hard enough to double him over. As he gasped for air they continued to hit him several more times until they finally let him go and he dropped to the ground wheezing.

"Stop it, stop, quit hurting him!" Lily screamed at the soldiers. She was thrashing about as the soldier held her tighter, until he suddenly threw her to the ground beside Gavin.

"The funs over boys," said their sergeant as he rode up. "Get them up and walking. It's a long way to the ships."

Several of the soldiers grabbed their arms and lifted them back on their feet. The soldier who had kissed Lily leaned into her ear and said "Don't worry honey, I'll find you later tonight." He laughed wickedly as he walked off, winking at her when he looked back.

Lily started walking as soon as she was back on her feet. She didn't want to look at Gavin, she was so embarrassed by what had happened. If she hadn't been so foolish as to not watch where she was stepping, none of it would have happened and Gavin wouldn't have been hit by the soldiers. She could feel him watching her as she carefully navigated the rough ground in front of her.

"It's not your fault," she heard him say as he walked beside her. She nodded that she had heard him but she didn't have the strength to answer him. She couldn't think about the soldier touching her. She let her body go numb, determined to just survive one day at a time.

Gavin woke on the second morning of their captivity from a sleepless night spent on the cold ground. He was hungry, thirsty and just plain angry. Where were the King and the rest of the island's soldiers? He remembered Versan saying that they were only a few days off. Was it possible they didn't know that the Empire had attacked Redin? Could Commander Versan and all of his men have been taken or killed? These thoughts went through his head as he helped Lily to her feet so that they could start this day's march. They hadn't been walking for more than a few minutes when he heard his name being called.

"Gavin, is that you?" a man called, as he lurched toward them, a bloody cloth tied around one foot. He was using a sturdy stick to keep himself upright but was obviously near the last of his strength judging from his clumsy gait.

"Daniel?" Gavin asked as he grabbed the man by the arm and helped steady him. He lowered his voice when he noticed one of the legionnaires close by. "Where's the commander? How many of us survived?"

"I don't know, we were separated." He stumbled as he spoke and would have fallen if Gavin hadn't still been holding his arm.

Gavin saw Lily start to reach for him and stopped her. "You can't," he said. "Remember what the apothecary said."

Before she could respond a legionnaire on horseback approached them. He called to a second legionnaire marching near them. "This man is too injured, he'll slow us down. Kill him."

Gavin didn't have a chance to react as the legionnaire drew his sword and plunged it into Daniel's chest. He pulled it out as Daniel's body fell to the ground and walked away; telling them to keep moving in a rough voice as he left. Gavin reached for his sword before he remembered that he no longer carried one. Lily had stopped and was staring at the body lying on the ground. He took her hands clumsily because of the bindings and urged her forward. If they stopped they would be noticed and he didn't want that. He would have to mourn the death of his comrade as they walked. His commander was gone, possible dead, but he had given Gavin a job to do and he would do it to the best of his ability. He would protect this woman beside him and try and get her safely away from the Empire's legions.

It took them two more days to reach the waiting ships on the coast. A freezing rain had started the day before and the ground had become so wet that the walking became almost impossible with their legs tied. They slipped and slid their way through muddy ground and the bindings on their ankles and hands became so wet that they chafed and caused their skin to bleed. Lily watched as the elderly fell behind and were either killed or just left to die. Everyone was cold, wet and miserable. They were also starving, as the bread had run out the night before and it was now late afternoon. Lily and Gavin stumbled behind the people in front of them, not even realizing they had reached their destination until they stopped and almost ran into them. They sat down in the wet sand, too tired to care, as the rain continued to fall around them. The only bright spot in the last two days was that the soldier had never bothered her again, although several times she had looked up to find him staring at her.

Gavin reached over and touched Lily on the arm. "Why don't you rest your head on my lap for awhile? You're exhausted."

"So are you," she said tiredly but she tipped sideways anyway and did as he asked. She kept her eyes open, though, and saw a man with a black robe heading their way. His hood was pulled so low that it left his face in the shadows but it appeared that he was staring at the slaves crowded on the beach as if searching for someone. Suddenly

Lily felt frightened; the man was still thirty feet off but something about the intensity of his shadowed gaze was alarming. In another moment he would be looking her way and Lily's instincts told her she should run, run as far and as fast as possible away from him. What her mind told her to do and what her body was capable of, though, were two different things. Even if her legs hadn't been tied and she wasn't exhausted, she was rooted where she sat in fear. She couldn't move even if her life depended on it. She started to shake and Gavin leaned over her to see what was wrong.

"Are you sick?" he asked. "You're shaking."

"That man," she said terrified, looking in his direction.

Gavin looked over at him. He hunched his body over Lily as if to shield her from his sight. "I don't know who that is but he doesn't feel right. Keep your head down." The man was just glancing his way when a soldier called his name and he turned around. Whatever the soldier said must have been urgent because the man walked quickly to his horse and mounted. As he rode away, Lily let out a shaky sigh of relief.

A short time later, Lily and Gavin crowded into the front of the slaves and were loaded on the first ship. Gavin wanted to get Lily as far away from the man in the black robe as he could. As they were stumbling up the gangplank Lily looked back and saw thousands of people coming over the hill above the shore. "Gavin, look, who are they?" she asked. He turned and stared in disbelief.

"The island is lost," was all he said.

They continued up the ramp and were forced down into the hold until it was filled to capacity. They were given a piece of hardtack and a swallow of water. They fell asleep to the lulling sound of water lapping against the sides of the ship. When they awoke they had already set sail and were headed for the Empire.

~

The hunter Sylvius was furious that he was called away when he was so close but the summoning had come straight from sub-minister Falx and one does not keep a sub-minister waiting. He knew the witch had to be on the shore somewhere in the midst of the slaves. He was confident that he would make it back to the boats before they left and if she was amongst the slaves she wouldn't be escaping anytime soon. The hunt wasn't over, merely delayed.

79

Chapter 9

It continued to rain as Lily and Gavin staggered down the gangplank of the ship. The crossing had taken several hours and it was late in the day when they reached the opposite coast. Sitting in the cramped hold had actually been a relief compared to all the walking they had done the three previous days. Gavin had put his arms around her and they had both finally felt warm as they dozed. Now they were back in the wet weather and Lily could feel herself starting to shake again. Judging from the looks of the pens they were being herded into, she wouldn't be getting out of the rain anytime soon.

The make-shift slave pens had been hurriedly constructed just after the Empire's soldiers had sailed to Camar. The locals in the small fishing village knew that the slaves wouldn't be kept long here before being sent to all parts of the Empire, so they had taken the payment given and stuck up some posts and wire. They were just up the beach far enough to prevent the tide from reaching them but not so far that they would have to dig in the rockier soil to secure the posts. They dug a latrine hole in one corner of the pen but didn't bother with a roof. It had rained the last two days so the slaves would be wet anyway, and after all, they were only slaves.

They were brought a watery, meatless stew by the villagers. The Empire paid them to feed the slaves but they didn't pay enough to waste meat on them. Lily ate what she was given; thankful to have a change from the hard bread they had eaten the last few days. The sun went down as they lay in the wet sand with her cloak covering them both. Lily slept fitfully beside Gavin through the night, listening to the moans and cries of the people around them. When they woke in the morning the rain had stopped and the soldiers were once again giving them hard bread and water. Lily sat up and took her share. The sun was peeking out from behind a cloud and she pushed her cloak off to feel its rays.

"What I wouldn't give for a warm bath," she said as she soaked her bread in the water to make it easier to chew. "I'm so damp and dirty I feel as if I've moss growing on me."

Gavin smiled and nodded his head in agreement. Lily saw him look over at a group of men watching the pen of slaves. One in particular was staring at Lily's uncovered blonde hair shimmering like gold in the sunlight. "Uh oh, I don't like the looks of that," he said. "I thought we'd have more time before they sold us but those men are probably slave holders. If they're here to buy slaves it's possible we'll be split up."

Lily hadn't even thought of that possibility. "No," she whispered fearfully and grabbed Gavin's hand. "We have to stay together. What can we do?"

"All I can think is that we'll tell them that we're married and hope that they like to keep married people together," Gavin replied. He squeezed her hand in his and Lily once again thanked the Maker for sending him to her.

Lily pulled her cloak around her again and pulled up the hood, trying to make herself inconspicuous. She watched the group of men as they looked over the slaves. One was obviously in charge by the way he gave orders and the arrogant look on his face. He was not a large man but he carried himself as if he was used to people obeying him and would have no problem punishing anyone who dared defy him. He seemed to be selecting slaves to buy, examining them and then sending them either back into the pens or on to a wagon some distance away. As she watched him, he turned her way and said something to the soldiers that were guarding them. One of the soldiers stepped into the slave pen and took Lily by the arm. When Gavin would have stood with her, the soldier pushed him back. "You're not needed," he told him. Keeping a tight grip on her arm he pulled her over to the man that had been staring at her. "What's your name slave?" the man asked.

"Lily," she replied quietly.

"Such simple names these Camarians give their children," he said mockingly as he began to circle around her. "Although you are as pretty as the flower you are named after so perhaps the name is appropriate in this case." Lily stood very still when he picked up a strand of her hair and rubbed it between her fingers. "At the moment you're a very dirty flower, though. I wonder what she'll look like cleaned up?" he asked the men who stood with them. Several of them chuckled at his comment.

81

"First, though, some rules. If I decide to buy you, you will always address me as master or master Elezar," he barked at her. "You Camarians will have to learn your place."

"Yes, master," she replied meekly.

"Much better," he said. "Now, tell me Lily what did you do before you became a slave?"

"I was a healer," she answered and then promptly added "master" before he could shout again.

"I already have a woman who acts as my healer but I'm sure I can find something for you to do," he said. He put his hand under her chin and tilted her head up, looking at her teeth and eyes, then told her to remove her cloak and made her turn around as he watched. The way he looked at her made her feel as if she was naked and she looked down, her face red. The slave owner seemed to think this funny and laughed. "I'll take this shy one. Chain her to the wagon, Darius," he said to a man standing behind her.

He started to walk away and Lily knew she would have to speak up quickly if she wanted Gavin to be bought with her. "Master," she said quietly. He turned back to her and looked at her as if he couldn't believe she would speak to him. She didn't like the look in his eyes.

"Yes, slave."

"Excuse me, master, but my husband is also here. He's a strong man and grew up on a farm. I'm sure he could be useful to you."

"Ahh, so you want me to buy him also. What will you give me if I do?"

Lily was perplexed by his question. He had to know that she had nothing she could give him except her abilities but she answered him as bravely as she could. "I don't have anything to give you master, except my skill as a healer which I will gladly give."

"I already own your skills, but there is something you can give me. Will you come willingly to my bed, slave?" He stepped closer to her and put his mouth next to her ear, his hand pulled her against him. Lily couldn't stop herself from stiffening in fear although she did her best not to pull away. If she wanted Gavin with her she would have to play his games. "I'll have you either way, but I prefer a warm, willing body in my bed." He rubbed his hand up and down her arm as he spoke. "Will you do that for your husband?" he asked in a quiet voice.

Lily stared at the ground. She held her hands tightly together to stop them from shaking and drew a ragged breath. It took all her courage to look this man in the eye and say the words he wanted to hear. "Yes, master," she said quietly.

"What did you say slave? I need to hear you say it, all of it."

"Yes, master, I will come willingly to your bed," she repeated softly.

"Excellent. I'll look forward to it," he said with a final leer at her. "Darius buy her husband and chain them both to the wagon and remove the leg restraints. I need to find another dozen slaves."

Lily and Gavin walked behind the wagon along with the other slaves that Elezar had purchased as it left the fishing village. Their feet were free but their hands were chained to rings attached to the back and sides. They hadn't spoken since they had been bought. Gavin had asked her how she had talked the slaveholder into taking him but she just shook her head and couldn't answer him. She was afraid to tell him, afraid he would think less of her for what she agreed to and also afraid he would be angry enough to attack Elezar or his men. She didn't want him to do anything that might cause Elezar to separate them.

When they stopped for the night, the slave owner came over to speak to the slaves. "There are several rules that I expect all of you to follow. You will always address me as Master. If you do not, you will be punished. You will do whatever I ask of you without question. If you do not, you will be punished. If you steal from me, you lose a hand. If you try to run, you lose a foot. If you try to run again, you die. You are my slaves now and will be until you die." With that he left to sit near the fire that his men had built. They had made a large pot of stew and after the men had eaten, the slaves were each given a plateful.

Lily and Gavin sat together and ate. She was so hungry that despite the situation they were in, it tasted like the best food she had ever eaten. She was filthy; especially her hands, but that didn't stop her. They, along with the other slaves, were still chained to the wagon by one hand but they could at least sit down and stretch their legs. There was very little talking as most of them were too tired to do anything but rest and Lily was disappointed that she didn't recognize any of the slaves taken from Camar. With their backs leaning against

83

a wagon wheel, Gavin looked at Lily and said quietly," Are you ready to tell me yet? It must be bad for you to be so silent."

She couldn't look at him as she said, "He told me he planned on taking me to his bed. He told me that if I would come willingly then he would buy you. I agreed."

She heard him take a deep breath and then let it out before he said, "Why?"

"We said we'd stay together and I can't bear to face this alone. He'll have me anyway. Please leave it at that." She set her plate down and looked up into his face, afraid of what she would see there but even more afraid not to know. Instead of anger or disgust, all she saw was sadness and when he put his free arm around her she leaned into him and quietly wept at the injustice of what had happened to them both.

Five days of walking brought them to Elezar's estate just as the sun was setting. They had passed through fields ripe with grain, sparse pine forests and rolling hills that were covered with the dried husks of wild flowers. Lily couldn't help but think that if the circumstances had been different she would have enjoyed seeing this new country. It was warmer here than Camar and drier. She knew that many of the herbs she struggled to grow in the wet island climate would grow well here. She was sure that if they could find a way to escape there would be plenty of wild plants to sustain them.

Lily watched as Elezar went into a large manor house, giving orders as he went. It was set on a small knoll and had a porch that went around two sides of it. There were several large trees in the front and she could see a kitchen garden around one side. Slaves were leaving the house and walking to a large building set some distance away.

Lily stood in the dirt with the rest of the new slaves waiting for what would happen next. She was dirtier than she had ever been in her life. The dust from the dry roads covered every inch of her clothing and hair and there hadn't yet been a time when they had been allowed to have water for washing. One of his men unchained them and led them away from the house to a series of buildings. "This is for the women, this one for the men and you two can have that smaller one in back," he said as he pointed at two large buildings with several smaller ones behind it. "You have five minutes to draw yourself some water from the well here and then we let the dogs out. You don't want to be outside with them, they'll tear you apart. When you hear the morning bell, come up to the manor and you'll be told what to do. I hope you all remember what happens to anyone trying to escape," he said with a nasty smile. "Now move."

They stood in line with the others and Gavin filled the bucket he'd been handed. They walked to one of the smaller buildings and Lily opened the door to their living quarters and went in with Gavin following. He shut the door and they both looked around. The shack was one room with a small window in the back wall, too small to crawl out Gavin noted, two pallets on the floor, two blankets, a basin for washing, a towel for drying and a chamber pot. Lily was relieved that the room was relatively clean. Gavin poured some water into the basin and they both washed their face and hands.

"What I wouldn't give for a bathtub full of warm water and some soap," Lily said. She started to unbutton her dress to clean herself further but stopped when she realized that Gavin was watching her. She had given some thought as they marched behind the wagon about the repercussions of pretending to be married and now was the time for her to act. She took a deep breath, turned his way and deliberately began to undo the buttons with shaky hands. She could tell she had surprised him as he stepped forward, stopped her and took her hands.

"Lily, what are you doing?"

"Gavin, I need to ask you to do something for me."

"Of course, anything," he said still holding her hands.

"Just listen for a moment." She wasn't sure how to get the words out and knew her face would be bright red before she was done but started in nervously, staring at her feet as she spoke. "I was taught that a woman remained a virgin until she was married. Up until now I've kept to that, but Elezar is going to take that from me. I don't want my first time to be with a man I fear. A man like him," she shuddered. "If I can't be with my husband, I would at least like to be with a man I like and respect." She forced herself to look at Gavin despite her embarrassment. "I'm asking you to be that man. Please."

Lily couldn't tell by the look on Gavin's face what he was thinking. Was he as uncomfortable as she was by what she was asking? Was she asking too much, maybe he didn't like her in that way. He leaned toward her, took her face in his hands and said, "Why can't you be with your husband?"

Now it was Lily's turn to be surprised. "What do you mean?"

"We have a tradition in the north of the island called handfasting. A man and a woman clasp hands and promise to stay together for a year as man and wife. After that time if they want they can marry, if not then they are free to separate. I know I'm only a simple soldier and I have little to offer you except my name and my protection, but if you'll have it, it's yours. Would you handfast with me and be my wife?"

Lily's breath caught in her throat. "But you barely know me," she said.

"It's true that if we were still on Camar I doubt I'd offer to handfast when we know so little of each other, but our lives have changed so quickly and we have no idea what's going to happen to us. I don't want to scare you but we could both be dead tomorrow if Elezar chooses and there's little we can do about it. If we can find some happiness here why not take it?"

Gavin still held her hands and Lily liked the feel of them against her own. She realized that she was very fortunate in the man that Commander Versan had asked to protect her. "I would be proud to be your wife," she answered him with a smile.

"There is one thing you should know, though, before we commit. I plan on escaping here as soon as I can. It will be dangerous for you if I'm caught and I don't want you to suffer from my attempts to leave."

"They already believe you to be my husband so what we commit to privately won't make a difference. Besides I want out of here as badly as you do. I'll be right behind you, helping in any way I can."

"Good," Gavin said then he leaned in and kissed her.

Lily had no experience with men and didn't know what to do next. Her life on the island had been sheltered in some ways. Her father died when she was barely fourteen and she had taken over caring for Jon and their homestead. She didn't have time to spend with friends and because they lived so far from town she had very few of those anyway so instead she had worked in her herb gardens and learned to be a healer. Her aunt had tried to find her a husband since she'd turned sixteen, concerned with her unmarried state, but Lily hadn't been interested. She'd known she would want to marry some day but she hadn't been ready. She had an innate need to heal people and now that she knew more about her powers she understood better the drive she always felt.

Gavin must have sensed her nervousness and misunderstood the reason for it because he stopped kissing her and asked her seriously, "Are you sure about this? It doesn't have to be tonight. We can wait."

"No, I don't want to wait. It's just that I've never done this before. I don't know what to do."

Gavin chuckled and said, "Don't worry, just relax. We'll do this together." He reached out and finished unbuttoning her dress then helped her to take it off. She stood there in her shift while he took off his tunic and then he led her over to the pallets and they lay down together. Within a few minutes Lily was no longer nervous and Gavin's mouth and hands were doing things to her that tugged at something inside her and made her want more. Now she understood why her aunt had five children despite the fact that they could ill afford them.

She'd never known this kind of pleasure and eagerly responded to his touches and the sweet taste of his kisses. When he stopped to slide her shift over her head she impatiently helped him. His clothes came off next and she marveled at how good it felt to lie touching skin to skin. She ran her fingers over his chest, playing with the soft brown hair that grew there, still surprised that she had the right to touch him in such a way. She expected the pain when it came but it passed quickly and she wrapped her legs around him as he moved inside her, amazed at the sensations it caused, not wanting him to stop. She clutched him harder as he moved faster within her until they both gasped with pleasure, then she lay still as their breathing slowed and Gavin rolled them over, pulling her with him, her head resting on his chest. She wrapped herself around him and smiled up at him to let him know how happy she felt right now. Then she closed her eyes, letting the sound of his heartbeat slowly lull her to sleep.

After their lovemaking, Gavin lay with Lily in his arms watching her sleep. The moonlight coming in the small window gave just enough light to see that she was smiling. He hoped that was his doing. He'd tried to be gentle and please her but the only women he'd slept with before had been whores and they didn't expect him to be gentle. She had responded to what he did, though, and seemed to enjoy it. He was still surprised when he thought about their handfast marriage. Surprised at himself for asking and surprised that she'd agreed. Under their present circumstances it had just seemed like the right thing to do. They were here under miserable conditions that would probably only get worse and he wanted to give her some small happiness and truthfully, he wanted it too. He remembered how he had desired her shortly after he had kidnapped her and thought at the time that she was too far out of his reach, and now she was his. Strange what life could bring. He would make the best of this, though, and try and be a good husband to her.

Lily made a small noise and nestled closer to him as she slept. The smile was gone; he hoped she wasn't having a nightmare although who could blame her considering where they were. That damn Elezar. What was he going to do when the man took Lily to his bed?... Nothing, he realized. There wasn't a damn thing he could do but get himself killed and how would that help Lily? It made his blood boil just thinking about it. He found himself holding her tighter as his anger flared. As if in response Lily opened her eyes, stretched like a cat and slowly rubbed her bare leg against his own. She pushed him gently on to his back and laid on top of him, rubbing against him, her long hair tickling his chest.

"Aren't you sleepy?" she asked.

"Not anymore," he said as he rolled her on her back with a laugh and proceeded to make love to his wife for the second time that night, confident now that he had indeed pleased her earlier.

Lily awoke to the sound of a bell ringing. For a moment she couldn't remember where she was until she heard Gavin's soft breathing. She lay with her back to him, his arm thrown protectively over her, his hand possessively cupping her breast. It felt right to her, being with this man that she hadn't even known two weeks ago. Thinking of him sent a tingle of pleasure through her and she rolled over and looked at the man she could now call husband. He was just opening his eyes and gave her a sleepy smile. "Time to get up?" he asked.

He moved over a little so she could sit up just as their door banged open. Darius stood just outside looking at them.

"You're expected to appear up at the manor in ten minutes, slaves. This is the only time I will tell you this. There will be punishment for those that are late."

88

Lily didn't want to dress in front of him but it quickly became obvious that he wasn't leaving. Gavin got up, handed her her shift and then stood in front of her to partially block Darius' view as he put on his own clothes. She could tell by the hard set of his jaw that he was furious. She had hoped to use some of last night's water to wash herself but gave up that idea and nervously dressed instead. She combed her fingers through her hair, took Gavin's hand and they stood waiting for Darius to move so that they could leave. He stepped aside, giving her a leering look as he did.

They walked to the central courtyard and waited there with the other new Camarian slaves. They were given a piece of hard bread and a water jug was passed among them. Thirty minutes had passed before Elezar finally stepped from the house to address them. Lily took a moment to really look at the man. He was dressed in fashionable clothing today, his dark hair pulled back in a short ponytail. His beard was trimmed close and if Lily had to guess she'd say he was around forty years of age. She looked down as his eyes passed over her, afraid of displeasing him with her stare.

"Well, Darius, where shall we place our new slaves?"

"We need more men in the fields, sir, as it will soon be harvest time."

Lily realized they must be further south than her home. The weather was warmer and many of the plants she had seen as they traveled were just going to seed. Whatever they were harvesting must be a late crop.

"Fine, fine," Elezar said graciously as if he truly cared what happened to them. "I'll want three of the women in with the house slaves. Those two to help with the cleaning and cooking," he said as he pointed to two of the younger, prettier women, "and then, of course, our little healer."

Lily cringed as he looked directly at her. She instinctively took a step closer to Gavin who put his arm around her.

"The other three may work in the fields with the men," he added. Lily noticed that they were women well past forty.

Elezar turned and went into the manor as Darius took the men and three older women and left the courtyard. Lily only had a moment to squeeze Gavin's hand as he left.

A large woman wearing a voluminous apron took Lily and the two other women into the house. "Now then, I'm Agnes," she said. "I'm in charge of the house slaves which is what you now are. Come with me." As they entered the house they stood in a large entryway with a sweeping staircase leading upstairs. Lily looked about her as Agnes kept up a steady flow of words explaining what was expected of house slaves. The words slid off her tongue so quickly that Lily wondered when she found time to breathe. There was an open door to the left and when Lily peered in she saw it was full of books, more books in one place than she had ever seen before. To the right were glass doors leading into a large room with a piano in its center with chairs and couches scattered throughout. One wall was solid windows letting in the morning sun. Lily had never seen anything like it. Elezar must be very rich, she thought, to have a house like this. Agnes didn't take them into either of these rooms, though, but went straight down a long hallway leading to the back of the house. She stopped in front of a green door and said, "Which one of you is the healer?"

"I am," said Lily.

"You're awfully young to be a healer. I hope you know what you're doing because our healer is mighty old and not long for this world. You go in to her now through this door and I'll get you two started on your tasks." As Lily opened the green door Agnes led the other two women further down the hall talking as she went. "I hope one of you can cook because the master is mighty particular about his food and he has me clean worn off my feet. He likes..." Her voice was cut off as Lily stepped in and closed the door behind her. Lily chuckled to herself, that woman certainly knew how to talk.

The room had a large work table in the center. There were bunches of herbs hanging from the rafters and a pot filled with a bubbling mixture was hanging from a hook over a small fire.

"Hello, is anyone here?" Lily quietly asked. No one answered and Lily thought the room was empty until a tiny, old woman stepped through a door on the far wall. She appeared to be very frail and walked with halting steps using a cane for balance. Her hair was totally white and Lily couldn't even guess at her age, she looked so old.

"Are you the healer the master told me about?" she asked softly.

"Yes, my name is Lily."

"I'm called Sara. I've been a healer on the estate for fifty years. I served the current master's father. I'll show you around my healing room and the medicines I have to use. Those that are sick or injured are brought in midmorning. We'll take care of them and then

I'll show you the herb garden. It needs harvesting and my health won't allow me to work in it anymore. That will be your job now, as well as treating the slaves that come in. In the afternoon we will make the ointments and syrups that I use."

The morning passed quickly by. Lily was familiar with most of the herbs that Sara showed her. There were only two patients that came in. One had a cut hand and Lily crushed calendula flowers in oil and put it on the cut. The other had a cough and Lily gave her mullein syrup to calm it. Sara watched her carefully and seemed pleased with what she did. They went outside and Lily worked in the herb garden while Sara sat on a bench under a tree and watched to make certain that she knew her herbs from the weeds. When Sara was satisfied that Lily wasn't going to pull up the wrong plants the two women chatted together.

"So you have a husband, do you?" Sara asked her.

Lily nodded. "That'll be a hard thing for you. The master will use him against you and use you against him. Remember that. If you do anything to displease him he'll beat him. He knows that will keep you in line better than him threatening you. He's a hard man just like his father. Don't displease him."

Lily thanked her for the advice and continued the weeding, more worried now than ever about their situation.

She was given a meal at midday in the kitchen but her dinner would be eaten in the slave quarters. The food was surprisingly good although what she was most thankful for was a hot cup of tea. She had been missing her herbal brews and was delighted to once more have access to the plants to make them. When the days work was done she left the manor house with the other two women from the morning. She now knew their names were May and Katherine. May was very pretty with striking red hair; Katherine had dark hair and liked to talk. As they crossed the grounds to the slave quarters, Elezar intercepted them and pointed to May. "Come back to the house with me."

"But master, we were just going to eat the evening meal," she said. Elezar's eyes darkened and Lily knew immediately that May was in trouble. She nudged her and nodded toward the house.

"Yes master, right now," May said and turned to walk back to the house.

Elezar stepped in front of her and said coldly, "Never walk in front of me." She fell behind him, not daring to look back at the others.

Lily and Katherine continued on to the eating hall in the slave quarters. She found Gavin and went to sit by him while Katherine joined a woman at another table. Agnes walked in with another slave, one carrying a large pot of stew and the other a basket of bread. They were told to form a line and carrying their plates they stepped up to get their dinner. As they sat and ate Lily told Gavin about her day with Sara and then what had happened to May on their way here.

"I'm worried he'll do something bad to her. She was foolish to talk back to him but it's hard to think like a slave. I'm used to being silent from living alone but most Camarians aren't. It's going to be harder on us, I think, than those that are natives of Trost."

"Two of the new ones were whipped today out in the field for speaking up to Darius," Gavin told her. "They were simply asking about a plant they didn't recognize. You're right; it'll be hard for us islanders to keep quiet if we have something to say." He leaned in close and said, "We need to start looking for a way to escape."

The bell rang outside and Agnes stood up and rapped on the pot with a large spoon. In a loud voice she said, "For those of you that are new, that's the evening bell. You have thirty minutes to get back to your quarters. You can draw water at the well for washing as you go, but remember they'll turn the dogs loose when the time is up and you don't want to be outside for that. Morning bell rings early, come back here to break your fast."

Lily and Gavin drew their water from the well as they walked to their quarters. Lily used the water to wash and when Gavin decided to join her they ended up spilling as much water as they used. They'd both removed each others clothing before they were through washing and once again made love with the moonlight shining through the small window of their room.

The next morning after breakfast, Lily went in through the back door of the manor house and made her way to the healing room. Sara was already there mixing up some ointment. As Lily watched she used a mortar and pestle to grind up coneflower, calendula and comfrey. She mixed it in a lanolin base and soon had a smooth cream that could be used for infections.

"We'll be needing this soon, I think," she told Lily.

"Will someone be coming in with a wound?" Lily asked.

"The young redheaded slave that was working in the kitchen. The master took her to his bed and she tried to fight him and then turned to weeping. Master won't stand for either. After he was through with her he beat her and then left her locked up in a shed all night. Your turn will come, husband or not, so you remember this. Let him do what he wants and you won't be hurt. They are worse things than being in his bed, much worse."

As she spoke the door opened and May was helped in by Agnes. She could hardly walk and didn't seem to be fully conscious. Her clothes were filthy from lying on a dirt floor all night and her once beautiful red hair was snarled and matted. When she lifted her head Lily saw that her nose was encrusted with dried blood and looked like it might be broken and her eyes were black and blue. They laid her on a pallet on the floor and carefully stripped off her gown and shift. Her body was covered in bruises with small cuts everywhere that oozed pus. Lily wondered what had caused the cuts and gave Sara a questioning look. "Master wears a large ruby ring. The metal prongs that hold the stone make the cuts. I see this whenever he beats someone."

Lily and Sara cleaned her gently and rubbed the ointment in. She whimpered as they touched her and thrashed about. Sara gave her a sip of poppy juice to ease the pain and help her sleep and then covered her in a light blanket.

Agnes had stayed to help them shift her on the pallet and she whispered confidentially to them, "His moods are getting worse. You don't dare say a wrong word or you'll get a beating. I don't know what we'll do if he goes over crazy like his father did. Be careful." She left them and Sara shook her head and sat down.

"I don't envy you Lily. He don't dare touch me at my age but you have a lot of years ahead of you. Keep your head down and walk lightly."

~

The hunter Sylvius surveyed the slaves with disgust. He hadn't detected the witch anywhere within the filthy camp for the past three days. He'd seen all the slave ships off the island and she hadn't been on any of them either. That only left two options, she had

93

escaped the camp or he had somehow missed a ship. He didn't like either option but he could at least check with the quartermaster. The man paled as Sylvius approached but held his ground.

"I need to see the transport documentation for the slaves over the last three days," he demanded. The man swallowed but went inside his tent and brought forth several scrolls. "Here they are my lord… I mean sir, reader," he stuttered and quickly pulled his hand away when Sylvius took the scrolls. Sylvius found what he was looking for in a few moments. He had missed not one ship but two; they had left when he had been called away almost three days ago. Worse yet each ship was sent to a different location so he would have to check both destinations. He cursed silently at his misfortune and threw the scrolls back at the quartermaster who flinched away.

Sometimes the longest hunts were the best ones, he reminded himself and smiled.

Chapter 10

Three weeks had passed since Lily had begun working with Sara. Despite the difference in their ages, they had quickly become friends. Lily had found that the older woman was a wonderful healer; always kind and generous and that she truly cared what happened to her patients. They treated different slaves each day for a wide variety of ailments and Lily was getting to know many of them by name. She never used her powers, only the herbs and potions that she and Sara prepared. It made her angry that many of the slave's problems were brought on by mistreatment from Elezar's guards, but despite the broken bones and whippings she occasionally had a bright moment, too, like the day she had helped Sara midwife a baby. According to the Empire, any child born to a slave was also a slave and became the property of the slave owner so Elezar encouraged the slaves to have as many children as they could. Sara did her best to work beside Lily each day but Lily knew as a healer that Sara was not well and she would miss her dearly when she died. She was afraid that the time was not far off.

Lily rarely saw Elezar and then mostly from a distance. She knew he was bedding Katherine and at least one other slave. They had learned from May's beating what was expected of them. She knew it was too much to hope that he had forgotten about her and when she mentioned this to Sara she shook her head. "He's like the cat and you the mouse. He's teasing you, letting you get comfortable before he pounces."

That night as Lily was cleaning up the healing room before leaving, Elezar stepped into the room. Sara had been sitting down chatting with Lily as she worked but she immediately stood up. "Good evening, master," she said. Lily stopped what she was doing and stood also, keeping her eyes on the floor.

"Tell me Sara, how is our new healer doing? Is she learning your ways of healing?" Elezar asked her.

"She does very well, master. She already knew a great deal when she came and is a very fast learner. The slaves seem to like her, she has a gentle touch."

"Very good," he said. "Lily, I'd like you to eat in the kitchen here tonight. Agnes will show you where you can bathe after dinner and then I would like you to come to my rooms."

Lily's mouth went dry when she tried to answer him and she couldn't speak. He was watching for her reaction so she nodded her head and barely whispered, "Yes, master."

As he turned and left the room Sara took her arm and led her over to the chair. "It will be all right. If you do as he asks he won't hurt you. Just put your mind somewhere else, and you'd better send a message to your husband with Agnes so he doesn't tear the manor apart looking for you and get himself killed."

Gavin was waiting in the dining hall for Lily when Agnes came up to him. "You're Lily's man?" she asked him. When he nodded she motioned for him to sit at one of the tables. She looked across the room to a burly man shaved completely bald that Gavin thought was the blacksmith and motioned for him to come over and sit with him.

"Lily won't be coming to your quarters tonight. She's been asked by Elezar to stay at the house with him. I think you know what that means," she said looking him in the eye. "You can't do anything to help her and if you try you'll only get yourself killed or maimed."

"We've all been through this," the blacksmith said. Gavin noticed that he had put his hand on Gavin's arm to keep him from standing. "If you're lucky it'll only be this one time. He does this to every woman he buys, he has to prove to them who's in charge. There's not a thing you can do but go back to your quarters and wait for her. She'll need you after he's through with her."

When he had come in he had been hungry after a hard day of work in the fields, but after hearing what they had told him, the thought of eating made him sick. He thanked them both and assured them he wouldn't cause any trouble. As he got up and walked outside he noticed that many of the men were giving him sympathetic glances. He didn't understand how they could tolerate this year after year; watching their wives, sisters, even daughters treated this way. As he circled the dining hall several times, he wondered if they'd forgotten what it was like to be free. He supposed maybe some of them never had been, maybe that was why they put up with the abuse. Thinking wasn't helping his anger, he was a man who was used to using his hands and right now he needed to hit something or someone in the worst way. He turned to walk to their quarters and spied the oak tree that sat behind the building. He knew it was stupid but he pulled back his fist, pretended it was Elezar's face and swung.

Before Agnes had left for the dining hall she had shown Lily where the tub was. Lily heated water on the stove and filled it, cooling it with water from the well. She sank into the tub gratefully. It had been so long since she had a bath. Her father had always said there was a bright side to every bad situation, this must be it today. She stayed in the water as long as she could, scrubbing herself clean, afraid of what lay ahead of her tonight.

She dried herself and put on the white gown that was left for her. She was so nervous now that she was feeling sick. She hadn't eaten any dinner, too afraid she would throw it up. She had wanted to ask Katherine how bad this was going to be but Katherine wouldn't look at her as she left that night and Lily thought it was probably just as well. She wasn't sure which was worse, knowing or not knowing.

She walked slowly up the stairs to the third door on the right and knocked softly. She heard him say come in and opened the door. Elezar was sitting in front of a small fire in his dressing gown. He smiled when he saw her and said "Ah, my little healer, you look lovely tonight."

Lily stood frozen in the doorway. She tried to move forward, tried to say something but nothing came out. She knew she had to do this to protect Gavin but she was paralyzed with fear. He got up, walked toward her and took her hand to pull her in to the room and she had to stop herself from jerking away from him. Her heart was hammering in her chest and she took shallow breaths as she tried to calm herself. Elezar walked with her toward his bed then released her hand and took her hair into both of his, murmuring to himself about how lovely it was.

"Your husband's a lucky man," he said as he continued to play with her hair, running his fingers through it until he suddenly jerked back on it almost pulling her over.

"What will you give me to let him live?"

"Anything," Lily gasped, "anything you want."

He let go of her hair and slapped her, causing her to stumble back. She was so shocked all she could do was stare at him in fear. He seemed to like that. "Are you afraid of me, Lily?" When she didn't answer he grabbed her arms roughly and shouted loudly, "Answer me girl, I asked if you are afraid?"

Lily stammered out, "Yes, yes I'm afraid," not knowing what he expected of her. This seemed to excite him and he pulled her to him and kissed her hard on the mouth. He grabbed her breast roughly and squeezed until she could feel tears come into her eyes. She heard herself whimper although she was trying not to make a sound and he took his mouth away and backhanded her. Reaching up she touched her cheek where he hit her and her hand came away with blood on it. She saw a flash of red on his finger and remembered the cuts on May that were caused by his ring.

The more fear he saw in her the more he seemed to like it. She tried to back away from him but he gripped her arm tightly and alternated between slapping her and kissing her, keeping her off balance and frightened. He laughed then and shoved her on to the bed, pushing her gown up around her hips. His robe came off next and Lily could see that the violence had aroused him.

Lily wanted to fight him. She wanted to push him off, knee him in the groin, anything to stop him but she knew it would be worse if she did. He would take it out on Gavin not her, so she lay as still as she could while he forced her legs apart and pushed himself into her. She remembered Sara's words of advice and tried to put her mind elsewhere, anywhere other than in this room. She kept silently repeating to herself, *don't fight him, don't fight him*, while he thrust himself into her again and again, hurting her more each time. Finally she felt moisture run down her thigh, then he stilled, rolled off her and growled, "Get out."

She got off the bed and almost ran to the door, her hand on the wall so that she wouldn't stumble. She had to hold tightly to the banister to make it down the stairs without falling she was shaking so violently. Agnes was waiting for her in the kitchen and silently handed Lily her clothes. She helped her change out of the white gown then asked her if she would like a cup of tea. Lily shook her head; all she wanted was out of this place. Agnes opened the door and Lily could see a man standing on the porch. "He'll walk you home, Lily. Keep the dogs from bothering you." The man reached to take her arm but Lily shook him off. She didn't want to be touched by anyone, not now, not ever again. She managed to walk to their quarters and get in the door, arms held tightly around her, holding herself together.

98

Gavin had been pacing in their small quarters for the last two hours. His hand hurt, he thought he had probably broken it, but he was glad for the pain. It was something to focus on instead of what was happening to his wife. He looked up as he heard the door opening and saw a man outside with Lily. She walked through the door with a haunted look on her face and just stood there watching him as if she didn't see him or didn't know who he was. The guard pushed the door closed and Gavin went to her and tried to touch her.

"Lily, are you all right?" he asked her.

She jerked away from him, and walked to the water bucket. "I need water, I need to clean myself." She stripped off her dress and shift and stood naked in the room with a cloth in her hand. He watched as she dunked it in the cold water and started scrubbing herself harder and harder as if she could wash away everything that had happened to her. He could see a bruise starting to form on her cheek with a small cut near it. There were more bruises on her forearms and breasts, and handprints showed against her pale skin. Gavin had to breathe deeply several times to calm himself down. He took the cloth from Lily and gently began to clean her. She tried to take it back but he shushed her like he would have one of his little sisters. "You're hurting yourself, let me help you. It's all right." He kept whispering to her, slowly washing her and eventually her frantic breathing slowed and she seemed to relax a little. She was starting to shiver so he put the cloth down, helped her put on her shift and wrapped her in one of their blankets. He led her over to their pallets and gently helped her down on to one, then sat beside her and covered her with the other blanket. He wanted to lie beside her and hold her but he was afraid she wouldn't want him to touch her. He carefully ran his good hand through her hair over and over until she finally looked up at him and tugged him down beside her, turning her head into his chest, she started to cry.

The first thing she saw when she opened her eyes in the morning was Gavin's hand. He was holding her with his right arm but his left was carefully lying on his leg, not touching her. It was swollen to almost twice its normal size and she could tell that it had bled sometime in the night. He lay awake watching her and she wondered if he had slept at all last night. She cleared her throat which was sore from last night's crying and said, "What happened to your hand?"

99

"I got in to a disagreement with an oak tree."

"The one behind our quarters?"

"The very same."

She knew what must have happened and shook her head lightly at him. "Let me see it," she said and took it gently in her hands. She felt the power come out of her as she thought 'heal' and watched as the swelling went down and the abrasions closed up.

Gavin tried to pull his hand away as he said "No, Lily, you can't," but she had already healed him.

"No one is here to notice, Gavin, it's alright. You wouldn't be able to work today with your hand like that and we don't want to draw any more attention to ourselves."

"I hope you're right." He flexed his hand, amazed at how quickly she could heal it. "Are you going to work with Sara today? Are you okay now? I don't want to leave you," he said as he looked at her closely. She knew he must have been frightened for her last night. He had held her when she had finally started to cry. It was like a dam had burst inside her, the tears just went on and on scaring them both, she thought.

"I'll be fine" she said with a forced smile, not sure if she was trying to convince Gavin or herself.

After breakfast Lily walked the short distance to the manor house uneasily. She saw the man who had escorted her to their quarters last night and went nervously past him, afraid he might say something rude to her. Instead he nodded once and walked her to the back door, holding it open for her. She thanked him warily, not sure what this meant, and went in to Sara. As soon as she saw her, she pushed the rape to the back of her mind and focused on the other healer.

Sara looked terrible. Her health had been failing rapidly for the last few days and she had taken to sleeping in the healing room on a cot because it was getting too hard for her to walk to her sleeping quarters. Lily hurried over to her and found that her breathing was labored and when she took her hand her pulse was racing far too quickly. She hurriedly got down some foxglove extract and gave her a small amount. Sara whispered a quiet thank you and patted her hand.

"It won't be long now, dear, and I'm quite ready to see my life end. I just want you to know how glad I am that you've been here for me at the last. I've so enjoyed working with you. You're a good healer and I know you'll be fine here without me." When she had finished speaking her eyes closed and she slept.

Lily worked in the healing room, keeping an eye on Sara as she did. Two slaves that had been injured in a wagon accident came in during the day, one with a broken arm and one with a smashed finger. When they saw that Sara was dying they knelt beside her to say thank you for all her years of healing them all. When they left they passed on the word that she was dying to everyone they saw.

Gavin heard the news of Sara's worsening condition when he stopped at midday to eat with the other workers. They were saying that they would like to have the chance to say goodbye to her and thank her. "Why don't you just walk to the manor house before we go to the dining hall and see if he'll let you? What harm is there in that?" he asked them.

"What harm?" one slave said, "mebbe none but the master'll have us whipped just the same. He don't like us to break our routine."

"But that's crazy. If we all go as a group he won't be able to whip everyone. I'll bet even his hired men would like to see her. She heals them too, doesn't she?" Gavin added.

The men muttered under their breaths as they thought about what he had suggested. There was more talk off and on during the afternoon and word was passed around among the rest of the slaves so that by the time the day's work was done it had been decided. Gavin noticed the men in charge listening to their plans but nothing was said to discourage them.

They walked up to the manor house as a group and stopped just outside. One of the slaves left the group to talk to Agnes and came back saying that she would send someone to tell the master what they wanted. As they waited for a response, a dozen of the hired men came to stand in front of the group. They kept their hands away from their swords, just stood watching to see what would happen.

Sara had dozed off and on through the day but never tried to speak again. Lily had tried to send word to Elezar several times but he

101

couldn't be found. By evening Sara was breathing so slowly that Lily knew she was near death. It was time for her to be leaving to go to the dining hall but she didn't want Sara to be alone so she went to the kitchen to speak to Agnes. She found her staring out the window at what appeared to be most of the two hundred slaves on the estate standing in the yard. Lily could see a dozen of Elezar's guards standing on the edge of the crowd. "What is it, what's happening?" Lily asked her.

"They say they want to say thank you to Sara, to give tribute to her for all her years of hard work. I've sent a slave to the master to see what he wants to do."

Just then Elezar came into the kitchen. "What's this?" he said brusquely looking at Lily and Agnes. "Why are you not working?"

"I...they..." Lily stammered, pointing out the window as she tried to speak. Elezar strode to the window, seeing the group of slaves for the first time. He pushed open the back door so hard that it banged against the wall causing Lily to jump.

"What are you all doing here?" he shouted at them. "Why are you not working?"

One older slave stepped forward. "We've heard that Sara the healer is dying, master, and we'd like to pay our respects to her. Our work for the day is done and we'd hoped that you would allow us to see her," he said respectfully bowing his head as he spoke.

Elezar stepped back in and grabbed Lily by the arm. "Why have I not been told that Sara was dying?" he asked abruptly.

"I...I looked for you several times, master, to tell you but I couldn't find you," she stammered. He put his face up close to her, trying to determine if she was lying. Apparently satisfied with her answer he walked back outside and shouted angrily to his men. "Get these slaves back to their quarters. They can do without food tonight and let the dogs out early. I want everyone inside. I'll have no more of this disobedience. If you have free time on your hands then maybe we need to have a longer working day." He stepped back in and looked at Lily. "And you, healer, get back in there and take care of Sara. When she dies I want to know." He stomped off back down the hall and into his library.

Lily looked out the door as the crowd of slaves was dispersed. She noticed that the men weren't using whips or swords, just walking behind the slaves as if sending them in the right direction. She saw Gavin in the crowd talking intently with a man she recognized as the smith from his burly build and bald head, and quickly stepped out on the porch. He looked up and walked over to her and she noticed that Elezar's men looked the other way and let him by. She hurried down to him, giving him a quick hug. "He wants me to stay with Sara and I'd like to. I'll be fine here; I don't think he'll bother me tonight."

Gavin started to object when Agnes stepped outside. "She's right. The master has known Sara all his life and he respects her as much as he can respect any slave. He'll want Lily to sit with her. He won't bother her."

Before Gavin left he told Lily that he was going to talk with the smith. "He stopped me from charging up to the house when Elezar grabbed your arm. It seems that the slaves are planning something." She nodded and went inside to sit with Sara.

The old woman was as comfortable as Lily could make her lying on the old cot in the healing room. Lily had hoped to speak with her again but she never regained consciousness. Sara died later that night with Lily beside her. She sent word to Elezar but he didn't come down to see her, nor was he there when she was buried the next day in the slave's cemetery. No one was allowed to be there, not even Lily. She spent the day tidying up after Sara's illness, cleaning the healing room. She opened the window to air it out and then brought in fresh lavender. When she was done there was nothing left of the old woman, only the memories. This is what it is to be a slave, Lily thought, to have nothing, to be nothing.

~

The hunter Sylvius had crossed the sea quickly but it had taken time for him to slowly track down the individual slaves from the first ship. He went from estate to estate reading their minds. He learned that there had been forty seven women carried over on the vessel but he had no way of knowing if any of them could have been a witch. He was halfway through the list of slaves when he came to one farm that held both a woman and a man from the slave ship. The man was clearly a soldier and as Sylvius read his memories he discovered he was a survivor of the town of Redin where Sylvius had first felt the witch's presence.

Excitedly he dug deeper into the man's memories and found that the man had seen the witch before but had never learned her

103

name. The soldier remembered her as a young pretty woman with long blonde hair, small in stature and that she was with a soldier called Gavin. Most importantly the soldier knew that the witch hadn't been on his boat. Now all Sylvius had to do was track down all the women from the second ship. It was only a matter of time, he thought.

Chapter 11

Brother Arius left Roh Vec at night fall. It was far easier to travel the usually crowded streets when people were sleeping, and though he didn't like to admit it, the press of bodies made him feel vulnerable. He didn't travel alone; twelve men were commissioned to go with him. Ten of them were common legionnaires who had volunteered for the task. He suspected it was for the pay bonus they would receive, but when he read their minds he discovered that they did it for various reasons.

The other two men were from within the order. They had no official title within the Empire, but the readers often referred to them as the watchers. Their sole purpose was to protect and serve the readers, and their training was quite similar. They were chosen when very young, were castrated and then trained to be the perfect guards. They were quite familiar with a readers basic abilities and he found that it was very difficult to read their minds without them detecting his presence.

The group rode south on the crowded main highway for two days before turning west on the night road and starting the long trek to Trost. It was called the night road because of how long the nights could be that far north. It took a few days for Arius to become travel hardened. He hadn't ridden a horse for extended periods of time since he was a child, and on the first few days he went to sleep saddle sore. He could have retreated within his mind to dull the physical pain but felt that if the others could endure it then so could a reader. The legionnaires refused to get within ten feet of him, but on the other hand the watchers couldn't be pushed away. He was impressed with how efficient they were at protecting him but sometimes wished they would give him some space. He spoke little in the first few days and spent most of the time in his own thoughts.

He found that he had mixed feelings during the beginning of the journey. On the one hand he felt free without other readers around. There was no one always touching his mind, reading his thoughts, making sure he was doing as he was supposed to. He could vent his anger and frustrations freely but he soon realized he didn't need to. He took the time to enjoy the vast space, the open plains and shallow marshes that stretched for as far as the eye could see. It reminded him of his childhood on the Roh Plains, herding cattle, and riding his steppe pony. Strangely such thoughts still brought him feelings of sadness and he quickly stopped thinking of the past. *I am the boy Tevarian no longer*, he reminded himself. *I am Brother Arius the essence reader, and readers don't trifle over petty emotions.*

On the other hand, after the first week, Arius realized that he was bored. He was not used to communicating with those outside of the order and felt he had nothing in common with the soldiers' crude conversations. His two watchers would only speak with him if they felt he needed help and otherwise continued to stay annoyingly close to him. Arius needed to be training his mind as he had for the last twelve years but the problem was that there were neither readers to train with, nor any books to be read.

He decided to get up before sunrise one morning to practice his Shai-Yi exercises and ponder how he could continue training his mind. The watchers immediately got up with him, as did the soldiers, who were nervously anticipating orders.

"Just make breakfast," he told the sleepy men and began warming up with his stretches. One of the watchers approached him with a slight bow. "Honored reader, do you require a sparring partner?" he asked.

Arius nodded and the two men warmed up before signaling they were ready. Arius was quite confident, because even though he was slightly smaller than his watcher, he had been training for twelve years and had even bested some of his teachers at the compound. The watcher lunged at him to tackle him to the ground. Arius let the tackle come and then using the man's momentum against him tried to fling the man behind him, but the watcher expected this and clung onto him forcing them into a roll on the wet grass. The watcher pounced on him and the grappling match began. Arius prided himself on his ground grappling skills and forcing people to submit but this man was more than his equal. Not only that but he used wrestling slams with his body that Arius was unfamiliar with and knocked the wind out of him. He held out for a minute but the watcher eventually bested him in a chokehold. They separated and sat panting in the grass.

Arius was slightly frustrated with himself when he suddenly recalled Tasitus's words, "*Remember to always obtain knowledge and wisdom from whoever you meet, be they reader, slave, or even your enemy.*"

"I can see that you are quite familiar with Shai-Yi," Arius said approvingly.

"That and many other forms of hand to hand fighting," the watcher responded with a bow.

"Like what?"

"Wrestling, takedowns, striking with the arm and leg, and even some pressure points and grips that can cripple men."

"Teach me," Arius said.

The days quickly fell into a routine. Though Arius didn't show it, he was thrilled to be training again; it was the only life he really understood. He threw himself into the exercises every morning and evening. Sometimes he would even stop them in the middle of the day to spar. While they rode he kept up a continuous stream of questions with both his watchers. When he felt he had obtained all he could through speech he read their memories so he could relive parts of their training. He discovered that they were trained with many different types of weaponry as well, and asked them if they would teach him how to use his short sword. Arius knew how to use daggers quite well but using a short sword was completely different. Because of his reader abilities he improved very quickly but was rarely able to best his two watchers.

As the weeks passed and they gained elevation, the marshes disappeared into plains, and the plains into rolling hills. The Kheight mountain range slowly appeared to their left further south, and with winter approaching they soon found themselves riding in light snow. The mountains were at least kind enough to block the worst of the wind that plagued the Roh plains behind them. They met few travelers along the night road and most of them were couriers who rode by without a word. Villages were less common than small border forts containing supplies and horses for military personal and they passed only one settlement large enough to be called a town and nearly everyone there were slaves working in the iron mines.

One evening before sundown they made an early camp so Arius could spar with his watchers. The snow had just stopped falling when one of the guards suddenly called out a warning shout.

"Riders, from the north!" he yelled as the legionnaires scrambled to get their weapons. Arius stepped forward and viewed the riders as they approached. There was about thirty of them bundled in winter steppe clothing. They were Northlanders, some of the last men not yet integrated into the Empire. It was relatively rare to see them this far south but the winter weather must have made them bolder. They were well armed with bows and lances and Arius knew that they had no chance against these men if a fight broke out. His mind scrambled for ideas and he decided that his power was their best chance of survival.

He reached out to as many minds as he could over the long distance. They faltered at his alien touch about one-hundred yards away and he took the moment to speak into their minds. *"I am Arius of the order of essence readers, if you come any closer I will see to it that none of your souls ever reach the spirit realm,"* he bluffed.

To make his point Arius took control of one of the riders and had him slit his own throat. The rider fell from his horse into the snow and his comrades looked at him in horror. The act over so great a distance left Arius feeling drained and he reached greedily for the dead man's essence as it left his warm corpse. He pulled within himself and immediately felt his inner strength renewed and then some. The snow would slow the horses and he estimated he could kill four or five riders before they shot him down with their bows. He readied himself but luckily after picking up their fallen comrade, the riders quickly turned and rode off in the direction that they came from.

"I don't understand?" said one of the legionnaires. "They outnumbered us three to one, why are they running? And why did that man kill himself?" Slowly all heads turned to Arius. "I gave them a warning," he said. "They won't be bothering us again, but we should double our watch just in case." He thought that the legionnaires would trust him more after he had saved their lives but instead their fear of him only grew after seeing him use his abilities.

A week later one of the soldiers took ill and Arius called the men to a stop at midday. He didn't mind the delay because it allowed him to practice and he thought it would give the sick man time to recover. By nightfall the man's condition had worsened and Arius could feel how his essence barely clung to his physical body, he knew his death was imminent. The sickly man was being held by another legionnaire. Arius was unsure how or why but the two soldiers had become fast friends.

He approached them both and the sick soldier cried out in delirium. "Don't let him near me! Don't let him take my soul!"

"Why would I take your soul? I have no need for it," Arius said with genuine confusion. His words didn't calm the soldier who kept babbling about not wanting his soul to be sucked away. Arius eventually left and went to his tent, the life of a reader was a lonely one and he knew he would have to accept that. He was no stranger to death but he couldn't help but feel slightly uncomfortable at seeing the soldier waste away in such a fashion. He would rather die by another's hand he decided.

The soldier died in the middle of the night. The feeling of an essence leaving its body woke Arius from his sleep. He watched it slowly ascend into the sky and onward towards the spirit realm. The soldiers were silent in the morning when Arius sought out the dead man's friend. "His soul made it to the spirit realm," Arius told him. He didn't know why but some instinct told him it was the right thing to do. "I just thought you might want to know." The man was visibly upset and walked away after choking back a sob when he heard his words. Arius left feeling as if he had made the situation worse.

Later that evening, however, the soldier approached him when he was sparring. "Thanks for telling me," he said simply. "I've been watching you train over these last few weeks and while I don't know much about wrestling like these two," he said acknowledging his watchers, "I could teach you a different style with your short sword, if you're interested." Arius was pleased and nodded his thanks.

After that many of the other legionnaires warmed up to him slightly, at least in the sense that they gave him advice when he sparred in the evenings. Arius was surprised to learn that the watchers and soldiers used the same weapon in completely different ways. The watchers had been teaching him how to use the short sword in a duel, emphasizing footwork, parrying and slashing, but the legionnaires taught him to cut and jab while trusting in a large shield to protect the body. When he had learned the basics of what the legionnaires were teaching him, he implemented them into his duels with the two watchers. The mixed tactics helped him improve and though the watchers were still his betters, everyone agreed it was only by a narrow margin. Arius felt confident that in the few remaining days of their journey he would have learned almost all that he could about these forms of combat.

Chapter 12

As soon as he left Lily at the manor, Gavin went in search of Smith. He knew he didn't have much time before they let the dogs out and he wanted to be back to his quarters before that happened. The smithy was easy to find but he wasn't sure if the smith would be there or even where his quarters were. He walked through the entry and immediately felt warmer. The fire had been banked but the place still radiated heat from the work that had been done during the day. The anvil was in the center of the room with the tongs, bellows and various other tools lying neatly on a shelf nearby. He liked how organized the smithy was and immediately his assessment of the blacksmith rose.

He stood for a moment listening and thought he could hear a quiet murmuring coming from behind a door at the back of the room. He knocked and the hushed voices went silent. The door was opened by Smith himself who, when he saw who it was, opened it wide and invited him in.

"You came," was all he said as Gavin walked through the door and saw that the small room was crowded with at least a dozen slaves, all of them men.

"I did. You said something about a plan and I hope you're talking about a plan of escape," Gavin said quietly. "I want out of this damn place and I'll do anything to help that happen."

Smith got a broad grin on his face. "I was hoping you might feel that way. There are a few of us willing to take a chance on escaping but not enough yet to make it happen. With you new Camarian slaves here, I'm hoping we might have enough numbers now. Would you be willing to talk to the other Camarians and see if they would join us?"

One of the other slaves stared at Gavin and spoke up. "Are you sure we can trust this man, Smith? He hasn't been here long and his wife is up at the house all day with Elezar."

Before Gavin could answer, Smith spoke again. "That's exactly why we can trust him. Would you want your wife around Elezar day after day?"

110

The man shook his head but continued to stare suspiciously at Gavin. "I don't know where you're from," Gavin said to the man, "but on Camar there are no slaves. Living like this is so foreign to us that I honestly don't think any of us will be here long. We'll either take our chances and run, or we'll die trying. I want out of here and I want my wife away from that fiend. He's raped her once already, and I'll be damned if I let it happen again." He had clenched his hands feeling the need to hit something while he spoke.

"There are no slaves on Camar?" one of the men asked. "Who works the fields?"

"If we own a piece of land, we work it ourselves or at least we did until the Empire invaded. I don't know what's happening there now and I'd sure like to find out. If we can escape, that's where I want to go. Anyone that wants to come with me is welcome."

"Before we go that far we need to escape the estate," Smith said. "Let's take it one step at a time."

"Do you have a plan already? How many men do we have that are willing to fight?" Gavin wanted to know.

"All of us here tonight, of course; plus another ten or so. If you convince the other Camarians to join us we should have close to twenty five. The problem is lack of weapons. We have several knives hidden away but we're mostly going to have to rely on our wits and our fists."

"What about the dogs? And what direction will you go once we leave?"

"We don't have all the details worked out which is why I'm glad you're here. Were you a soldier on Camar?" When Gavin nodded yes to the question, Smith continued, "Good, I thought you might have been. I hope you can help us with the final plans. As to what direction we would head, we should go north. There are too many legions to the south and it's too heavily populated."

They spent the rest of their time together discussing possible escape plans. Gavin listened carefully to all Smith told him and considered how it would all work with his plans of returning to Camar. He made it back to his quarters before the dogs were let out and lay there most of the night thinking. He wondered what had happened to his family when the Empire came in. He grew up in the heavily forested mountains in the north of the island and was sure they had probably escaped into the hills. His father was canny in the ways of the forests and could disappear without leaving a trace.

He wished Lily hadn't stayed at the manor with Sara because he had so much he wanted to tell her. He was sure she would want to go back to Camar and knew she would be relieved to know that plans for their escape were being made. He thought about his brothers and telling them of all that had happened to him and then he thought about introducing them to Lily. That brought a smile to his face. He finally fell asleep lost in memories of his family.

Lily didn't see Gavin until dinner the next day. She was tired from sitting with Sara until she died and wanted nothing more than to eat her meal and then lie down and rest. She was surprised at how Gavin hurried her through the dinner until she finally gave up trying to finish and took it back to their quarters.

"What's the hurry?" she asked him as they sat on their blankets, backs against the wall as Lily tried to finish her dinner.

"I went to see Smith last night," Gavin said quietly. "They're planning an escape and we're part of it. I spoke with most of the other Camarians today in the fields and they also want to help. The plans are not all set but some time in the next few weeks we should be able to make the attempt."

Lily set her food down, unable to finish. "I can't believe it. We could actually be free of this place?"

"And the best part is many of them want to join us when we return to Camar. Eventually I'd like to help rid the island of the Empire. We won't be able to go straight there, of course, but I hope within a few weeks after our escape we can head west and try to make it back."

Lily pulled her knees up and rested her head on them in thought. "Gavin, I don't want to go back to Camar."

Gavin looked at her in surprise. "I know the Empire is there, but it'll be alright. We'll find a way to sneak past them and head north to my family. They'll take us in until we can sort things out. You'll like them."

Lily smiled at him. "I'm sure I'll like them and I'd like to meet them someday but I need to head into the Northlands before I can think of going back to Camar. Remember, Samuel told me that my mother might be there and I need to find out. I also need to find…something…else," she stammered. The words of Joan's prophecy came to her, "*You will find what you are seeking to the north, you must follow the black book.* " but she found that she couldn't put it into words to share with him.

Gavin appeared to be thinking about what she had said and interrupted her attempts to explain. "The Northlands? You really want to go that far? We'll be heading north at first, of course, but I didn't plan on going that far."

"This is really important to me. I thought my mother was dead for the last twenty years and now I find out she might be alive. I've got to find out. Can't you see that?"

Gavin had a disappointed look on his face as he said, "I can see how that would be important to you but have you considered how hard that will be? We'll be almost into winter by then and we'd be dealing with bad weather and heading north straight into it."

"I know it won't be easy but I at least need to try."

"Well, as Smith said the other night, one step at a time. First we have to escape and then hopefully we'll know where to go from there," he said as he picked up her discarded dinner and proceeded to finish it for her.

Lily let it go at that. She didn't want to go back to Camar where she'd have to go back into hiding again to heal like she did here in Trost. If Samuel was right about the Northlands, perhaps she could practice her healing without being afraid and she wanted that badly. She'd have to convince Gavin it would be worth it and hope he would agree.

Chapter 13

The slaves still came everyday to be healed, only now Lily did all the healing herself. Most times it was something minor that she could do with the herbs she had available, or there were the occasional broken bones to set. Since Sara had died Elezar had been rougher with the slaves than usual. There had been some beatings and one man had been tied to a post and given twenty lashings. While Lily cleaned the wounds and applied her herbal ointment she had used a small amount of her power to take away some of the pain and hasten his healing. She made sure that no one noticed what she had done and she didn't tell Gavin, knowing he wouldn't like it.

Lily had done her best to put that horrible night with Elezar behind her. She tried to avoid him as much as was possible and when she had to see him she kept her head down and spoke respectfully, not wanting him to take offense at anything she said. It helped that she knew there were many other women on the estate that had had the same experience and she saw that they had coped with it. It also helped that she had Gavin to turn to. She thanked the Maker once again that he had been chosen to protect her.

One day, two weeks after Sara's death, a woman ran in clutching a screaming toddler. Lily took him from the mother and gasped when she saw that he had been badly burned. His shirt was in smoldering tatters and the skin on his arms and chest was bright red, the burned edges blackened from fire. His mother was sobbing incoherently as she tried to explain what had happened.

"He's just learned to walk and I turned my back for a moment, just a moment it was, and he was out the door. By the time I found him he was already at the smithy and tried to grab a hot coal." She was sobbing so hard now that Lily had trouble understanding the rest of what she said. "By the time the smith saw him his sleeve had caught on fire. The smith threw a bucket of water on him but he's burned so bad." She looked at her son's burned body and sobbed even harder

Lily laid the screaming child down on her work table. She tried to get the shreds of his clothing off to see what she could do for

114

him but it stuck to his burnt skin. He thrashed his little body from side to side trying to escape the horrible pain she knew he must be feeling. She had no herbs or ointments that would help with a burn this bad and she knew that she had to use her powers. Gavin wouldn't like it but she was sure he would understand. A slave burned this badly would probably be killed if he didn't die first and there was no way she could allow that to happen to this innocent child. She looked up and saw that a small crowd of slaves were in the doorway, Agnes among them. The mother turned as a man hurried in and stood staring at the child, desperation in his face. He put his arms around the woman and said "Is there anything you can do for my son?"

"Yes," Lily hesitated, "but I must ask that what I do be kept a secret between those of you that are here. If our master finds out…" Lily couldn't even finish, it scared her so much to think of how he would use her abilities. Agnes shooed everyone in the hallway out to the kitchen.

"Let the healer do her job," she said, "she won't need us watching." As she shut the door to the room she looked at Lily and said, "Don't you worry, I'll mind the door." The child's parents stayed in the corner holding each other up and watching. Lily nodded to them knowing they wouldn't want to leave.

Lily put her hands on the child and opened herself to her power. She watched in fascination as the blackened skin fell off and was replaced with new pale, pink skin. She kept her hands on him until the room started to sway, then let go of him and gripped the edge of the table. The child had stopped crying and his parents came closer and gasped when they saw what she had done. Lily's legs suddenly gave way and the father grabbed her under her arms just as she started to fall. He helped her to a chair and knelt in front of her, saying quietly, "You know I have nothing to give you but if I can ever do anything for you, you just have to ask." The child's mother picked the little boy up and also knelt in front of her. "Anything," she said in a hushed voice.

After they had left, carrying their now quiet son between them, Agnes came in to talk to Lily. She hesitated, seemingly at a loss for words, an unusual situation for her. "What are you that you can heal a burn like that?" Agnes asked in wonder. "I've never seen anyone healed like that."

115

"Can I trust you Agnes to not say anything to the master about this?" Lily asked her.

"Don't you worry, there's no one that was here today that'll say a word. We know what he'd do with you if he found out," she answered.

Lily hesitated a moment before she spoke. "As to what I am, let's just keep calling me a healer. I can heal with a touch of my hands just as my mother could. I don't use the power I have often, because it will be dangerous for me if it's discovered. There are people who would kill me if they knew. I only use it when I know my herbal medicines won't help."

"Well, all I know is it's a miracle."

"What's a miracle?" asked a voice from the doorway. Lily looked up to see Elezar standing there looking like the benevolent master. How she hated that look. "It's my estate surely I should know if we've had a miracle." He cocked his head to the side and gave them an oily smile. Lily's heart beat faster as she wondered how much he had heard.

Agnes jumped right in with an answer, always quick on her feet with words. "Only that Miss Lily didn't hit her head when she fell. She took a dizzy spell and toppled right over a few minutes ago. Didn't you Lily?"

"Yes, I'm feeling better now though," she said shakily, as she stood up from the cot.

"Perhaps you're with child?" Elezar asked with a hopeful look on his face.

Lily knew he would like that, more free slaves to work the estate. "No, master, actually I just started my monthly bleeding. Sometimes it makes me light headed. I'm sure that's all it is." It was a little lie but it would explain the dizziness and in case he was thinking of raping her again she knew this would keep him away a little longer.

Elezar got a look of distaste on his face. Lily wanted to hit him when she saw it. Only a man such as him would find a woman's life giving cycles distasteful. It was all she could do not to say something nasty to him. "Well, maybe next month," was all he said as he left the room.

Agnes and Lily gave each other a look, and then Agnes turned to more practical matters. "If you're feeling better it's almost time for dinner so you'd best get over to the dining hall. I expect your husband will have heard what happened and he'll be worried about you."

116

Lily knew she was right about that and she wasn't looking forward to what he would have to say to her. Why couldn't the man understand that as a healer there were times she felt the need to use her powers? She headed outside thinking she'd better head Gavin off before he came looking for her.

Gavin was in the dining hall waiting for Lily. The story of what she had done was spreading among the slaves like wildfire. Each time he'd seen someone talking about her, he had joined them and begged them not to let any of the hired men hear about it. If Elezar heard, he was certain he would either try to make money off her or he would turn her over to the Empire to make a name for himself. He wanted them to understand how important it was to keep this only among the slaves. Suddenly everyone stopped talking and the hall became completely silent. Gavin looked up and saw that Lily had stepped into the room and was walking toward him. She stopped uncertainly when she realized that everyone was staring at her. He went to her quickly and put his arm around her.

"Why is everyone staring?" she whispered.

"They all know what you did today. I don't think they all know quite what to think about it."

Just then Agnes walked into the room with dinner. "Why is everyone so quiet," she said with her usual aplomb. "Grab your plates and get in line if you want food."

The crowd did as she asked and soon the hall was as noisy as usual. They got their food and Gavin and Lily found a table to sit at. While they ate, some of the slaves came up to them one by one and thanked her for what she had done. Others seemed to want to touch her hand as they spoke to her. Agnes came over to them after she had finished serving the meal to reassure them. "You've given us all hope, Lily, that maybe we can have a better life. That someone cares about us even if we are only slaves. No one will give you away; you're too special to us now."

They left soon after they had finished eating and walked back to their quarters in silence. Gavin could tell that Lily had something on her mind. He knew she could probably tell that he was not happy with the situation she had put herself in. As soon as he closed the door she turned to him. "I can tell that you're upset with me so you'd better speak your mind."

He took a deep breath before he spoke, hoping he wouldn't sound as angry as he was feeling. "Did you have to heal the child that way? Don't you realize how dangerous it was? We might have half the Empire looking for you as far as we know."

"Nonsense, we don't know for sure that anyone noticed what I did in Redin." Lily snapped back. "Samuel was just guessing when he said they had a reader with the soldiers and anyway I had no choice today. That boy would have died if I hadn't healed him and he would have died slowly and very painfully. I couldn't stand by and watch that and I don't think you could have either. I know you're worried about me but we have to take some chances in this life or we don't have a life. I'm a healer, Gavin, I have to heal when I can, in whatever way I can".

Gavin could see that Lily was breathing hard by the time she had finished speaking and her hands were clenched. He was sorry that he had upset her but she didn't seem to realize the danger this put her in so he answered her in a louder voice than he intended. "Lily, we're in the Empire now and you can't ignore the dangers. These readers Samuel told us about could be anywhere. For all we know Elezar invites them to dinner once a month. You can't just throw your power around and not expect it to be noticed."

He heard Lily hesitate before she spoke again. "I don't regret saving that child's life. I would do it again even if a reader was in the next room. Some things are more important than staying safe. I know you worry about me and I'm sorry but I can't promise to never use my powers."

"Can you at least promise me that you won't use your power any more than you have to?" he said in exasperation.

"Of course not, only in the worst cases," she said apologetically.

Gavin paced around the small room for another moment or two before he stopped and stared at her. "Do you know another thing I hate about this place?" When she just raised her eyebrows questioningly at him he continued. "I can't even go to the tavern for a drink to cool off after an argument."

Lily laughed at him and his anger was gone, although the worry remained.

Lily was in the healing room one afternoon when Elezar came in. Lily looked up nervously when he banged the door open.

"Where are the sleeping herbs that Sara used to give me," he shouted at her.

"I don't know of any herbs that Sara gave you master," she replied, "but I'm sure I have some that will help you sleep. Just let me find them for you." Lily started searching quickly among the jars for the valerian.

"You're lying to me slave. Don't you want me to sleep well?" he said in a quiet, menacing voice. He walked toward her, his fist raised and she backed up until she bumped into the wall.

"Of course I do," she said, holding the jar of herbs in front of her.

"What? You don't want me to be able to sleep?"

"No, that's not what I meant. I…I do want you to sleep well, of course," she stuttered so nervously that she hardly knew what she was saying. His arm was still raised and she cringed when he brought it closer to her face.

"Then where are they?" he screamed at her, standing so close that the spittle from his mouth hit her in the face.

Lily still held the jar in front of her and tried to show it to him but Elezar was pressed so close to her that she couldn't lift it between them.

"I have them here. I just need to make a tea with the leaves," she said.

Elezar put his mouth up to her ear and said quietly, "Perhaps instead you'd like to come to my bed again and help me sleep."

Lily looked into his eyes and couldn't speak. If she said yes he would rape her. If she said no he would have her punished and probably rape her anyway. She was tired of his bullying, tired of being a victim but she didn't know how to protect herself and she didn't know how to protect Gavin from the repercussions of her answer.

"What do you think, Darius? Does she look eager to share my bed?" Elezar asked and Lily realized that his hired man was also in the room. She heard the other man laugh.

"Maybe she'd prefer your company Darius, or maybe I'll let you have her after I'm done with her. Would you like that Lily?" he asked as he picked up a strand of her hair and wrapped it around his hand. "Would you like to spend some time with Darius?"

119

Lily had no trouble answering this time. She had already seen evidence of how rough Darius was with the slave women that Elezar let him have when they came to her for healing. "No," she answered firmly, determined to take whatever punishment he would mete out.

"No? Well then, I guess there's only one thing to do." He backed away from Lily and motioned Darius over. "This slave needs to be reminded who is the master here. I want her whipped," he said and walked out of the room.

Darius came over to her with a nasty smile on his face and grabbed her hands, turning her around so that he could tie them behind her back. When he was done he pulled her toward him so that her back was against his chest. His hands came around her and he began to rub her breasts. "I'll enjoy taking you after Master Elezar is done with you," he said. Lily tried to pull away but his grip was too strong and he merely laughed at her attempts. She was afraid to stand up to Elezar but she didn't feel that way about defending herself from his hired help. When he shoved one of his hands inside her dress, tearing off the buttons as he did, she flung her head back and hit him firmly in the chin.

"Bitch," he swore and let go of her. "You'll pay for that." She lurched forward and looking back at him saw a drop of blood on his lip. She tried to dart away but he grabbed her and slammed her against the wall, one hand holding her neck and the other reaching under her dress. She began to struggle but with her hands behind her back she couldn't push him away and his hand on her neck tightened. She was having trouble breathing and her struggles were getting weaker when she heard Elezar's voice.

"Darius, what are you doing? Get the woman out here," he shouted.

Darius released her and shoved her roughly ahead of him. "I'll have you soon," he said, "and if your husband tries to stop me, he'll die." He laughed then and pushed her out the door and down the hallway to the back of the house.

When they stepped outside, Lily's arms were stretched above her head and her hands were tied to a ring attached to a post that stood in the center of the yard. Darius unbuttoned her dress and pushed her shift to her waist leaving her bare from the waist up. He leered at her as he undressed her but with Elezar watching this time, he didn't touch her. Mouthing the word *"soon,"* he walked over to stand beside the master. It was just before the dinner hour and the slaves were

120

coming in from the fields. Lily knew Elezar liked to make a spectacle of any slaves he had whipped so as to frighten the other slaves into submission. When the slaves saw who was tied to the pole, they started to mutter angrily. Since healing the little boy, Lily was a favorite among them and they were not pleased to see Elezar punishing her.

Lily was so frightened now that she barely heard Elezar as he shouted to the slaves. "This slave is being punished for forgetting who is the master here," he said. "But because I am a benevolent man she will only get ten lashes instead of the usual twenty." He motioned for his hired man to begin. Her back was to the watching slaves and as she waited for the sting of the whip she hoped Gavin was still in the fields. She knew he would never stand by and watch her whipped and would probably get himself killed trying to help her.

The first lash stung, the second hurt even worse but by the third lash Lily felt like her back was on fire. She gasped each time they struck and felt the tears running down her cheeks although she wasn't aware that she was crying. When they were done she could feel the blood dripping down her back. She had treated men who had been given twenty lashes and as she hung there she wondered how they had stood it. They untied her and she fell to her knees. She pulled up her shift to cover herself and then tried unsuccessfully to stand. One of the slaves stepped forward to help her and soon she was surrounded by others helping her to get to her quarters.

As she lay face down on their blankets, her back was uncovered to help with the pain. One of the women went to get her some food and another brought water and gently sponged her back. Her medicines were at the house so she didn't have anything to put on the wounds to help them heal and take some of the pain away. It was dark now and still Gavin hadn't come. As much as she wanted him with her, she was afraid of what he would do when he saw what had happened. As she lay there taking deep breaths, she heard Agnes come in.

"What did he do to you, Lily?" she asked as she walked in and then gasped when she saw her back. "That man, what was he thinking to injure our only healer? Idiot." Always practical, her next question was, "What can I do to help?"

"There's a green jar on the second shelf in the healing room with a salve in it that I use for injuries such as this." Lily said quietly. "Could you bring it here without getting yourself in trouble?"

121

"Of course, but where is your man? He isn't off trying to get himself killed I hope."

"Her man is right behind you, Agnes, what's happened here? Why are people crowded outside our door?" Lily heard Gavin say as he stepped inside.

When he saw her back he began to swear. He turned around and started out the door when Agnes grabbed one arm and the smith, who was just behind him, grabbed the other. The smith was a big man with bulging muscles from his years of forging iron and he held Gavin with a steel grip. He was going nowhere unless the man let go of him.

"I'll kill him," Gavin swore savagely and tried to jerk away. "Let go of my arm Smith, I don't want to fight you but I will kill that man tonight."

"No, you won't, not tonight." Smith sternly replied. "You'll wait until we're ready, as we planned. Tonight, you'll stay here with your wife and take care of her. I feel for you, but we've all had loved ones injured and we've endured it, as will you."

When the smith was sure that Gavin wasn't going to leave, he let go of his arm. "Are you calm now, man? Can you hold your temper?" he asked him.

"I'll be fine, you can leave. I won't do anything stupid," he muttered angrily.

Agnes slipped out the door to get the salve for Lily, leaving Gavin and Lily alone. Gavin closed the door as the last few slaves left for their own quarters. Lily turned her head and saw that he had knelt down beside her. He looked like he wanted to touch her but was afraid to hurt her. "Gavin will you help me please?" Lily asked him.

"What can I do?" he said, again reaching for her but stopping before he touched her.

"I've never tried to heal myself before and I'm not sure where to start. Could you just help me sit up and hold me while I try?" Gavin did as she asked, keeping his arms around her and holding one hand as she reached her other hand to touch her lower back and then pushed out with her power. There was a strange pattern to the healing; she went from feeling fine, to feeling exhausted, then back to normal. This went on for several moments until she stopped using her power. She had never felt anything like it in all the healings she had done. She lay down again and looked at Gavin. His face was pale as he slowly fell forward to lie beside her.

"Gavin, what's wrong?"

"I don't know. I just need to lie down for a bit. I feel like I've been run over by a horse," he said laughing lightly.

"Do you think it's because I was touching you?" Lily wondered. "But that doesn't really make sense, I've touched you many times and it's never tired you before." She heard him snicker at that. "You know what I mean, what makes this time different, I wonder?"

"Maybe because you were healing yourself? I don't know. Why did Elezar have you whipped anyway?" he asked.

"He said I had forgotten who the master was," she answered.

"What did you do?" he asked, surprised.

"Nothing really, I think he might have had me whipped regardless. I don't think he's happy that I'm so well-liked and he needed a way to keep me in my place."

"You may be right at that. I can't wait to leave this place and I *will* kill him before we go. I won't leave him alive to come after us."

Lily turned over on her side and touched the scar on Gavin's face. "How did you get this?" she asked him wanting to change the subject and quiet his thoughts of killing.

"My first skirmish riding with Commander Versan. We were fighting against one of the northern lords over some piece of land or another. The other man was faster and bigger and I was barely holding my own. He tried to take off my head and it was so muddy that I slipped backward on my ass which probably saved my life. Versan ran him through before he could kill me." He stopped speaking for a moment, staring quietly at the little window in their room. "I hope the commander made it out of Redin. He's a good man."

Thinking about Versan had calmed Gavin's anger and Lily was falling asleep beside him. They both turned over and she spooned in behind him, enjoying the warmth of his body

They were both asleep when Agnes quietly opened the door bringing the salve that Lily had requested. When she saw her healed back she shook her head in awe. "Another miracle," she whispered as she gently closed the door taking the unneeded salve with her.

Chapter 14

"You have to admit, these Islanders have some spirit," Jacobo said with a chicken bone between his teeth.

"No more than all the others we've defeated," General Gavrus disagreed. He stood near a castle window that overlooked the capital city of Felmar on the island of Camar. He had occupied the city about a month ago with two of his four legions. The first snow had come that night blanketing the houses in white. Though it was the biggest city on the island it was not even half the size of the imperial cities. Gavrus found that he disliked the place, though he disliked most cities. He preferred to be in the field with an army at his back. The walls here were old and poorly constructed, and the city didn't even have a proper sewage disposal.

"I don't recall the Tornes or the Altiats giving us this much trouble. There are pockets of resistance springing up everywhere, and we even heard reports that the slaves we sent over are quite rebellious." Jacobo pressed.

"That's because the Tornes and the Altiats got to watch us come closer and closer each year. Always we conquered and by the time we reached their lands they knew their defeat was inevitable. The problem with the Camarians is that they haven't figured out they're beaten yet."

"You're wrong Gavrus," came the raspy voice of King Rubin slumping on his throne. He was uninjured from the battle; clean, and well fed. However at closer inspection one could see that his eyes were ringed with lack of sleep. Close behind him stood a single black robed reader, his hand resting lightly on the stone throne inches from the king's shoulder. "My people will always keep fighting, just as I will." he said

"Rubin, so good to hear your voice," Gavrus said with surprise. "Would you care for a drink?" he said and offered him some wine.

"You know I won't," he spat. Gavrus nodded to the reader and Rubin stiffened as the reader took control of his body. His eyes glassed over and slowly he reached out and took the goblet from Gavrus's hand. He drank awkwardly and spilled down the front of his rich robes. He handed the goblet back to Gavrus and then the reader released him and he slumped back on to his throne.

"My people will never accept your rule, Gavrus, and he," he said indicating the reader behind him. "He won't be here forever to make me your puppet. Believe me general when he slips, and he will slip, I will kill him, and then I will kill you," King Rubin said with a fire in his eyes.

Gavrus smiled briefly, he couldn't help but like and respect the king's will to fight the inevitable. "Rubin, I'm going to tell you a little story that is quite personal, though I'm sure nearly all the legionnaires under my command know at least part of it. You see, I was born a slave within the Empire. My grandfather fought against the Empire and received a sword in the gut for his troubles. A sword quite like this one," Gavrus said drawing his short sword. He held it out to Rubin who glanced at it with a deadly hunger in his eyes. The black robed reader simply tapped him once on the shoulder and Rubin shuddered and looked away from the weapon. Gavrus sheathed the weapon and began to pace around the room speaking as if he was giving a lecture to a student.

"My father was only a child at the time, and when the Empire conquered his land he became a slave hand in the fields. His life was short and meaningless; he died on the lashing post. His only achievement was spilling his seed in some whore who gave birth to me." Gavrus paused and took a sip of wine before continuing.

"I too seemed destined to live the life of a slave, and like you Rubin I fought against such a fate. I fought so hard that one day I killed one of the guards with my bare hands. So there I found myself on the chopping block, looking at the same fate as my father and his father before." Gavrus shivered at the memory, it had been cold then too. He could still feel the icy burn of the snow on the chopping block touch his face.

"But fate is a fickle thing," he continued. "For at that moment, when they had the axe raised above my head, a group of legionnaires happened to pass by. There was a captain amongst them who asked for my life. Apparently, he and his men were quite bored and wanted to see some sport. They promised the local officials that I would be dead by nightfall and after a few coins exchanged hands I was off to the legion." Gavrus suddenly laughed to himself.

"You have no idea how happy I was Rubin; I knew I was still going to die, but this time I could do it on my feet! Actually I suppose you can relate with the feeling," he said with a smile at the king, but Rubin only stared back blankly.

"They took me to the camp that evening and gave me a short sword and armor. They placed me in the center of a large circular wall. I figured they would pair me against one of their men in single combat, but instead they brought forth a tiger. A bloody tiger," he murmured more to himself than to the king. Instinctively his hand went to the worn piece of tiger pelt that hung from his belt at all times.

"Have you ever seen a tiger Rubin?" he asked the king but didn't wait for an answer. "I've been all across the Empire and I can tell you that it's the closest resemblance to death in its physical form. Well, besides our mutual friend here," he said giving a nod to the reader who remained as silent as ever. "Staring at that tiger made me realize something I hadn't before. I knew that if I continued to fight the Empire I would only find a shallow grave. If, however, I joined the Empire, well then not only would I live but I could make a difference. So I told the captain that unless he gave me something in return I would lie down and let the tiger eat me, denying him and his men their sport. To this day I think he knew I was bluffing but he humored me and asked me what it was I wanted. I told him that if I killed the tiger and survived that I wished to serve as a legionnaire under his command. He laughed at me but granted my request." Gavrus looked down at the faded pelt around his belt and stroked it thoughtfully.

"I was as surprised as they were when I discovered that I had killed the beast," he said quietly. "The event did not leave me unscarred." He lifted his shirt to reveal the claw scars across his chest and the bite marks in his left arm. "I don't know how I survived the wounds but the captain was true to his word and I became a legionnaire. That is how I became known as The Tiger or Tigris. Look at me now Rubin; you know how many lives I've been able to save? All because I made the decision to join the Empire, not fight against it."

"Yes, but how many have you enslaved to the life you so hated," Rubin asked.

"The weak allow themselves to be enslaved," Gavrus spat. "Growing up in the slave camps will teach one that. All I do is set everyone we conquer on equal footing. Some of your men are weak Rubin, and they will serve the strong through slavery because it's their fate. Others are strong but foolish and as long as they resist the Empire's might, they will die as I almost did. But others, others will realize that it is their fate to rise above the weak and accomplish great things. You could be one of those men Rubin, think of all the good you could do for your people. I feel we are much the same you and I, both of us are strong willed men who can take control of our own fate. Don't turn yours toward a meaningless death," Gavrus pleaded.

"I think your fate is about to take a turn for the worse, General," the king said. Gavrus shook his head and smiled at Jacobo.

"Alright Jacobo, perhaps your right, maybe these islanders have some spirit," Gavrus said.

"You know, I could have sworn the last time you told that story you killed two tigers," Jacobo grinned.

"Oh, of course, of course, how could I forget and did I mention that I killed the second one bare handed." Both men broke out laughing. Just then the door to the throne room opened and a courier came quickly inside.

"Urgent message for General Gavrus from Nazbar," he said. Nazbar was both a city and a province. It was located directly south of the region of Trost, at the eastern end of the Empire. In the west there were several massive cities but in the east there was really only Nazbar, making it a sort of unofficial capital. Gavrus quickly scanned the letter, than threw it to Jacobo in disgust. After he read the letter Jacobo looked at Gavrus in confusion.

"It says they wish to reward you. I don't understand why you're so upset."

"Oh come on Jacobo. You know as well as I the bull shit that happens within those walls. This isn't a reward, its punishment."

"Perhaps they're going to make you high general of the entire east." Jacobo suggested. Gavrus considered the option briefly before dismissing the possibility.

"There are too many old men in line for that position already. No they're more likely to assign me a new position in Laharah or Moorim, where I can sit on my hands and do nothing. They'll say that my experience is required to train the new legions." He sneered and then slammed his fist into the table. "Damn it! I fought hard to get this position Jacobo, you know I did! Whoever is the general of Trost region gets to stand toe to toe with the Northland rebels. Out here is where it's happening! Out here a soldier stays sharp because his enemy is near. Out here a man can fight for his destiny. Those men in the east and south are just herdsmen, watching over fields of slaves and growing fat."

"What do you intend to do?" Jacobo asked. Gavrus sank down to a nearby stool and put his face in his hands. Dark treasonous thoughts entered his mind but one glance at the reader standing near Rubin and he dismissed them.

"I will go of course. One cannot fight the inevitable," he said with a small smile and looked to Rubin.

"You'll be missed," Jacobo said gravely. Gavrus threw back his head and laughed.

"You're a terrible liar my friend. My misfortune means that you're in charge. Don't tell me you didn't want it." Jacobo smiled guiltily at being caught. "And why not," Gavrus continued to himself. "It's high time someone younger took over. I have at least created a name for myself." Gavrus stood and Jacobo stood with him.

"When are you leaving?" Jacobo asked.

"Now before I change my mind." Neither man was good with goodbyes and they each stood awkwardly for a moment. Gavrus eventually sighed and gave Jacobo a strong hand shake. "It's been an honor, General Jacobo," he said, emphasizing the word general. Jacobo simply nodded once in return. Gavrus turned and walked towards the door.

"I'll put in a good word for you at Nazbar," he said loudly. "Oh and one more thing, I suggest that you send the fifty-fourth legion back to Trost. The veterans shouldn't be bothered with the uprisings here, its bad for moral." With that he strode through the door leaving Jacobo behind.

Gavrus traveled with his personal group of twenty body guards. On horseback it only took them two days to reach the shores of Camar. It snowed almost every night for brief periods of time, but the ground was not frozen enough to keep the snow from melting by midday and leaving the ground a muddy mess. There was a single ship waiting for them and they dismounted and slowly walked across the wet sands, leading their horses. The sea gale blew fiercely across his face forcing him to place a hand in front of his teary eyes. The cold seemed to pierce straight through his furs as if he were walking naked. *At least it will be warm back in Nazbar*, he thought.

"Tigris, look." One of his men pointed down the beach to where an old woman was quickly hobbling towards them. Her long, white hair was blowing freely in the wind and one hand held her cape tightly closed as if she was afraid the wind might tear it from her. The other hand had a firm grip on an old gnarled cane to aid her as she walked. When she got close one of his men drew his sword but Gavrus ordered him back.

"Are you lost old mother?" he asked standing before his men, wondering what this old woman could want with him.

The old woman stared into his eyes causing an uneasy feeling to go through him. "You became a more perfect version of what you faced Tigris," she said. "You would be wise to remember this in the near future." She turned, then and without another word she hobbled away as quickly as she came.

"Should we go after her Tigris?" one of his men asked.

"No," he said slowly still watching her go. He shook his head and focused on the task at hand. "Come on, let's get off this freezing rock," he said as they went aboard the ship that would carry them off the island they had so recently won.

~

Sylvius eventually arrived at the small fishing village where the second slave ship had docked. The tiny area was filled with rows of posts and wire, signs that a large amount of people had moved through recently. Fortunately there were still a few guards left to question. Even with reading their minds and their quick fearful responses, it still took time for him to find the quartermaster who had received the first shipment of slaves. It was then by reading his memories that he finally discovered that the blond woman had been sold to a man named Elezar. He apparently had an estate only a few days to the south. The hunt was finally drawing to an end.

Chapter 15

General Gavrus and his chosen twenty had a safe crossing to Trost. As soon as they had collected their horses, they mounted and left, heading south for Nazbar. Trost was predominantly used for farmland and the further south one went the richer the soil was. They passed large estates run by the rich as well as smaller holdings belonging to retired soldiers and freemen. The first three days were uneventful. They hunted small game to supplement their rations and camped at night under the stars. Gavrus would normally have enjoyed the trip and the freedom of traveling quickly but his mood was soured at the thought of meeting the officials at Nazbar.

Dawn seemed late in coming on the morning of the fourth day. The sky was overcast and dark and before they had finished their rations, the rain had started. They mounted and rode off in a slow drizzle but before long they were riding in a solid rain, their hoods pulled low. Gavrus noticed a prosperous estate just east of them and thought of stopping to commandeer food and a dry place to wait out this rain, but decided against it. By the time they had bullied the owner they would have wasted half the day. They had ridden for less than an hour beyond the estate when they spotted a grove of trees in the distance.

Gavrus turned to his guards and said, "Let's take shelter in the trees up ahead and rest the horses. Maybe we'll find some cover from this damn rain." Another ten minutes brought them to the edge of the grove. Gavrus was behind two of his guards when he leaned over to scratch his calf and heard something whistle by his ear. He knew that sound well and instantly shouted "shields!" to his men. As he yelled he grabbed his own small leather cavalry shield and held it in front of his body. He felt an arrow smash into it a second later, the tip piercing through just inches above his forearm. "Charge them!" he yelled

The onslaught of arrows slowed quickly as Gavrus and his men charged into the woods. He had his sword drawn and his shield held high, confident that his elite guards could defeat any small force. The number of attackers appeared to be less than his own guard and they quickly cut most of them down, but the grove concealed more men than the initial archers and new enemies sprang forth in woodland clothes carrying swords and spears. One man charged him from the side and jabbed at him with a short spear. Gavrus deflected most of the strike but felt it pierce his leather armor and cut across his side. He brought his sword down quickly and the man collapsed. Gavrus searched for more threats but found none, the attack was over as quickly as it began. "Search the woods for anymore of these vermin," he told his men.

Gavrus dismounted and examined the wound in his side. It was little more than a scratch and he held a torn cloth on it to stop the bleeding, he wasn't worried about it slowing him down. "Are any of them alive?" he asked.

"This one's still breathing," Titus, the commander of his personal guard answered, and pointed to a man that had been stabbed in the gut.

"Good, I want answers," Gavrus said walking to the man. He was feeling dizzy and slightly nauseous as he leaned over him to question him. "Your miserable attempt at an attack has failed. Who sent you? Answer and I'll make your death quick; refuse and you'll die very slowly."

The man laughed at him weakly, "Aye, general, my death is already assured but then again so is yours. You may see a failed attack but I see success in our mission."

Titus grabbed the man and held his knife to his throat, pressing hard enough to draw blood. "Answer him or I'll carve you up in small pieces while you watch."

"You don't think this scratch will kill me, do you?" said Gavrus with contempt.

"Actually, general, it will. You see, we poisoned all of our weapons. You've only a few hours to live." Gavrus felt himself grow cold and the man laughed again.

"Who sent you? Who wanted me killed?" he demanded grabbing his tunic roughly. The man coughed up blood before responding.

"Oh, you've become far too popular with your legions and they don't like that," he grinned; his teeth were stained red with blood. "I'll tell you, one warrior to another." Gavrus resisted the urge to hit him in the face. "You need look no further than your friends in Nazbar." With that the man coughed up even more blood and slumped forward as he whispered, "Sorry, general, no time left for torture." He slid sideways and hit the ground, dead.

131

Gavrus looked around at Titus. "Find out how many of the men were hit."

Titus walked away and Gavrus sat on the ground next to the dead body of the assassin. He pondered the man's words. He had no friends in Nazbar so it was most likely a jealous general or a high official. His mind raced trying to pinpoint who it could be but then he realized it didn't really matter. Someone in the Empire wanted him dead and it appeared that they had succeeded. Poison, he thought, bloody fucking poison. A man didn't die from fucking poison; he died on the battlefield with a sword in his hand. He wondered how much time he had left. The man said hours, he had to think of what to tell his men, the ones who wouldn't be dying with him. Damn, he was feeling so sick and his head was spinning. He looked up to see Titus watching him. "How many?" he asked.

"Six dead and eight more have wounds such as your own. The poison is already starting to work, no doubt. What would you have me do, General?"

"I suggest you wait here and see how many of the men survive. According to that bastard," he nudged the dead body next to him, "I only have a few more hours to live. Some of the men might last if the wounds are small or they didn't get much of the poison in them. Bury us or burn us, I don't care, but if you value your life don't tell anyone what's happened here. Whoever wants me dead won't leave any witnesses."

"General, there's still a chance you might survive," Titus said quickly. "Let me send some of the men in search of a healer. We passed an estate less than an hour back, if they ride hard they can be there and back in under an hour."

"Do what you will, Titus, I put you in charge now. Just make sure the men make it back to the rest of the army." He laughed weakly to himself, "I guess fate has a way of catching up, eh Titus," he said, suddenly feeling weak. "The Empire wanted me dead years ago as a slave and now they'll get their wish." He felt his eyelids drooping and his hand went to the piece of tiger pelt at his waist.

Lily was in the manor house kitchen talking with Agnes as they ate their midday meal. She glanced out the window and saw two armored soldiers in legion red riding quickly toward the house. Her heart hammered against her ribs the nearer they got. Agnes noticed her distress and asked, "What's the matter with you girl, you look like you've seen a ghost?"

"Soldiers from the Empire," Lily stammered out.

"What's that to us? They come by occasionally, although we haven't had any here in six months or so. My but those two look to be in a frightful hurry. Why are you so frightened of them?"

Lily couldn't tell her that the Empire called her a witch and wanted to kill her, so she just said, "We were taken by soldiers on Camar, they frighten me." She wondered if they had somehow sensed her power and had come for her, but Samuel had said that it was a reader who could sense her and they didn't have anyone else with them. Just then Elezar came into the kitchen and grabbed Lily by the arm. "Come with me," he barked at her.

"But…" she started to tell him about the soldiers nearing the house, but he took it as a refusal to come with him.

"Apparently it's time for another lesson of who's in charge here," he said as he began dragging her down the hall to the stairs. Just then there was a loud pounding on the door. A slave ran forward to open it and the two soldiers stepped in.

"We need your healer at once," one of them shouted, looking at Elezar.

"My healer is busy at the moment," Elezar told them coldly. "You may come back in an hour and have her."

At this point Lily wasn't sure what she was more afraid of, being drug back to Elezar's bed or being taken by the soldiers. She knew she must look terrified to the two men as they were staring at her. Caught, she thought, after all this time and with Elezar holding her arm she couldn't even attempt to run, as futile as that would probably be.

"Is this her?"

"Perhaps," Elezar answered. Lily couldn't believe the arrogance of the man. How could he hope to go against the Empire? What was he trying to gain?

One of the soldiers stepped forward and grabbed Lily's other arm. "We're in a hurry, she's coming with us." He drew his short sword with the other hand and pointed it at Elezar. "One way or another, your choice."

Elezar slowly released Lily's arm. "I'll expect to be recompensed for this and I expect my healer back in one piece, and if not, I'll want proper reimbursement. Healers are hard to come by."

The soldier still held on to Lily as he said, "We need to leave now. Grab whatever you need quickly, healer, there's not much time."

Lily started walking down the hall to the healing room. "I'll need to know what's wrong with whoever I'm treating so I can bring the proper herbs."

The soldier looked cautiously around before answering in a whisper, "Poison," he said.

Lily stepped into the room and started putting herbs into her bag. Lobelia to make him vomit if there was still time or ground charcoal to neutralize the poison. She really needed to know what kind of poison she was dealing with but doubted that the soldier would know. She just grabbed whatever she thought might be useful while the soldier tried to hurry her up. Obviously whoever she was treating must be very ill.

Within minutes they were on the horses and heading down the path with Lily sitting behind one of the soldiers, hanging on tightly. She hadn't asked how far they were going so had no idea of how long this ride would last. It gave her time to think, now that her initial fears had subsided. Obviously these soldiers weren't here to kill her or she'd be dead already. They wanted her to heal someone, but the more she thought about it, why should she? These were the men who had captured her, tore her from her home and sold her into slavery putting her in the hands of a man like Elezar. They might not be the very same soldiers but they represented them to Lily, and now they needed her help. She must take this time while they were riding, to consider how best to use this situation. If she was going to be forced to heal someone who represented all she hated, then she needed to get something out of this. There was only one thing that she wanted, one thing that would make healing a Roh Vec soldier and an important one she was guessing, worthwhile; freedom. She needed to figure out a way to gain their freedom, hers and Gavin's and all the slaves on the estate.

Gavrus woke to see a young blonde woman bending over him. He was disoriented and couldn't remember where he was or why he was lying on the ground. A skirmish, he recalled, he had been in a skirmish and had been wounded. He tried to sit up but his head felt so thick that he couldn't get it off the ground. At least the rain seemed to

134

have stopped. "Who are you?" he asked, his words slurring as he spoke.

"There now," said the blonde woman gently, "Don't try to sit up, just let me touch you so that I can see what's wrong." She put her hands on his head and then turned to Titus and said, "Help me remove his tunic. I need to see the wound."

Titus started to pull his tunic over his head. Gavrus tried to help but he couldn't get his arms to work right. This woman must be a healer. He should tell her not to bother, he knew he was dying. She took her hands from his head and touched the wound. She looked straight at him as she said, "I can heal you, sir, but in exchange for your life I would ask something of you."

"What is it you want?" he asked weakly, not really caring.

"My freedom and freedom for the slaves on the estate where you found me," she said determinedly.

"You are in no position to negotiate," Titus answered. His hand dropped to his blade and he gave her a menacing stare. "How about we just promise not to kill you in exchange for the general's life?"

"Go ahead," the woman answered staying very still. "But if I die so does your general and you'd better decide very quickly because he hasn't got long to live. I can feel him fading."

Gavrus summoned his remaining strength and took a closer look at the woman. She had courage, he'd give her that. She reminded him a little of himself when he was faced with the tiger so long ago. He hadn't had anything to lose and apparently she felt she didn't either and was willing to bargain with her life for what she wanted, just as he had. Of course he doubted that she could heal him, he couldn't even feel his limbs properly anymore, but he'd be damned if he'd just give up and let whoever wanted him dead, win. What the hell, there couldn't be that many slaves on that estate.

"I agree," Gavrus said, "but only if you can really heal me."

The woman heaved a sigh of relief as Titus moved his knife from her throat. She sat up and placed her hands on his side which immediately stopped throbbing. "I can heal the sword wound, but the poison has moved throughout your body." She put her hands on his abdomen and then moved them up his chest. His body suddenly felt hot, like he had a fever and the woman's face had paled when several minutes later she finally removed her hands. She crawled a few feet from him and retched in the bushes.

135

He felt good, so much better than a few moments before. He slowly sat up, not wanting to risk falling over if he got dizzy again. The woman had stopped retching and sat up, pushing her hair out of her face. "I must tell you, general, that I probably won't be able to heal all of your men." Titus gave her a dark look and fingered his knife. "I'll try but as you can see, the healing tires me and I think the poison is making me sick. Bring me the sickest first and maybe the others will last long enough for me to rest between healings."

Gavrus nodded, not doubting her words. He didn't understand how she did it but he knew the fact that he lived was nothing short of a miracle. If she could save any of his soldiers, that too would be a miracle. He knew each of these men personally but as a general, Gavrus was used to giving orders that chose who would live and who would die. He quickly followed her advice and let her heal the worst men first, so that she might be able to save as many of his men as possible. In the back of his mind he was also trying to determine what to do about his assassination attempt, but he reminded himself that he had made an agreement with the healer, an agreement he meant to honor. "One thing at a time," he muttered to himself, "one thing at a time."

Lily had never felt so sick in her life. She had continued to throw up between each healing and knew she would never be able to save all the soldiers. If only it didn't take so long to regain her power between each injured man. She was worried that if some of them died these men might not honor their agreement. As she recovered between healings, General Gavrus paced back and forth harassing her with questions. How many guards were there and where were their quarters? Where did they patrol? Did they use dogs? Where were the slaves held and how many were there? No detail seemed to be too small or too insignificant. When he had finished questioning her he conferred with Titus and his men and they devised a plan.

It was twilight when Lily finished her healing. Two of the men had died before she could recover enough to save them. The soldiers seemed grim but it appeared they felt no resentment at the loss of their two comrades, if anything they all seemed to be looking at her in awe. They offered her food and drink and after she had finished Gavrus came over to speak to her.

"I haven't yet asked your name, healer."

136

"It's Lily, my name is Lily."

"Lily," he said, "A Camarian name." He got a thoughtful look on his face. "It seems I owe you my life. You have an incredible gift and if you ever find yourself in need of protection, I will gladly take you in as a healer in my army."

"I thank you for the offer, general, but I don't think working with the Empire would be good for my health."

"I don't offer you a place with the Empire, just with me and my men," he said, a dark look crossing his face.

"I'll bear it in mind but my husband and I have already made plans for the near future," she told him, all the while thinking that although the general seemed honorable, she still didn't trust him.

"I see," he said looking slightly disappointed. "Well then, we're ready to leave when you are."

Lily nodded to him and they mounted their horses to head back to the estate. The general filled Lily in on their plans while they rode. The general and one of his men would take her straight to the house, distracting Elezar in conversation, while his men would come in from the back of the estate, some to take out the patrolling guards and others to silence the dogs. Meanwhile Lily would slip away to her healing room, supposedly to put away her bag of medicines but actually she would leave out the back door and find Gavin to let him know what they were doing. They would meet up with the soldiers who were carrying weapons enough to arm a dozen slaves and from there, if all went well, it should be over quickly and quietly. A night raid, the general called it.

"It sounds like it should work, general, but you don't know Elezar. He's unpredictable and I would suggest you take more than one soldier into the house with us and be prepared to defend yourself. He may be quite reasonable or he may attack you. I know he'll be furious with me because we're getting back so late."

"I'll deal with him when the time comes; you just carry out your part of the plan."

They could see the lights of the manor house in the distance when they halted. Gavrus sent most of the men to circle around to the rear while he, Lily and two others would wait twenty minutes and then ride in. They were sheltered in a small stand of oak trees and wouldn't be seen by any patrolling guards if they came out so far.

When the time was up they slowly rode toward the house. They dismounted and walked up to the door with Lily behind the general. After a slave opened the door, they went in and waited for Elezar to appear.

"So, you've returned my property, I see," Elezar said as he stepped out from the library. He walked straight over to Lily and grabbed her by the arm.

"Yes and I'd like to talk to you about your property. Would you be interested in selling her?"

Lily stared in Gavrus in shock. Was this part of his plan, if so he hadn't discussed it with her, or was he turning on her? Elezar saw her alarm and laughed.

"I'm not sure that my little healer wants to go with you and I'll warn you that she will be very expensive. I like her, she's been very useful," he said leering at her. He put his hand on her neck and gently squeezed before he pushed her toward the stairs. She shuddered despite herself.

"Step into the library and we'll discuss possible terms," he said as he ushered Gavrus toward the door. "You, slave," he said looking at Lily, "go up to my room and wait for me. I'll be needing you tonight before I sell you to the general."

Lily kept her head down and started toward the stairs as the door closed. As soon as it was shut she looked up and headed down the hall instead. One of the soldiers stayed by the library door and the other accompanied her. She didn't speak until they were out the back door and half way across the grounds. "He's really a bastard, isn't he?" the soldier commented. Lily nodded and said "My quarters are this way. We need to find my husband and let him know what's happening."

While they hurried she listened for any signs of the dogs, but apparently the soldiers had already taken care of them because she heard no barking. They reached her door and she knocked quietly so as not to startle Gavin. He opened the door and when he saw it was her a look of relief passed over his face. It ended quickly, though, when he saw the soldier standing behind her. "Quick, let us in," Lily told him as she pushed past him and entered their room. Gavin put himself between Lily and the soldier and stared at him, then at her, trying to discover why she was with a Roh Vec soldier.

"Close the door, they're helping us." At these words Gavin looked at her as if she had grown two heads. "I know it doesn't seem possible but I healed their general and half of his men so he's agreed to help free us."

"Us, meaning…?" Gavin questioned her.

"All the slaves on the estate. Some of his soldiers are dealing with the guards right now and getting rid of the dogs. He has weapons for a few of you. We need to find the smith and let him know so that the slaves will be ready to leave once the guards are dead."

"Where's Elezar?" Gavin wanted to know.

"The general's with him keeping him busy while he waits on word from us that everything is secure," the soldier told him.

"He'd damn well better not kill him, I get that privilege," Gavin said as he opened the door and looked around to see if all was well. They stepped out and hurried to the smithy to spread the word. As they went they saw that several of the guards were already dead, lying where they fell on the ground. The general's soldiers hadn't wasted any time in following their orders.

In a short time, the guards were all dead and only Elezar still lived. The slaves were all standing on the grounds, their meager belongings on their backs along with what food could be stolen from the house. Agnes had gladly emptied the larder of everything edible and divided it out amongst them all. The general still had Elezar in his library, supposedly discussing the purchase of his healer. Gavin turned to Lily, "It's time to end this. I'm going to get rid of Elezar, stay here with the smith." He was glad that she didn't say anything, just nodded as if she understood. He was afraid she might tell him to be careful or fret over him and he wasn't in the mood for that. His mind churned with hatred for Elezar and he wanted to drink it in and use it against him.

He walked through the silent house past several closed doors until he saw a soldier standing guard outside one of the rooms. He looked at him, hoping the soldier wasn't going to challenge him but instead the man nodded at him, turned the knob and pushed the door open. Elezar was seated behind his desk with the general opposite him. "What do you want slave?" he said when he looked up and saw Gavin in the doorway. "Who allowed you to walk in here uninvited? I'll have you whipped for this or maybe castrated," he said slyly," and then your little wife will be happy to spend her nights with me."

Gavin stepped into the room. He looked at the general who said, "Is everything taken care of?" When Gavin nodded he asked, "Are you Lily's husband?"

"I am."

"Will you be needing this?" he asked holding out his sword to him.

Gavin smiled for the first time that night as he thanked him and then turned to Elezar, the sword in his hand. "I can wait while you arm yourself. I like a fair fight," he said as he rocked gently on the balls of his feet, passing the sword from hand to hand in preparation. It felt good to have a sword in his hand again, though this one was much shorter that what he was used to. Elezar grabbed a sword that hung in a scabbard on his chair. He came around the desk and faced Gavin.

"You think a slave can best me. I'll show you who's master here," he said as he lunged at him. Gavin sidestepped and laughed at him as he parried the blow.

"You'll have to do better than that," he said as he reached out and sliced down Elezar's arm cutting through his tunic and drawing blood. Elezar lashed out again with his sword but Gavin once more stopped the blow and this time sliced down his chest. As they exchanged blows over the next few minutes it was obvious to Gavin that Elezar had been taught how to use a sword but he was out of shape and Gavin had no doubt that he could kill him easily. He wanted to do this slowly, to cut him bit by bit until his body screamed in agony. He wanted to make him suffer like he'd made his slaves suffer over the years but there wasn't time. They needed to leave before they were discovered.

Gavin looked at Elezar and said "I'm tired of playing with you, the game is over," as he knocked Elezar's sword from his hand and drove his own through the man's heart. When he was sure that he was dead, he cleaned the sword on Elezar's pants and handed it back to the general. "Thank you," he said and walked outside to find his wife.

The slaves were still gathered in the yard when Gavin walked from the house. Lily saw him come toward her, a grim look on his face. "He's dead," he told the waiting slaves. Two of the men went into the house and brought the body outside. They dumped it on the

140

ground and the slaves all gathered around it; some walked close and kicked it, others spit at it. Lily had no desire to go near the body and stood back beside Gavin and General Gavrus. One of the soldiers walked up to the general with a bloody rag wrapped around his arm.

"Sorry sir, one of the guards was a little quicker than I thought he'd be," he said when the general asked him what had happened.

Lily went over to him and removed the dirty rag. Since the general already knew what she could do, she didn't even hesitate, she just healed the soldier.

Gavrus looked at Lily and shook his head. "My offer still stands. You would be invaluable to me as a healer and your husband is good with a sword. He'd be welcome in my army. Are you sure you want to strike out on your own?"

Gavin overheard what the general had offered. "Our course lies to the north for now with these others," he said looking at Smith and the group of slaves standing with him.

"If that is your wish," he said looking disappointed. "I have business to the northwest. If our paths cross again, I will welcome it." He gave a slight bow to Lily, called to his men and left.

Lily watched them ride away until the darkness swallowed them. She picked up her pack which she had filled with medicines and food and prepared to say goodbye to most of the slaves. Only a dozen were going with Gavin and Lily, the smith being one of them. The majority of the slaves were separated into small groups, each going their own way, most to join their families in various parts of the Empire. A few would head south to Nazbar to lose themselves in the crowds of a city, but most would disappear on small homesteads to try and regain the lives they lost when they were taken as slaves.

Lily walked over to where Agnes stood. "Where will you be going?" she asked her.

"I'm going to try and find my sister. She has a home in the foothills to the west of us; at least she did five years ago. I'll miss you Lily, you and your man would be welcome to come with us."

"Thank you, Agnes, but we're going north with Smith. Maybe we'll see each other again," she said and gave her a hug.

"I hope so, girl, take care of yourself," the older woman said, "and may the Maker go with you both." She turned then and walked off with two dozen other slaves all heading west.

Lily reached for Gavin's hand and looked up at him. "Ready?" she asked him. He leaned in and kissed her making her look at him in

surprise, eyebrows raised. He laughed and said, "I was born ready."
Lily laughed with him as they walked hand in hand toward freedom.

~

The hunter Sylvius arrived at the estate at midday. It had taken him some time, but he had finally found the manor that the witch had been taken to. Riding in, he thought it odd that he didn't see any workers in the fields. As he got closer to the main house he noticed buzzards circling the area and as he watched, several landed just west of the house. He rode closer to investigate and saw there was a body on the ground and as he looked he saw several more not far away. He dismounted and strode through the house seeking anyone who might be able to tell him what happened. When he realized he could sense no one, he walked around the grounds checking out the slave quarters only to find everything deserted. He found it hard to believe but it almost seemed that the slaves had rebelled and killed their owner.

Leaving the bodies to the birds, he mounted his horse again and rode farther out on the grounds searching for footprints or anything that could tell him where everyone went. He found horse tracks heading northwest and footprints heading in every direction imaginable. It appeared his search was not over. He chose a likely looking group of prints and followed it, heading east this time.

Chapter 16

The last two weeks of the journey flew by and before Arius knew it they were reaching the other end of the Kheight mountain range and entering the region of Trost. The land dropped and the temperature warmed. Wet snow still covered the ground but it was clear that the winters weren't as hard here as they were in further east. Trost, Arius decided, was far different from the eastern end of the Empire where he had lived his entire life. Great oak and pine trees sprung out of the ground almost everywhere. The winds were calmer and far less frequent. The others claimed that this land was gentler than the northeast, but Arius didn't entirely agree. He felt that almost every grove of trees was hiding unseen dangers.

It was a particularly foggy morning that had Arius on edge when they saw their destination. It was a small town located in a minor valley and circled completely by a wooden palisade. Arius hadn't expected another Roh Vec but its quaintness still caught him off guard. He had come to expect more grandeur wherever readers dwelled. The walls and buildings were all made of lumber cut from the surrounding area. Little traffic walked its streets for which he was thankful, and the town didn't smell nearly as bad as Roh Vec had. A second circular wooden palisade was built around a vast clearing in the center of town. Arius immediately knew it was the hunter's compound and went straight there. The nine legionnaires departed from his group when they reached the compound gate, but his two watchers rode with him. The inner compound was designed similar to the one at Roh Vec, but much smaller. There was a barracks for the guards, who all seemed to be watchers like the two men with him. A row of shabby slave huts, a storage building, and a two-story building for the readers. One thing that was quite different from Roh Vec was the teeming vegetation growing about the grounds. Oak trees ringed around a snowy field and there was even a small garden area near the main hall.

Arius rode his horse toward the building and was soon met by two readers and several servants. He dismounted and gave a low bow, they returned the gesture. Before they said a word to him, however, they addressed the two watchers. "Your service to this reader is finished, you may join the watchers here in protecting the compound." The watchers bowed and left, giving their horses to the servants. Then the readers reached out to Arius with their minds. It had been almost two months since he had communicated telepathically and he recoiled slightly at their initial touch.

"*Greetings brother Arius, I am brother Brucus and this is brother Hardalio. We were expecting you a week sooner, did you face troubles?*" Brucus was slightly shorter than Arius and his robe was tight around his thick muscular form. Hardalio was the exact opposite, he stood a full head taller than Brucus and his robes hung loosely from him.

"*Some,*" Arius replied, not wishing to inform them the delay was his fault because of the training each day. He was slightly surprised that they already knew of his coming, the couriers it seemed were very efficient with their work.

"*No doubt you must be tired from traveling and would like to rest,*" Brucus said.

"*On the contrary, brother, I have become quite accustomed to the life on the road.*"

"*It is good to hear that, brother, because as hunters we spend much of our time traveling. In fact almost all of our brethren are abroad as we speak. Sub-minister Falx and eleven others still remain on Camar, and we've received word that one of our brothers has recently landed back in Trost pursuing a witch. We are the only two remaining in the compound,*" Brucus said.

"*Are there no other hunters in Trost?*" Arius asked in surprise.

"*Just us fifteen, but with you we are sixteen. It used to be that the hunters were the most common group of readers within the order, but through the years we have eliminated nearly all of the heretics and witches and thus sadly reduced our own necessity. Inquisitors, dominators, and seekers are far more important nowadays.*" Arius was beginning to realize that brother Brucus enjoyed lecturing and would probably make a decent teacher at Roh Vec.

"*Still, we play a very important role here in Trost. We border the Northlands where the last peoples resisting the Empire dwell. It is also the last safe place for heretics and witches to hide from us.*"

Brucus paused and Hardalio, who had yet to say a word, suddenly asked. "*Is Tasitus still the head master at Roh Vec?*"

"He is." Arius replied and Hardalio thanked him and then fell silent again.

"Hardalio and I were just going to train in the field, would you care to join us?" Brucus asked. Arius nodded and they began to walk down to the large open circle of trees. While they walked Brucus continued talking of the hunters as if there had been no interruption at all.

"We hunters train quite differently from other readers in two ways. First we focus on mastering the arts of a common assassin, such as swordsmanship, archery, tracking, and stealth." Arius was going to tell him about his sparring sessions with the watchers but didn't wish to interrupt Brucus and kept the thoughts in his mind.

"These skills allow us to work independently without the aid of non-readers. Second, but far more important, is our ability to work together with our fellow hunters. We are the only group in the order of essence readers trained to kill heretics and witches, and this is done best when we can overwhelm a single target. All the other groups within the order can worry about politics and the welfare of the Empire."

At this point they had arrived in the center of the field and Brucus paused with his telepathic communication. Arius took the opportunity to ask a question of his own. *"Brother Brucus, in the compound at Roh Vec we learned very little about witches; do the hunters know more?"*

"I'm afraid not. A live witch hasn't been captured in over a century. We only understand that our essence powers do not work against them and that they can kill with a single touch."

"But how will I know when I see a witch?" Arius asked

"You will know," the quiet Hardalio said out loud. The answer seemed to satisfy the two hunters so Arius didn't press any further. Hardalio gave Brucus a nod and they each removed their hoods, revealing their bare tattooed heads. Arius was surprised to see that Brucus was only a few years older than himself, while Hardalio was probably in his late forties. Arius also removed his hood and squinted as the sun hit his eyes.

"Brother Arius when was the last time you did any domination training?" Brucus asked.

"Perhaps six months ago. We didn't have many available slaves to use so we didn't practice very often," Arius explained.

"Forgive me brother I did not phrase the question correctly. When was the last time you did any domination training with another reader?" Brucus was referring to the last time Arius and another reader had controlled one another, not just slaves. They never allowed students to practice with one another, but they did practice with the teachers so all students understood how to defend one another.

"It's been a few months," Arius replied.

"That will change. Learning to defend yourself from a heretic's mind is the most important part of being a hunter. Next is being able to attack his mind and take control of his body as you would a non-reader. We train in this task at least once per day. If you feel you are ready we can begin now."

Arius swallowed nervously but nodded that he was ready. He had only practiced dominating a few times in the twelve years at the compound and found each experience to be unpleasant. It took an enormous amount of will power and energy to try and dominate the mind of another reader. Arius had never successfully beaten his teachers and losing control of his body made him feel helpless and weak. Afterwards it took days to recover his mental energy.

"We must warn you Brother Arius, the first time we practice this with a new hunter we hold nothing back. We will attack you at the same time, try to hold out as long as possible. We only do this so that we can see how we should start teaching you."

"I am ready," Arius said grimly.

Brucus acted first, throwing the full force of his will against him. Arius felt a great pressure against his mind, as if he was deep under water. He pushed back mentally already feeling weary from the effort. To his dismay he realized that Hardalio hadn't even joined the battle of wills. When he struck, the pressure against Arius's mind doubled, and seemed to come from different directions. They clawed hungrily at his mind, seeking to take control of his body. Arius knew he could only withhold them for a few more seconds and quickly decided to improvise.

He charged at Hardalio who was closer and tackled him to the wet snow. The older man was caught by surprise and for a brief moment he stopped reaching for Arius's mind. Arius took the moment to counterattack and try to take control of Hardalio's mind. His attack was pathetically weak, however, because he was still trying to fend off Brucus's mental assault. Rather than block his mental press

146

Hardalio somehow deflected it off to the side. Arius wondered how he did it.

Hardalio physically threw Arius off of him and each came quickly to their feet. Arius felt pressure in his head mount as Hardalio once again resumed his attack. He tried to fend them off, tried to form a protective shield around his mind but they struck hard and in quick succession. The pain was incredible, he felt as if his head would explode but still he fought on, refusing to yield.

Hardalio came forward then and struck at him with his fists in the same manner that the watchers had taught him. Arius blocked the first two blows but his arms seemed slow, and his vision was slowly turning black. The third jab caught him in the chest knocking him off his feet. As he concentrated on controlling his fall, he felt them seize control.

The pressure on his mind stopped and he felt numb. He had no control of his own body, not even his eyes. If they chose to do so they could pick freely through his memories and even his thoughts. In vain he attempted to retake control but it was as if he was reaching for something miles away. No reader truly understood it, but once someone was dominated it was almost impossible to retake control. If they had been his enemies his best hope was that they would tire of controlling him, giving him a chance to retake control of himself, but if they were his enemies he knew he would already be dead.

They released him quickly and he slowly regained control over his body. He had a splitting headache and he felt incredibly exhausted. He found he was sweaty from the mental exertion. Hardalio and Brucus came over and helped him to his feet. Arius noted that they too had sweat on their brows.

"Forgive me brother Hardalio," Arius said breathlessly. He was so tired that he wasn't sure he had the strength to communicate telepathically. "I should not have tackled you as I did, I just felt…"

"There's nothing to forgive brother," Hardalio interrupted him. His voice was soft and reminded Arius of sub-minister Tasitus. "When we hunters train against one another we use all our skill sets, for so will the heretics. Your performance was actually the best I have ever seen for a first try. If sub-minister Falx were here I believe he would agree with me."

"Thank you brother," Arius said, bowing at the praise. In truth he thought he did very poorly, he couldn't have resisted them for much more than a minute.

147

"There is still room for improvement, however, when you are ready," Hardalio continued.

"I can barely think straight," Arius admitted.

"It is always that way after being dominated," Brucus chimed in, his voice rich and booming in the quiet clearing. "It is the best time to continue training. For example; let's say you just killed a heretic but there are other enemies still alive. If you don't kill someone quickly and take their essence you will be overwhelmed. We are only mortal men without our abilities. Come, we shall go and try right now while your strength is down." Arius nodded weakly and followed them across the field towards the slave pens. As they walked Brucus once again broke into a telepathic lecture.

"The recent invasion of Camar has been most fortunate for our compound here. We have plenty of available slaves and criminals that are brought here from the surrounding regions. I've been told that crime rapidly diminished in the area when people heard that readers were the executioners. It's a shame really, we could use the additional essences for training."

They approached the slave huts and Arius noticed several hanging cages near the wooden palisade. The nearest one contained a filthy boy not much older than ten. He was half asleep until he saw the hunters approach. He screamed and scurried to the opposite side of the cage his eyes wide in fear. "No please, I didn't steal anything I swear! I'll do anything you ask, I... No... I..." he stuttered.

"Wait here," Brucus said and walked to the edge of the gate. Slowly he pulled out a dagger and held it out to the child. The boy was shaking now and urinated in his tattered trousers.

"No please I don't want to die! Please! I didn't do anything wrong! Please!"

"Take control brother Arius," Brucus said telepathically. Arius tried to reach out but his headache only worsened and he shook his head in defeat.

"I don't think I can from this distance," he whispered to Hardalio next to him.

"The Northlanders excel with bows, Brother Arius. There may come a time when you have to reach even further away to save your own life," Hardalio told him seriously.

"I don't want to die!" the boy sputtered, tears streaming down his face.

148

Arius closed his eyes and reached out to the child again. The effort caused him immense pain and he was worried he would pass out. Finally he grasped the boys mind and his pleas stopped. Quickly, he had him grab the dagger from Brucus and slice his own throat. Arius wrenched the boy's essence towards himself the instant it left the boy's body. He sighed in relief when he absorbed it within his own essence. Instantly the headache left him and he felt moderately rejuvenated, not quite full strength but close enough to continue training. He opened his eyes and found that he had fallen to his hands and knees, though he had no memory of it. Brucus stood before him and pulled him to his feet.

"Brother Arius, you have an incredibly strong essence and will make an excellent hunter and I don't say that lightly. Come let's try sparring again."

Readers were supposed to be above such things as petty emotions but Arius couldn't help but feel elated. Perhaps he would be promoted into the core before the decade was out, he thought.

"This time just you and I will spar, but only at half strength," Brucus said. *"I will first teach you how to defend yourself and then how best to strike me. Now, I am going to reach out to your mind and I want you to block me."*

Arius felt Brucus push at his mind and exerted his own will to the same level of strength effectively blocking the weak mental push. It felt as if they were each channeling their power directly at one another.

"This is a simple push contest that any reader can do. In the end it will exhaust us both but it is also the fastest way to dominate someone. Whoever has the stronger essence will most certainly be the victor, so the best time to use this method of attack or defense is if you feel substantially stronger than your opponent. For instance, if you were to absorb the essences of several of these slaves you would be far too strong for me to contend with you in this manner." Brucus stopped his gentle push and Arius stopped as well.

"Now this time when I strike, I want you to deflect my push off to the side." Arius understood what Brucus wanted because Hardalio had done it in his attack in their first sparring contest. Yet, when Brucus began pushing at him he was unsure how to deflect it and ended up just blocking him as before. After several failed attempts Brucus stopped and Arius couldn't help but feel frustrated with himself.

149

"You must push in two places at once Brother Arius," Hardalio said. *"Do not be discouraged, this can take time to learn. Try to remember what it was like to hold off Brucus's mind while striking at mine, as you did before."* Arius took Hardalio's advice and when Brucus pushed at him, he blocked it with half of his mind while reaching out towards Brucus with the other half. Only instead of attacking his mind he tried to brush his stream of power aside. The effect was perfect, instantly he felt the push on his mind cease as Brucus was now reaching out into nothingness.

"Very good brother, you are a fast learner," Brucus said. *"Now I am going to attack your mind again and I want you to stop me, but this time I won't just come straight at you. I will try to slip past your defenses, not just power through."*

Arius tried to prepare himself but there was no way he could have been ready for the fierce onslaught. Whenever Brucus struck at his mind, it seemed to come from a different direction. Arius tried to completely shield his mind but Brucus would strike hard in one place forcing Arius to push back, only to have Brucus strike at another area of his mind. He was kept busy blocking or deflecting for the next hour. He lost control of his body twice to Brucus but with Hardalio's help he learned to detect the incoming strikes. As he learned, Brucus craftily began to add in feint strikes from one angle and then striking hard from another. Arius was never beaten again, however, even when Brucus mentally struck at his mind from two places, something that was quite difficult to do.

They eventually stopped and had him practice attacking Brucus. Arius found that he was far better at defending his own mind than trying to dominate another's. He couldn't strike very quickly and he found that he got tired much faster. Hardalio said it was perfectly normal and that when two trained hunters sparred against one another it was quite rare for one to actually dominate the other. That was why training in weaponry was so important.

The training was very tiring and by the end of the day they had killed eleven slaves. Both Brucus and Hardalio told him that he was the fastest learner they had ever seen in the hunters but Arius still felt discouraged that he had been effectively dominated three times. He went to sleep wondering why Tasitus and the other teachers at Roh Vec had taught him so little, especially how to properly defend his own mind.

Chapter 17

Over the next three weeks Arius trained harder than he had ever trained before. There was no reading of books or study like there had been in Roh Vec, everything was hands on. He began to learn the arts of an assassin, warrior, and hunter. He was already quite adept in close combat but he found he was lacking in several other skills. His archery was awful, he knew little of stealth, and he had no idea how to track even the simplest of creatures.

Often times he trained with the watchers for basic skills but every day he would practice domination sparring with Brucus and Hardalio. Arius quickly proved to be their equal in protecting his mind from their control but he still was never able to dominate either of them on his own. They often practiced several times a day, each time requiring the essences of several slaves to rejuvenate their powers, but slaves were easy to come by now that the island had been captured.

He found that he liked the small town much more than Roh Vec. Brucus said it was named Nightgrove because it was built along the night road where the trees were thickest. It was far warmer than the capital without the incessant wind but it still inherited its fair share of snow. There were far less people and the smell of dung was rarely strong. While he had enjoyed his freedom away from the other readers on the long journey, Arius found that it was comforting to once again have company with whom he had something in common. He could ask Brucus and Hardalio questions that he wouldn't have felt comfortable asking many of his teachers at Roh Vec.

One evening, after their latest sparring session, Arius and the others went up to the compound and warmed themselves in front of the fire. As they watched the crackling flames in silence Arius asked Brucus a question that had been troubling him since his first day at Nightgrove.

"Brother Brucus, do the heretics train as we do?"

"An excellent question brother," Brucus said, obviously quite content to begin another lecture. *"While we don't know much of the heretic's forms of training, we have found them to be competent*

warriors of both body and mind. However, history has proven time and again that we are the stronger fighters. Hardalio has defeated two heretics in his time, perhaps he can give you more incite." Arius turned to the ever quiet Hardalio expectantly but it was some time before he answered.

"The heretics I faced were much like you Brother Arius when you first sparred with us. Equally strong in essence, as we are, but they lacked the experience of domination sparring, so I was able to outwit them. That doesn't mean you should underestimate them Arius; if you find yourself outnumbered you should retreat and find help." As Arius contemplated Hardalio's words another thought came to him.

"Brother Hardalio, you say we should not underestimate our enemies even though we train everyday to kill them. What of the other readers, the seekers and dominators, surely they would be defeated by a heretic? Are our enemies so few that we only need fifteen hunters positioned against the very border of the Northlands where they dwell?" Hardalio threw another piece of wood on the flames before answering.

"We are unsure how many heretics or witches there are, only that their numbers are so few that they don't feel confident enough to attack us here at Nightgrove. We are actually quite exposed this far north, and the closest legions are two days away. As for the other groups within the order, many new readers are taught some of the domination skills that you have been taught in the last few weeks, but we as hunters perfect them."

"Why didn't they teach us how to properly defend ourselves at Roh Vec?" Arius asked. To his surprise Hardalio laughed, the sound was so foreign in the compound that even the twin watchers posted as guards turned in surprise.

"You will have to ask Tasitus that the next time you see him, though it has been my experience that the teachers at the school like to keep many secrets among themselves, perhaps for their own protection," Hardalio said.

Arius had other questions but felt that now was not the appropriate time to ask them, so he excused himself and went to his bunk. He awoke at first light to find that the compound was a bustle of activity. Watchers and slaves alike were saddling horses and weapons and rations were being packed up. He sought out Brucus and Hardalio to ask them what was happening and found them standing in the center of the activity, seemingly oblivious to what was happening around them. At seeing him, Brucus reached out to his mind.

"It is good you are awake brother. You have been training hard and now it is time to see that training pay off. We are going across the border."

"What? Already? Why? Arius asked in surprise.

"One of our brothers, a seeker, has detected a heretic amongst a group of Northlanders skirmishing with the eighty-second legion. We leave as soon as the watchers have prepared our mounts."

Arius found that he was suddenly anxious, perhaps even a little nervous. He had already faced dangers on the night road but the idea of facing a heretic, an equal, set him on edge. He hid his feelings from those around him, though and asked calmly. *"How did the seeker find the heretic?"*

"That is not our concern," Hardalio stated flatly before Brucus could answer. *"As hunters we have only one purpose, killing our prey. Come, the horses are ready."* They rode out of town with the watchers surrounding them, scattering the scared townsfolk in the streets. Arius read the emotions of the watchers around him and felt only determination and purpose, their strength fortified him. Any force that opposed these men would have a serious fight on their hands.

The eighty-second legion was positioned in a wooden fort about two days west of Nightgrove. The hunters rode hard and made it to the fort by nightfall, their horses sweaty from the exertion. There were about three dozen heavily armed watchers who rode with them. The Legion commanders met them outside the fort and Hardalio exchanged a few quiet words with them. After a few moments they were allowed entry but it was clear that the legionnaires were uncomfortable being around the black robed hunters and similarly clad watchers. They were given a wide berth by all who saw them and allowed to rest around a few large campfires to one side of the fort. At first light they left the fort in search of their prey.

The legionnaires knew roughly where the Northlanders had been striking from but once they learned that there was an enemy essence reader with them, any attempt to attack the small raiding party had ceased. They headed north for an hour to the border which was marked, not by man, but by the thickening of the forest. Arius had been uncomfortable around the great trees in Nightgrove but the wall of trees before him was especially daunting. They must have stood 200 feet tall and were so big around that Arius doubted his arms would reach from side to side. They stood so close together in places that they reminded him of the crowds of Roh Vec, only this time Arius couldn't read their thoughts. Who knew what manner of man or beast could lie hidden in the darkness behind those foreboding limbs. Even the horses seemed spooked by the forest and Hardalio had them dismount.

They gave their horses to a small group of legionnaires who had guided them to this point. "Their trail is just over there," the commander said, pointing to an area of well trodden snow. "They didn't even bother to conceal the damn thing. They know we won't go in after them. It's their ground and battles will be fought by their rules. Can't say I envy you, soldiers who go into those woods never come out the same."

Hardalio turned to the commander, gave him a cold stare and said in loud voice. "Keep your insecurities to yourself commander, we are hunters of the Empire and we fear nothing." With that he turned and strode towards the woods; Arius, Brucus and the watchers falling in behind him.

The watchers formed a protective ring around the three hunters while a few ran ahead to scout out the trail. Arius was amazed at how fearless these men truly were, perhaps even braver than Hardalio was. He knew that they been trained specifically to serve the essence readers and whoever had trained them had done an excellent job. Once again he remembered Tasitus's words, *"Remember to always obtain knowledge and wisdom from whoever you meet, be they reader, slave, or even your enemy."* He made a mental note to thoroughly read the memories of one of the watchers when they got back.

They traveled slowly through the forest so as not to get separated. The trail they followed wove in and out among the dense underbrush. The branches of the cedar trees grew thickly out from the base of the trees and seemed to push them back in places, forcing them to forge new ground. The place felt unnaturally quiet and their footsteps seemed loud on the soft snow. The black robes they wore boldly stood out against the white world around them and Arius wondered if they should have brought more camouflaged clothing. Few used any form of communication other than hand gestures and

Arius suddenly wished Brucus would break into one of his usual historical lectures just to ease the silent tension. All of a sudden Hardalio froze and held up a fist, all the watchers immediately drew weapons and got behind cover.

"Arius, Brucus, carefully reach out with your minds, I can feel the essence of someone up ahead," Hardalio said. Tentatively Arius felt out as far as he could, and sure enough he could feel the essence of someone a little over one hundred yards ahead, in fact he thought he could feel several. Both he and Brucus nodded to Hardalio and he spoke quietly with the nearest watcher. They quickly formed a wide line and slowly began advancing through the trees.

"Arius, if the heretic is here, leave him to me and Brucus, just focus on disrupting the Northlanders," Hardalio said. *"But don't forget to protect your own mind."* Arius nodded his understanding and kept reaching out with his mind. He detected at least a dozen other essences by now and began to detect more the closer they got. Suddenly he felt the familiar humming power of an essence reader and his blood ran cold. The heretic was instantly aware of the probing at his mind, and whatever chance they had at a surprise attack was gone.

"He knows were here," Arius said out loud. Hardalio barked an order and the watchers sprang forward, swords drawn, arrows notched in bow strings. Arius hadn't even bothered to bring his bow because he couldn't hit a damn thing, but he did carry four daggers and his short sword, which he now drew. He charged through the branches with the watchers and into a clearing. The Northlanders were waiting for them and the ambushers became the ambushed. There were even more of them than he had originally thought, probably more than their own force. The Northlanders were huge bearded men that towered over the short Imperials; even the shortest of them seemed slightly taller than Arius. They wore thick furs and carried heavy battle axes and long bows. They gave fearsome war cries and charged the watchers as they entered the clearing.

One particularly ugly Northlander with a red beard came straight for him, yelling at the top of his lungs. Arius watched as he lifted his giant axe and swung it down at his head. The swing was obvious, however, and seemed to be coming at Arius in slow motion. He easily sidestepped the man and plunged his short sword into his side near his kidney believing that would bring him down. The man merely grunted in pain, however, and grabbed at the surprised Arius

155

with one hand. The physical contact forced Arius to enter his enemies mind and he took control of his body before the warrior could use his axe in the other hand. He had the man drop his weapon and fall to his knees, where Arius slit his throat and let him fall.

He quickly found that he would be far more helpful in the battle if he used his power rather than his physical skills. He took control of one warrior and had him swing his axe into the back of his unsuspecting comrade. He controlled another to simply bash himself in the head. It didn't take long for Arius to feel fatigued but he realized that there were dozens of silver shimmering essences floating up from the fallen dead. He gathered several of these which boosted his power well past its normal strength, and continued to wreak havoc with the enemies' minds.

It was then that he noticed a bright blue light coming from his left. He looked to see Brucus lying on his back with an arrow through his chest, his essence shown bright blue as it left his body and traveled to the spirit realm. Arius had only seen the death of one other essence reader in his life time and had forgotten just how stunning the shimmering blue light looked. Only the essence readers could see its beauty, however, so the battle continued without interruption.

Arius spotted the archer who had slain Brucus, and reached out to take control of his body, but as he reached he instantly realized that the archer was the heretic. He looked no different from the other Northlanders except that he had a metal breast plate. The heretic struck at him with his mind and Arius felt the familiar painful pressure against his temples. He swiftly began deflecting the heretic's mental attack as he had been taught and even counter attacked with a few clever mind jabs of his own but it was quickly apparent that the heretic's power was far stronger than his own. Arius realized that he must have absorbed quite a few essences to achieve such power.

He struggled to keep the powerful reader from overcoming his defenses, hoping that Hardalio would soon come to his aid. The heretic also seemed to know that there was another hunter and tried to dispatch him quickly. He struck out even harder with his mind and notched an arrow in his long bow. Arius flung himself to the snow as the arrow whizzed by his chest, missing by mere inches. In that brief second he understood that he had to either kill the heretic quickly, or flee for his life. He had little chance of victory but knew he would never make it to the core, never stand before the Emperor if he ran in fear now. He gained his feet and charged for all his worth at his enemy. The heretic notched another arrow and Arius knew there was no way he would be lucky enough to dodge a second arrow.

By chance he noticed a Northlander not far from the heretic and desperately grabbed control of his body. The effort of controlling him and holding back the powerful mental assault on his mind was exhausting but desperation pushed him on. He made the Northlander turn and charge at the heretic, forcing him to fire his arrow at his comrade. The Northlander fell and Arius released his hold over him. The heretic dropped his bow drew a large two handed sword and roared at him in anger. Arius met the larger man with his short sword in hand. The pain in his head mounted the closer he got and he began to see stars in his vision, he had mere seconds before he would lose control. The long blade came flashing at him and he parried the strong strike with his right arm. The force of the blow nearly knocked him to the ground, but he quickly recovered and ducked a slash at his head. With his left hand he pulled forth one of his five concealed daggers. Just as he felt himself lose control of his mind he jabbed hard and hit something solid.

The pressure in his head subsided but he could barely keep his eyes open, he was so drained. He knew he couldn't pass out here in the middle of a battlefield, he had to stay awake. In vain he tried to grab a lost essence and replenish his power, but he didn't have the mental strength left and collapsed in blackness.

A second later he jolted awake with a power coursing through him like he had never known. His essence felt ten times stronger, as if he had just absorbed the life force of a dozen grown men, but it was more than just that. Not only had the strength of his power increased, but somehow his abilities were more honed as well. Before, the concept of dominating two non-readers at once would have required an enormous amount of skill and practice, but now he felt as if he could control four people as easily as he could one. He reached out and dominated the nearest Northlander near him, than another, and another. He laughed out loud to himself, three men dancing to my every whim and I feel as if I could do this forever, he thought to himself. He felt good, no, better than good, he felt great, as if he could take on the world itself.

He laughed again, and decided to see just how far he could push his new abilities. He dominated five, six, seven, eight, and at nine he finally felt he was at the extent of his power. He killed them and pulled their essences towards him, adding to his mental strength.

It was only then that he realized that some of the men he had killed had been watchers, and why not, he thought, they can be replaced easily enough. Their power is helping me kill even more Northlanders, so really they are serving their purpose even better than before. As if he was justifying his actions Arius quickly reached out and began having the Northlanders kill themselves in groups of five or six. He loved how easy it was for him, and he began to pull all the available essences towards him so that he could kill with even more ease.

Within seconds the battle was over and a dozen watchers stood about completely bewildered by what had just happened. Arius had a sudden urge to take their lives as well but resisted when he saw Hardalio striding towards him. Strangely he wanted to kill him as well and take his powerful essence but something in the back of his mind told him not to.

"Arius how did you do that? I was about to call a retreat but then you somehow just controlled everyone at once," Hardalio asked. Arius only half heard him and didn't bother with a response because he had no idea what happened either. Why did it matter anyway, it had happened, so now was a time to look forward to new possibilities, not dwell on the past.

"Arius, are you all right? Your mind feels strange to me," Hardalio continued. Arius was getting annoyed with the old man's constant questioning, why was he always asking questions?

"Be quiet old man, I need to think," he said rudely for all to hear. Hardalio's eyes widened at his response but Arius didn't take any notice. How should he use his new powers, he wondered? He should probably kill all the heretics first of course, that would ensure that he would become a member of the core within the essence readers, but then what? Surely he was the most powerful reader who ever lived, so it made sense that he should lead the order. Yes, that was it; he would become head minister Arius, leader of the order of essence readers.

"Brother," Hardalio said cautiously, his voice filled with suspicion. "I know the heretic is dead, I felt him die, but I never saw his essence like I did Brucus's. Did you?" Something about the way the man spoke brought Arius back from his thoughts. Come to think of it he didn't recall seeing any blue light and the body lay only a few feet from him with Arius's dagger in his heart. Slowly he came to the obvious conclusion; he must have absorbed the heretic's essence. The

158

idea sparked some memory within him and he suddenly recalled words Tasitus had hammered into him constantly when he was at the compound, "*Those that absorb the essence of a witch will meet death instantly; those who absorb the essence of a reader will face insanity, followed by a slow death.*" The words sparked hot anger in Arius. What did Tasitus know? Nothing! He was always keeping secrets; the readers in general were always keeping secrets. They hadn't even taught him how to properly defend his mind! They were afraid of him he concluded. They had even wanted to kill him when they first brought him there! He wasn't insane; they were just holding him back. Well now he knew his true powers, now he would show them that he should be feared!

Arius looked up to find Hardalio reaching for a new arrow and placing it on the string of his bow. As he began to raise the weapon Arius leapt forward tackling the older man to the ground. The few remaining watchers looked on in confusion; they were unsure which reader they were supposed to be helping.

As they wrestled in the wet snow Arius struck with his mind, his overwhelming power brought Hardalio under his submission within a few seconds. He stood, panting, and controlled Hardalio to rise as well. He drew forth his dagger and handed it silently to Hardalio. The older hunter slowly drew the blade across his own throat and collapsed to the ground. Arius reached out and took the glowing blue essence as it rose from his corpse. His power exploded again as he took in the essence of the hunter, the feeling was incredible and he wished it would never end.

"Reader, what happens now?" Arius looked to see one of the watchers before him. He was clearly shaken at seeing Hardalio kill himself and it was the first time Arius had seen one of the watchers truly afraid. He suddenly found that he was laughing and opened his arms to the sky, relishing the moment.

"What happens now?" he said finally. He reached out with his power and took control of the remaining few watchers and had them quickly kill themselves. "What happens now," he repeated to the corpses. "Is that I do whatever I damn well please. For not even the gods could stop me now."

He looked about the lifeless clearing for a moment or two, picked a direction, and began walking. The snow began to fall and his bloody boot prints were soon hidden as he made his way through the ever vigilant trees.

Chapter 18

Lily, Gavin and the slaves they journeyed with, walked north through the night. They had started off in high spirits, just the thought of their freedom keeping them moving quickly but Lily was so exhausted by the time they stopped that all she could think about was putting one foot in front of the other. They found a grove of trees to make camp in, planning on sleeping during the day and traveling at night. They weren't sure how much time they had before what they had done was discovered but they hoped at least three or four days might pass before anyone found the abandoned manor with its dead owner. Smith had come with them, most of the Camarians, and six other slaves.

The sun was just rising as they dropped their packs and sat to rest. Two of the men went in search of water and the others pulled out blankets and food from their packs to eat a cold meal and then to sleep. "Do you think we should set a watch on the camp today?" Smith asked Gavin. "I doubt anyone will find Elezar's body for at least a few days."

"I don't think we should take a chance of being discovered. I don't want to be hanged because we got careless. I'll take first watch," Gavin told him. The men nodded their agreement.

Lily noticed that they all seemed to consider Gavin the leader, even Smith. It may have been because he was in the army or possibly because the Camarians outnumbered the rest and wanted to follow one of their own, but it was more likely because he had been the one to kill Elezar.

They slept through the day, the watches changing every two hours, and saw no sign of pursuit. As they cooked a simple meal over the campfire, they discussed what to do now. Lily wanted to head straight north and was still hoping to convince Gavin to go to the Northlands with her, but Smith and some of the others wanted to free more slaves on some of the estates. Smith's brother was a slave on an estate a few hours further on from where they were camping and he wanted to liberate him. Lily watched Gavin as he thought this over.

"How are you thinking we could free more slaves?" Gavin asked Smith.

"We knew the layout of Elezar's estate and how many guards he had. Even without the soldiers I'm confidant that we would have succeeded eventually but it would be much harder going in blind on a strange estate."

"You haven't been here long enough to know that most of the estates are almost identical. The Emperor had these built years ago and gave them to his favored followers. Elezar inherited his from his father who got it from his father, as have most of the owners these days. The layout will be the same on this one."

"Would you have us kill all the guards and the owners? They may not all be as bad as Elezar and his men," Lily asked. "I don't like the thought of killing more people." Several of the other slaves nodded their heads in agreement.

"Not necessarily," Smith answered. "There are more of us than there are guards. We could sneak in after dark, tie up any guards we find, set the slaves free and be gone before anyone even knows we were there."

Another slave spoke up, "We've all got family that are slaves. I say yes and if we have to kill the bastards I say yes to that too."

"I don't want the Empire to have any more reasons to hunt us," said a second slave.

"We'll already be hunted for murdering Elezar. If we're going to be hung for murder we might as well make it worthwhile and take as many of them with us as we can," said a third, angrily.

Lily listened as the slaves around her continued to argue. Gavin spoke up and said, "If you're sure about the layout of the estates then I say we do it. No one should have to live like we have for the last few months."

There was more muttering until he held up his hands for quiet. "I'm not saying that we murder anymore. We go in and free the slaves but try our best to do it without killing. We've got surprise on our side and larger numbers. We'll only kill if there's no other way. Agreed?" After a few moments thought, they all nodded in agreement.

"Good then, it's nearly dark, let's pack up and head toward the estate. We should reach it in a few hours which will give us time to look about and hopefully contact your brother," Gavin said, looking at Smith. "Then tomorrow night if it looks good, we'll free the slaves. If we're going to do this, we don't want to waste any time."

161

They gathered their things and after several hours of travel they neared the estate. Gavin and Smith went on together to speak with his brother, leaving the others to set up camp. Lily was nervous while Gavin was gone and was relieved when they returned without trouble. They told the others, "There are only twelve guards, four on the night shift and eight on the day and no dogs. We had no problem sneaking past them tonight. We'll tie up the night guards and lock the rest in their quarters while we release the slaves. If we have no trouble, we'll kill no one. For now, let's sleep the rest of the night and most of the day. We'll need to head out immediately after the rescue and we'll have another seventy people with us. They'll branch off over the next day or two in other directions but we'll have to push them the first night."

Everyone nodded in agreement and settled down for the night with Gavin once again taking the first watch. Lily wondered where he got his energy. She was so tired from the walking and the stress of their escape that she felt exhausted. It must be something that soldiers trained for, she thought. She fell into a restless sleep until Gavin joined her two hours later. She was glad she had put their blankets on the edge of the camp for a bit of privacy because it soon became obvious that he didn't have sleep in mind when he lay down beside her. She tried to stop his hand from unbuttoning her dress, self conscious with everyone sleeping around them, but he only laughed quietly at her, grabbing her hand with one of his while the other continued undoing the buttons.

"Gavin, everyone will hear us," she whispered nervously.

"Only if you keep whispering so loudly," he murmured in her ear. "If we have to wait until we're alone for me to make love to you, we're going to be waiting a long time. Now, keep quiet and let me pleasure you. No one will even notice."

After one more futile attempt to keep her buttons untouched Lily soon realized she wasn't going to be able to stop him. "I didn't realize I married such a stubborn man," she told him, gasping a little as he began kissing his way down her throat. His mouth was inches away from claiming her breast when he stopped and looked up at her.

"Do you really want me to stop?" he asked seductively, feathering little kisses on to her breast and causing her to shiver in anticipation of his next move. Wrapping her legs tightly around him she answered him without words.

They slept until late afternoon and then everyone began preparing for the escape. All the men would go on the raid, armed with the knives and swords they had taken from Elezar's estate. The women stayed behind making sure that all their possessions were packed and ready to go.

As it neared midnight the men left camp and made their way toward the estate. It took very little time to take out the first three guards that were patrolling the grounds. Using the element of surprise, they simply came up behind them, hit them on the head and had them tied and gagged before they moved on to the next one. It had been done so silently that the sleeping guards in their quarters hadn't tried to get through their now locked door. There was only the guard at the house left to take care of, so Gavin headed that way with Smith, his brother and two other men. They wanted to take him quietly so they didn't wake the slave owner. As they neared the house Gavin signaled two of the men to go around the back while he and the other two went to the front. Gavin spotted the man just as Smith's brother came from behind him and ran toward him, sword in hand. The guard saw him and drew his own sword and they began to fight. The guard yelled for the other guards as he fought and almost immediately a light appeared in an upper window.

"Damn it," Gavin yelled at Smith. "Go help your brother take that guard down. You other men come with me; we've got to stop your master." He ran up on the porch as he yelled to them and kicked the door open. He saw a man and a boy of about sixteen starting down the stairs. They both had swords in their hands. A woman and a young girl stood at the top looking down at them.

"Stay where you are and you won't get hurt," Gavin yelled at them. "I don't want any more bloodshed but if you fight me I will kill you."

"What's going on here? Who are you to give me orders in my own home?" the man said furiously. "Where are my guards?"

Several of the slaves had now entered the house and stood behind Gavin, Smith among them. He looked at Gavin and nodded his head letting him know that the other guard was taken care of. Gavin noticed that his hands were bloody.

"I'm the man who is freeing your slaves. Your guards are all tied up or dead, you have no one to help you. You and your son put your swords down and we'll tie you up as well and leave."

One of the slaves behind Gavin spoke up. "Why can't we just kill them all?" he said angrily. "They've treated us like animals for years, I say we treat them the same and slaughter the family." Several of the other slaves with him muttered their agreement and started to step forward.

"No," Gavin shouted at them, raising his sword, "I won't have any more blood spilled if we don't have to. It will only bring the Empire down on us faster if we kill all the slave owners. We only kill when it's necessary." He looked at the slave owner and spoke, "Will you agree to put down your swords? I swear no one will hurt your family if you do."

The man lowered his sword but his son leapt past him on the stairs and charged at Gavin. Although the boy knew how to wield his sword he was no match for a man trained as a soldier and Gavin had soon disarmed him and held his sword point at his throat.

"That was either a very brave act or a very stupid one. There's a time to fight and a time to realize you're outnumbered. How will your death help your family? Now, sit in that chair," he then pointed to the slave owner. "You too, and your wife and daughter." When they had all sat in the straight back chairs that were scattered about the room, Gavin had them tied to the seats.

"We'll be leaving now along with your slaves. I think you'll discover that slavery may be coming to an end. It's time for you to learn to run your estates with paid help. I'm sure you'll be able to get out of those ropes in a day or two. If you come after us, prepare to fight, I won't be merciful again," he told him harshly.

When Gavin had walked outside he turned to Smith and angrily said, "What the hell happened out here? I told your brother we wanted no killing and he ran at that guard screaming for blood. Where is he anyway?"

"The guard raped and killed his wife two years ago and he wanted payback. I should have told you, I just didn't realize what he was going to do," he told him as they walked to the side of the house. "He may have paid for it with his life, though; the guard wounded him pretty badly." Gavin saw Smith's brother lying on the ground beside the dead guard. Several other slaves were with him and he could see that he was bleeding from a deep cut to his stomach.

"Has anyone signaled for the women to join us?" Gavin asked them. "Lily can help him when she gets here."

"Yes, they should be on their way," one of the slaves answered.

Gavin looked up just then and saw Lily hurrying up to him. "This is Smith's brother, can you help him?" he asked her. She nodded and knelt down beside him. The slaves backed up a few feet and watched her as she put her hand on the man's wound and healed him. They looked at her in amazement and started whispering among themselves. Smith helped his brother rise and held him while he got his bearings.

"All right let's get going," Gavin shouted to the assembled slaves. "We've got a long way to march tonight." He looked at Lily and asked, "Are you all right? We really need to leave."

She took his arm. "I'll be fine if you'll let me lean on you. Let's go."

Over the next two weeks they marched steadily north freeing slaves as they went. The slaves that they freed usually stayed with them for a day or two and then broke off in small groups to search for family or friends. They were given weapons from the estates when they left and many of them planned on freeing even more slaves. Gavin tried to impress on them the idea of freeing them without violence and tried to follow his own orders whenever they could. As the slaves left, Gavin often wondered what they had started. Perhaps slavery really could be abolished in Trost. He liked that he was a part of such an important cause.

Lily still wanted to go to the Northlands to search for her mother. Whenever Gavin asked if others wanted to join them, they got mixed reactions. Most warned them against going, saying that there were monsters and strange people living in the north. There were quite a number of stories that they were told to try and convince them not to go. Smith might have gone with them but he was committed to freeing as many slaves as he could and didn't want to leave. Gavin had to admit that he didn't want to go north either although not because he was afraid of what they might find in the Northlands.

He had tried to explain to Lily how he felt one night as they sat alone by the fire. "Don't you feel that what we're doing here is more important than searching for your mother right now? You

165

haven't seen her in twenty years, can a few more months matter that much?"

"I know it sounds selfish, but it's not just my mother that's sending me north. I want to find other healers like myself. I want to know that I'm not the only one that can do what I do."

"Don't you think that I want to find what's happened to my family? If I'm willing to wait to go to Camar then why can't you wait for the Northlands? It makes me furious to think of the Empire controlling our island but I know what we're doing here is just as important," he said, impatient with her attitude.

"I'm sorry. I know you're getting angry with me and I obviously don't seem to be explaining it well but I just know I have to go and I have to go now. I want you to come with me but if you feel you can't then I'll go alone. I won't blame you but I will miss you," she said looking sadly at him.

The look she gave him tore at his heart. He felt so conflicted on what to do and then he remembered the old woman he had met in Lily's woods. What had she said? *I lay this burden on you, help her find her purpose.* One look at Lily and he knew what he had to do. He'd agree to go with her into the Northlands and he'd stay with her as long as she needed him.

They sat in front of the fire with Smith the evening before they planned on leaving. "How can I convince you two to stay with us?" he asked them. "Gavin, you've been in charge of the raids we've done together and Lily, you're our healer. We need you with us. Why is it so important for you to go north? You could be killed by the wild men that live there. It's said even the trees in the forest are odd. My brother knows of a slave who escaped to the north. He returned to tell stories of a creature that is three times the size of a bear and can kill you with one swipe of his paw."

Now that Gavin had made his decision to go with Lily he decided to make the best of it and laughed at Smith as he said, "And we have a story on the island of a sea creature that comes out of the sea on the full moon, turns into a beautiful woman and entices a man to sleep with her, then takes him into the sea and drowns him. My oldest brother claimed to have seen one but he was well into his cups and trying to impress the girl he was courting at the time. I've never met one, however and I doubt that I'll meet with your creature either.

I'm not one to listen to tales, Smith, unless I've had one too many ales in me."

"What about the wild men, then? Even the soldiers from the Empire are afraid of them. I've heard tell that the Empire has lost whole legions of soldiers in the Northland, that's why they don't try and conquer it anymore."

"If these wild men like to kill the soldiers of the Empire, then I'd like to meet them. Maybe I'll bring a few back with us to help with the rebellion, what'd you say to that?"

Smith gave a low noise in his throat and then shook his head at them. "I can see there's no changing your minds. So you'll be leaving in the morning then?" he asked. "If you think you'll come back this way, I'll tell you that we plan on heading west from here. We'll continue freeing slaves whenever we can and we'll be looking for a safe place to hole up in for the rest of the winter. Head west to find us if you can."

Lily and Gavin agreed to search for them come spring and left Smith by the fire to go to their blankets. They wanted to get an early start in the morning. After all the stories he had heard, true or not, Gavin wasn't heading into the Northlands in the dark; they'd be traveling by day now.

Lily stood under the tall trees feeling like she had come home. The cedars and firs had begun appearing randomly as they crossed the rolling hills of Trost, gradually increasing in number until they were so numerous that she knew they must have entered the Northlands. A few maples and alders fought to survive in the dim light filtering through the much taller evergreens and ferns grew from every crack and crevice alongside mushrooms and other fungi that preferred the dark, moist earth. The trees themselves were immense, taller than any she had ever seen on Camar and their girth was such that even with her arms stretched wide she couldn't reach from side to side. Moss grew thickly on the ground and hung from the lower branches of many of them giving them the appearance of an old woman with long straggly hair. Although the sun was shining when they left the plains, the density of the forest only allowed patches of light here and there and the overall effect was rather dark and ominous. Many people would have found it forbidding, Lily knew, but when she laid her cheek against the bark of one of the massive trees, she could feel the heartbeat of the forest and knew it welcomed her. She was certain she would find her mother in this enchanted place.

Looking back at Gavin she saw him eyeing the huge trees with trepidation. "How are we ever going to find a trail in here, the undergrowth is so thick and the tree branches hang so low," he said.

Lily turned back to the forest and saw a line of small moss covered stones marching into the murky depths, clearly marking a faint trail that led through the trees. "What do you mean?" she asked him. "It's right here in front of me."

Gavin blinked several times and then shook his head. "That's odd," he said uncertainly, "I didn't see that a moment ago. I must be more tired than I thought." He tightened his pack and followed Lily up the path. She looked back at him as they walked and noticed that he cast worried looks over his shoulder often, as if he thought they were being watched. When they stopped for the night, though and nothing untoward had happened to them he seemed to relax slightly.

Over the next few days they both enjoyed the freedom of being together without being surrounded by other people. They spent each night now wrapped in each others arms, partly for warmth and partly for pleasure. Lily learned that Gavin was an expert with a snare and they enjoyed rabbit most days along with the food they had brought with them. He even managed to catch a fish in the still flowing stream they crossed one day.

They had been in the Northlands for a week and the weather thus far had been cold and clear, when it appeared that their luck had changed. Heavy, wet snowflakes had been falling since morning, leaving several new inches on the ground, and now the wind began to pick up as they walked up the trail. The trees had a heavy covering of snow on their branches and they had to be careful as they walked under them. Gavin took Lily's hand to help her over a log across the trail.

"Careful here, the log is slick. Although I guess if one of us slipped and broke a leg you could heal it."

"Yes I guess I could," Lily said and laughed as he lifted her up and kissed her before setting her down on the other side of the log. She wrapped her arms around him and kissed him back. "Hmm. Do you think it's too early to stop for the night?" she asked him as she ran her hands up his back.

Gavin leaned in and held her closer. "I suppose we could or I could just lay you down and have my way with you right here. Of course, we might be covered with snow before we're through but don't worry, I'll do my best to melt it off you," he said as he waggled his eyebrows suggestively at her.

Lily leaned in as if she was going to kiss him again and then scooped up some snow and threw it at him instead. Laughing, she tried to run but only made it a few feet before he caught her and dropped snow down her back. They grabbed at each other and played until they were both out of breath. Standing from where she had fallen in the snow, Lily slowly backed away as Gavin leaned down and packed a snowball together with a dangerous look in his eye. Before he could throw it, though, a large limb dumped snow all over him. "No fair," he said, shaking his head to get it off, "the trees are on your side." Lily helped brush the snow off him, laughing at their silliness as they picked up their packs and continued on their way.

The usual dim light of the forest began to brighten and Lily saw that they were making their way toward a clearing. The canopy of trees parted before them, the lower moss covered limbs producing a lush archway more beautiful than any mason could ever hope to duplicate. The sky above was overcast with a few wispy clouds but even that limited light still reflected brightly off the snow causing Lily to shield her eyes until they adjusted. A single magnificent oak tree stood in the open; it was nearly as tall as the fir and cedar trees that surrounded it. Its great gnarled limbs were reaching off in all different directions twisting menacingly this way and that, as if warding off the rest of the forest. Icicles were dripping from the oak's leafless fingers and a single ray of sunlight suddenly breached the clouds and hit the tree, cascading through its branches to the snow below and causing each icicle to twinkle. Lily caught her breath as she stared at the beautiful image, yet at the same time she found the tree, the clearing, and the ray of sun a little out of place, like a rose amongst weeds. The tree looked special, as if it held the answers to questions she hadn't ever asked, hadn't even thought of.

She was about to voice her strange thoughts to Gavin when she felt him stiffen in apprehension and push her behind him. She followed his gaze across the clearing where a man in a black robe stood, his hood shadowing his face. He didn't move or speak and his hands were concealed within his black robes. He had noticed them now, she could feel his eyes on her from beneath his hood and Lily felt the hair stand up on the back of her neck as a chill ran down her spine causing her to shiver. Gavin stiffly drew his sword and Lily felt

169

an irresistible urge to take his hand. He jumped slightly at her touch but then his fingers wrapped around hers. He gave her a brief worried glance and then they looked back at the black robed figure. He was coming towards them now with slow, menacing steps across the snow. Gavin let go of her and charged the man in black. Lily watched him run across the meadow that she had thought so beautiful just a few moments ago and cried out after him, suddenly overtaken by a foreboding that something terrible was about to happen.

Chapter 19

Gavrus and his few remaining guards rode north through the night with all haste. He knew he couldn't hide within the Empire, he would eventually be caught, and the idea of running just wasn't an option. Maybe he could go to Nazbar as if nothing had happened but he hated the big cities, hated the politics and cowards waiting in the dark with little knives. He could retreat to Camar and live there, he thought hopefully, but then dismissed it as the same as hiding, besides Camar was a relatively poor country and its people were already hostile to him. His hand went absentmindedly to the tiger pelt at his waist while he thought and rethought possible actions. He looked down at the faded fur and suddenly words came to his mind.

"You became a more perfect version of what you faced Tigris. You would be wise to remember this in the near future." He couldn't recall where he had heard the words but now he understood them. When he had faced the tiger, death had seemed imminent but he had fought because he had had no choice. He had used his victory to make a name for himself and became one of the best generals within the Empire; only now he was facing the Empire. He knew what he had to do, but the impossibility of the task was too daunting to even think about.

The sun was beginning to rise and the horses were sweating with exhaustion when he spotted a shallow wooded gorge to the east away from the road. A small stream ran through it and the young oak trees would conceal them from anybody traveling on the road making it an adequate camp area. Even better, there were no estates in sight. They dismounted and let the horses drink and Gavrus ordered the men to rest. He alone stayed awake, his mind too restless to let him sleep. He had nearly died hours before and now he was plotting how to stay alive and his plan would rely heavily on his men remaining loyal to him. He looked over at the sleeping Titus and wondered if he would follow him into certain death.

His legionnaires had fought countless battles risking life and limb for a few coins and the promise of a small plot of land; he felt certain he could offer them better if his plan succeeded. But would they follow him, he wondered? He would know soon enough, and he suddenly realized that this would be one of the last times he could rest peacefully. He laid his head back against his thick blanket and listened to the stream flow by. Sleep came but it was anything but peaceful, dark robed assassins and treasonous men haunted his dreams.

He awoke midday to find that many of his men were already awake and watchful. Some had broken out rations and were eating but no one had been foolish enough to light a fire. They acted as soldiers in an enemy land which by all accounts they were.

"Titus, everyone, gather round," he said. "I'm sure you have all been wondering what happens now. Someone in the Empire wants me dead, and we all know that the Empire always gets what it wants. Perhaps it's pointless of me but I plan to make it hard for them. I'm going to continue heading north and gather the legions loyal to me. My goal is not only survival but to win. In short, I plan to defeat the Empire and create a better one." The circle of soldiers was uncomfortably silent as they considered the implications of what he was saying.

"I chose each of you personally to be in my elite guard because of your skill, intelligence, and loyalty. But I know many of you have families and friends within the Empire so I offer you all a choice this one time. Stand with me or against me." Gavrus rested his hand on the hilt of his sword and stared around the circle of legionnaires. They exchanged nervous glances with one another and few met his eye. Titus stepped forward.

"Sir, we've been discussing it amongst ourselves while you slept. We figure that the Empire will probably kill us anyway for all that we have seen. We're with you, sir, what are your orders." The rest of the group nodded in agreement and Gavrus let out a sigh of relief.

"We head northwest to the coast. Before I left Camar I told Jacobo to send the fifty-fourth legion back across the channel to Trost, we need to find them as soon as possible."

"Are you sure he followed your orders, he may have been behind the plot," Titus said.

"No, I know Jacobo and I know how he thinks. The legion will be there," he said definitively. Titus nodded and then barked, "You heard the general, we have an army to build. Get ready to ride."

Five thousand men were easy to track and in three days they approached the fifty- fourth legion only a few miles from the sea. The wind was blowing strong and carrying a light snow with it; Gavrus could just make out the sound of the quiet flutes before the legion came into view. They were stretched out marching in a long column; thousands of footsteps were churning the shallow snow into the dirt leaving a muddy trail behind them. It didn't take the nearest scouts long to spot a group of riders.

"One more thing," he said to his elite guard. "If asked, don't mention the assassination attempt. It's best to keep it a secret for as long as possible." As the scout rode closer he noted their military attire and visibly relaxed on his horse.

"Greetings comrades, what is your business with the fifty- fourth?" he asked casually.

"Is that how you address your general soldier?" Titus barked. The young scout jumped in his saddle when he spotted Gavrus.

"General Tigris...that is General Gavrus, sir, I didn't mean to..."

"State your name and rank legionnaire," Gavrus interrupted.

"Ruso, sir, legionnaire second class."

"Very well legionnaire Ruso, I need to meet with the legion commanders immediately."

"Yes sir," he said and they began riding towards the legion. Gavrus quickly analyzed his chances of survival. He was greatly outnumbered but even if the generals knew of the assassination attempt they would never risk killing him in front of the troops. Gavrus slowed his horse, forcing his guards and the scout to slow with him.

"Is everything alright?" Titus whispered to him. Gavrus nodded reassuringly and then called the scout to him.

"Ruso, are there any readers with the fifty-fourth?" he asked

"No sir, we haven't seen any of the black robes since they left Camar."

"Good, let's approach the legion from the rear; I want to see some of the men first." The closer they got, the sound of the flutes playing a marching tune grew stronger. As they approached the rear of the column, legionnaires turned to see who the group of riders were. Gavrus took his time and let himself be seen by the men, he even stopped to acknowledge some of the lower officers that he knew by name. Wherever they went there were whispers of "the tiger," or "look it's General Tigris." Gavrus had a special fondness for the fifty-fourth legion and the men knew it. It was the same legion that he had joined after he had survived the ordeal with the tiger. When he eventually worked his way up to becoming a general, he hadn't forgotten the fifty-fourth and made them his crack troops. Not a man in the fifty-fourth was younger than twenty six and all were experienced in battle. In all three campaigns he had led, the fifty-fourth was tasked with the most important assignments.

As they made there way down the line of soldiers, somewhere back down the column someone began the chant. "Tigris, Tigris…" slowly it built in volume and traveled up the line till it swept past Gavrus and up to the head of the army. Gavrus laughed aloud and raised his sword to the praise. "I don't think we need to worry today," he said with a grin to Titus who remained as grim and serious as ever. The flutes had stopped playing and the column quickly came to a halt as soldiers turned to see him ride by.

A group of horsemen from the front of the army turned and rode back to meet him. Gavrus recognized Decmitius the legionary commander of the fifty-fourth. Decmitius led with an iron fist of discipline and Gavrus felt that the man never learned how to capture the spirit of the legionnaires. Still he was an excellent soldier who liked to lead from the front and Gavrus had been the one to recommend him for the position.

Decmitius shouted at the soldiers as he rode towards Gavrus, "Back in formation! Keep marching! You look like a bunch of star struck girls! You there, keep blowing that damned flute or I'll see you personally flogged!" He continued in such a manner till he reached Gavrus. "General, I would appreciate a little forewarning the next time you decide to rile up my men," he said, a little red in the face.

"Don't be so harsh Decmitius. They're returning home from a great victory, they deserve a little liveliness along the way," Gavrus said with a grin.

"We are only three leagues from the Northlands; I will let them enjoy themselves when we are safe within friendly walls," he countered still visibly cross. "Can I ask why you are here general? Jacobo informed me you left for Nazbar under urgent orders."

"I did, but those orders have changed," Gavrus lied smoothly. "I promise I will explain soon enough but first I need to speak to the men."

174

"All of them? You would have me break formation this close to the Northlands?"

"I'm sorry, Decmitius, but I must insist, you will understand soon enough."

"All right Gavrus," he answered grudgingly. He departed and began giving orders. Soon the flutes changed their tune and the legionnaires began forming into a large square formation. Gavrus quickly rode to a shallow hill alongside the legion so that all could see him. "Gather round, gather round," he shouted. When the legionnaires had stopped moving he took a deep breath, reassured himself and began.

"Fifty-fourth, welcome home!" They cheered in response. "You legionnaires have earned your rest one hundred times over, and I personally asked for a bonus in pay for each and every one of you!" Again they cheered and he held his arms out to quiet them. "I told them that since the time I was a raw recruit the same few legions have held the border and kept them safe. I told them that we had fought three campaigns in the last decade which have filled the fields with slaves and their coffers with coins. I told them that we fought and died for them, while they got rich and fat. I told them that my legionnaires deserved their fair share and that it was high time they got it! And I also told them that they better listen because my legionnaires were the bravest and best soldiers in the Empire!" The legionnaires roared in response and many of the men were nodding at what he was saying.

It took almost half a minute before they quieted. He put on his best somber face before continuing. "My legionnaires, I have failed you," he said in a quieter voice. Immediately the mood became serious and the legionnaires huddled closer so they could hear what he had to say. "I told them all those things and they turned me down. They said that my legionnaires were obviously greedy and needed to be reminded of whom they served. Soon they will cut your pay and incoming supply by half and you will return to your post along the deadly Northland border," Gavrus smoothly lied. The legionnaires were now shaking their heads and murmuring angrily to one another.

"Worse yet they said I was a traitor to the Empire for saying such things. They told me I was to be decommissioned and some inexperienced general from the west was to take my command. My legionnaires I have failed you," he repeated louder over the growing cries of protest. "I thought that we had bled enough. I thought that our

175

sacrifices would be noticed by those at Nazbar and at Roh Vec. I thought the twenty thousand slaves that we took at Camar would be enough to satisfy their gluttony. I thought that keeping the barbarous Northlanders out of their homes would be enough to secure some small respite!" The legionnaires were getting seriously angry now, and Gavrus knew he had them.

"My legionnaires I have failed you. I must return to Nazbar to be decommissioned…" but he could say no more for the legionnaires were shouting so loud that he could no longer hear himself. "Don't go Tigris," shouted some, "We won't be treated like this!" others yelled. Gavrus held up his hands and they slowly quieted.

"Legionnaires I sympathize with you but if they have not heard my pleas then how will they hear yours?" he asked knowing someone would speak the obvious

"We will make them hear us!" yelled one. "They can't decommission us all! For the fifty-fourth!"

"A single legion may not be enough," Gavrus shouted over the noise.

"Then we will get our comrades to join us!" someone shouted to the approval of all.

"And who will lead these men?" he asked waiting for the invitation.

"Tigris, Tigris, Tigris!" The chant built and Gavrus smiled as he realized he had just started his own rebellion. Now all he had to do was control the flames.

"And why not?" he yelled joining in the uproar. "I haven't seen any of the rich land holders on the front lines! Haven't we bled enough for them?"

"Tigris, Tigris, Tigris!" the chant continued and Gavrus strode down the hill towards a pale faced Decmitius.

"You're either with us or against us general," Gavrus said with Titus and his guard nearby.

Decmitius just shook his head sadly. "Perhaps the soldiers don't see it but you've just guaranteed all their deaths."

"Only if we lose," Gavrus said with a grin.

"But you're talking about rebellion! Look at your history, Gavrus, there hasn't been a successful rebellion in four hundred years!" Decmitius tried to reason with him.

"It's already done, are you with me or not?" Gavrus asked.

He sighed and eventually responded, "I would rather die with the fifty-fourth than against her, so yes, I'm with you."

Gavrus grinned and then motioned to Titus to bring him his horse. Together they began to ride across Trost and the army followed, marching to the eerie sound of the flutes.

Chapter 20

Arius stumbled through another thicket of trees; the low branches clawed at his face and dumped snow on his hood and shoulders. He brushed himself clean with shaking hands and cursed the forest for the tenth time that morning. It had been two days since he had killed Hardalio in the clearing and only now was he truly aware that he was hopelessly lost. His powers had waned back to his normal strength and so had the clarity of his mind. He knew he had killed his comrades in cold blood but the memory seemed hazy as if it had only been a dream. He imagined that he could be severely punished for what he did, but the order needed to know the power they could obtain absorbing just one reader's essence. It was power that could very well end the Northlanders resistance; hopefully the order would see that and forgive his rash actions. First, however, he had to make it out of this damn forest alive. He had only eaten some scavenged nuts over the past two days and knew that if he didn't find proper nourishment soon he would be in serious trouble. He knew it was only his imagination but there were times when he felt like the forest was a living thing trying to push him back each time he attempted to go forward. Even as he thought this, a root appeared in front of him and he tripped, falling heavily into the snow. As he lay there panting in exhaustion, one of the branches that had been jarred by his fall dumped a foot of snow on his head. He jumped up and broke off the branch just to spite the tree, but his actions only managed to dump even more snow down on him. He swore loudly and trudged on without the slightest idea where he was headed.

Another hour of cursing brought him out of the dense trees and into an open meadow. He had been walking with head down trying to keep the snow out of his face when he sensed a presence. Looking up, he saw a man and a woman about thirty feet from him on the other side of the clearing. The man was an ordinary non-reader. He didn't appear to be a Northlander if his size was any indication, as he looked to be about Arius's height or perhaps a bit taller. When he looked at the woman, though, he felt nothing, as if she had no essence at all. He considered the possibility that she was a hallucination but then dismissed it as quickly as the thought entered his head. She was alive and she had power, of that he was certain. He stared at her and realized that the aura he sensed from her was just different from any he had ever seen. If a reader's aura was a deep tone hers would be much lighter and definitely harder to sense. Suddenly he realized that she must be a witch and he remembered that Hardalio had told him that he would know immediately if he ever encountered one.

The man pushed the woman behind himself and drew his sword, watching Arius to see what he would do. Arius took the time to analyze the situation. If she was indeed a witch, then she was his enemy and she needed to die. He recalled brother Brucus's words, *"We only understand that our essence powers do not work against them and that they can kill with a single touch."* If he couldn't control her he would simply control the man and have him kill her.

He extended his power and forced the man to turn toward the woman. He was about to have him raise his sword against her when she suddenly took the man's hand. Arius jerked back as the connection he had forged with the man was broken, shattered as if it had never been. What happened, he wondered! He had never experienced this before even in the domination duels with other readers. The witch must have some way to block his power.

He started to walk slowly toward them, now, his dagger hidden up his sleeve. If he couldn't use his powers he would do this the traditional way. The man was running toward him, sword extended and Arius knew that his dagger was too short to block the attack. He would have to use his wits and guile. He kept the dagger hidden until the last moment. The man struck recklessly, assuming he was unarmed and would be an easy kill. As he swung his sword toward him, Arius sidestepped, and thrust his dagger into the man's belly, gutting him. He would die slowly, but he would stay down while Arius killed the witch.

He looked up to see that the woman was running toward them. "Gavin!" she screamed, a look of sheer terror in her eyes. Arius pulled another of his daggers out and cautiously approached her, wary of her touch. When she saw his dagger she stopped just short of him, her arms held out, for protection or to kill him, he didn't know. He lunged toward her hoping to catch her off guard, but somehow his feet slipped on the snow and he fell toward her, his arms flailing as he tried to keep his balance. He grabbed the witch's hand as he slid and a burning pain seared through his body, more intense than anything he

179

had ever experienced. Then he was falling, falling into darkness, surrounded by phantoms reaching out to touch him.

He saw himself as a child of six standing with his father in the family yurt. A small cook fire of cow dung made the air pungent and hazy but it kept the night's cold at bay. Arius's grandfather lay on his deathbed at one end of the cramped yurt. Arius's mother knelt beside him with a babe in her arms, tears streaking down her face at the pending death of her father. When the old man breathed his last, his essence left him and slowly drifted upward to the spirit realm.

It was the first death Arius had ever seen. He tugged at his father's arm, "Da, what's that light?" he asked pointing at the shimmering silver essence of his grandfather. His mother gave a slight gasp, and his father's shoulders suddenly slumped and he sighed deeply. Arius thought that he looked incredibly old and tired. He dropped to his knee and looked his son in the eye, "That is your grandfather Tevarian, he is going to the next life." Then he gave his son a hug and held him close, the two parents exchanged a worried look.

As quickly as the memory came, it ended. Arius convulsed in hot pain, his body twitching against his will. His eyes didn't seem to be working for he was surrounded by blackness. He knew that he needed to get up, that he had to kill the witch before she killed him. He tried to use his power to dull the pain but to his dismay found he couldn't. The familiar sanctuary that was in his mind was gone; he had no power, no way to reach beyond his mind. Perhaps he was already dead and he was traveling to the afterlife. Another memory surfaced from the depths of his mind.

He was seven now, sitting on a wooden stool and milking one of the family cattle. It was late in the evening and the sun was just setting over the windy Roh Plains when his mother called him. He pulled the milk bucket away so that the cow didn't tip it over and skipped over to his mother. Her belly was swollen with another child and Tevarian's baby sister Elizabell crawled on the grass nearby. Tevarian immediately saw that his mother had been crying and ran to her.

"Ma what's wrong?" he asked, wanting to comfort her.

"Oh Tevarian," she cried and scooped him into her arms. For a while she just held him close, slowly rocking him back and forth.

Eventually she asked, "Tevarian, do you remember where grandfather went?"

"Yes, he went to the sky. Da says that's where we all go for the next life."

"That's right Tevarian, you see, your father has gone to the sky now too," she said as fresh tears fell down her face.

"When's he coming back?" Tevarian asked quietly. His mother choked up and replied, "I don't think he is coming back." Slowly recognition came to his eyes as he grasped what his mother was telling him. She began sobbing and held him as only a mother could. His little sister, hearing her mother, began to cry as well. His mother picked her up and held her against her chest.

"Did he go like Grandfather did?" Tevarian asked.

"I don't know," his mother smoothly lied, "but I need you to listen to me very closely. These silver lights you see in people, the ones your father has been teaching you about. Well, you and I need to keep that a secret, so you can't tell anyone that you see them. Never point to them or even look at them, just pretend that they aren't even there. Can you do that for me Tevarian?" she asked very seriously. He nodded and they sat outside their yurt and watched the sun slowly set to the west.

A third memory quickly followed the second. He was twelve and was riding on the back of a young pony. He'd been helping the other herdsmen for some time and they had finally allowed him to have his own mount. He spent almost every waking moment riding the beast, knowing that when he was skilled enough they would let him ride with him the next time they guided the herd to a town. Then he would be a real man, and he would be allowed to take a woman. There was already gossip amongst the families that he was to be promised to Ruslan's second daughter Sasha. Every time he thought of her he felt butterflies in his stomach.

His mother's yelling tore him from his thoughts and he turned on his pony to see her running towards him. He rode to her and dismounted when they were close, he was concerned that she had run this far from the yurt.

"Mother what are you doing way out here?"

"Tevarian, listen to me!" she said breathlessly. The look of fear on her face surprised him more than her words. "There are men coming for you and they're going to take you away."

"What men? Where?" As he spoke he looked over her shoulder and saw the dust of several horses coming their way. His mother slapped him hard across the face. Tevarian was so stunned that he didn't even notice the sting of pain on his cheek. His mother had never hit him before, not even as a child.

"Just listen!" she hissed. "You cannot run from these men, they are too powerful, if you do they will kill you. They are going to take you to the capital to train you as an essence reader."

"A what?" he asked but she kept speaking.

"While you are at the capital they will make you do things to innocent people, bad things. Whatever happens, whatever they do to me or your sisters, you must do as they say. If you disobey them in any fashion they will kill you, do you understand?"

"Yes, but…"

"Your father and I thought we could keep you safe out here but we were wrong. We didn't want to believe the old woman when she told us, but a foreteller cannot lie. You are meant for so much more Tevarian, you will accomplish a great deed. Promise me that you will survive no matter what it takes," she said sternly.

"Mother I don't…"

"Promise me Tevarian."

"Fine, I promise to survive. Now..." he was cut off by the noise of the horses approaching and his mother held her hand against his face.

"I love you Tevarian," she whispered, a single tear rolling down her cheek. Then she turned and together they watched a group of riders in black approach. There were four of them and a fifth empty horse. The first dismounted and pulled back his hood. His forehead held a black tattoo of a triangle with a book at its center.

"You will come with us, or we will kill your family," he said. Then the memory faded and Arius was left to the darkness and pain.

He didn't understand why these memories were surfacing in his head, and he didn't want to relive them either. For over a decade he had suppressed them at the school with his power until they were all but forgotten. Now they brought forth a guilt that hurt as badly as the pain coursing through him. How had he become so lost he wondered? He'd forgotten his own name, forgotten where he came from, gods help him he'd killed his own mother, he'd killed his little sisters, and for what? Was becoming a more powerful reader and getting into the core so important to him that he destroyed his own past? He no longer knew who he was and he wept for the things that he had done.

Slowly, after what seemed like an age, he felt the burning pain subside and he opened his eyes to the white, snowy world. He lived, that much was true, but the reader Arius was dead and Tevarian hadn't been alive for twelve years.

Lily had seen Gavin fall and immediately ran toward him. She saw the robed man coming at her with a knife. As he lunged toward her she automatically flung her hands up to protect herself and felt him grab one. She felt a rush of heat similar to what she felt when she healed, and watched in surprise as he suddenly collapsed with a cry of pain. She had no idea what had just happened, all she could think about was getting to Gavin. He laid in the snow a few feet away, blood seeping into his tunic from a wound in his stomach. She knelt beside him and lifted the tunic, putting her hands on the deep cut and pushed out her power to heal him. The cut immediately started to close and Gavin moaned softly and opened his eyes. "Where is he?" he asked as he tried to sit up and began searching for his sword.

Lily pointed to the man lying in the snow. "He's over there, but I don't think you have to worry about him attacking again."

"He's a reader, of course we have to worry about him. I'm going to kill him before he does anything else," he said as he slowly stood up. "Are you all right?" he asked as he helped her stand, rubbing his hands down her arms and looking her over for wounds. "I was afraid he was going to kill you."

"I'm fine," she said and walked over to the man. He was curled up in a ball on his side and shaking violently. They both watched him for a moment and then Gavin raised his sword and prepared to strike him.

"No, Gavin, you can't, look at him. He can't hurt us, he's helpless." She reached out as if to touch him but stopped herself when she remembered the rush of power that had passed between them before he collapsed. "What makes you think he's a reader?"

"Look at his face. One of the slaves told me about the tattoos they put on themselves. He said if you ever saw a man with a tattoo like that," he pointed at the triangle on his face, "you'd know it was a reader. I've got to kill him, Lily, or he'll kill us," he said heatedly.

183

"Haven't you heard the stories about these monsters? They kill people so that they can steal their souls."

Lily didn't care about his tattoos. "No....I.....No, you can't," she stammered.

"Why not?" he said and looked at her incredulously.

I feel something," she stammered and clutched at Gavin's sword arm. "I touched him just before he fell and I think I did something to him. I felt power rush into me. I don't know what it was exactly but I know you can't kill him. I can't explain it but I feel a connection to him."

"You feel a connection to this monster?" he asked incredulously. "Listen to me; I don't think you understand what he's capable of. Just before he knifed me he took control of my body. For just a moment I had no say in what I did. I don't know what happened but he lost control and that's when he stuck me with his knife. He just tried to kill us both and you feel sorry for him?"

"I do feel sorry for him but I also feel a sorrow in him." She stared down at the stranger in the snow. "I know I'm not explaining this very well but there's something wrong inside him."

"He's a murdering bastard, that's what's wrong with him," Gavin said, exasperated. "If I don't kill him then what do you want to do with him? We can't let him run loose in the woods or he's liable to come at us again,"

"Couldn't we tie his hands and take him with us? Perhaps the people that live here will know what to do." She put her arms around Gavin and held him. "I'm sorry," she told him, "but I know in my heart that this is the right thing to do."

"I'll do what you ask for now because I trust you," he sighed, "but if he makes any threatening moves, I'll kill him. I won't ask your permission, I'll just do it. Agreed?"

Lily tightened her arms around him and shivered as she said, "Agreed."

Lily walked back across the meadow and picked up the packs that they had dropped. Gavin wasn't willing to leave the man alone, even for a moment. He kept his knife out, ready to use it if he felt he needed to. The man had opened his eyes and was watching her as she returned. She knelt beside him and reached toward him but Gavin grabbed her hand just as the man jerked away, fear in his eyes.

184

"Don't touch him, I want you to stay away from him," he said brusquely.

"I was just going to check him for fever," she said. "He looks ill." She turned then to the man. "What's your name?" she asked him. "Can you tell us?"

"Arius," he said, weakly. He got a confused look on his face and spoke again. "No, its Tevarian, my name is Tevarian."

"Well, Tevarian, we need to move on and you're going to get a chill if we don't get you up out of the snow." She looked at Gavin. "You may need to help him get up."

Gavin didn't look pleased but he extended his hand and helped Tevarian rise. He then told him to put his hands behind his back and tied them with a bit of rope from his pack. "Walk," he said harshly and they started across the meadow and into the trees, heading north.

Lily watched as Tevarian did whatever they told him to do. He walked where they told him, stopped when they told him. He seemed extremely weak, however, and walked as if in a daze. Apart from telling them his name he had yet to say another word. As they traveled she thought about what had happened in the meadow.

"Gavin, I've been thinking. I healed you in the meadow and I'm not tired, and I wasn't tired even after I did it. I felt as if I had twice the power I usually have and didn't use a tenth of it. In fact, I feel better now than I have in a long time. I don't understand it. Do you think he could have anything to do with it?" she said and nodded toward Tevarian who was walking in front of them.

"You said you touched him?"

Lily nodded. "He grabbed my hand. That's when I felt the power pass between us."

"Like when you heal?" Gavin asked, with a concerned look on his face.

"It was similar."

Lily looked up to see that Tevarian had stopped and was staring at her. "You heal people?" he asked her.

"I do," she answered.

"I thought…" he said as he shook his head. "More lies, Tasitus? " he muttered to himself. Lily and Gavin looked at each other in bewilderment and Tevarian said, "It doesn't matter," then turned and trudged forward. Gavin shrugged his shoulders, held out his hand to her and followed Tevarian through the snow.

~

The hunter Sylvius could not believe his misfortune. He had tracked down a group of slaves and discovered that the witch was heading north. He rode after her party as fast as his horse would allow but the turmoil slowed him down. Estates were either abandoned or burning and he struggled to find supplies and a fresh horse. When he finally was able to continue he tracked her party to the Northlands, where it was evident that she and one other man had traveled into the great forest alone.

For two days he attempted to pursue them but every time he followed their tracks he wound up lost and confused. He was forced to find his way back out of the dense forest and start tracking them from the beginning. It was as if the trees themselves were determined to throw him off his prey. They clawed at his face, tripped at his feet and dumped snow over the tracks. When his rations dwindled he finally accepted that she had escaped him and went to report his failure to sub-minister Falx. He expected that the other hunters had returned from Camar by now and began to make his way back to the hunter compound at Nightgrove.

As he rode out of the forest he looked back and spoke quietly to the trees. "You can have her for now, but she can't take you with her." Eventually she would have to leave, of that he was certain, and next time she wouldn't be so lucky.

Chapter 21

The next few days brought more snow and freezing temperatures to the three travelers as they walked further north. The forest was beautiful to look at, the branches of the trees sparkling white with the heavy snow sitting on them but Lily was cold all the time and the fire they lit each night did little to warm her. Camar had snow in the winter but nothing like the deep, wet snow here that soaked through her boots and made her feet ache with pain from the cold.

Lily checked herself and Gavin for frostbite each evening when they stopped but so far Tevarian wouldn't allow her to touch him. On the third evening since they had found him she told him that if he wouldn't let her look then he at least should check his own feet. "Move closer to the fire," she said, "so that you can see if your skin is discolored." Ignoring her suggestion to move nearer to the firelight she saw him take a red rock out of his pocket. She was surprised to see that it gave off a reddish glow and moved closer to see it better.

"What is that?" she asked. "How does it give off that light?"

Tevarian looked up in surprise. "You can see the light?"

Lily laughed and said, "Of course I can. Anyone could see that bright glow."

Tevarian held the rock toward Gavin. "Can you see it?"

"See what?" Gavin replied. "What are you two talking about?"

"The rock is glowing with a soft red light," Lily told him.

Gavin shook his head. "All I see is a dark gray rock."

Lily looked at him in surprise. "But what is it?" she asked Tevarian again.

"It's called a crystallus, a glow stone. I was told only readers could see it glow but once again my information is incorrect," Tevarian replied quietly. Although Lily tried to get him to tell her more about it he put the stone away and didn't speak again. She sensed that he was afraid of her but couldn't understand why.

At midday on the fourth day as they trudged through the ever deeper snow, Lily heard a dog bark off to their right. Gavin was breaking trail through the snow but stopped and reached for his sword at the sound. The snow was coming down heavily and as Lily looked around she suddenly saw six men materialize out of the white mist. They were huge men, each a half a head taller than Gavin, with barrel chests and full, bushy beards. They wore bear pelts as capes and each was armed with a battle axe and a bow. Before Gavin had a chance to draw his sword, there were six bows trained on them. One of the men said something in a language that Lily was not familiar with and pointed an arrow at Tevarian, a look of anger on his face.

"Lily, we need to show them that we don't want a fight. Raise your hands away from your body so they see that we hold no weapon," Gavin told her.

When he heard Gavin speak, the man who had spoken earlier said, "Empire?" He pointed an arrow at Gavin in a threatening gesture.

"No, no we aren't from the Empire. We're from Camar," Gavin told him, shaking his head and continuing to hold his arms away from his body in a gesture of peace.

The man now pointed at Tevarian and said "Essendai?" in an even angrier tone.

Gavin looked at Tevarian and told him to raise his tied hands. "They don't seem to like you, reader, you'd better show them your hands are tied or they might shoot you. Not that I would mind, of course, but I wouldn't want to be shot with you because they thought we were allies."

Once the men saw that he was tied they surrounded the three of them and urged them to walk with them further north. "Come," the man said.

Another twenty minutes brought them to a clearing in the woods. A wooden palisade surrounded a large building made of logs. As they walked through the open gate Lily saw many men working on various jobs in the yard. A man was chopping wood in one corner with two boys picking up the logs and stacking them. She could hear the ringing sound of a hammer on an anvil off to her left and chickens, goats and children ran everywhere creating a myriad of noises. Smoke was rising from the chimney of the building and Lily could smell meat cooking somewhere. As soon as their small party entered the enclosure all activity stopped and everyone, including the children, turned to stare at them. The man that had spoken with them said something to one of the children, sending him scurrying into the building. When he came back out he was followed by a man that, by the look of him, must be in charge here. He was well over six and a half feet tall and had the same full beard as the other men but instead of a bear cape, he wore a wolf cape with the head and feet still attached. He looked a few years older than Gavin and stood like a man that was well used to fighting. Lily would have thought him handsome if the look he gave them wasn't so filled with menace.

This man walked over to Lily and Gavin and said, "What do you want here?" in a brusque voice. Lily was relieved that he was speaking in the common tongue.

Lily spoke up. "We're travelers from the island of Camar. We were captured as slaves by the Empire but escaped and are traveling north in search of my mother."

"Why are you with the black essendai?" the man asked angrily.

Lily and Gavin looked at each other, perplexed. "What is essendai?"

"The black essendai," the man said again pointing at Tevarian. "Only the essendai or the essarai can control the black ones. Which one of you has the power?"

"We don't know what these words essendai and essarai mean," Lily told him.

"The essendai have the power of the mind and essarai have the power of the hands."

Power of the hands, Lily thought. She looked at Gavin. "Do you think he means healers?" Gavin shrugged as he continued to watch the man warily.

"I'm a healer," she told the man. "A healer can heal your body with her hands. Is that what you mean?"

"Show me," he said and took out a large knife. Lily stepped back nervously, not sure what he intended, but watched as he pushed up the sleeve of his tunic and slashed his forearm. His blood dripped on to the white snow as he held it out to her, obviously wanting her to prove that she could heal him.

She stepped closer to him and put her hands on his bloody arm. The man watched as the bleeding stopped and the gash closed and then he broke out in a broad grin. "Essarai," he said looking at her. With both hands he touched his fingertips to his forehead then put his hands palm out as he bowed slightly in an obvious gesture of respect. "Welcome," he said to her. "Who is this man you travel with, is he essendai?"

189

"No, he's not essendai, this is my husband," she told him. The man's eyebrows rose as he said, "You've married a man without power? But what of your children? They will be weak."

Lily didn't know how to respond to his statement. Gavin looked slightly affronted, but before either could reply the man spoke again.

"Forgive me, it's not for me to question an essarai. Come inside and warm yourselves and share a meal with us." He looked at one of his men and pointed to Tevarian as he said, "Put that one in the byre. See that he's secured."

Lily started to object to this treatment but Gavin nudged her and shook his head. She knew he didn't want her to question them when they had been accepted by these people thus far and she also knew he would have been happy to have them kill Tevarian. She decided she'd leave it for now, at least until she could get answers to the many questions she now had.

Several hours later Lily pushed back from the table, comfortably full and finally warm from the roaring fire that was blazing in the huge fireplace at one end of the hall. Lily guessed that the hall was filled with close to sixty men, women and children, all eating off several huge tables that ran down the center of the room. Rolf, their host, had seated her at his right hand, in honor of her status as an essarai, and had been regaling her with stories throughout the long meal.

"Have you heard about the monsters we have that live in the high forests?" he asked her in a grim voice. "Twice the size of bears with teeth as big as my hand and always hungry for the blood of humans, they prey upon travelers. They come upon them at night when they are sleeping and creep among them searching for their favorite prey." His voice became quieter, forcing Lily to lean closer to him to hear his next words. The noise in the room had quieted while everyone listened to the story. "Do you know what he does when he finds them?" Rolf leaned even closer to Lily, looking intently in her eyes. She shook her head, mesmerized by his story.

"He eats them piece by piece and then pours himself a mug of ale," he said loudly, laughing at Lily and taking a deep drink from his own ale. The other men in the room roared with laughter and everyone held their mugs high and took a drink. Lily saw that Gavin was laughing along with the rest of them.

"We were told that the monsters were three times the size of a bear," Gavin said to Rolf, "and liked to eat the Empires soldiers."

"That sounds like your father, Rolf," one of his men yelled.

"Sounds more like your mother," Rolf yelled back.

"Are there really monsters in the forest?" Lily asked him nervously.

One of the men pointed at Rolf. "Well, of course, just look at Rolf."

The laughter and the stories continued, but Lily noticed that the women had begun taking the children off, presumably to sleep somewhere. As things quieted down Rolf turned to her to tell her their plans for next day.

"Tomorrow we will leave at dawn for Jorval where I will take you to see Eurik. He is our wise man and an essendai. He'll be able to answer all your questions."

The thought of another long journey did not appeal to Lily and she yawned as she thanked Rolf for his kindness. He laughed at her and said, "Don't worry little essarai, we will ride horses on this journey. You'll get to see our beautiful country in all its white splendor. I'll take very good care of you or Eurik will have my head. We don't have many essarai and we treasure those that we have."

"Why are there so few of us left?"

"Again, that is not for me to answer." Lily yawned once more as he spoke, hoping it didn't offend him. "If you are tired I offer you my bedchamber to sleep in tonight. If you would like I offer myself to keep you warm or you may choose any of the men here. They would all be honored to share your bed."

Lily could feel her cheeks turn bright red as she realized the meaning of his words. Gavin, who was seated beside her, tensed, but said nothing. One more question for their wise man, she thought. She reminded herself that this culture was different from her own and she didn't want to offend this man who had treated them so well so she chose her words carefully.

"I thank you for your offer, Rolf, but I'm very tired from the long journey we have been on. If it's all right I would like to sleep with my husband tonight."

"Of course, I'll have you shown to my chambers." She felt Gavin let out his breath in relief at her side.

Lily had one more thing on her mind that she needed to discuss with Rolf before she left the hall. "May I ask a favor of you?" When he nodded at her she continued, "The man that came with us, Tevarian, has he had food tonight? Is he safe where he is?"

"The black essendai? You want us to feed him?"

"Yes, I do. It's important that he be kept alive. I need to ask your wise man about him. I'll need him to ride north with us."

Rolf looked at her like she was insane but he turned to a servant behind him and spoke in their language. The man nodded and left and Rolf turned to her and said, "It will be done."

Lily thanked him again and she and Gavin were led from the room by a servant to a large chamber with an enormous bed in the center of it. After she left, Lily leaned her head against Gavin's chest and sighed. "I hope I didn't say anything wrong in there. I was nervous that I might be breaking one of their customs every time I spoke. They seem similar to us in some ways but quite different in others."

"I don't think it's possible for you to say anything wrong to them. Didn't you notice that they treat you with great reverence? I'll have to call you Queen Lily from now on," he teased.

Lily pushed away from him and said tartly, "Perhaps I should choose one of them to warm my bed after all. I'm sure there's still time," and started toward the door. She didn't get far before Gavin had picked her up and dropped her in the middle of the huge bed with a laugh.

"Oh no, my lady, you're all mine, this night and every night. I only hope I don't lose you in this bed."

Lily removed her gown and crawled under the thick furs that covered the bed. "Just look for me in the warmest corner. This is a cold country."

The snow had stopped sometime during the night, Lily noticed, as she left the hall the next morning. She was wrapped in warm furs given to her by Rolf and was wearing a thick pair of wool socks inside her boots. She was determined to stay warm as they rode north. Ten of Rolf's men were already mounted and ready to go as she and Gavin came out. Lily looked up at the horses, her eyes going higher and higher until they finally reached their heads. He must be eighteen hands high, she thought. Was everything in this country enormous? How was she going to mount a horse this big and once she got on, how would she stay on?

Her eyes must have been huge because Rolf laughed at her as he came toward her. "Don't worry, little essarai, they're really quite gentle," he said. "May I help you mount?"

"Please," she replied and he picked her up as if she were a child and put her on the horse. She looked at Gavin, who had already mounted his own horse, and smiled weakly. Glancing beyond him, she saw that one of the Northlanders was bringing Tevarian out of the byre. His hands were tied in front of him but he appeared unharmed.

"You still want to bring this man with us?" Rolf asked her.

"Yes, I do."

"He'll have to ride or he'll slow us down. I'll take his horse's lead rope myself. I'll have one of my men keep an arrow on him at all times. If he causes trouble he dies."

They rode all day stopping only once at midday to eat and give the horses a rest. Their pace was steady but not too strenuous for the animals. Rolf rode beside Lily, pointing out places he wanted her to notice and showing her how far his holdings extended. He had over two hundred people spread throughout his lands, most of them living on small farms away from the main homestead. He was very amusing and she enjoyed the ride much more than she thought she would.

"Do you like the forest?" he asked her as they rode through the tall evergreen trees.

"It reminds me of my home, only the forest I grew up in was not this old. The trees feel as though they're welcoming me to the Northlands," she told him.

"Of course they do, you're essarai," he answered. When she asked him to explain what he meant by that he once again refused, telling her to wait for Eurik.

When they had stopped for the night and had eaten their evening meal, they sat around a campfire and talked. Rolf asked Lily and Gavin to share what had happened to them before they came to the Northlands. They told him about the war in Camar and then about being sold into slavery and their escape with the help of General Gavrus.

"The Empire is built on slavery," one of the men said as he spat on the ground.

"I'm surprised that this general would help you escape. If more slaves would fight back, it might change the way things are," another man agreed.

The talking quieted for a moment and Lily heard a wolf howl in the distance.

"That reminds me," she said to Rolf. "I've wondered why you wear a wolf cape while all your men wear bear."

"That's easy," he said. "It's because of my name." Lily looked at him questioningly.

"The name Rolf means wolf in our language. My mother named me this because she knew I would be as cunning as a wolf."

"More like your father used to howl at the full moon every month," one of his men joked and began howling with his friends. Rolf cuffed him and everyone laughed. Lily loved the easy camaraderie that these men had with their leader. They were big men and used to battle, she was sure, but they also knew how to joke and enjoy life. Even if she never found her mother, she was glad she'd made this journey and had a chance to see the Northlands and meet its people.

When they were ready to sleep, Rolf once again offered to share his furs with Lily. Lily once again refused as politely as she could. She turned to look for Gavin and found him standing right behind her with a frown on his face. He stared at Rolf for a moment then took her arm as they walked to where he had placed their sleeping furs. He sat down on the furs and took off his boots.

"As we were riding today the men explained to me that they were taking bets on how long it took Rolf to get you to share his bed. They told me that the culture is very different here. Men and women who are not married to each other share beds and husbands and wives take other lovers as well. Apparently essarai and essendai are very much sought as lovers and essarai are almost expected to take essendai as their lovers. They couldn't explain why to me though. I'm not considered much of a husband for you," Gavin said in a too calm voice.

Lily knelt down beside him and whispered, "Their culture is not my culture so unless you want me to go to another man's furs, I suggest you move over. I'm freezing." Gavin reached out for her, pulling her on to their makeshift bed and did his best to keep her warm.

The next five days passed much the same as the first. Lily loved being surrounded by the massive trees and could almost pretend she was back on Camar. They came to a large lake the evening of the fifth day and Rolf told them that they would reach Jorval by tomorrow evening. When they arose in the morning Lily could just barely see the far end of the water. It was long and narrow and such a deep blue color that she could see the clouds reflected in it. She felt as if she were looking into a mirror and as she stared she couldn't tell if she was looking into the lake or at the sky. There were mists rising above the water on the opposite side and the snow rimmed the lake like a string of pearls she had once seen in the marketplace. She was sorry when they reached the end of it at midday, but looking ahead she could see farmsteads in the distance which meant they were nearer to the town of Jorval. As they passed the first of them a Northlander stepped out of the door and watched them. When he saw Rolf he gave a nod of acknowledgement but it was the way he looked at Tevarian that scared her. 'If looks could kill' was an old saying that she had heard her father use many times, and it seemed to apply quite well here. She began to understand why Rolf was hesitant to bring Tevarian along.

They reached the edge of Jorval in the late afternoon. Rolf had kept up a steady conversation with her throughout the day, telling her about the town they were approaching and the man named Eurik who was in charge of the essendai here. He told her that he was a fair man and he was sure he would treat her and Gavin well. As they reached the center of town she saw that it held a large marketplace. The sellers were loudly hawking their wares and from the sound of it some serious trading was going on. It made her miss her market days in Redin when she saw a bunch of herbs being traded for a live chicken and a length of wool for a wooden bucket. When they first entered the square the noise of the animals and the stall holders was almost deafening but as they continued to ride, the sounds got quieter and Lily saw that the people had stopped their haggling to stare at their group or, more specifically, to stare at Tevarian.

A man strode toward Rolf, stopping them, and said something to him heatedly in the Northlander language. Rolf pointed at Lily and answered back in the same language. She recognized the word essarai which caused the man to bow his head slightly in her direction and motion their group forward. He marched in front of them, his back radiating his anger even as he led them from the market square, then stood and watched as they continued on. Lily saw that Rolf and his men were no longer talking and joking as they had been earlier. They moved in closer around the three of them as if to protect them.

There were six streets that branched off from the center; they took the furthest north. Although they had not had bad weather since they left Rolf's landholding, the streets were covered with hard packed snow, making the horse's hooves crunch as they walked. It was still so deep that it hid the refuse that always built up where many people lived and gave the town the appearance of being very clean. The air was smoky from all the hearth fires but at least it masked the usual pungent odor of the waste that came from too many bodies living in close quarters. If not for the unfriendly reception they were receiving Lily would have liked the town very much.

As they rode they passed many houses built side by side. Some were made of logs but most were wood and thatch. There were often people watching them from the houses, all of them looked angry when they saw who rode with Rolf. A few of them began to follow them and in a short time they had a small crowd behind them. As before in the square, Lily watched them as they stared at Tevarian. As she looked around her she saw that they were approaching a large building and hoped it was their destination. It was two stories high, twice the size of Rolf's dwelling and made of logs so great that their diameter was almost as tall as she was.

Standing outside the building was a man much smaller than the typical Northlander although he wore furs as was characteristic of everyone she'd met thus far. He looked to be in his late forties with gray hair and a neatly trimmed beard. He had a certain air of authority about him and behind him stood five men and three women. As they drew near, the man spoke sharply to Rolf, and then said something to the men and women standing behind him in the language of the Northlanders. Instantly two of the men came forward and forced Tevarian from his horse. They each grabbed an arm and almost dragged him into the building, although he put up no resistance. Before Lily could react, two more men had approached Gavin. He moved his horse closer to Lily and started to draw his sword but then left it in the scabbard and slowly dismounted with a strange look on his face. Without a word to her, or even a backward glance, he walked off between the two men, his stride stiff and precise.

Two of the women now came forward and told her to get off her horse and come with them. They looked at her sternly as if they didn't approve of her. She looked to Rolf for help but the friendly camaraderie they'd had earlier was gone and he wouldn't meet her eyes. She dismounted and followed the women into the building. She saw a large hall as they entered, filled with tables but empty of people at the moment. Windows were set in recesses down both sides of the room and the sunlight gave the room a friendly atmosphere, at least it would have if Lily hadn't been so terrified. There was an enormous fireplace against one wall with a fire blazing in it. The women led her down a short hallway and into a small, windowless room. As soon as she stepped in, they backed out and she heard the door being bolted from the outside.

The room had a small table in it with two chairs. There was a fire burning in a fireplace set in one wall with a large bear skin rug lying in front of it. A beeswax candle burning in a saucer on the table illuminated the room. The aroma given off by the wax made Lily miss her home on Camar and made her wonder what she had gotten them into by insisting on coming to these Northlands. Perhaps they should have listened to Smith and the stories he had told about the wild men of the Northlands instead of heeding the words Joan had spoken. If anything happened to Gavin she would never forgive herself. She moved closer to the fire for warmth, her arms wrapped around herself, wondering if it was the cold or her nerves that was causing her to shiver.

More than an hour passed with Lily pacing the floor of the small room and worrying about Gavin. Why didn't they come and tell her what they wanted? From all Rolf had told her as they rode, she didn't think they would kill her or Gavin but what about Tevarian? She barely knew the man but she felt to blame for the condition he was in, although she still didn't know what had really happened to him back in the woods. She felt responsible for him; he had no choice when they had taken him with them. She hoped she hadn't prevented Gavin from killing him just to bring him here to his death. As her thoughts focused on him, though, she knew with a strange certainty that he was still alive. It was almost as if she felt his heart beating in time with her own. As she concentrated on the odd sensation, it helped to calm her and she stopped her pacing and sat at the table to wait.

Time passed and the room began to get chilly as the flames burned low. Lily stood and put a log on the fire from a small pile beside the hearth. Rubbing her arms for warmth she began to slowly pace again as she wondered how long they were going to make her wait here in solitude. Suddenly she heard the bolt being lifted, the door opened and Gavin walked in. Without a word he sat in one of the chairs, his eyes staring straight ahead. A Northlander stood in the doorway but before Lily could open her mouth with questions, he stepped back, closed the door and once again she heard the bolt put in place. Gavin shook his head and then leapt to his feet. He grabbed Lily and looked her over, as if making sure she was all in one piece.

"What happened to you, are you all right?" Lily asked him frantically.

Gavin sat back down rather shakily. "It was the strangest thing," he said. "I was sitting on my horse ready to defend us with my sword, when I suddenly found myself walking with these men. I knew I should be back protecting you but I couldn't seem to stop myself. They were controlling my body, just like Tevarian tried to do in the forest. They must be readers. We went into a room just like this one, and they sat me in a chair and stared at me. For the last hour and a half they just sat and stared. Sometimes the men would change but they never said a word. I think I was awake, but it seemed like I was dreaming."

"What did you dream about," Lily asked as she sat across from him and took his hands in her own.

"I think I saw the battle at Redin and then we were on the estate with Elezar. After we killed him we were freeing the slaves and heading north. I saw our fight with Tevarian in the meadow several times. It kept replaying in my head over and over. I saw you touch him and he fell again and again." Gavin slumped forward, releasing Lily's hands and holding the sides of his head. "Damn, my head hurts."

"Here, let me help," Lily told him as she reached for him, intending to heal him.

Gavin jerked back out of her reach. "No, I don't think you should use your powers here. We don't know what these people want. We can't let on what you can do."

"Gavin," Lily said softly, "It's too late to worry about that. Rolf knows all about me, I'm sure he's already told them everything. You might as well be comfortable while we wait to see what they're going to do with us."

Gavin moved closer and let her heal him. Exhausted from all that had happened that day, they lay down together on the rug in front of the fire. Within minutes they had both dozed off.

Chapter 22

Tevarian was taken by the heretics into a small dim room. He cared little about what was happening around him, but it had been impossible not to see the stares the people gave him. He hadn't needed his power to feel the anger they held against him, he could almost taste their venomous need for revenge. Since the witch had destroyed his power some part of him had been clinging to the notion that he might survive, but upon entering this town he knew it was only a matter of time before they killed him, this room was as good a place as any.

The man motioned him to sit on a short stool and they both sat in silence. Then, surprisingly, he reached forward and unbound his hands. Tevarian could think of five different ways he could strike the heretic but without his power it was pointless. Even if he struck him down, the others would kill him, but truth be told he wasn't sure he really wanted to live anyway.

"What is your name?" the man asked. Tevarian just stared at him; there really was no point in responding, the heretic could just read his mind anyway.

"Very well," he said sternly. "My name is Eurik and I'm going to be reading your memories and as you well know it's going to take some time. Resist and this can be a painful ordeal, comply and it will go by faster and much more comfortably."

With that, the man Eurik reached out and set his hands on either side of Tevarian's head. The familiar touch of another essence readers mind was very different without his powers. Instead of the instant awareness that somebody was touching his mind, he could barely even detect Eurik's presence, let alone identify who was reaching out to him. No wonder non-readers were rarely aware of his touch at Roh Vec. If they didn't know what to look for it would almost feel like someone was watching them from a distance instead of touching their mind.

Surprisingly, Eurik didn't dominate his mind like he expected, rather he gently reached in and began to draw forth Tevarian's memories. He began with Tevarian's earliest memories of

200

his mother and then continued onward. Tevarian watched his early life replay in his mind, nothing seemed too insignificant to Eurik. They watched him create a mud slide into a bog on a wet spring day with the other herd boys. The children took turns running at top speed and then threw themselves head first down the slide. They watched as he stood up for his younger sisters when they were bullied by other children and helped them pick flowers for his mother.

To Tevarian's amazement Eurik made no attempt at hiding his own emotions. He seemed sad when a tragedy befell the small group of herding families and happy when something good happened. He even smiled when Tevarian took a bet from one of the older boys and jumped on the back of the herd bull butt naked in the middle of the night. The beast bucked him off and preceded on such a rampage that it knocked down two of the yurts while he ran for his life. He received the paddle from his uncle shortly afterwards in front of the whole community, still stark naked. Tevarian felt strange watching his old life again, he had forgotten the joy and innocence of his youth but he knew the memories they were going to view soon enough and felt only regret.

Eventually they came to the memory of Tevarian when he was twelve and the readers came for him. He recalled it well because it hadn't been far from his mind since the witch touched him. His mother was telling him how he had to obey the black riders approaching him and saying something about him being meant for more. The readers arrived for him and quickly took him to the Roh Vec compound, in exchange for his family's life. Suddenly Eurik stopped and looked at Tevarian in surprise.

"This memory has been altered," he said.

"What?" Tevarian asked, sure that he had heard him wrong.

"It's the most skilled work I've ever seen but someone has altered your memory," Eurik concluded

"How is that even possible, I am, I mean, I was essence-touched at the time. No one can alter the memory of a reader without them noticing." For the first time in over a week Tevarian suddenly found that he cared about something, even if he were going to die soon he wanted to at least properly know his past.

"I'll try to find your true memories if I can," Eurik said and placed his hands on his head again. For some time Tevarian felt nothing but then slowly a memory came forth hidden from his mind for twelve years. Once again his mother caught him on his pony and warned him of the coming riders. The black readers rode up and Tevarian saw five riders, only he had always remembered their being just four and an empty horse. The first man dismounted and removed his hood revealing his reader tattoo.

"Kill the woman, I'll take care of the heretic," he said, eying Tevarian. His mother screamed and before Tevarian could do anything he felt the attack of another mind against his own. This had never happened to him before but he understood the push that came against him and instinctively pushed back. A great rage welled up inside him at these men who were going to kill his mother. He resisted the trained readers attack and charged at the essence reader with a roar. The man drew a dagger and prepared to stab him, but in that moment against all odds Tevarian somehow overcame the readers mind. He tackled the reader as hard as a twelve year boy could and in the process the dagger was turned inward and pierced the man's chest. The other readers froze in amazement; the nearest overcame his shock and hit Tevarian over the head, knocking him out cold.

His next memory was lying in a dungeon just before he was brought before the council of readers who would decide his fate.

"That is all that was altered I think," Eurik said. "They must have changed your memories later." Tevarian nodded, he was sure he knew right when it happened. Shortly after Vetrix and the council of readers decided that he would live, or rather after the strange black robed man decided that he was to be trained, the guards brought him before a single reader. They forced him to drink a strange liquid and everything became hazy and surreal.

Eurik must have been reading his thoughts for he said, "If they drugged you that would make it easy to alter the memories of an untrained mind."

"Why would they alter my memories?" Tevarian asked aloud.

"It seems to me," Eurik said stroking his beard, "that they couldn't very well train you if you knew you had the power to attack your teachers. I'm amazed they didn't just kill you." Tevarian was unsure what to think of the knowledge he had obtained. On the one hand he was amazed that he had killed a reader at age twelve with no training but on the other hand his survival meant that he became the abomination that had killed his own family and countless other lives. In the end he realized it didn't matter; he couldn't cheat fate twice, he would soon be executed.

Eurik continued to read his memories but Tevarian paid little notice, they were looking at his life in the school and those were not memories he wished to see. To his surprise Eurik seemed to skim through these memories, even though he could be learning how essence readers were trained. He seemed to focus on how many slaves they killed in the compound and how often it happened. The more memories he viewed the angrier the older man seemed to get. At one point he stopped and took his hands off Tevarian's head.

"Do you even know how many men and women you've killed?" he asked.

"No, why?" He wasn't really sure why Eurik was so upset, they were only slaves and death at the compound was just the way it was.

Eurik began to pace angrily across the room muttering under his breath. Often times he stopped to look at Tevarian and then would continue pacing, muttering about morals and how he had a difficult choice. Eventually he calmed down and they resumed looking through his past.

Finally they came to the memory Tevarian was dreading most of all, the day of his graduation. He was forced to once again watch as he killed his sisters and his mother. The boy that he once was came forth and he felt tears coming to his eyes. Eurik stopped and Tevarian calmed himself, for some reason he didn't want the older man to see him cry. If he were to die, he would do so understanding he had created his own fate.

"Don't blame yourself too much, they turn boys into monsters. You aren't the same person that you once were." Eurik's words struck a nerve within him. Of course it was his fault he thought angrily. He could have chosen death; he should have chosen death the moment he was brought to Roh Vec. What did this man know? Just because he read a few memories didn't make him an expert on his life! Tevarian resisted the urge to strike the older man in hot anger. Instead he turned the heat into a cold hatred, a hatred of himself and what he had become.

"Let's finish this," he said coldly. Eurik looked weary and disappointed but placed his hands on his head and continued the reading. He watched Tevarian travel across the Empire and train with the hunters. Eventually they came to the battle in the forest. When Eurik watched Tevarian kill the heretic and absorb his essence his hands fell to his sides. He walked to the corner of the room and wept silently.

Finally Eurik collected himself and resumed the reading. He watched as Tevarian killed everyone in the clearing, and he seemed particularly interested when the witch came and took his power away from him. After that there was only the journey to their present location. When he finished, both men sat in silence for some time.

"It's morning," Eurik said. There were no windows in the room and while Tevarian felt exhausted he wondered how Eurik knew that it was already morning.

"You have lived two lives," Eurik said standing up and stretching. "The life of Tevarian and the life of a reader. One of those lives has a future, the other has much to answer for, yet you are still one man." Eurik stroked his beard and paced for a few minutes before walking out of the room and bolting the door behind him. Tevarian was left alone to ponder Eurik's strange words.

Lily woke to the sound of someone clearing their throat loudly. She still lay next to Gavin on the bear rug next to the now cold fireplace. They both sat up as the older man from yesterday entered the room. At closer inspection Lily noticed rings under the man's eyes and suspected that he had been awake all night.

"Good morning. My name is Eurik," he said with a tired smile. "I came to apologize for the poor reception you received yesterday."

"Poor reception?" Gavin said incredulously. "That's what you call how we were treated?"

"I understand you're upset and believe me we try to be gracious hosts, but it's not everyday that a black essendai and an unknown essarai come to this city." Upon seeing their confused looks he quickly added, "The black robed man Tevarian, whom you saw fit to bring with you, just so happens to be our greatest enemy. When we saw you with him we just assumed the worst. Please let me make it up to you," he said genuinely. "How about breakfast? Gavin we have bacon that I'm sure you would enjoy, and Lily I'm sure we'll have something you desire."

"How do you know our names?" Lily asked.

"And how do you know that I like bacon?" Gavin added.

Eurik chuckled and shook his head, "Forgive me, the night's activities have left me tired and I forgot you don't know what an essendai can do. An essendai is the same as a reader in the Empire. We have the power to read people's minds just as you Lily have the power to heal people. I've read Gavin's memories and I know quite a bit about you both since you've been together but Lily, I can't read your memories, so your life before Gavin is a blank to me."

"Why is that?" Lily asked him.

"The essendai can't read the memories of the essarai. I believe I can answer that best by quoting from our sacred histories. That should explain your question but I think your black essendai friend Tevarian would also benefit from hearing this," he said as he motioned them out the door and down the hall to another door that was bolted from the outside as Lily's had been.

"Do you not have your sacred histories written in a book?" Lily asked him. She was remembering the words of Joan and wondered if that could be the black book she was referring to.

"No, we have no books in the Northlands. All that we need to know, we essendai remember."

"No books at all?" Lily asked in surprise.

"We haven't found a need for them here," Eurik replied as he unbolted the door they stood in front of. They walked in to find Tevarian sitting in a chair. His eyes were closed but as soon as they shut the door behind them, he opened them, staring blankly at them all.

"Tevarian, I know you must be as tired as I am," Eurik said to him, "but I'd like you to listen as I quote from our sacred histories. I think they might surprise you." Eurik cleared his throat and closed his eyes as if remembering something that had happened long ago. When he spoke the tiredness seemed to leave his body to be replaced with calm conviction.

"In the beginning the Maker formed our world and created man and woman to care for it. They cultivated the land and ruled the beasts and the Maker came down and walked among us and saw that it was good. But in time man became corrupt and fought amongst themselves, so the Maker created essendai that they could bring justice to the troubled world. The essendai were sent to read the thoughts of mankind and distinguish between those with good intent and those with evil intent. Those of good intent were honored by having their souls received into the spirit realm. Those of evil intent had their souls consumed by the essendai so they were forever denied the peaceful sleep of the spirit realm and the Maker saw that it was good."

"Many years passed and then a time came when it was deemed that some essendai were as corrupt as mankind and used their powers for evil. A war was fought between the essendai who followed the Maker's word and the essendai who had forsaken the Maker and the land slipped into darkness. Many people believed that the Maker had abandoned them. They prayed to the Maker to once more walk among them and give them aid and their pleas were heard. The Maker sent the essarai to the world to aid those of good intent and harm those who chose evil. The essarai were immune to the essendais' powers and in time defeated those they fought against. From that time on, essendai and essarai worked together to bring justice and healing to the world. And the Maker saw that it was good."

Lily had listened quietly as Eurik recited the histories but when he had finished, she asked a question. "We have holy books on Camar who tell us of the Maker but I've never heard of essendai or essarai nor have I heard that the Maker ever walked among us. Is it true?"

"Obviously you now know that essendai and essarai exist but yes, it is said that the Maker at times walks this earth with us. We don't know what guise he wears; it's been told to us that the Maker can appear as either a man or a woman and that he only comes in times of great change."

Lily thought for a moment then shook her head in amazement at all she had learned. "I came here searching for my mother and now find a community of people with powers similar to mine. How many essendai and essarai are there?"

"There are twenty seven essarai and nineteen essendai living here now. We believe there are others hiding in the Empire and we are always searching for them. I saw in Gavin's memories that you were looking for your mother. What is your mother's name? I should be able to tell you if she's here."

"Her name is Katherine."

Eurik thought for a moment before he replied. "I don't know any essarai by that name but we did have an essarai that lived on Camar years ago. She's not here right now, but when she returns we can ask her if she knows of Katherine."

Lily nodded her head in disappointment just as Gavin's stomach let out a loud rumble. Eurik laughed and said, "I think it's time for breakfast and I have an announcement I must make to the others. Tevarian, I'd like you to remain here and food will be brought to you." He opened the door and once the three of them left the room, he once more bolted it.

As they stood just outside the door Eurik spoke. "One more thing, Lily, I'm curious why you decided not to kill Tevarian?"

"Didn't you read Gavin's mind?" she asked him.

"I did, but I'd like to hear it in your words. I'm a little tired and it's not clear to me."

"After I touched him, I felt a burst of power between us and I was aware of a connection to him. I couldn't just let Gavin kill him; he was so defenseless at that moment."

"Then why didn't you kill him later or let Rolf kill him?"

"Well, I..." Lily thought this over and suddenly her thoughts turned strongly to Tevarian. "It's like I can feel him, like we share something between us. I know that doesn't make sense, but I can't explain it any better."

Eurik contemplated what she had said and got a thoughtful look on his face. "Thank you for telling me," he said.

"Can you tell me what's going to happen to him?" she asked.

"We're about to find out."

They walked out into the large room that Lily had seen briefly last night, only this time it was filled with people. There was a long rectangular table placed in the center of the hall as well as other smaller ones scattered throughout the room. On the long table there was food; freshly baked bread, thick creamy milk, and platters of bacon and eggs. If Lily hadn't already been hungry, the aroma alone would have caused her to want to eat.

Many people were sitting at the tables eating a morning meal; others were just milling about and talking. There was an air of tense expectation in the room and as soon as they entered, all eyes turned toward them.

Eurik held up his hands for silence and instantly all talking stopped. "I'm afraid I have terrible news," he said looking downcast. "Folkvar is dead." A gasp went around the room and Eurik quickly added, "The black essendai is responsible for his death. His soul never made it to the afterlife." Cries of dismay and anger followed and Eurik waited until the room got quiet again before continuing.

"The black essendai is called Tevarian. I have read his memories," Eurik told them, "and it is my decision that for the time being, this man will live."

There was dead silence after Eurik's announcement and it seemed as if they were waiting for him to say something more. A moment passed and when it was obvious he was through speaking the room exploded with noise as people stood up voicing their opinions. A chair was knocked to the ground, a table pushed back and someone thumped their fist on the table as they had their say. Some demanded why he wasn't to be killed on the spot, others wanted to know what was going to be done with him, and still others lapsed back into their native tongue and Lily had no idea what they said. Eurik listened patiently until everyone had quieted.

"Tevarian," he said emphasizing his name, "will remain in this community as our prisoner and will be accompanied by an essarai and an essendai at all times. He will not be harmed in any way; these are my wishes so long as I remain first essendai."

One of the essendai spoke for the group, "We will not go against you Eurik if your cause is right but will you at least tell us why you see fit to spare this man's life?"

"I no longer believe that Tevarian is our enemy," he answered, once again emphasizing his name. Once more they broke into words of protest. "He's a murderer, they all are," one said. "Justice requires that he die for his actions even if he is a changed person," said another. "Think of your sister killed by their hand only a few years ago, is this what she would want?" a third said. Eurik waited until they quieted. "My decision stands. Will you stand with me or depose me as first essendai?" For a moment or two the room was awkwardly silent and the essendai and essarai exchanged glances with one another.

Eventually one of the essarai spoke up. "We have chosen you as first essendai, Eurik, and will all respect your wishes, but we will bring this before the first essarai when she returns. If she believes that he should die then we will force it to a vote." One of the essendai quickly added, "In the meantime I would like to read this black essendai's memories and judge him for myself." A few other men nodded their heads in agreement.

"Of course, I hope you come to the same conclusion as I do." Eurik said. He now motioned Lily and Gavin forward and continued to speak. "This is Lily, she's an essarai from Camar, and will be our guest. She doesn't know much about our traditions and has never met another essarai or essendai before. Please answer her questions if you can." He then looked at Gavin as if recalling that he was there.

"Oh, and this is her husband Gavin," he said. Lily saw a number of people giving them very odd looks after Eurik's statement and a few muttered 'husband' questioningly.

Eurik led them both to the main table and sat down next to them, piling their plates high with food. He introduced them to several of the people around them. One, a woman about her age, was called Greta and a man a bit older was named Harald. Although they gave them a polite good morning, no one was very talkative after the news they had received about their friend's death, so they sat quietly and ate their meal. Lily felt like an intruder sitting among these grieving people, moreover she felt somewhat responsible since she was the one who had brought Tevarian to them.

When they had finished, Eurik turned to Lily and said, "I hope you'll get a better understanding of who we are and what we are trying to do here as you learn more about us. If you choose to stay with us and become a member of our community, you'll be welcomed. Our numbers are small and the Empire diminishes them even further every chance they get. We'll be sending out messengers to contact the rest of our essarai and essendai for a funeral for Folkvar, and while we wait I would like you to explore your surroundings and meet others like yourself. I'll have Greta go with you wherever you like."

"Thank you, I'd like that," Lily replied. Eurik sent Harald with food for Tevarian and asked him to guard him for the morning and then turned to Greta, asking her to be Lily's guide for the day.

Greta gave a sad smile to Lily and said, "I'd be happy to. We've put your belongings in one of the rooms upstairs, including your sword," she said looking at Gavin. "Perhaps you'd like to clean up before we go out." When Lily and Gavin both nodded in agreement, they all looked once more at Eurik.

He gave a long sigh of weariness and said, "I need to go to my bed now, I'm not as young as I once was and last night was very long." He stood and headed toward a stairway leading to the upper story. He turned back toward them with his foot on the first step and said simply, "Enjoy your day," before disappearing up the stairs.

Chapter 23

Lily felt much better after washing up and combing her hair. Their room had a window facing east and the sun gave it a warm feeling as it shone through the glass. The bed was covered in a handmade quilt with a tree design as its center. She marveled at the intricacy of the pattern and thought it was appropriate considering the forest surrounding them. She was reminded once again of Camar and wondered how her country was surviving the invasion of the Empire. When Gavin had buckled on his sword they went downstairs and found Greta waiting for them.

They walked out the front doors into the cold, crisp air of a wintry morning. The sun was out and the sky was clear, it was a beautiful day. Lily looked around and saw that the essendai's compound was situated at the edge of the town. There were several large outbuildings on either side of the building they had just come out of and far behind it were the trees of the forest.

"What are in these other buildings?" Lily asked Greta.

"This one to the east is for lodging visitors. Rolf and his men are staying there now. Behind it are the stables for the horses and behind that we have a barn for the domestic animals. We raise goats and chickens for their meat and milk. We also have gardens but they're hidden under the snow. We try to raise most of our own food and trade with the townspeople for the other things we need."

As they continued walking, the snow crunching under their feet, Lily pulled the warm furs Rolf had given her closer and tucked her hands into fur mittens. "This building to the west of us is for the children," Greta said. "When we have a child, we have to watch it carefully to see if it will have power and that doesn't usually show up until after they're at least six years old. If they do, they stay here and we raise them together so that they can be instructed to use their powers safely and wisely."

"What if they don't have any powers?" Lily asked her.

"That depends on who the parents are. If both parents have power but their child does not, then they usually choose to foster them

211

out. If only one parent has power then the child will go with the parent without powers. Rolf has had two sons with two different essarai but neither is essendai. He will raise them to be warriors, like himself, and the oldest may become leader of his clan when he dies."

"Does no one marry here?" Lily asked incredulously, as she picked her way carefully over an icy patch of snow.

"People without power often marry but we essarai and essendai rarely do. But what does that have to do with having children?" Greta asked. "Even if we're married we're encouraged to have children with other mates. I think you don't understand that children with powers are rare. There is more of a chance if an essarai mates with an essendai for the child to be born with power which is why we so often sleep together."

"That's why Rolf was so surprised that Lily and I were married," Gavin said.

Greta looked slightly uncomfortable as she answered him. "If Lily had grown up here your marriage would have been discouraged. Although I have slept with Rolf, I would never marry him. There would be no advantage for me. I live here with the other essarai and travel with them for healings. I wouldn't be able to live with him and if we had a child with power they would come here to live, so you see it wouldn't make sense for me to marry him."

Now I understand the surprised looks when Eurik told them that I was married to Gavin, Lily thought. To them he's just someone to sleep with, a potential father for their child but not someone to spend their life with. As she looked at Gavin and thought about how much they had endured in just the short time they had been together, she felt sorry for the women here. They wouldn't know the comfort of having someone you knew you could trust by your side, no matter what happened. She took Gavin's hand while Greta kept talking; wanting to feel his presence.

"The other thing you should know, Lily, is that we don't often have children. I don't know if our powers interfere with conception but at most we might have two or three children in our lifetime."

They walked past the building with the children and Lily saw that several of them were outside making snow people. They were laughing and obviously having fun.

"How many children live here now?" Lily asked her.

"There are fifteen boys and girls here; only five have power that we know of but the other ten are still young so it's too soon to tell. One of those with power was born to parents where neither had powers. That also happens but it's even rarer. They brought him to us as soon as they realized he was essendai."

"Wasn't it hard for him to leave his parents?" Lily asked with surprise at the same time that Gavin said, "How could his parents just give him up?"

"This is our way of life and even the children know what is expected. Besides, he is essendai, he will be treated with honor all his life. His parents will also be treated with respect because of him."

While they talked they had slowly been walking the perimeter of the grounds and had ended up near the visitor's lodgings. Lily could see that Rolf and his men were behind the building sparring in an open space. Beyond them was more of the forest. "How far does the forest go?" Lily asked Greta.

"It continues north until it meets the great ice mountains but if you went east for a few leagues you would reach the plains where the horse people live. They're Northlanders, like ourselves, but with some differences. They claim that they're born in the saddle and learn to ride as babes," she laughed. "I don't know if that's true, but it's true they are the best riders I've ever seen and they raise the best horses. In the old days the Northlanders of the forest and the Northlanders of the plains were enemies, but now we're all united in our fight against the Empire. There are several warriors from the plains staying here now with Rolf and his men. We come and go often to see the people of their tribes."

Lily noticed that Gavin was staring at Rolf's men as they sparred with each other. "Do you want to go and join them?" Greta asked him. "I'm sure they'd welcome a new soldier with different fighting skills and I want Lily to join me at the healing center anyway." Lily felt like Greta was trying to send Gavin away but couldn't fault her for the idea especially when she saw how Gavin's whole demeanor seemed to change as he considered it. She could tell he wasn't impressed with what they were learning about the essarai.

Gavin took Lily's arm and pulled her to one side as Greta waved at one of the warriors. "Will you be all right without me? As friendly as they are this morning, I don't completely trust these Northlanders," he said quietly.

"I'll be fine," she said with a smile.

Touching her briefly on the cheek he nodded and went to join Rolf and his warriors.

As Lily and Greta walked away from the men, Greta asked her, "So, tell me Lily, is Gavin a good lover?"

Lily stopped walking she was so astonished by Greta's question. "What?!"

"I just assumed that must have been why you married him. Would you mind if I asked him to sleep with me?"

Lily was almost speechless with astonishment. How could she answer this in a way that Greta would understand without hurting her feelings? "I don't think you understand what marriage means on Camar," she said carefully. "When two people are married they don't share a bed with anyone else. At least they promise not to, although occasionally it happens, but that usually means the end of the marriage."

Now Greta was the one to look astonished. "Really? How unusual. If you're going to stay here in the Northlands with us, you might want to consider accepting our customs, especially for your children's sake."

Lily didn't know what to say so decided that saying nothing might be best. She had no intention of sleeping with anyone but Gavin. As they continued walking she noticed that three of Rolf's men were now following them as they headed in the direction of the town center. She wondered if they were acting as guards and hoped that she and Greta weren't in any danger. As they walked, Greta said good morning to many of the people they passed and received cheerful greetings in reply.

"Where did you say we were going?" Lily asked her.

"I'm taking you to the healing center where we see the sick each day. We all take a turn working there and today is my day. I hope you won't mind helping?" Greta asked her.

"Not at all, I'd love to help." Lily looked over her shoulder at Rolf's men who still followed them and said, "Greta, why are those warriors following us?"

"It's their turn to help in the healing center. You'll see, we're nearly there," she replied.

They had almost reached the marketplace that they had ridden through yesterday and Lily once more felt homesick for Camar as she listened to the trading of the townspeople. She smelled meat pies from one of the stalls and fresh bread from another and even though she had just eaten, the aroma made her hungry. The fish monger had several large trout strung on a line in his stall and was telling anyone

214

who would listen how fresh they were. They turned a corner and she came to a stall that tugged at her heart. She saw a young woman selling herbs standing next to another woman selling cloth. Instantly her memories of time spent with Bridgett came back to her and she wondered if Bridgett and her family had survived in Redin. She was almost relieved when they left the square and entered a large building just off to one side of the marketplace.

As she entered the building Lily smelled the calming scent of lavender. She knew the essarai wouldn't use herbs in their healing as she used to, but evidently they still knew their benefits. The lavender would help to calm anyone who was nervous about their healing or nervous about their illness. It also helped to calm Lily since she was feeling a little overwhelmed.

The building had a row of chairs down each side of the room. Most of the chairs were filled with people. Some of them had an obvious injury such as the man who was holding his arm at an odd angle as if it were broken or the woman holding a bloody cloth to her foot. Others, though, looked quite healthy to Lily and she couldn't imagine why they were there unless it was to help the injured. There seemed to be a healthy person sitting next to each of the injured, as far as she could tell.

As Lily watched, an essarai walked over to the man with the broken arm and touched it. The look of pain on his face instantly gave way to one of relief as he stretched out his arm, bending it back and forth. The essarai swayed slightly and then leaned over the healthy man sitting next to him and took his hand for a moment. She straightened almost immediately, the look of fatigue gone from her face. The man she'd touched stayed in his chair, leaning his head against the wall, looking as if he had just run ten miles. She watched as this procedure was repeated with the woman with the bloody foot.

Lily turned to Greta, hoping she could explain what Lily had just seen, when Greta asked her, "Would you like to heal this man here? His foot was run over by a wagon wheel and several of his toes were crushed. He also broke his arm as he fell and has a gash on his forehead as well. Rolf's warriors can help with this one, since he has so many injuries."

The man was apparently too injured to sit in one of the chairs and was lying on a blanket on the floor. He quietly moaned as he waited for their help and looked at Lily pleadingly as she knelt beside him. She had no idea how Greta thought the warriors could help her so she ignored them, although they had come over to stand beside her as she first touched the man's crushed toes. She poured her power into each of them and was pleased when they appeared healed. She felt tired but moved on to his broken arm at once, certain that it was also causing him pain. When she had healed his arm she was beginning to feel a little light-headed but reached for the gash on his forehead, knowing that it wouldn't take much power to heal. She sat down next to him and put her head in her hands while she tried to regain her strength.

Greta had been watching her as she worked and when Lily looked up she saw a look of bewilderment on her face. "Why haven't you been using these warriors to help you as you healed?" she asked her.

Now it was Lily's turn to look confused. "How could they have helped me? I don't understand."

"Do you mean to tell me that you heal without replenishing your powers?" Greta asked her in surprise. The other healer in the room had come over to stand with her and was also looking at Lily. "Tell me, when did you first know you could heal?" Greta said.

"I was twelve years old and I healed my brother's broken leg."

"And after that?"

"I healed a young boy in the town I lived near. Gavin saw me heal him and then took me to the army encampment to help his commander. His legs were paralyzed and afterward I healed other soldiers with various problems. I did the same on the slave estate and then I healed some soldiers that had been shot with poisoned arrows."

"How many men were poisoned?" Greta asked her.

"I saved the general and six others, so seven total," Lily answered. "I didn't have the strength to save the last two."

"You saved seven men without replenishing your powers?" the other healer asked in astonishment.

"What do you mean? I don't understand how I can replenish my powers except with rest," Lily replied.

"When we do a healing," Greta explained, "we usually have someone without power with us. After, or even during the healing, we take life force from them to replenish our powers. It's impossible to heal seven men that are gravely ill without help unless you are an incredibly powerful healer. How did you do it?"

"I threw up after each healing, because of the poison I think and had to rest between each one. I was very tired afterwards. That's why I couldn't heal the last two soldiers. My powers were gone. I wish I had known about using another's life force. Can you teach me how to do it?"

Both Greta and the other healer were shaking their heads in amazement. "We'll show you right now," Greta answered her. "Take hold of one of the warrior's hands." As Lily held his hand, Greta continued, "Now feel his strength and pull gently on it. Just take a little, in fact you might want to hold on to two of them so you don't take too much from either one. It will tire them, but it won't hurt them unless you pull too much or pull too fast. Slow and gentle is best."

Lily felt awkward holding the hands of these two huge men, but took both their hands in hers and tried to do what Greta told her. At first nothing happened. "I don't understand what to do," she told Greta.

"Close your eyes and feel their life force. Just think about letting it flow into yourself. Take a deep breath and relax."

Lily tried again, drawing in a deep breath and thinking of their life force coming into her just as she thought of healing when she healed. She could feel herself getting stronger as she pulled power from them. When she felt herself again, she let go of their hands. They both looked a little tired and sat down in the chairs to recover. Lily felt wonderful. She smiled at Greta, "That was amazing," she said.

The other healer left to return home and Greta and Lily spent the day healing. Lily was amazed at how easy it was to heal when you could immediately replenish your power. They stepped into the marketplace at noon and each bought one of the meat pies whose smell had enticed her on the way over. It tasted even better than it smelled and was soon followed by a piece of apple cake.

The day went by quickly and as she and Greta left the healing center, she asked her why Rolf's warriors would volunteer to give up their life force to the healers.

"It's how they repay us for giving them food and shelter when they're here and, of course, healing them when they're injured. Warriors are injured a lot," she laughed. "Nearly everything we use in the Northlands is obtained through trade. We don't use coins like the Empire. We healers give our abilities to heal and in exchange the warriors let us use their life essence. The townspeople do the same."

What a different life style these people lived, Lily thought, as they walked back to the community in the early evening. Greta continued to greet most of the people they met, and Lily even recognized a face or two from the healing center. She had a good feeling about the Northlands and hoped she and Gavin could stay.

Gavin walked away from the two women with relief. After yesterday's treatment, the last thing he felt like was a tour of this community. He was not comfortable with people reading his memories and didn't want to be around the essendai and he felt as if the women were staring at him for some reason. Just like in the slave camps he felt like he was nothing. When they had been with Smith freeing the slaves, he had felt like the soldier he was, doing something important. Although it made him feel guilty thinking it, here he would once again just be the healer's husband and nothing more. He was feeling more and more frustrated and needed a way to work off his anger.

Rolf looked up as Gavin got closer. Gavin saw that he was watching two of his men fight with axes within a circle drawn in the snow. "I'm glad to see you still have your head, Camarian. I didn't realize they would take you off as they did or I would have warned you."

"You mean they don't treat everyone new like that?" Gavin asked him, also watching as the two men hacked away at each other. He wondered how many shields needed replacing at the end of the day.

Rolf was still watching his men and yelled at one of them to get his shield up higher before he replied to Gavin's question. "I knew they wouldn't like the black essendai riding in with us but I thought since your wife was essarai it would be all right. What did they do to you?"

"They read me like a book, cover to cover, and I couldn't do a thing to stop them," Gavin said, watching as one of the men's shields quickly split in two and the two men separated, the winner clapping the other on the back.

Rolf shuddered and rolled his head from side to side. "I hate it when they read us," he said, then yelled at his men. "Hans, you idiot, next time keep that shield higher and he won't be able to hit it so hard."

"Why do they read your thoughts?" Gavin asked him. "Don't they trust you?"

"It saves them time when we've been on the borders fighting the Empire. They don't have to ask us questions, they just take what they want to know. It's efficient, but tiring, and if they spend too long at it your head aches afterward."

"I noticed," Gavin replied as he watched two more men step into the circle, each with an axe and shield. "How can you stand to be around them? Do they always know what you're thinking?"

"They're not always reading us, but they can whenever they want I suppose, and they have to be fairly close to you to do it. I'm glad they're on my side, though, because without them we'd lose to the Empire quickly. They're all that prevent the Empire's readers from controlling us every time we meet."

Gavin grunted noncommittally, on his side or not, he didn't like them.

"You ready to have a go with an axe?" Rolf asked him.

Gavin watched as the two bashed away at each other, denting the shields they each held. "I've never fought with an axe and from the size of those I'm not sure I could do much more than chop their foot off."

"Aye, you are a little small for one, perhaps we could get you a hatchet instead," he laughed at Gavin and clapped him on the back. "Take out that sword then and show me what a fighting Camarian looks like."

Gavin was more than happy to comply and soon the two of them were swinging their blades at each other. Rolf was six inches taller than Gavin and heavier, but Gavin was much quicker so the sparring was more evenly matched than he expected in the beginning. It wasn't long before the other men had made a circle around them and watched eagerly to see who would win the bout. Ten minutes into the sparring Gavin was beginning to tire and knew that he was no match for this big Northlander. He began to throw out insults at Rolf, hoping to distract him, until Rolf retaliated with a few of his own causing them both to laugh. Gavin tried to circle behind Rolf and trip him up but his scheme backfired and Rolf managed to dump Gavin into the snow on his rear. He was laughing so hard he had trouble rising but after he was up and standing Gavin held out his sword and bowed to Rolf, "I call a truce," he said laughing. "I will admit that you are the better fighter if you'll allow me to prove that I am the better drinker."

Rolf shook his head at Gavin and said, "I'm afraid you'll lose that boast. Nobody out drinks me and at the moment I'm so dry I feel as if I just crossed the great plains in a dust storm."

He clapped his arm around Gavin and headed him toward the building. "That, my friend, was a fine fight. You know how to handle that sword of yours. If I can't get you to use an axe with me then tell me, what other weapons do you commonly use on Camar?"

"The lords of my country like to battle against each other and they all have walled cities, so we use the longbow quite often. We stand outside the walls and shoot flaming arrows in the thatch of the roofs. Once the town is on fire, the lords are generally more willing to talk. The battles end quickly if we're lucky."

Rolf laughed, "I would imagine they would. Are you skilled with a bow then?"

Now it was Gavin's turn to laugh. "I'm the fourth child of eight; the three older are all brothers. My father was a poor man and I was always hungry for meat that I wouldn't get unless I caught it myself. I learned very early to shoot; I especially liked roast goose and fat turkeys."

"It just so happens that we have some of our cousins from the plains staying with us and they're more skilled than I am at the bow. Would you like to test yourself against them?"

Gavin agreed and soon he and two others were walking around the back of the building to the targets that had been set up there. Gavin was surprised by how short the bows were that the Northlanders used and chose the longest he could find. The two men from the plains chose much shorter bows. They started shooting fifty paces from the target but when all three men hit those easily, they moved back. A few more shots and they were at two hundred paces. Again they hit the targets and again moved further back. At two hundred fifty paces one of the Northlanders missed the target so now Gavin shot against the remaining man. At three hundred paces he pulled back and released his arrow, watching as it once more hit the target. He held his breath as the other man shot, his arrow falling just short of the target. The men watching gave a great cheer and pummeled him on the back.

The Northlander turned to him and said, "You're good with that bow but can you shoot from horseback? That's why we use the shorter bow, you should try it sometime."

"I'd like that," Gavin told him.

"I like the way you fight, Camarian, we'll make a Northlander out of you yet. If you decide to leave Jorval, you're always welcome to join me," Rolf told Gavin as they walked toward his quarters. "I'd be glad to have you fight beside me. What are your plans? You can't want to stay up there much longer," he nodded his head toward the main building, "with the essendai reading your every thought."

"I won't like living under the same roof as them but Lily won't want to leave and I don't want to leave her alone. I'll stay for now until she can find out more about her mother."

Rolf handed Gavin a mug of ale. After taking a long drink and wiping the foam off his mustache he said, "I'll tell you seriously, though, that you won't be able to stay with Lily. Our culture doesn't allow for essarai to marry a man that's not essendai and even then, marriage is not encouraged."

"Why do they care who she lives with? If I take care of her and protect her, why should it matter to them?"

Rolf's eyebrows rose at Gavin's words. "Do you really think she needs your protection? Didn't you see what happened to the black essendai when she touched him? Besides, it's all about the children."

"Greta said the essarai don't often have children. If Lily and I had a child I wouldn't give it up for them to raise. On Camar a man and woman raise their own children," Gavin said defiantly as he lifted the pitcher and poured them both a refill.

"If the child has power it's better for them to be raised here where they can learn to deal with it. If you're going to stay in the Northlands you'll have to eventually accept our ways. You'll have to let her go." After another long drink which effectively emptied the full glass, he added, "Besides, there are so many beautiful women here in the Northlands. Why don't you move your things in here with us? I'll be happy to keep Lily warm," he said as he waggled his eyebrows at Gavin.

"Do you always tell a woman's husband that you want to sleep with his wife?" Gavin asked, amazed at how brazen these Northlanders were but smiling as he said it.

"You might as well agree to it, with a handsome man like me it will happen eventually. You Camarians are much too worried about who you sleep with. I don't understand how Lily can refuse me as she did on the way here."

"Maybe she finds me even more handsome than you," Gavin told him taking a long swig from the mug. "Women find scars very appealing, you know," he said as he rubbed the scar on his face.

"She certainly seemed to find it very appealing on the way here from the noises coming from your furs."

"I was trying to be very quiet, did we bother you?" Gavin asked him with a very sincere look in his eyes.

Rolf snorted so hard he spewed his ale on the table. "More like tried to rub my nose in it, you mean."

This caused them both to start laughing and soon they were trading stories like old friends. Gavin hadn't been this relaxed in a long time but even as he laughed and joked with Rolf, his mind kept returning to Lily and their marriage. It was becoming obvious to him that if they stayed in the Northlands and accepted their customs, they couldn't be together. He'd gotten her here safely, maybe it was time he should start thinking about what was best for him. He'd give it more time and consider Rolf's offer to join him and his warriors. If it came down to sharing her with the other man, though, he didn't think he could do it. He just wasn't raised that way.

Chapter 24

Tevarian stood at the window in the common room and looked down at himself. They had taken away the black robe he had worn for the last few months, the robe he had earned by murdering his family, and replaced it with sturdy clothes that the Northlanders wore. The wool pants and tunic kept him warm and the felt hat covered the tattoo on his forehead as well as his shaved head. Although his hair had begun to grow back it still wasn't very long and his head got cold very quickly in the Northland winter.

Since Eurik had read his memories, he had been passed among the other heretics, or essendai as they called themselves, until his head had begun to ache. It had been five days since he had been brought here by the witch and her mate and he hoped they were almost done reading him. Very few had taken an interest in his early life as Eurik had and many ripped straight into the memory of him killing the heretic. Reliving his memories every day had been exhausting and although he knew they had hoped to get useful information about Roh Vec, he was unsure how valuable his memories were. Most of the time he felt as if he were floating in a haze and now that they had stopped reading his mind he wasn't sure why they kept him alive.

Tevarian went to the single window in his room and looked out at the setting sun. In the distance he could just make out a huge pile of wood that was obviously being prepared for a bonfire. The door opened and he turned to see one of the essendai enter the room. Tevarian couldn't recall if this man had read his memories or not but then he struggled to remember much of anything since losing his power.

"You're to come with me," the man said quietly. "Eurik wants you to see this. I suggest you keep that tattoo hidden and stay quiet." The essendai stepped outside the door and then turned and frowned at him as if he couldn't make up his mind about something. "My name is Harald, if you have questions I've been instructed to answer them." Tevarian really just wanted to know when they were going to kill him, he was tired of the waiting, but he kept his mouth shut.

Harald motioned for Tevarian to follow him and they both went out into the cold, fast approaching night. After several minutes of walking they neared the field behind the main building. It was full of people, both those with power and those without. He recognized the large warrior Rolf standing alongside many others he assumed must be from the town. The essendai stood as a group off to one side with the essarai among them. They carried nothing that marked them as men and women of power other than an aura of authority. Harald joined this group with Tevarian following behind. Those without power kept a respectable distance from both groups. No one spoke and in the quiet he could hear the distant hoot of an owl and the neighing of a horse from the barns.

Atop the pile of wood and branches lay a body, draped with an embroidered covering. It was still light enough to see that it was dark red and had gold thread sewn around the outside border. The threads twisted together in intricate designs, patterned to look like knots. In the center of the cloth was more embroidery, this design was even more beautiful, with a tree at its center. The branches were covered in golden leaves and had golden birds sitting on them. The roots of the tree were interwoven, similar to the knots that surrounded the cloth. It was then that he realized the body must be the heretic he had killed.

As the setting sun dipped below the trees it sent out a ray of light that danced on the golden embroidery, making it appear that the cloth was already on fire. As Tevarian watched, four essendai now stepped forward, each holding a burning torch, and thrust them into the pyre. As the fire took hold among the branches someone began to play a flute. The melody was haunting and lasted for several minutes before he heard a woman's voice join in. Her voice, light and pure, seemed unnaturally loud against the crackle of the flames. Tevarian had never known such emotion and even though he didn't understand the words, he understood the sadness and grief which they symbolized. As the song continued he could feel tears flowing down his face and noticed he was not alone in that regard. She sang until the sun had completely set in the sky, the fire burning brightly behind her.

Tevarian wiped his eyes and saw Eurik walk forward and begin to speak. Because of the silence of the night, his voice carried so that even those at the farthest edge of the crowd could hear him. Tevarian couldn't understand the words, as he spoke in the Northlander tongue, but he could tell by the reactions of those around him that they were moved by what he said. He saw some people smiling, others crying and many holding on to the person standing next to them. Strangely he thought of Roh Vec and the readers and wondered why they never held funerals when one of the brothers died.

When Eurik had finished speaking, people began to drift away from the funeral pyre. Four essendai stood at each corner; Harald told him that they would stay until the fire had burned to ashes. Everyone else now began to walk back to the main building where tables with food had been set up. Tevarian could hear someone tuning an instrument and guessed that the dinner would be followed by dancing. He remembered as a child when his grandfather died there had been food and music, but not the grandeur or reverence he had witnessed this night.

"Can I ask you a question?" he said suddenly. Harald looked at him sharply but nodded his consent, "Can you tell me what the embroidery on the coverlet meant? The golden tree?"

"It is the tree of life. The roots symbolize the connection to the other world where spirits dwell; the trunk is the mortal world where we live and the branches that stretch to the sky show our connection to the heavens where the maker dwells. The trees are very important to us, which is one reason we choose to live among them in the forest. They provide us with food, shelter and wood for burning. They are a life source for us. This forest surrounding us has been here for centuries. We use it sparingly and it protects us with its presence."

Tevarian thought back to how oppressive the forest had felt to him when he was stumbling through it. How it seemed to want to push him back as he tried to go forward. He wondered if that was what Harald meant by protection. As he thought about all this he noticed that the music had started again, only this time a lute, flute and drum played together creating a light joyful beat. He watched as the men and women whirled about dancing to the music. It brought back more memories of his childhood, the adults of his tribe dancing after a wedding.

As he watched he saw a swirl of blonde hair as one of the women wove in and out of the line of dancers. He realized it was the witch that had captured him, Lily, they called her. She seemed to be enjoying herself, clapping her hands and laughing as she danced. He suddenly felt good, almost happy; he wanted to go dance as well.

"Pretty, that one, isn't she?" said Eurik, who had seemingly come out of nowhere and noticed Tevarian's stare.

"I…what?" he stammered, the strange moment of fleeting happiness leaving him.

"It's perfectly natural," Eurik said as if explaining to a twelve year old. "Even we essendai whose power limits our emotions cannot hide from the pleasures of the bed chamber. I imagine that it must be hard for you now that your powers are gone."

"It makes no difference that my powers are gone," Tevarian said defensively.

"So you found her attractive before, then?"

"What…no I wouldn't…that is, I've never found her attractive at all," Tevarian replied definitively.

"Do the readers of the Empire not take women to their beds?" Harald asked, joining the conversation.

"No... I mean yes, there are brothels for that sort of thing." Tevarian shook his head in confusion. "Why is this important? You've already read my memories, what else do you want from me? Why don't you just take my life and be done with it?" he asked angrily.

"Harald, why don't you go enjoy yourself, I'll stay with Tevarian," Eurik said. Harald looked uncertain but followed Eurik's wishes. "Walk with me reader," Eurik told Tevarian. They went away from the dancing and laughter and out to the night air. The wind nipped at the tops of the trees and the music became fainter and fainter. Eurik eventually stopped walking and looked up at the stars. Tevarian stared at them as well and looked for constellations he knew. The sky seemed smaller with the trees crowding around the town. Tevarian remembered his life on the plains where one could see the heavens touch the earth. Still, even with the forest so near, he could make out Pelgarius, lord of horses, and Poseset, bringer of the rains. He hoped his sisters were somewhere up there in the vast spirit realm. He knew his mother wasn't there and she would never go there, even when he died. He remembered her telling him the names of the gods of old and found it strange that Eurik and the Northlanders only had one god.

"Do you still want to know why we haven't taken your life yet?" Eurik abruptly asked, and Tevarian nodded. "Because I am the leader of the essendai and I wanted you kept alive. While the lead essarai is away they won't disobey my orders, though I imagine a vast majority of the populace would like to see you dead," he said and Tevarian thought he saw the older man smile for a moment.

"I imagine your next question is why did I want to keep you alive?" Eurik said and Tevarian nodded again. "I don't actually think you're an evil person, Tevarian, I think you were twisted into one, and have the ability to change. That, however, makes little difference because your actions demand justice. What ultimately influenced my verdict was Lily."

"Lily? What did she have to do with this?" Tevarian asked in confusion. Thinking of Lily again made him feel strangely happy although he wasn't sure why.

"No, I don't suppose you would remember because you were stunned from her touch. She and…oh what is his name… Gavin," Eurik remembered," had a chance to kill you but she decided against it. Since it was she who took your power, I feel it isn't my place to give final judgment on your fate."

Tevarian pondered this and then asked, "Why did she keep me alive?"

"Why don't you ask her for yourself?" Eurik suggested. "Either that or you can wait until your powers return and try to read her mind," he said laughing. "Although I think we both know how well…"

"Are you saying my powers will return?" Tevarian interrupted.

"Of course, I assumed you knew," Eurik said in surprise. Tevarian's obvious bewilderment made Eurik laugh. "Honestly you readers, with all your history books and papers and you don't even remember what an essarai can do. We have nothing in writing in this country and we remember the time before the Empire."

"Can you tell when they will return?" he asked.

"It depends on how hard Lily pulled at your power. Why does it matter?"

Tevarian opened his mouth to speak and then he realized he had no answer. Why did it matter? What would he do with them if they did return?

"I can see you have some things to think about," Eurik said. "I'll take you back to your room. The next time you see Lily ask her why she spared your life. You may find the information interesting."

After the funeral, Gavin had pulled Lily into the dancing before she knew what was happening. She worried that the dances would be different from the ones she knew on Camar but discovered that they were much the same. The music pulled at her and made her feel as if she hadn't a care in the world. She knew she danced with Gavin and Rolf, but most of the time she was flung from person to person and didn't care who twirled her about. By the end of the dancing she felt as if she never wanted to leave the Northlands. Gavin pulled her to him and gave her a hug. "You look happy," he said smiling at her. "I didn't know you could dance so well."

"I used to dance with my cousins at my aunts house and at weddings and such but I haven't danced in a long time. I'd almost forgotten how much fun it is." She looked about her at the Northlanders. "I love it here, the people are so full of life," she said. The music had stopped, the food was nearly gone and everyone was leaving. She was pleased that Gavin seemed much more relaxed than he had been since they came here. Their arms around each other they walked across the main room to the stairway, talking and laughing. Suddenly she felt Gavin stiffen and pull her a little closer. Looking around she saw that two essendai were standing across the room staring at them. She recognized most of the essendai that lived here now, but these two must have just come in for the funeral as they didn't look familiar. They continued to stare, making Lily uncomfortable and she could tell that Gavin was just plain angry, although as he stared back at them he gave them a small, rigid smile.

When they had closed the door to their room behind them, he let loose his resentment. "You realize they were probably reading my thoughts, don't you?" he said, his voice tight with anger.

"Why do you think that?" Lily asked him.

"It's what they do. Rolf told me they read the warriors memories and that they could be reading mine anytime they're near me. I hope they enjoyed the thoughts I was sending their way tonight," he said.

"What were you thinking?" she asked warily.

"I was thinking about the sex we had last night and all my favorite places to kiss you." He sat on their bed and removed his boots. "I hope they have trouble sleeping tonight."

Lily could feel her face turn red even though there was no one but Gavin there to see. "You didn't," she exclaimed looking at him.

He looked at her, surprised by her embarrassment. "Are you ashamed that they should know that we sleep together?" he asked her with an edge to his voice.

"Of course not but they don't need the details," she said, her voice a little shriller than it should be.

Gavin stood up and walked over to where she stood. "I need to know how long you want to stay here. Your mother isn't here and we don't know if she's even alive. I want to rejoin with Smith and fight the Empire for our freedom. I'd even like to take a ship to Camar and try to reclaim the island. I don't like these essendai, I'm ready to leave anytime." He had a grim look on his face that let her know just how unhappy he was.

Lily gaped in astonishment at him, no longer upset with what he had done. "I'm sorry. I didn't know you were so unhappy here," she said anxiously. "Can you just wait until spring? Maybe the essarai that lived on Camar will be back by then and we can ask her if she knew my mother. I'm learning so much about what I can do, I can't leave yet."

"Spring, then," he said brusquely as he removed his outer clothes and crawled into their bed. He rolled on his side, putting his back to her. Lily got into bed and spooned in behind him as she always did for warmth. She barely touched him, though, afraid he might not want her to; afraid he was still angry and not wanting to fight with him. In time, his breathing relaxed and she could tell he had fallen asleep. Lily lay there for a long time with sleep evading her, wondering what the future held for them.

Chapter 25

One week after the funeral, Eurik called Lily and Gavin over to his table at breakfast one morning. Since their argument, nothing more had been said about leaving the Northlands but Lily knew that Gavin didn't relax until he left the common room each morning. He spent his days sparring with the warriors, practicing his archery or working in the stables with the horses. She thought the repetition of mucking stalls and currying horses helped ease the tension caused by his distrust of the essendai.

"Lily, you've settled well into the healing aspect of your powers, how would you like to learn more about what you can do?" Eurik asked her as he slathered butter on a thick slice of homemade bread.

"Of course, anything you think I should learn," she replied, taking Gavin's hand so he couldn't go off without her. They hadn't seen much of each other for days and she wanted to spend some time with him this morning. He looked impatient and she could tell he wanted nothing more than to leave the hall.

"We're sending a group north to several of the villages for healing and justice and then it will circle out on to the plains to do the same at a few of their camps. I'd like to send you with them. You'd be gone about three weeks," he said.

Lily saw Gavin frown when he heard three weeks but before he could comment, Eurik spoke again. "Gavin, you'd be welcome to go along with the warriors who act as guards. There will be one other essarai and one essendai also going. There are many wild beasts that roam these forests and in particular we watch out for the arktos. Their fur is so pale that they're hard to see in the snow and they can attack before you even know they're there."

"How many warriors will be going?" Gavin asked, clearly intrigued with the idea of beasts to fight.

"We usually send at least a dozen. Some of Rolf's men have volunteered although Rolf has duties that will keep him here."

When Gavin nodded his assent, Lily agreed to go as well. It would be good to get away and she knew Gavin would be better for it, even if there was an essendai coming too.

"Good," Eurik told them. "I know its short notice but they'll be leaving in about an hour. You only need to bring warm clothes; the food has been taken care of. Good journey," he said as he went back to eating his breakfast.

Lily and Gavin went back to their room to pack their clothing for the trip and in less than an hour were at the stables ready to leave. The essarai going with them was a woman named Signe that Lily had worked with before at the healing center. The essendai traveled often and had only come for the funeral, so Lily and Gavin hadn't met him yet. His name was Anvindr. The warriors were all from Rolf's holding which she knew pleased Gavin.

They set off before noon with the sun shining and the sky as blue as Lily had ever seen it. As always she felt at peace the minute they rode into the forest. The warriors ranged ahead and behind the essendai and essarai providing them protection from any animal that was foolish enough to attack an armed band of humans. They were so far north that they didn't fear harassment from the Empire's soldiers.

Lily was bundled up in her warm furs and let the horse she was riding have his head as he picked his way up the snowy trail. She was sure he knew the way far better than she did. As she rode she heard Gavin laughing with one of the warriors up ahead of her. Secretly she hoped this journey might soften his opinion of the Northlands and let him reconsider wanting to leave in spring. She had hoped to spend more time here with him.

They rode through the forest most of the day, stopping occasionally to rest the horses and eat cold food. By nightfall they were halfway to the village that was their first destination and stopped to make camp. As they sat around a campfire that night, talk turned to the arktos that Eurik had mentioned.

"They're twice the height of a normal bear and much more intelligent. They work together in packs, culling out the weak and old just like a wolf does. They circle their prey until they separate it from the rest of the herd and then go in for the kill," one of the warriors said.

"Aye, they do," joined in another, "but they don't just eat the four legged. They'll kill a human just as quickly if they can get you alone. With a large enough pack they'll even attack a band of four or five men."

"It's the howling that I don't like," said the first warrior again. "They howl when they catch your scent and keep it up until they attack."

Lily was getting nervous with this talk of beasts eating men and moved closer to Gavin, who obliged her nervousness by putting his arm around her. "What weapon is best for killing them?" he asked.

"Their reach is so long you don't want them to get anywhere near you so don't use your sword. Arrows are best or a spear if you have it. An axe will work but if you're that close to them you may already be dead," one of the warriors said with a laugh.

"Keep the fire going tonight," Anvindr said as he prepared his furs for sleep. "No animal likes fire."

The warriors muttered their agreement and took that as a cue for everyone to prepare for bed. Lily lay close to Gavin as she burrowed into her furs hoping she could sleep with thoughts of arktos in her head.

They got up at first light and continued on their way, reaching the village just after noon. It was a small village, with a dozen log cabins set back from a river. The river was narrow but deep, supplying water through chopped holes in the ice for the villagers. Lily watched as a boy drew a bucket of water from the hole and disappeared into one of the cabins. The village elder, who looked to be over sixty years of age, came out to welcome them and soon had ushered the two essarai into one of the cabins.

They were brought basins of warm water to wash in and then a warm mug of honey mead. Lily removed her outer furs as she stood in front of the stone fireplace drinking the warm brew. Those that needed healing were brought in one at a time and Signe told her that they would take turns healing them. With each person that needed healing, a young adult came too, offering their life force to the healers. There were only a few from the village that needed their attention but others had walked in from surrounding homesteads and it was over an hour before they had finished.

Signe put her furs back on and told Lily that they would need to go back outside for their part in performing justice for the village.

232

Lily still wasn't certain what this entailed, but decided to stay quiet and observe instead of questioning Signe.

Outside was a group of villagers waiting patiently beside Anvindr. When the essarai came out, they looked up nervously. Anvindr motioned to the village elder to begin. Two men from the group then stepped forward and the village elder spoke.

"This man," he said pointing to a large black bearded man wrapped in a bear skin, "is accused of stealing a bull from his neighbor. What do you have to say for yourself?"

The man stepped forward. "He promised me the bull to breed with my cow then never brought it. I merely borrowed it for a week, let it breed and then returned it. The animal wasn't injured."

Anvindr stepped in front of the man and stared at him for several minutes. Lily saw that the man was obviously nervous and was beginning to sweat before Anvindr was done.

"He speaks the truth, yet there is more to the story. Where is the grain you offered in trade for the breeding rights?" Anvindr asked him.

"I never..." he started to say then realized who he was speaking to and stopped. "I will bring it to him tomorrow," he said.

Anvindr now looked at the other man standing next to him who so far hadn't spoken a word. "Will this be acceptable to you?"

"Yes," he replied and both men now walked off. Lily watched as Anvindr handled several more cases in the same way and then justice was done. She wondered why Signe had wanted them to watch but gave it no more thought when they were invited into one of the homes for a meal prepared for them. Because the homes were small they were fed separately from the warriors and Lily didn't see Gavin. After the meal Signe took her aside to speak with her.

"I should have thought to explain this earlier but I forget that you're still new to our ways. When we come to the villages the essendai is expected to sleep with any woman who would be appropriate for having his child. Usually it's the village elder's daughter or perhaps a niece." She lowered her voice a little more and continued. "We as essarai have the option of sleeping with the elder or again a close male relative. It's not required, you understand, but it's seen as an honor for the elder. In this village, it would be the elder's son that would be the obvious choice." She motioned to two men slightly older than Lily talking by the fire. "The one with the red hair is the son."

Lily drew a deep breath and expelled it before speaking. "I'd rather not."

Signe looked at her. "So, is it true that you only sleep with your husband?" she asked. When Lily nodded she just shook her head. "I'm still of an age to bear a child, I'll offer myself to him but I think you're a fool." She softened the last statement with a soft laugh and sauntered over to the redhead. He smiled at her and they walked out the door together.

Anvindr left a few minutes later with a young woman and now Lily didn't know what to do. Was she supposed to sleep in the barn with the warriors? She would have been fine with that but had a feeling the elder wouldn't like it. While she struggled with her dilemma, the elder came over to her. Only he and his wife were still in the cabin with her. "We offer our bed to you," he said pointing to a bed in the corner of the cabin.

Lily was appalled that this old couple would sleep on the floor while she took their bed. "No, please let me sleep in front of the fire on furs. I'll be fine," she argued gently with him.

The old man straightened his shoulders, head high, clearly affronted with the suggestion. Lily realized that she had made a mistake and quickly spoke again.

"I would be honored to use your bed for the night," she said. "Thank you."

The old man smiled at her and lay down next to his wife in front of the fire. Lily climbed into their bed, alone, wishing Gavin could share it with her but realized that would probably insult someone, somewhere.

Morning came and they were off to the next villages. Each one was similar in that they performed healings and justice, were given a meal and a warm place to sleep. Signe sometimes slept with the elder or his son, but not always. Nothing was said when Lily chose to sleep alone each night. Anvindr, on the other hand, had no problem fulfilling his obligations and Lily heard the warriors commenting on his prowess as they rode through the forest one morning. Most of them had also found village girls willing to spend a night with them in the barn, so they weren't complaining. She had been told that they would spend tonight in the forest, being too far from the next village, and truthfully she was relieved. She would enjoy being curled up next to Gavin for a change.

Midway through the day, Gavin rode up alongside her. She smiled when she saw him, and was puzzled by the worried look on his face.

"Is everything all right?" she asked him.

"I want you to stay close to me today as we ride," he told her as he scanned the trail in front of them. "I have one of those feelings I get that something is going to happen. Something doesn't feel right, that's all I know."

Lily nodded and looked around at the forest. Everything looked fine to her, but she knew that Gavin was often right with his sixth sense. It had snowed heavily last night and the horses were having a harder time than usual breaking new ground. The warriors were trading off making the trail, trying to give the lead horses a rest. She saw that they were coming to a clearing in the woods, a meadow with a frozen stream running through it. Suddenly she heard a strange noise in the distance and realized it sounded like howling. Her first thought was wolves, but then realized it didn't sound right.

One of the warriors roared, "Circle, form a circle around, backs to the center. The arktos will be here soon, that howling didn't sound far off. Spears and arrows ready."

Lily was amazed at how quickly the warriors, including Gavin, formed a circle around herself and Signe. Anvindr joined in the circle with the warriors, a spear in his hand. Gavin looked back at her and shouted, "Stay in the circle and you'll be fine." She wondered if that was his sixth sense or if he was just trying to calm her. She hoped it was the former because she was anything but calm, in fact she was terrified. The howling continued, getting louder as the arktos got closer, and she understood why the warrior had said he hated the howling. It was the most frightening sound she had ever heard and the anticipation of what was going to burst from the trees only made it worse.

Moments later, five white shapes loped into the clearing. They were the largest animals Lily had ever seen; easily twice the size of a bear, with teeth that must have been as long as her hand. "Shit, five of them," she heard one of the warriors say.

They had run in on all fours but now stood on two feet, beating their breasts with their paws and howling even louder than before. They circled the horses watching as the warriors shook their spears at them. She saw Gavin put an arrow to his bow and shoot. The arrow sped true and would have been a killing shot but the beast dropped to all fours so quickly that it was only nicked in the shoulder. The horses were starting to panic making shooting that much harder.

The beast that had been shot now ran forward, enraged by pain and tried to attack the warrior nearest him. Gavin had strung another arrow and shot him again, this time hitting him in the leg. Four more arrows in succession and the beast was finally down but he had managed to knock the warrior from his horse and his blood now stained the snow.

The other four beasts, emboldened by the first beast's attack and perhaps enticed by the fresh smell of blood now decided to attack as well. Everything became mass confusion and Lily desperately tried to stay on her panicked horse. When he tried to break loose and run into the beasts, she slid from the saddle and let him run. He was too big for her to control, she hoped he would return if the beasts didn't kill him. Now that she was down she ran frantically to the mauled warrior who had fortunately fallen into the relative safety of the circle and quickly healed him. He opened his eyes in surprise and she helped him to his feet. Lily looked around and saw that two of the beasts were now dead but the other three were still fighting with the men. They were too close and moving too quickly for arrows to be much use so the men were using their spears. The beasts lashed out with their huge paws, snapping many of the spears in half and sending some of the warriors flying into the circle.

Signe was still on her horse trying to control it, so Lily reached out quickly to the men on the ground, healing three more. She knew she needed to renew her power before she could do more so she turned to Signe, thinking she could help her off her horse and let her take over the healing. Suddenly the horse broke free from the circle, Signe still on her back, and ran off into the woods. Lily abruptly sat hard on the ground, so weary she couldn't stay on her feet. She looked up and saw that another beast now lay dead and she watched as the warriors used their swords on the last two, weakened as they were from the spears. It was over. The men that were still standing began checking on those that had fallen and carried them over to where Lily sat in the snow exhausted.

Anvindr, who appeared to be unhurt, and one of the warriors rode off in pursuit of Signe and her runaway horse. Lily could see from where she sat that all of the men were still breathing and turned to Gavin who stood over her.

"I won't be able to heal them unless I can replenish my powers. Is anyone able to share their power with me? You must be unhurt, or I'll weaken you too much." Lily told the warriors.

Gavin knelt beside her. "Use me," he said. Lily looked at all the blood covering his clothing and questioned him.

"Is none of this blood yours?" she asked.

He actually laughed when he told her no; it all belonged to the beasts. He had never offered to share his life force with her before and she wondered how he would deal with it. She took what she felt was enough from him and had him sit down. She healed three more men, then took enough power from another warrior to heal the rest. When she was done she sat in the snow next to Gavin.

"How do you feel now?" she asked him.

"Tired, but alive," he said and took her face between his hands and kissed her.

Two days had passed since they had fought with the arktos and now they were once more leaving a village, only this time they were also leaving the forest as well. They were headed for the plains and although Lily would miss the trees, she was also looking forward to a change. Signe had been amazed that Lily had healed all the warriors without help and kept telling Lily that she must be a very powerful essarai and asking her questions about her powers that Lily couldn't answer. Even the warriors were looking at her differently and Lily was getting tired of it. Gavin laughed when she complained about it to him and called her Queen Lily again. She really hoped the change of scenery would take the focus off her.

Anvindr had told her that they would only have one stop on the plains but would see many more people. Because all the tribes were nomadic, they all gathered several times a year in one location and the essarai and essendai came to them. They would probably camp here for several days, possibly even a week, depending on the number of men and women that could come.

They left the trees by mid afternoon and Lily looked out on an unbroken plain of white. The Ice Mountains could be seen far to the distant north as sentinels watching over the plains. There were a few scrub trees and rolling hills but Lily knew the warriors would be navigating by the sun overhead. The butte they were headed for was only two days away and they had told her that by late afternoon tomorrow it could be seen.

They had brought eye guards carved from antlers to wear as protection from the constant sun shining on the snow and they now stopped to tie them on. They felt odd and looked even stranger but they did help with the glare. A thin slit had been cut in the antlers to let in just a small amount of light, enough to see by but not so much as to harm the eyes. By the end of the day, Lily was glad to take them off and rub her weary eyes.

True to their word, the warriors pointed out the butte the following afternoon and by the next mid day they could see the tents of the people living on the plains. It looked like there were several hundred in all shades of brown. Made from tanned hides that had been scraped and stretched to dry in the hot sun, they almost looked like a vast herd of animals from a distance. Another afternoon of riding and they rode into the center of the camp and were greeted by the elders of four of the tribes. It had been explained to Lily that there were twelve tribes but that not all of them came together in the winter. Many of them lived too far to the north and east to make the trip safely this time of year.

Anvindr was known and liked by the tribes and they were quickly shown to a large tent that had been set up just for them. Lily hoped that meant she wouldn't have to be fending off the elders' sons while they were here. Even Signe seemed happy to have a stable location to drop their things. She put her pack next to Gavin's and almost immediately water was brought for washing, followed by food to eat. Lily was sure they wouldn't be healing tonight so after the meal she collapsed on their furs and didn't wake up until morning.

As she stepped out of their tent the next day with Signe, she saw that their healing would take place in a smaller tent across from the one they slept in. She looked closely at the tents and saw they were made from the hides of an animal she wasn't familiar with and were stitched together so cleverly that they prevented the snow and rain from getting through. The healing tent had a small fire burning in a fire ring, and enough space for ten or twelve people. Those in need of healing were brought in two at a time, one for each of the healers, with two more people to replenish their powers.

They worked steadily at their healing for the next few days and Lily knew that Anvindr was also busy listening to complaints and requests for justice. Unlike them, he did his work in an open area in the center of camp. The people of the tribes liked to watch as he dealt with their complaints. It was almost like the atmosphere of the market, with talking and laughter as they watched the guilty parties being chastised for what they had done. Animals were traded, food was eaten and children ran everywhere, completely unrestrained.

On the second day there, Lily was taking a break at midday when one of Rolf's warriors stepped over to speak to her. "You might want to see this," he said and motioned for her to follow him. They walked to the far side of the tents and Lily saw a few dozen of the plainsmen racing their horses across the snowy plain and shooting arrows at targets set up for them. The warrior pointed to one man in particular and as Lily watched him she thought he looked familiar. He had just made a spectacular shot and one of the other men rode up to him, pounding him on the back in congratulations, accidentally knocking his wool cap to the ground. With surprise she saw it was Gavin who had made the shot.

"He's good with that bow," the warrior said, smiling at her. She went back to her healing, happy that Gavin had been so readily accepted by the warriors.

On the afternoon of the fourth day, Anvindr requested that the healers be present for a serious complaint. A man from one tribe had been accused of murdering a man from another tribe.

When they stepped out of the healing tent, Lily saw that most of the people of the tribes were present and that the atmosphere had completely changed from the previous day. There was no laughter or running children, and a feeling of apprehension clung to the crowd. Anvindr stood in the center of the mass of tribesmen, none of them within twenty feet of him and all of them watching him intently. Behind him stood four elders, one for each of the tribes. As she watched they opened a pathway through the crowd and a man was brought forward struggling, his arms held by two burly warriors. He was pushed to his knees before Anvindr and held in place. A moment passed and his struggling stopped as Anvindr stared at him, reading him. When he had finished, he looked up and projecting his voice so that everyone could hear, he said loudly, "This man is guilty of murder." The crowds that had been watching suddenly went completely silent. Lily could hear a woman weeping softly not far from where she was standing. An older woman spoke quietly to an elder and then walked forward and kissed the man on the forehead. He was still motionless and Lily was sure that Anvindr was controlling him.

Anvindr now looked over at Signe, motioning her forward. She walked over to the guilty man. First she looked at the elder who nodded his head at her, then at Anvindr who also nodded.

She took both of the man's hands firmly in her own and looked him in the eyes. He stared back at her, never moving. Lily was sure that Signe was drawing out his life force but didn't understand why she was doing this when she wasn't performing a healing. It wasn't until he started to sway and eventually fell slowly sideways that she understood what was happening. She watched as Signe eased his fall and continued to hold his hand as he lay on the ground. She looked to one of the elders who then stepped forward and checked to see that his heart had stopped beating. The elder spoke in a strong voice so that all could hear. He simply said, "Justice is done."

Lily realized she had just witnessed an essarai kill another person. She knew she had to be careful when she drew life force from people, but she had never realized that she could go so far as to actually kill someone. She turned slowly and walked back to their tent in shock. She looked at her hands, horrified that she had this kind of power.

She felt warm arms wrap around her and knew that Gavin had come in behind her. "Did you see what happened, what I'm capable of?" she asked him quietly, still staring at her hands, her voice shaking with emotion.

"Just because you're capable of it, doesn't mean you have to use that power," he said. "That man was a murderer, he deserved to die. Signe acted just as the law would have on Camar."

Gavin turned her around so she was looking at him. "That power can be used for good as well as evil." When she shook her head at him in disbelief he said, "If you had known that you had that power, you could have stopped Elezar from hurting all those slaves. Think of the women he raped, you could have saved them from that, you could have saved yourself from that." He pulled her in closer until she was pressed against his heart, listening to its steady beat. "I

240

know you, Lily; you'd never use it unless you were protecting someone else."

She knew he was right, knew she could use this power for good, but she also understood now why she had sometimes seen fear in the eyes of the people of Jorval. She had thought it was the essendai they feared; now she realized they feared the essarai too. When they returned to Jorval, she had questions for Eurik. She wondered just how much of the history he hadn't shared with them.

Chapter 26

Tevarian side stepped to avoid a pair of laughing boys sledding down the street. Most people laughed with them as they passed and no one scolded them for blocking the road. Tevarian had noticed that most people seemed carefree in the town of Jorval. He had spent the last few days wandering and exploring what the Northlanders called a city. It was only slightly larger than the town of Nightgrove where the hunters trained but Tevarian found that he liked Jorval. The smell of wood fires and the snow hid the smell of dense human population, and the trees didn't seem as daunting from inside the town. In fact, Tevarian almost felt like they were protecting the town like a bird nest sheltering an egg. By far his favorite part of Jorval was its people. The mood was almost always light, no one was ever rushed or being ordered about and best yet, as long as he wore his cap to keep his tattoo covered, no one ever paid any attention to him. As a reader in the Empire people were meant to see him and fear him but here he could walk around as a normal person. Harald was always with him, of course, but in time he came to give Tevarian plenty of space when they walked around town.

Tevarian passed by a butcher shop and watched people come and go with various meats and other items. It still amazed him that no one in the Northlands used any coin. The butcher seemed to know most of his costumers by name and exactly what they required the moment they walked in the door. Tevarian stood and watched for so long that the butcher called out to him. Tevarian couldn't understand him but politely shook his head and continued on his way.

"It's not so bad," Eurik said.

"What?" Tevarian said, jumping in surprise at seeing the old man suddenly walking with him. He decided that Eurik was much more agile and stealthy than he looked.

"Life here, it's not so bad." Tevarian stared at him in confusion. "I've read enough legionnaire's minds," Eurik continued, "to know that most people think that life is cruel up here in the Northlands. It can be hard in the winter but we always make it through. If we chose we could take slaves as the Empire does, then all of our people could eat well, but what of the slaves?" Eurik paused and Tevarian realized he was waiting for him to answer.

"What of them? They're just slaves," Tevarian said, unsure what Eurik was getting at.

Eurik shook his head sadly. "Yes I suppose they are. Slavery has existed before the Empire and will probably exist after."

"How can you claim to know such things when nothing is written down?" Tevarian asked. "Surely all your histories cannot be memorized to perfection."

Eurik tapped his head, "It is the essendai's task to pass memories down to the next generation. I believe you experienced this at Roh Vec did you not?" he asked. Tevarian then recalled how high minister Vetrix had shown him the memory of his induction into the order. "We don't remember every bit of the past," Eurik continued. "That amount of information would be simply overwhelming; but we do pass on the most important memories."

"Like what?" Tevarian asked, suddenly interested.

"Oh… times before the Empire, the creation of the Empire by the Emperor, and the war we've been fighting for the last four hundred years," Eurik concluded.

"Tell me of the early Empire and of the Emperor."

"Haven't you already read about it in your history books?" Eurik asked.

"Of course, its one of the first things we were taught at the compound. Four hundred years ago the Emperor inherited the small kingdom of Daskon in the south east. His land prospered but he saw how poor the rest of the world was, and how war plagued all lands. Worse yet the readers and witches were killing each other into extinction. The Emperor then formed the order of essence readers and vowed to bring stability to the world," Tevarian finished.

"And what of the essarai or witches, what does his history say about them?" Eurik pressed.

"Only that they are the greatest enemy to the Empire and to the order of essence readers."

Eurik shook his head sadly and muttered under his breath before speaking. "There are some half truths in this history that your Emperor has created," Eurik told him. "Almost a thousand years ago the essarai first came to the world in order to overthrow those essendai who had become corrupt. The war was long, lasting several generations but ultimately the essarai and good essendai defeated the

243

evil essendai. From that time on, essarai and essendai chose not to rule over the people; rather they formed a college on the plateau of Karegik, the city you now know as Lundburrow. For the next five hundred years they allowed local rulers to lead their people while they would travel the lands giving justice and healing to kings and commoners alike."

"Things changed four hundred years ago when a young essendai named Marsilius came to the college. He was the first son of the king of Daskon and, like you, Tevarian, he came to the college at a later age than usual. Having royalty in the college was rare but not unheard of; as long as they understood that, because they were essendai, they could never rule. When Marsilius left the college he went back to Oska, the capital city of Daskon, and stayed there. He asked if he could start a small sub college in Oska and the college granted his request. Other small schools had been started in the past and as long as they were closely monitored they served as places of healing and justice that troubled people could go to. Still, his young age and the fact that he wanted to start a college in his home town should have warned them."

"Soon after he left they sent a party to investigate his college but a great war began between many powerful lords and our people never returned. The essendai lost communication with all of Daskon for nearly a decade. When the war drew to a close and the roads were safe to travel again, Marsilius returned as king of Daskon with an army behind him. His soldiers were fresh, young, and ready to fight, for the war had never entered their lands. No army could stand before his and he quickly expanded his lands threefold. The essarai and essendai tried to reason with him at first, they told him that he was repeating the mistakes of the evil essendai by taking power for himself. He tricked us by saying that he just wanted to bring peace and order to the people after such a long war. He claimed that he would step down from power and lured almost a third of our college into an ambush on the great Kheight Lake. As far as we know not a single person survived," Eurik said solemnly.

"After that he quickly sacked Lundburrow and killed even more essendai and essarai. With much of the populated world conquered, Marsilius retreated within his own Empire for many years. The college was greatly weakened and with few of the remaining countries strong enough to oppose Marsilius's Empire it was decided that we should wait and rebuild our forces. It took nearly a decade but we eventually convinced enough of the western kings to unite and march against the Empire. Again we underestimated Marsilius and his army as he handed us a crushing defeat. We hadn't realized how effectively he was training his new readers in the arts of warfare, and his experienced legions were more than a match for the western allies."

"And then what?" Tevarian asked when Eurik stopped. "What of his long life or is that also a lie."

"No it's not a lie. After we were defeated it was decided that we should wait in hiding until Marsilius's death. We had hoped that with his death his Empire would fall into discord and we could return." Eurik shook his head sadly. "When age did not take him we realized our plight. For the last four hundred years we have sought ways to destroy him but without success. We did learn a few helpful things through the years however," Eurik said as he watched the two sledding boys come flying by again. "We learned that his body does age and that he has somehow harnessed the power of both an essendai and an essarai."

"How is that possible?" Tevarian asked in astonishment.

"I don't know," Eurik said, "but it has been pondered for hundreds of years."

They continued to walk in silence as Tevarian considered the history Eurik had told him. Though he had read the histories of the Empire many times, recent events made him inclined to believe much of what Eurik had said. Suddenly a thought occurred to him. "When I killed your friend at the battle in the woods, I absorbed his essence and my powers intensified. Is it possible for an essendai to absorb the powers of an essarai in the same way?"

"That's a logical guess," Eurik said, "but the dragas only works between essendai. In the ancient wars some of the evil essendai tried to take the souls of the essarai; all that attempted it died. I don't know how Marsilius has accomplished this feat but I feel certain that both his long life and his ability to use the powers of an essarai are somehow tied together."

"Dragas?" Tevarian asked curiously.

"The powers you received when you absorbed Folkvar's essence. Long have the essendai known of this ability but we Northlanders use it only under the most dire circumstances. The power you gain is tremendous but the desire for more consumes you and you must be very strong to control it instead of it controlling you.

You're familiar with the effects. I can't blame Marsilius from keeping this secret from you and the other readers."

Tevarian contemplated this as they walked back to the community together. Eurik suddenly asked him, "Did you ever get a chance to talk to Lily?"

It took Tevarian a moment to realize what Eurik was talking about. "No, I haven't, perhaps I'll look for her when we get back." "You'll have to wait; she left yesterday to travel as a healer to some of the smaller communities in the Northlands. She'll be gone another few weeks."

Although he had rarely spoken to her, he felt somewhat disappointed by Eurik's words. He wondered what her answer would be when he asked her why she spared his life. "Will I still be alive in a few weeks?" he asked him, half in jest.

Eurik looked at him seriously. "You will be as long as I'm still first essendai."

Tevarian continued to take walks through the town each day, sometimes accompanied by Eurik and other times with Harald. He enjoyed getting out of the essendai community where he still received dark looks from many of the other essendai. The townspeople didn't know who he was and greeted him each morning when they passed by. They often times saw Rolf and his men training in the yard and Tevarian looked intrigued by their different fighting styles. Eurik must have noticed this and spoke to him about it.

"I know you'd like to be working with the warriors, but I don't want anyone else to know that you were with the black essendai. Your tattoos would surely give you away, and the less people that see you for what you are the better."

Tevarian was disappointed but he understood. At least Eurik allowed him the freedom of the town and didn't keep him confined in his room.

One day when they were on their way back from town a strange feeling of danger overcame Tevarian. "Something's wrong," he said trying to keep his voice down as he searched the area around him looking for trouble.

"What do you sense?" Eurik asked, stopping in the road trying to find whatever was worrying Tevarian.

"I don't know," he said, the feeling getting stronger. Somehow he knew it was coming from the northern woods. As it intensified he knew that it wasn't himself that was in danger but someone else. He felt an overwhelming need to act, to try and save this person and he began to run towards the forest.

"Tevarian wait!" Eurik cried, but Tevarian wasn't stopping. He rushed by a woman carrying a basket and nearly knocked over a young boy coming out of his house. He sprinted into the trees using his arms to push away the low branches. He stumbled onward falling into the snow repeatedly but pushing forward all the same. He thought he could hear noises coming just ahead of every tree he passed, the roars of beasts and cries of men and women.

"I'm coming," he yelled and then was tripped up by one of the trees. He hit the snow hard and shivered as it went down his shirt and clung to his face.

"I can see that," said an old woman standing over him. Her hair was white and she carried a cane in her right hand. Her left rested tenderly against the tree that tripped him. "I must say this is one of the strangest meetings I've ever had," she said with a smile.

"What?" Tevarian said in total bafflement, wiping the snow from his face. It was then that he realized that the feeling of danger was completely gone, as if it had never happened.

"I just can't recall meeting anyone as they were lying in the snow," she said still smiling. "You've grown into a handsome young man, Tevarian."

"Who are you?" he asked as he struggled to stand and brush the wet snow off himself.

"That's not important," she said seriously as she looked off into the trees. She spoke again. "I kept my peace while your mother was alive but now that she is gone it is time I revealed your fate." Her voice deepened as she continued. *"You must return home; sever the apex and restore the triangle."* With that she turned slowly and walked off through the trees. She looked back over her shoulder and said, "You'll need help, don't go alone."

"Wait, I don't understand," Tevarian said, and started to follow her. He looked away for just a moment, grabbing a tree trunk as he slipped in the snow, and when he looked for her again she had vanished. He walked behind the tree she had stood next to, but she wasn't there. Puzzled, he heard Eurik and Harald running toward him, Eurik's voice calling him.

247

"Tevarian, where are you?" Eurik asked.

"I'm here," he said as he stepped from behind the tree. "There was a woman, did you see her? She spoke to me."

"What woman, what did she say?" Eurik asked.

Tevarian stared at Eurik as he tried to remember. He knew what she had told him but he couldn't put together his thoughts with words to tell Eurik. He felt baffled and the more he thought about it the more confused he became. "Read my thoughts," he told Eurik. "I can't seem to put it into words."

Eurik stared at him for a moment and then his face took on a puzzled look. "I see nothing except your fear as you ran from me," he said.

"Perhaps it's a trick," Harald said. "Could he be blocking us?"

Eurik shook his head. "No, his powers haven't returned. I don't know what happened." He looked at Tevarian, "As long as you don't run off again, there won't be a problem, and Harald, let's not mention this to the others for now."

Eurik had told Tevarian that they could continue their walks in town after his encounter with the strange woman, but Tevarian didn't want to disturb Eurik again, so he stayed close to the community but did his best to avoid the other essendai. He was sitting by a window thinking about what the old woman had told him when a large crowd came through the main doors. Eurik was at the head of the group taking long strides to keep pace with a blonde haired woman only a few years his junior. The whole group was speaking rapidly in the northern tongue and Tevarian didn't need his powers to see that there was an argument happening.

The woman stopped in the center of the room, asked a question and a finger was pointed at Tevarian. She strode toward him like a thunderstorm. He sat up in his chair and did his best to stare her in the eye. She came forward and knocked the hat from his head so all could see the reader tattoo on his forehead. She put her palm to his head and he gasped as an explosion of pain rocked through his body. She released him and he sagged weakly in his chair. She said something to Eurik who responded in the language of the Empire.

"I didn't have him killed because it wasn't my place to decide his fate." Tevarian saw her checks grow red when Eurik spoke in the common language.

248

"Then who's place is it if not the first essendai?" she asked angrily, also changing languages.

"An essarai brought him here after she drained him of his power," he explained. "He nearly killed her but she decided to spare his life. I didn't feel I could decide his fate after that, at least not without the entire council here."

"An essarai came here on her own! She's probably with the Empire, where is she now," she demanded

"Calm yourself Katya; she's out in the villages healing with Signe and Anvindr. We trust her, she had a man with her and we read his mind." When Eurik said this, others nodded in agreement.

"Fine, I will speak with her when she comes back, but in the meantime I'm here and I say he dies," she said pointing angrily at Tevarian.

"And I say he doesn't," Eurik countered coldly.

"Then it comes to a vote," she said and the room fell awkwardly silent.

"So it does," Eurik said, "but not until all of us are here."

"Fine, but until then I see no reason to have him sitting out in the open with his hands unbound!" With that two of the essendai grabbed an unsteady Tevarian out of his chair and took him back to his bolted room.

Chapter 27

"So, what now general?" Decmitius asked with a slight edge to his voice. Gavrus had come to hate that glib face over the last three weeks. Every single delay the army went through only made the man scream silently "I told you so." At first, things went perfectly. Gavrus and the fifty-fourth met up with two of the four legions in Trost. The legion's enthusiasm easily sparked their comrades into following him, and the legion commanders were soon to follow. These men had served under him for ten years and were far more loyal to him than to the Empire, but it hadn't taken long for things to go wrong.

Three days before, the Empire had sent an envoy to his army demanding that he step down as the general of Trost and return to Nazbar to be court-martialed. He refused of course and the envoy had declared him and all those who stood with him traitors to the Empire. This opened the eyes of many of his soldiers as to just what kind of enemy they were facing. Without the grain support from the Empire he was also forced to take what extra food he could from the local farms, which was very little this far north. He had three of the five legions in Trost already but he needed to get his last two legions before he could turn south; unfortunately the Empire had reached them first, and they had been evading him for the last three days. Now in the early evening he could see them in battle formation not more than a mile away. Their backs were up against a shallow gorge which sloped into a short but steep cliff on the far side.

"Gavrus?" Decmitius said still waiting for an answer. "Your orders?"

"Prepare to make camp," he said looking out at the enemy force.

"Sir?"

"You heard me Decmitius, start making camp," he repeated.

"But we've finally cornered them and we outnumber them three to two, we should…"

"Will you follow my orders or not?" he interrupted, his calm breaking way to anger. Decmitius turned red but stormed away and began to have the three legions break out of the square battle formations. His other officers were similarly flabbergasted but followed his command and in no time fires were being built and tents were being pitched. The two enemy legions still stood in battle formation and showed no signs of moving.

"Sir, I would never go against your orders but isn't Decmitius in the right? We've been chasing them for three days and this is a battle we could win," Titus said.

"These men are not our enemies Titus, they may not have been involved in the Camar invasion but they fought with me on my first two campaigns and they've held the northern border with their brothers. I didn't come all this way to kill my own men."

"How will you sway them, surely the generals know of your betrayal and have been filling the legionnaires' minds with propaganda."

"All I need is a chance to speak to them, and a night for them to think it over."

"It won't be easy to get close, what if they have a reader?" he asked worriedly. Gavrus had been brooding on that very problem for over the last hour. To him a single reader was more dangerous than ten legions. He didn't understand everything about their powers, but he knew if they were ever able to get close enough they could take over his mind and he would be dead in seconds. At Camar the readers had been able to take control of King Rubin at almost one-hundred yards. Since he had taken the fifty-fourth he had ordered any readers approaching his army to be killed on site. Fortunately they hadn't met any in the last two weeks and now he felt he had found a reasonable solution that would allow him to speak to the men at least once.

"All right, here's what we'll do," he said and told Titus his plan.

Half-an-hour later, he, Titus and his personal guard were riding across the plain to the two enemy legions. None of his men had any weapons though they kept their hands on their empty scabbards to make the enemy think they did. Without any actual weapons Gavrus knew any readers would have a difficult time making his men kill each other. Two of the men were also given black robes so that from a distance they might look like readers. He hoped that would make any parties think twice about intercepting his squad before it reached the army. When they were getting close he ordered the men to stop and went forward on his own.

He carried his standard of a golden tiger in one hand so that all could recognize him from a distance and kept his other on his reins. His legs were tied to his horse in such a way that it was impossible for him to dismount or fall off. Another rope was tied around his horse and was connected to several of the other horses. If he moved either hand or started doing anything out of the ordinary, Titus and a team of horses could pull his horse back if need be. There was plenty of slack in the rope so he could advance well away from his guards so that they would be safe from any readers. The sun was getting low by the time he got within shouting distance. It was then that it occurred to him that he had no protection from arrows, but there was no turning back now.

"Legionnaires, why have you turned on me? Me! Tigris, who has brought you victory again and again!" he cried.

"It is you who have turned on us," came the reply. "You have rebelled against the Empire." Gavrus pinpointed the source as the two legion commanders who were acting generals of the force.

"You're misinformed general. It is the Empire who has betrayed us. Too long have they used us as nothing more than a tool so they can get rich!" He continued shouting some of the same reasons to turn against the Empire as he had to the fifty-fourth legion but it didn't take long for the rival commanders to figure out what he was trying to do.

"Spare us your lies Gavrus, or we'll have you shot," they yelled.

"Fine, but consider this; every one of you who stands with them," he pointed his standard at the two generals, "stands against me and the fifty-fourth. You're outnumbered and I have no desire to see anyone die for so poor a cause. I will attack at dawn." He turned and rode away as quickly as he could before any order could be given to the archers. Behind him, the usually well disciplined legionnaires stirred uneasily as his words echoed inside their minds. His guard made it back to their camp without any problems where Decmitius was waiting for them.

"The camp is complete, general," he said gruffly. "I have one legion standing guard while the other two rest."

"As cautious as an old woman Decmitius, that's why I like you," he said sarcastically. Decmitius gave him a stare that said the feeling was mutual.

"Now what?" he asked.

"Now we wait."

The first deserters began showing up as soon as it got dark. Gavrus had warned the sentries to not attack any incoming group unless they were attacked first. In the beginning they only came in small groups but just before dawn everyone could hear the sound of a large force approaching and hundreds of torches were visible. Decmitius quickly had all three legions up and ready for an impending battle. For a moment Gavrus was worried that he had put too much faith in the loyalty of the legionnaires, but then he realized that if they had wanted to attack they would have approached much faster and stealthier. He smiled when he saw a small group come forward bearing a white flag. He walked out with Titus and Decmitius to meet them.

"What do you think they are carrying in those sacks?" Titus asked him. Gavrus's eye sight was not quite as good as it used to be but as they got closer he could indeed see that each man carried a heavy sack in each arm.

"What is your decision?" Gavrus asked when they were close enough. One man stepped in front of the group and dropped the contents of the sacks he was carrying. They were filled with bloodied heads that rolled about as they hit the ground. The men behind him followed suit until there were almost one hundred heads lying on the ground.

"We're with you Tigris," the man said. "We've already dealt with those who oppose you, including the legionnaire commanders," he said tossing another two heads into the pile.

"Name and rank legionnaire," Gavrus asked.

"Captain Luscar, thirty-first legion, reporting sir."

"Captain Luscar, do you represent the legions now?" Gavrus asked.

"I do sir."

"Very well then, it seems that we are in need of more officers. I am promoting you to legion commander of the thirty-first," he said. "Have the legions fall in and prepare to march, we have a lot of land to cover today."

"Yes sir!" Commander Luscar said with a smile. Luscar strode back towards his men and held his hands in victory. The two legions gave a great cheer and marched forward to join their comrades. Gavrus smiled as he realized he had just increased his army from fifteen thousand men to twenty-five thousand. Beside him Decmitius was frowning and looking at the heads on the ground.

"Those two legions just killed their commanders and probably most of their high ranking officers. How can we trust them the next time they disagree with orders they don't like?" he asked. It irked Gavrus how easily Decmitius could turn his mood sour, but it irked him even more knowing that his reasoning was sound.

"We'll select new officers, half will come from their own ranks and the other half will come from our three legions. I'm sure you know experienced and well disciplined men in the fifty-fourth so I'll let you decide whom to promote Decmitius." He couldn't resist adding, "Does that satisfy you?"

"If we don't maintain discipline then we won't have an army, we will have a mob," he said coldly and once again Gavrus hated the fact the Decmitius was probably right.

"Why did I ever promote him to legion command?" he asked Titus as Decmitius walked away.

"Because he notices black, when you only notice white, sir," Titus answered. Gavrus looked at him in surprise but Titus had already turned away and was giving orders to some nearby soldiers. That was something Jacobo would say, he thought to himself and wondered what was happening on the island of Camar.

General Jacobo looked up from the morning reports on the table to see one of his captains come into the room.

"Sir, may I have a word in private?" he asked, glancing nervously at the reader standing next to an exhausted looking King Rubin. Jacobo nodded and they stepped outside the room.

"Sir, we've just received word from Trost, it's about Gavrus."

"He's still in Trost?" Jacobo asked in surprise.

"Yes sir, he sent a letter with a runner from the fifty-fourth. I wouldn't have read it myself but the runner instructed me to. Here have a look," he said, handing him the letter. Jacobo read it in quick, stunned silence.

"Rebellion," he breathed.

"There's more sir, an envoy from the Empire is here and he brought a reader with him. I got a look at one of the tattoos on his face and I believe he's an inquisitor."

"An inquisitor," Jacobo said, barely keeping the fear out his voice. There was only one reason to bring an inquisitor.

"What do you want to do sir?" the captain asked

"How much time do we have before they arrive?"

"Minutes," the man answered. Jacobo put his sweaty palm against the hilt of his sword as he considered his options.

"Ok, you must go to the legions right away. Tell every legionnaire you meet that the tiger is in trouble and that they need to prepare to march to the ships as soon as possible."

"What about you sir?"

"Not your problem captain, take the back way out and ride hard." The captain quickly exited and Jacobo walked back into the main hall and sat heavily. A month he thought, he had been the commanding general for nearly a month. It was probably the shortest span of time for any general to lead an army. He didn't look up when the envoy, inquisitor, and a few guards walked into the room.

"General Jacobo, I come with grave news from Nazbar. We...," the envoy began.

"He won't help us," the inquisitor interrupted, his eyes blaring into Jacobo's skull. "There was a captain here not long ago, he must be killed. He went that way," he said pointing at the stairs. A few guards quickly rushed to find the captain.

"One lousy month," Jacobo muttered. He stood and drew forth his sword with a sweaty hand. "A man could do worse," he said with a grin and charged the inquisitor. He made it two steps before he lost control of his body and everything went black.

It took Gavrus and his five legions a week to make it back towards central Trost from the Northland border. Their pace was delayed as they were forced to fan out and take what food they could from the surrounding farms. He was amazed to find that much of the land was in chaos. Farms were abandoned or burning and many of the storage facilities they went to had been raided. At first he feared the Empire was plundering the lands to starve his army but as his long range scouts began returning, he soon learned otherwise.

"There's a what?" Decmitius asked in disbelief.

"There's been a slave uprising, and if my scouting reports are correct its spread all across Trost," Gavrus repeated as Decmitius sat down on a stool within the command tent.

"Unbelievable," he said, stunned by the news

"We could use this to our advantage," Luscar said. Gavrus knew little of the former captain but he had found Luscar to be both shrewd and ambitious, in fact he was almost too ambitious. It had only taken a few hours as a commander for Luscar and Decmitius to dislike one another, though that wasn't unusual with Decmitius. "They'll inevitably push south towards Nazbar and clash with the legions there. That would give us a chance to strike after the legions have weakened their forces in battle."

"We don't have the strength to strike at Nazbar yet," Decmitius said, "They have ten legions they can muster to our five."

"The slaves can overwhelm a few of those legions and they aren't nearly as experienced as our legionnaires are," Luscar argued.

"This isn't my first campaign boy," Decmitius said coldly. "They're still trained legionnaires and we…"

"Enough," Gavrus said cutting off what he knew would surely be a long fought argument. "Save your bickering, they aren't going south; they're coming north towards us."

"Why would they do that, they've already taken most of the grain with them. What could they possibly want?" Decmitius said.

"Perhaps they're heading for the Northland border?" Luscar said hopefully. Gavrus shook his head.

"We spotted them yesterday; I believe we are their target. If we remained stationary they would reach us by nightfall tomorrow." Both men went silent as they digested his words.

"How many are there?" Decmitius asked.

"Sixty, maybe seventy thousand," Gavrus said.

"We could defeat a group that size," Luscar said hesitantly, "depending on how unruly the mob is and how many are women and children."

"But at what cost?" Decmitius said quietly

"The rebellion," Gavrus murmured and both men turned to look at him. "I have no doubt that we could defeat this force, but win or lose if we engage this slave horde with our current army, we would be left too weak to engage the legions of Nazbar."

"What do you plan to do?" Luscar asked.

"We'll continue marching west until we're close to the coast and hope that Jacobo and his three legions can meet up with us."

"What makes you think he'll come?" Decmitius asked.

"He'll come, he has too."

Chapter 28

Lily walked into the common room followed by Gavin. They had just ridden in from the last leg of their journey and she wanted nothing more than a hot bath and a soft bed. She saw Eurik across the room talking with a stranger, a woman somewhere near his own age. She was about Lily's height with hair of a similar color, although hers was touched with gray. They appeared to be having a disagreement and the woman seemed quite angry, emphasizing her words by shaking a finger in Eurik's face. Lily was surprised that anyone would treat the first essendai in such a way. As they crossed the room to the stairs, Eurik saw her and called her over.

"Here she is," he said, "this is the essarai I told you about."

"This is the one that brought the black essendai here?" the woman said angrily. She looked at Lily, making eye contact. "Why would you do such a thing? He should have been killed immediately. What were you thinking?" she said in a voice that was easily heard across the room.

Lily was tired of this question and didn't think she much liked this angry woman but tried to answer civilly. "His powers were gone and he was barely able to take care of himself. We were headed north and we merely brought him with us, not knowing what else to do. We had never heard of essendai or essarai and didn't know anything about the Northlands." She decided not to mention the connection she had felt with Tevarian, not wanting to make the woman any angrier. She felt Gavin come up behind her and slip his arm around her for support.

"Who is this man standing with you? He doesn't appear to be essendai, he has no right to be here," she stated bluntly.

"This is my husband," Lily answered, still trying to keep her anger in check.

The woman looked at her and then Eurik, dumbfounded. "Why in the maker's name would you marry so young… and to a common man? Eurik, how did you allow this?"

Eurik stepped forward and spoke to the woman. "Katya, this is Lily and she is from Camar. Their customs are different, as you should know since you once lived there." He turned then to Lily. "Lily this is Katya, she is the first essarai."

Lily heard the woman draw a deep breath as she looked at Lily more closely. She stood and stared at her for several moments while everyone waited quietly. "You look familiar somehow," she said, her voice a little calmer than before. "How old are you?"

"I was born twenty years ago," Lily answered.

"And your father, what is his name?"

"His name was Jon, as is my younger brother's."

Lily was surprised when Katya reached for a chair and sat down abruptly. "Can it be?" she asked shakily. "After all these years …" she paused and took a deep breath, "and you're an essarai?"

"What are you talking about Katya?" Eurik asked.

"I think this must be my daughter," she told him.

Lily stood there under her scrutiny not quite certain what to do. She had been searching for her mother and should have been delighted to finally find her, but instead she was torn. This angry woman was not what she had envisioned. She was prepared to give her the benefit of the doubt, though, until she spoke again.

Her mother was once again looking at Gavin. "This won't do at all, though," she said, shaking her head. "Essarai do not ever marry those without power. We must get you out of this marriage. What was your father thinking to allow you to marry so young? He must know of your powers."

Lily had had enough of this; now she was angry. "My father died when I was fourteen years old," she said angrily. "Something you would know if you had ever bothered to try and contact him. I have raised myself and my brother for the last six years. You have no say over anything I choose to do. You gave up any rights when you left us and never sent word to the man who loved you to even let him know you were still alive."

"Jon is dead?" her mother asked, her voice suddenly quiet.

Lily's heart was beating furiously as she tried to calm herself. Her mother truly looked upset at this news and she felt that this wasn't the time or place to discuss it. "Can we go somewhere privately and talk?" she asked her mother.

Katya seemed to come back to herself, looking about the room and realizing where they were. "Yes, … later…, there are more important things to discuss right now." She took a breath and continued. "I was about to tell Eurik that we have a slave rebellion

258

happening to the south and something odd is happening with the Empire's legions."

Gavin, who had stayed behind Lily throughout the argument between mother and daughter, now stepped forward. "What's happening with the slaves?"

Although Katya looked at him disdainfully, she answered his question. "We aren't exactly sure, but they seem to be leaving the estates and disappearing into the countryside and, for whatever reason, the northern legions haven't crushed them yet."

Eurik now joined the conversation. "I've forgotten that you and Lily were involved in the rebellion. Tell us what you know."

Gavin turned to Eurik and quickly summarized their involvement with the slaves. When he mentioned Smith, he noticed that Katya listened more closely.

"Our scouts have mentioned a man named Smith who seems to be a big part of the rebellion. They say he escaped his slave owner and has been freeing slaves throughout Trost. Could this be the same man, do you think? If you know him, you could talk to him and get him to join our warriors against the Empire," Katya said eagerly, apparently deciding Gavin might be of some value after all.

She turned to Eurik. "This is the chance we've been waiting for, we need to gather all the essendai and essarai and send them south with the warriors immediately."

She looked back at Gavin once more and said breathlessly, "What's your name? Would you be willing to go south with the warriors and see if this Smith is the same as the one you knew? We could leave tomorrow."

Gavin looked more excited than Lily had seen him in a long time. "My name is Gavin and yes I'll go with the warriors. I've wanted nothing more than to fight with the slaves since we started the whole thing."

Eurik stepped forward, hands held out as if to stop them. "We need to slow down," he said. "Katya we can't decide this quickly on something that affects us all. It would be impossible to gather everyone swiftly enough to leave tomorrow."

Katya thought this over for a moment and then spoke again in a slightly calmer voice. "We could send Gavin and whatever warriors are available, tomorrow. They could search for this Smith and make contact with him leaving an obvious trail for us. We'll gather as many of us as can be here quickly and follow them in a few days. You can wait for the rest of the warriors. Some will have to stay behind for the town, of course, but I say that most of us should go. Don't you see that this chance won't come again? Our numbers are too small to fight alone, but with the slaves we can make a difference in the harm we cause the Empire."

Lily watched Gavin nodding his head in agreement with everything Katya said. She knew that if her mother had her way, Gavin would be riding out first thing in the morning. This wasn't how she had expected to spend her first evening back in the community. She knew that Gavin would leave to help the slaves; it's what he had wanted from the start. He had only come to the Northlands to help her.

Eurik sent for Rolf and when he arrived they all sat at a table to discuss what would happen in the morning. Lily went upstairs to clean up and put away the few belongings she had taken with her. She hadn't been there long when she heard a soft knock on the door. She opened it to find her mother standing there.

"May I come in? I'd like to talk with you."

Lily could feel her heart start to pound with nervousness as she pulled the door open wider to allow her mother to come in. She motioned to the one chair in the room, but her mother chose not to sit. She walked over to the window instead and looked out on the courtyard below. It had started to snow again and she stood and watched it fall without speaking. Lily also stayed silent, waiting for her mother to begin.

"How did your father die? Why didn't you heal him?" she asked abruptly.

"He was in town when it happened," Lily answered. "He was helping to repair the wall that surrounds the town and one of the blocks fell on him, crushing him. By the time they brought him home, he had been dead several hours. Even if I had known how to heal, I couldn't have saved him."

Her mother gave a soft sigh and sat on the bed. "What do you mean you didn't know how to heal?" she asked her.

Lily told her the story of healing Jon and her father's insistence to never use her powers again. "There was no one to tell me differently, if not for Gavin I still wouldn't know what I was capable of and I certainly wouldn't be here now."

Katya now asked her for the whole story and Lily told her all that had happened over the last few months. She was sad when she told her about Samuel and angry when she heard all that happened at the estate. She was pacing the room by the time Lily had finished. "I should have taken you both with me but I was being hunted by the Empire and I didn't want you in danger."

"Why didn't you send word that you were here? Samuel told me you had planned on sending for us when you were safe. Until Samuel spoke to me, I thought you'd died when Jon was born."

Katya got up and began pacing the floor as she spoke. "When I arrived back here I realized that fighting the Empire was more important. I know that sounds cold but I knew that Jon would be a good father to you both and children with powers are so rare when we mate with a man other than essendai that I truly didn't believe either of you would have any. Why not let you grow up on Camar and live a normal life?"

"Why did you marry my father if you didn't want that same normal life you're speaking of?"

"Marry? I didn't marry your father, we just had children together." Katya looked up suddenly as if remembering something. "What happened to your brother? Is he still on Camar?"

"I don't know where he is. He left a year ago, said he was tired of living a quiet life and wanted to find some adventure." She shrugged her shoulders. "Perhaps he's more like you than I am. Why did you go to Camar anyway and how did you meet my father?"

"I went to Camar in search of other essarai. We were off the coast of Camar when a storm came up and our ship went down. I managed to swim to shore and was helped by a local fisherman but no one else survived the wreck. When I felt better, I decided I might as well continue with my original plans and search for essarai." Katya had continued pacing as she spoke and now used her hands to emphasize many of her words. Lily wondered if she was always in motion and realized that it reminded her of her brother Jon.

"I went inland and began my search. I would occasionally heal someone in payment for food and a place to stay and I began to get a reputation. I was always on the move so I thought I would be safe, but people started to notice and some shared the Empire's opinion of witches. I ended up hiding in the forest where you grew up and your father found me. He let me share his home which kept me safe and in return I acted as his wife and gave him two children. He knew I would have to leave one day."

"Did you love him?" Lily asked her.

Katya sighed and sat next to Lily on the bed. "He was a good man and I cared about him very much. I'm sorry he's dead. I never expected to see him again but I'm sorry he's gone. I should have come looking for you sooner, but…"

"I know, the Empire was more important," Lily said bitterly.

"Damn it, Lily, if I'd known you were essarai I would have come long ago," Katya said loudly.

"Somehow that doesn't make me feel any better," Lily said. Suddenly she couldn't take this conversation any longer. "I'm sorry, but I really need to rest. We just got back from a three week journey and I'm tired."

Katya walked toward the door and opened it but before she stepped out she turned back. "I still don't agree with you marrying so young, but at least he wants to fight," she said, and walked out.

Lily had been in bed for over an hour before Gavin came in and it had given her plenty of time to think. She knew what she wanted for this last night with her husband and it wasn't arguments and tears. He would leave tomorrow and she might never see him again. She didn't want to go with him or even with the other essarai when they left in a few weeks. The words of Joan's vision came back to her, "*You will find what you are seeking to the north, follow the black book.*" It seemed she had discovered at least part of the vision. She had made it to the Northlands and found her mother, but she still hadn't discovered the black book. That was one reason she didn't want to leave but there were others. She still felt like she had a lot to learn about her abilities as an essarai and she loved being able to heal others without fear of reprisal. The people here actually wanted her and the others to use their powers.

And then there was Tevarian. She didn't know what this bond she felt with him meant, but she couldn't stand by while they killed him. She had to stay until the council made a decision and hopefully they would let her speak in his favor. All these things added up to her not leaving the Northlands. She hoped Gavin would understand.

The moonlight streaming in the window gave plenty of light as Gavin washed up and removed his clothes. She lay in bed watching him, enjoying the sight of the muscles in his arms and chest. He had gained weight since coming to the Northlands, both from finally having plenty of food and from working with the warriors, and all of it was muscle. She knew he was aware of her gaze when she saw his shoulders tense and he looked toward her, probably waiting for her to say something about his leaving her tomorrow. Instead she flipped back the furs, inviting him to join her as she lay in their bed wearing nothing but what the maker had given her. She watched as his body responded immediately and saw him smile as he climbed into bed beside her.

Before he could speak, she was kissing him, touching him, and urging him to touch her in all the places she liked best. She wanted him inside her and shifted her body under him until he entered her. Their lovemaking was passionate and wild, exactly what she wanted for their last night together. When they were each spent, they lay wrapped around each other, their breathing slowing, naked bodies pressed tightly together. "You're a clever woman, Lily," Gavin said drowsily. "Here I was expecting you to argue with me to try and get me to stay, instead you love me so well I never want to leave."

Lily laughed quietly. "There's nothing I could say that would keep you here. I don't want to argue. When you're gone and you think of me, this is what I want you to remember."

Now it was Gavin's turn to laugh. "If this is what I remember each time I think of you, I won't be able to sleep at night," he said as he rubbed his hand up and down her back. "I don't think I've ever told you how thankful I am that I saw you that day in Redin. I don't regret a moment of the time we've had together. I love you, Lily."

Gavin had continued to rub her back as he talked and she leaned back so she could see his face in the moonlight still shining through the window. She ran her fingers over the scar on his face. "Did you know that when I first met you, your scar scared me? It made you look like a brigand who regularly kidnapped young girls and brought them to army camps," she said, making him chuckle. She looked up, meeting his eyes and she could tell that they both knew what would happen when he left tomorrow.

She heard a tightness in his voice as he asked, "Will you be coming then when Eurik brings the rest of the warriors?" She wondered if he was worried that she would come or that she wouldn't.

"No, I won't," Lily said as she played with a tangle in his hair. He had let it grow longer since they had been in the Northlands and he looked more like a Northland warrior now than a Camarian soldier. She was having trouble speaking and her voice came out so quietly that she wasn't sure if he would hear her. "I love you, Gavin. I've

263

been so happy being your wife but it isn't going to work if we stay in the Northlands, is it?"

Gavin shook his head at her. "No, and I can't stay here. I'm sorry Lily, I've tried but there's nothing for me here but you. As much as I love you I need a purpose in my life and this slave rebellion is it. If we can free the slaves it will weaken the Empire and then there's a chance we can take Camar back from them. There's so much to do and I can't help by sitting here in the Northlands. Besides, you know our marriage will never truly be accepted here." He took a deep breath, "I think we should end our handfast. If you're going to stay here it will help you to fit in."

Lily nodded as the tears flowed down her face. Gavin pulled her closer and held her while she wept. The thought of never seeing him again kept her weeping for a long time. What if he died in the rebellion, would she ever know what had happened to him? She was only able to stop crying when she remembered that this wasn't how she wanted him to remember her. She took a deep quavering breath and got herself under control. "Will you stay tonight?" she asked him.

Gavin wiped the tears from her face and gave her a small smile. "And miss the chance of sleeping with a woman who's not my wife? Rolf would never let me forget it," he said kissing her. Lily returned the kiss, glad that she at least had one last night with this man who had been so much to her.

Gavin looked at Lily as the room slowly lightened in the early morning. He had always loved to watch her while she slept, her face relaxed and at peace. A part of him would have liked to slip from the bed, not waking her, leaving quietly so that he could remember her like this. He didn't want to see the sadness on her face that he knew would be there when they parted. He knew his leaving was the right thing to do but that didn't make it any easier. At least he felt he had fulfilled what the old woman had told him to do. He still remembered her words so clearly, *"I lay this burden on you, help her find her purpose."* Here in the Northlands he was certain that Lily had found her purpose. She was a healer and up here she could be one without fear.

As if she could sense him watching her, Lily's eyes opened. He ran his hand through her blonde hair remembering the first time he had seen her in the marketplace. In Camar her hair color was rare and he had thought it looked like gold when she stood in the sunlight selling her herbs. They had been through so much together, how was he going to leave her knowing that they would possibly never see each other again? He could hear noises now outside the window and knew it was time he got ready to go. They both got up without a word and dressed. Gavin took Lily's hand and left their room for the last time. As they headed downstairs he could hear Rolf's laughter coming from the common room. They grabbed a plate of food and all too soon it was time to go.

The sun had just risen as he rode off through the town with Rolf and his warriors. He watched Lily as they left. He could still smell the scent of her, feel the softness of her hair as she hugged him one last time, listen to her quietly tell him she would always love him. Rolf rode up beside him ready to tell him the latest bawdy story he had heard in town. He pushed his horse a little faster and turned his thoughts to what awaited him south. He had to put thoughts of Lily behind him; time to move ahead.

Lily watched as Gavin and the warriors rode off in the early morning light. She stood with Eurik who still didn't look entirely happy with this turn of events. Katya was beside several other essarai and had given last minute instructions to the warriors concerning where they would eventually meet up. Lily knew she planned on following them as soon as the decision had been made about Tevarian.

She hurried to her room hoping to avoid another conversation with her mother and lay down on the bed to rest. She hadn't gotten much sleep last night between their lovemaking and her tears and she didn't feel like being with other people this morning. She knew their decision was the right one but she didn't think she would ever be content with it.

Several hours later Lily awoke to the sound of loud voices downstairs. She straightened her hair and clothing, washed her tearstained face and opened her door to hear what was being said.

"What do you mean he's gone?" she heard Katya yell. "How did he get out of a locked room? Are his powers back?"

Lily's heart sped up as she realized they must be talking about Tevarian. She didn't want to argue with her mother again, but she felt responsible for Tevarian being here and wanted to find out what had happened. As she came down the stairs her mother was still shouting.

"He could be anywhere! We'll have to send an essendai in every possible direction to find him. He knows where we are and he'll send the Empire here. Damn it, he should have been killed the minute he got here!" she shouted as she walked around the room, waving her arms and yelling at Eurik and anyone else who would listen.

Eurik reached out and grabbed her hands, effectively stopping her pacing as he tried to reason with her. "Katya, calm down, I don't think finding him will be a problem."

"What are you talking about, old man?" Katya asked him.

"Lily, come here," he said to her, calling her over from the base of the stairs where she had been standing. Suddenly everyone was looking at her, making her very uncomfortable. She walked over to him and he said, "I think you'll be able to tell us which way he went."

Katya suddenly turned to her, the set of her shoulders and the angry look in her eyes telling her what would happen to her if she was responsible for his leaving. "Are you saying she let him out?"

Lily took a step back. "Of course not, that's not what I meant," Eurik said looking at Lily in a sympathetic way. "Lily will be able to find him because I think Lily and Tevarian share the Drasana with each other."

"What? How can you be sure?" Katya asked.

"What is that?" Lily asked him warily.

"It's a special bond between essarai and essendai that is so rare that I haven't heard of any in my lifetime. It usually happens when both people are under extreme emotional stress. The connection was most likely formed when Tevarian tried to kill you and you took his powers. When you touched him, the bond was formed. We call the bond that you share, Drasana."

Lily looked from Eurik to Katya, completely confused. Was this what she had been feeling with Tevarian?

"Lily I want you to just think of Tevarian and tell me if you know which direction we can search for him."

Lily had no idea what he was expecting her to do. "Just think of him?" she asked. When he nodded, she tried to think of nothing but Tevarian. She closed her eyes and thought of him as she'd seen him when she and Gavin had first encountered him in the meadow. The black robe pulled low, covering his face. Then she remembered him standing at the funeral dance, dressed now in the clothes the Northlanders wore. Suddenly she turned to the southeast, certain that was the way he had gone. "He's that way," she said, still doubtful as to how she knew. "At least I think he is."

If everyone had been watching her before, they were openly staring at her now.

Katya shook her head in amazement and spoke to Lily. "What a waste. The Drasana formed with a black essendai, especially when we have to kill him. At least we can find him now."

"Wait," Lily said, "are you saying I can track him like, like..?"

"Like a hunter tracks his prey," Katya finished for her. "But don't worry, we won't send you alone. He trusts you so it shouldn't be too hard to draw him close enough to kill him."

"That hasn't been decided by the council yet, Katya. If she can bring him back alive, I think that she should," Eurik said. "At least you can leave now and join Rolf and his warriors with all the essarai and essendai that want to go."

He and Katya continued to argue back and forth for a few moments but Lily had stopped listening. Her head was spinning with all that had happened in the last week. She had found out she had the ability to kill, the Northlanders had decided to try and join with the slaves to war on the Empire, and she was no longer married but still loved a man she might never see again. Now she was to lead the search for a man she barely knew and if she found him she would have to decide if he lived or died, that is, if he didn't kill her first. She headed up the stairs to repack her things and prepare to leave. She thought of Tevarian again, and once more felt herself drawn to the southeast. At least she'd know which way to go, but once she found him, then what?

Chapter 29

Gavin, Rolf and Katya were two days out of the Northlands when they saw one of the scouts approaching from the south. With them were thirty of Rolf's warriors and a half dozen essarai and essendai. The rest of the community would follow when the warriors from the Northlands had all gathered. Gavin knew that Katya hoped they would come within a few weeks but he thought she was being optimistic. The Northlands was a large territory and the warriors on the plains were spread far out.

The scout rode straight to Katya and with both hands he touched his fingertips to his forehead then put his hands palm out as he bowed slightly in the gesture of respect that Gavin had seen used for the essarai. "They're camped just over the next ridge."

Katya settled her horse, her hands holding the reins loosely. "How many do you think?"

"A rough count would be sixty thousand, mostly men, but I saw women and children as well. They've posted guards but they don't appear to be well armed."

"All right, we ride in together. Gavin, you lead, maybe some of the slaves will recognize you," Katya said.

Gavin nodded and turned his horse in the direction the scout had indicated and rode over the ridge. They followed a rough path and soon the camp was in sight. They rode down the hill two abreast so as to look less like they wanted to fight, Gavin and Katya in the lead. He hoped by having himself and a woman first, the slaves wouldn't be quite so startled as he knew they would be when they got their first look at the Northlanders. "If only they weren't so damn big," Gavin thought not for the first time, and the furs they wore made them look even bigger.

The sun was shining brightly in the early afternoon and Gavin shaded his eyes, amazed at the sight in front of him. He had expected a camp much like those he had spent time in with Commander Versan on Camar. Instead he saw what looked like a mob of refugees spread over a vast amount of the countryside. Gavin had never seen this many people in one place. Looking from where he was on one side of the camp, he couldn't see where the other side ended. There were makeshift tents set up haphazardly throughout the encampment. He saw women and children in front of many of them tending to cook fires. Men of all ages were milling about, looking to the few horses that he saw or just standing in groups talking. They wore a motley collection of clothing, most in the standard garb the slaves wore, but others wore a collection of fancy coats and hats along with their old clothes. He supposed that they had taken their master's clothing along with anything else they could steal. When he thought about the conditions of some of the slaves, he didn't blame them. As they neared the camp, those people closest to them stared in their direction, some with fear in their eyes, others just looked curious. Several men now approached them, the first held a knife in his hand, the second had a thick stave but the third was carrying a pitchfork. They yelled at the Northlanders to halt and held their weapons in a formidable manner, showing them that despite the oddity of the weapons, they would use them if necessary.

Gavin and Katya stopped their horses and waited for the men to come to them. "I'd like to speak with whoever is in charge here," Gavin said. "We were told it was a man called Smith. It's possible he and I were slaves together on an estate southeast of here. Will you bring him here or should we go to him?" He spoke decisively, not wanting them to consider fighting rather than talking.

The men talked quietly among themselves for a moment before one of them spoke. "Give us a name and we'll see if he wants to talk to you."

"Tell him Gavin wants to speak to him." The guard rode off toward the center of the camp while Katya sat impatiently beside him. This woman was going to be a problem if she didn't curb that temper of hers, Gavin thought, watching her muttering under her breath. He hoped Smith would welcome their help or she'd cause trouble.

It wasn't long before Gavin saw Smith riding toward them. His distinctive bald head and burly build were obvious even from a distance. Gavin saw the scowl on his face turn to a grin when he met his eyes. He rode directly up to Gavin, causing their horses to bump each other, and grabbed him by the arms.

"It is you," he said his grin getting wider. "I didn't believe them when they told me who wanted to talk to me." He looked behind them at the warriors sitting silently on their horses. "Damn, looks like you found those wild Northmen we talked about and from the looks of that wild hair of yours, looks like you joined them. I can see you have a story to tell. Where's that pretty wife of yours?"

Gavin had told Rolf about he and Lily ending their marriage but wasn't ready to share the news with anyone else, including Katya, so he decided to just tell part of the story. "She'll be staying in the Northlands for now but we'll have ten thousand warriors joining us in the next few weeks if you'll have us," Gavin told him. "We're here to help with the rebellion. This is Katya," Gavin gestured to her sitting beside him. "She's essarai, like Lily, and in charge of this band of warriors, myself included."

Smith raised his eyebrows at Gavin's words and greeted Katya. "Come to my tent and we'll hear your story. I have others that'll want to know what's happened to you and why you're here."

The sun was sitting a little lower in the sky by the time Gavin had finished telling Smith what he and Lily had encountered in the Northlands and Katya had explained what the essarai and essendai could do for the slave rebellion. If possible, the grin on Smith's face had gotten even bigger by the time they were finished.

"Damn I'm glad you're here. You can see what I've been dealing with for the last month. There must be sixty thousand of us here and at least a third are women, children and elders who can't fight. Of the rest of us only another third knows how to use a weapon properly and there are only so many weapons to go around. Half of the men are using farm tools and sticks to fight with." They all sat on the ground around one of the many campfires since none of the tents were big enough to house all the warriors and the men Smith had wanted to hear their tale. They had just finished telling him once more that they had over ten thousand warriors that should be arriving in the next few weeks.

"Not for a few weeks, you say? Damn, I wish it was sooner." He reached over and grabbed a hat to cover his bald head. The weather was warmer this far south but it still cooled down considerably as the day wore on. "We've got ten legions coming up from the south behind us and five legions just to the northeast of us not even a day away. The plan is to attack the smaller army so that we can help ourselves to their weapons before we have to fight the larger one. We could use those extra men right now."

Katya looked at Smith in surprise. "Do you realize that the northern legions are under the control of General Gavrus, the one they call The Tiger? He's been in charge for the last ten years and has won virtually every battle he's fought. Taking his five legions won't be easy."

Gavin had been staring into the flames as he listened to Smith outline his plans but his head jerked up at the name Katya mentioned. "Did you say Gavrus?" he said looking at Katya.

"Yes, do you know the name?" she asked.

"Lily healed a general named Gavrus when we were on Elezar's estate. It was him that helped us escape. He offered both Lily and I the chance to join his army."

"What!" Katya exclaimed as she leapt to her feet, startling the men sitting nearest to her. "My daughter healed a general in the Empire's army? A black essendai and a general, does that girl not know who the enemy is?!"

Gavin watched as she walked away from the fire, her hands pulling on her hair, and then marched back toward them. He tried to explain why Lily healed Gavrus. "She offered to heal him in exchange for his freeing all the slaves on the estate. She said he was very near death and didn't seem to expect her to be able to save him. When she did, he offered to do anything she wanted. I'm sure he would remember her and possibly me since he loaned me his sword to kill Elezar, the man who bought us."

"Elezar? Eurik told me he read your memories of the time you spent as slaves. Is that the man who raped my daughter?" Katya asked with a hard edge to her voice. Gavin nodded. "You killed him?" Gavin nodded again. "Good," was all she said but she gave Gavin a small look of respect.

Gavin pulled his thoughts back to the present, "Doesn't it seem odd that he hasn't tried to attack you before now?" he said looking at Smith. "And Katya, didn't you say that you had reports of his unusual troop movements? Lily said he had been attacked with poisoned spears. Who would want to kill him so badly that they would use poison?"

A strange idea began to form in his mind as the others continued to discuss their situation. He decided to put it before them and see what they thought of it. "There's something strange going on with Gavrus. What if I try and talk to him, maybe I can convince him to leave us alone or at least look the other way when we fight with the other army. If that doesn't work I'll at least get a good look at his troops and where they're positioned."

271

Everyone looked at Gavin like he had gone crazy. "You want to walk into the legion's camp and try and talk to their general?" Rolf asked him.

"I'd hate to lose you when you're here to work with me again," Smith joked.

Several of the Northlanders tried to talk him out of it but Katya got a thoughtful look on her face and said, "It's not a bad idea. The problem will be convincing his sentries to let you in to see the general."

"It's still plenty light out, if I go in slowly and alone, I don't think they'll attack one man. If anyone has a scrap of white cloth I could tie to a stick, I'll take that too and besides, I've got a feeling that it will work."

Smith told someone to find the white cloth and Gavin prepared to leave. "Lily will never forgive me if I let you get yourself killed," Rolf told him. "Yell if you need us. We'll be close." Gavin gave him a nod of thanks and mounted his horse for the short ride to the legions' camp.

When Gavin told the sentries that he wanted to speak with General Gavrus and that he knew the man personally, they looked at him in disbelief, but after taking his sword and knife, they escorted him into camp. He saw that there did indeed seem to be at least five legions as he looked out over a sea of red clad soldiers. He was stared at by many of the soldiers but no one attempted to harm him as he walked between the two sentries, an arm held roughly by each of them. When they reached what appeared to be the largest tent in the camp, they handed him off to a soldier of higher rank, according to the insignia on his tunic, who then asked him for his name.

"Tell the general that the husband of the woman who healed him recently, would like to speak with him."

The soldier raised his eyebrows at that but sent the message by way of one of the guards standing in front of the tent. Moments later he was ushered inside, his arms once again held by two of the guards.

Gavrus looked up from the camp stool he was sitting on, a look of surprise on his face. "It looks like you've been busy since we last met, judging from the number of slaves you're with. Where's your wife?"

Gavin couldn't tell by the impassive look on the general's face what he thought of sixty thousand slaves sitting just over the ridge from him or what he thought of Gavin showing up unexpectedly. He wondered if he could get a reaction out of him if he gave out bits of information. Would he leave the slaves alone if he thought he had a Northland army to contend with? "She's still in the Northlands with our new friends. They'll be joining us soon."

Aha, Gavin thought, as he watched Gavrus's fingers tap nervously on his thigh, the Northlanders worry him. "Why are you here?" Gavrus asked him bluntly. "Is there something you wanted from me?"

"I'm here to speak for the slaves, General, and to remind you that there's nothing more dangerous than a trapped beast." Gavin noticed that Gavrus got a puzzled look on his face as if he wasn't quite certain what he was talking about. Was it possible that Gavrus didn't know that ten legions were heading north, he wondered? "If you engage us now, you will lose a lot of men as we greatly outnumber you and since we'll be fighting for our lives we may surprise you with our fierceness. But if you were to look the other way and allow us to leave before the southern legions arrive, we'd both gain."

Gavin watched Gavrus closely as he looked at his other generals. He was positive that hearing of more legions coming was news to Gavrus. Several of them had surprised looks on their faces although Gavrus was as impassive as ever. What was going on with this man? Why wouldn't he know that more legions were on the way? As he thought this over, he was distracted by a man stepping into the tent. He appeared to be a common soldier bringing a message for one of the generals but something wasn't right about him. Gavin's sixth sense kicked in and he knew with certainty this was a reader. Had they been trying to fool him into thinking he was safe here but in reality planning something? Whatever it was, he wouldn't have this reader taking his mind if he could help it.

He stepped closer to Gavrus and pointed out the man angrily. "Has the Empire taken to disguising their readers now? I thought I was getting safe passage to talk with you General. What kind of tricks are you playing?"

He watched as Gavrus jerked his head up and yelled to the other soldiers in the tent. Suddenly the tent was in chaos, with several of the soldiers jumping the reader. A soldier, obviously under the

273

control of the reader, stepped toward Gavrus, a knife in his hand. Gavin, who stood closest to Gavrus, jumped forward, grabbed the knife and punched the man in the jaw, knocking him over.

Another soldier saw the knife in Gavin's hand and obviously assuming he was after Gavrus grabbed him and tried to wrestle him to the ground. As Gavin was trying to stay upright he heard Gavrus yell "kill him" and wondered if he was about to die. He shook off the soldier that had grabbed him and was preparing to defend himself with the knife he still held in his hand when he looked over and saw one of the soldiers stab the reader in the heart. His blood began pooling on the ground and except for the sound of harsh breathing coming from many of the men, the tent became ominously quiet.

Amazingly, Gavrus had remained seated throughout the whole confrontation. Gavin watched him, the knife still in his hand, to see what he would do next. "It seems I owe you my life," he said looking at Gavin. "How did you know he was a reader?"

Gavin shrugged, "I have a sixth sense about things. He felt wrong." Gavin was certain now that his life was safe so he handed the knife, hilt first, to a soldier who had been eyeing him nervously. He turned to look straight at Gavrus to gauge his reaction to what he was going to say next. "But I have to ask myself why a general in the Empire would be killing the Empire's readers. We have a saying on Camar; 'the enemies of my enemies are my friends'."

Gavin watched as Gavrus studied him. Once more he noticed him drumming his fingers on his legs. "I'm beginning to think that you and that mass of slaves over the ridge don't really want to fight with me. Am I correct?"

"Do we want to fight? No. Will we fight if we have to? Absolutely," Gavin answered him, deciding it was time to be open and see what they could gain by honesty. "I'd like to ask you the same question and I also wonder if you know that ten legions are coming this way and will be here in as few as two days?" He stood with his arms crossed, daring the general to be honest with him in return.

From the way the generals all looked at each other, he could tell that this was news to them. "Are you certain about this?" Gavrus asked. When Gavin nodded, the expressionless look he had been wearing finally gave way. "Damn it," he said angrily. "You've been frank with me, so I'll return the favor. I've broken with the Empire. They want me dead and I no longer trust them."

"So, will you fight them?"

Gavrus began to pace in the narrow tent. "I'd be a fool to put my five legions against their ten."

Gavin rocked back on his heels, arms still crossed. "What if I could add another forty thousand men to that and thirty battle hardened Northerners."

"Are you the head of that mob that you can offer this?"

"No, but I can arrange for you to meet the heads tomorrow morning, say, one hour after sunrise."

Gavrus looked at his generals and then nodded to Gavin. "Do it."

Shortly after sunrise Gavin, Katya and Smith rode halfway to the legion's camp to wait for Gavrus. With them came the rest of the Northlanders and the essendai. The essarai had offered to heal for any slaves that needed it and had stayed behind in the camp.

Neither Katya nor Smith were happy about this meeting and both thought it unlikely that Gavrus would agree to join forces with them. "He agreed to the meeting, didn't he?" Gavin said as he dismounted and chose a comfortable looking rock to sit on. They were at the base of a small boulder strewn hill, the chosen spot for the meeting. "He doesn't want to meet those ten legions on his own and he has nowhere to hide twenty five thousand men. I won't say he's desperate yet, but in another day he will be." Just then they heard the sound of hoof beats and Gavrus, followed by his personal guard, approached them.

He sat on his horse somewhat arrogantly, waiting for someone to speak. The tension was building as they all stared at each other when Gavin said, "It might be easier to discuss things if you all got off your horses and joined me." Smith gave a snort that could almost be called a laugh and dismounted, followed by Katya and Rolf. Gavrus then got down and they all walked over to stand near Gavin. He introduced them all and not surprisingly, at least to Gavin, Katya was the first to speak.

"Are you really willing to fight alongside the Northerners that you've been trying to exterminate for the last four hundred years?" she asked spitefully.

"So long as they follow my orders and keep their daggers sheathed when my men need to sleep," he answered coldly, to which Katya smiled ruefully.

"So our night raids have been successful."

"If you ever have the guts to come out of your rotting forest and fight with honor we'll be waiting," he challenged.

"Honor!" she spat and would have continued but Rolf came forward and put a heavy hand on her slim shoulder. He glared at Gavrus but at this point Smith decided to join the conversation.

"I'd like to know how well your soldiers will fight next to those that have been slaves. If they're going to treat them as if they're chattel, I want no part in this."

They continued to argue like this until even the stoic Gavrus was red in the face. Before the situation worsened, Gavin decided to step in. "You three can continue to argue but the southern legions will reach us tomorrow and unless one of you has a better idea, I suggest you put aside the past and we try to survive tomorrow."

"I'm willing to try it as long as I'm in charge of the battle plans. I've had the most experience and I won't put my men in harms way trying to follow someone who doesn't know what they're doing," Gavrus said, giving them all a hard stare, particularly Smith.

"How do we know that you won't put the ex-slaves in the worst positions and hold your men back from the fiercest fighting?" Smith wanted to know.

"Because I want to win and that's not the way to do it. I give you my word I'll choose the best plan of attack and follow it."

Katya looked over at the essendai who were waiting by the horses. "Harald," she called. "Is he telling the truth?" Harald walked over to her and stared at Gavrus, reading his thoughts.

"Readers!" Gavrus yelled pulling his sword from its scabbard. His personal guard ran forward to protect him at the same time that Rolf's warriors also ran to protect Harald. Before anyone could strike the first blow at Harald, Gavin stepped in front of him and yelled "Stop!" so forcefully, that to his surprise, everyone did.

"It's not what you think," Gavin said loudly. "They can do the same things as readers but they don't. They're called essendai; they act as judges in the Northlands, using their abilities to tell truth from lies."

Gavrus looked at Gavin in disbelief. "I don't care what you call them, I don't want them near my men," he said angrily.

Harald now spoke. "Use reason general, you know the Empire is going to have readers they'll use against you. You'll need the help of the essendai and the essarai to counter them." Gavrus swore, seeing the truth in his words.

"Fine, but if we do this I want full command. No questioning my orders or any of that bullshit. We engage this army by my rules or you fight them on your own." Gavin looked at both Smith and Katya waiting for their decision. Slowly they nodded in agreement to his terms, Katya being the last to do so.

"Good. Now first I want to know what the hell an essarai is and then I want to know about this legionary force that is approaching." They spent the next several hours putting together a plan that would work for the impending battle.

Chapter 30

Tevarian rubbed his eyes and looked down at the small town of Nightgrove one more time just to make sure it was really there. The last five days seemed a blur in his mind and somehow he had ended up here, back at the hunter's town. He'd been sitting in his room in Jorval in the middle of the night, when the door suddenly opened. Eurik was standing there and tossed him his black reader robes.

"I think its time for you to leave," was all he said, and before Tevarian could say anything he walked away. He had thrown on his robe and quickly tried to follow but he nearly tripped over a long rope placed conveniently next to a window in the hallway. It then became clear to him that Eurik was helping him escape. He hurriedly tied the rope off and scampered down the building. He found a horse tied close by with a bag of food and didn't hesitate. He rode south as quickly as he could and for once the forest didn't hamper his every movement. Somewhere during those five hazy days his powers returned to him but oddly that didn't comfort him at all.

He stood overlooking the town of Nightgrove wondering what he should do. He remembered the old woman's prophecy. *"You must return home; sever the apex and restore the triangle."* The woman's words made no sense. He no longer had a home and who knew what the triangle was. Going back into the Northlands was definitely not an option and going back to the readers would probably get him killed as well. He had little desire to live in the Empire and the idea of trying to live in some remote village seemed cheap after all he had been through. After several minutes of indecision he decided he would need to get supplies from the town anyway and rode down the hill to Nightgrove.

With his black robe the gate guards let him in without question. The town seemed different from what he remembered. It was the tail end of winter now and much of the snow had melted but Tevarian felt colder here than he had at Jorval. It was the people he realized, Jorval's populace had been a friendly active group that had reminded him of his childhood, but here things seemed lifeless. Few people exchanged greetings, the children weren't laughing, the shop keepers were rude, and the only beings in a hurry were the occasional slaves scurrying by so they wouldn't get whipped. Worse, since he was in his robes, everyone shrank back from him in fear. He tied his horse to a post and tried to buy some salted jerky from a stand but the butcher simply backed away. Tevarian sighed and took a few pounds worth and then realized he had nothing to pay the man with anyway.

"I'm sorry, I'm afraid I have no money with me," he said, but this only made the butcher back away further. He turned and gathered more supplies from a few other stands with similar reactions from the shop owners. With his power back their fear radiated off of them like the smell of rotten fruit. He had a sudden wish not to have his powers, to be normal as he had been in the Northlands, but he realized it would never be. Wherever he went, however he dressed, his powers would remain, just like his memories.

He suddenly recalled something Eurik had told him. "You have lived two lives, the life of Tevarian and the life of a reader. One of those lives has a future, the other has much to answer for, yet you are still one man." Tevarian set his supplies on his horse but did not mount it; instead he began leading it towards the center of the town where the hunter compound was situated. Eurik was right, he had lived two lives as one man, and if he did indeed have a future as Tevarian he was going to spend it redeeming the time he had spent as Arius the reader.

He strode towards the center of town and laughed to himself as a suicidal plan came to his mind. He guessed his chances of survival were one in a thousand, but then he had thought his death was imminent before and he had survived. He checked himself once and realized he had no weaponry, so he commandeered a short sword from a nervous guard patrolling the street. As he approached the central compound wall he tried to loosen up his muscles. He had trained very little in the Northlands but at least his swift journey had kept him lean.

The watchers of the compound were hesitant to let him through at first and Tevarian read their minds to discover that they were suspicious of his facial hair. His hood covered the hair he had grown on the top of his head but he had also grown a light beard in his time in the Northlands which was unheard of amongst the readers. He pulled back his hood to reveal his tattoo and they let him pass. He signaled for two men of the watchers to follow him and they came along obediently.

Around the compound he noticed that some of the watchers were using slaves as archery targets while a pair of hunters were essence sparring nearby so they could use the fallen souls to rejuvenate their powers. He presumed the other hunters must be up at the main hall but he made a mental note to remember these two. He walked his horse up to the hall and tied it to a post just as two readers came out of the building to meet him. They reached out to his mind and he allowed them to speak to him.

"I am sub-minister Falx. With whom am I speaking?" Tevarian had not felt another mind against his own for some time and did his best to mask the anxiety inside him.

"I am Brother Arius," he answered as calmly as he could.

"Arius...yes the new reader from Roh Vec. We heard from the legionnaires that you went across the border hunting a heretic. Where are brother Brucus and Hardalio?" he asked.

"I am afraid I am the only survivor, sub-minister," he said bowing his head. *"We were ambushed and I was gravely wounded. They took me prisoner but I escaped four days ago."*

"Prisoner! That is unheard of, how did you manage to escape? Did you learn valuable information?" Falx pressed.

"I have much to tell, but forgive me sub-minister I am feeling rather faint at the moment, could I rest first and then talk to you?" he said, swaying slightly for effect.

"Of course brother, come eat and rest. Then we will discuss your journey."

Tevarian held out his hand and Falx took him by the arm to guide him to the main hall. Tevarian knew it was time to act; he used his other hand to grab his sword and plunged it into the unsuspecting Falx. At the same time he used his power to take control of the watchers behind him and forced them to dispatch the completely stunned hunter next to him. He wasted no time gathering both the reader's souls and absorbing them.

Once again he felt an explosion of power burst through him but this time he was expecting it and quickly harnessed it to his will. He refused to let the Dragas consume him as it had once before, and focused on the task at hand. He could feel several essence readers and well over two dozen watchers and servants in the main hall. Tevarian strode through the door, reached out with his mind, took control of as many watchers as he could and started turning the building into his own small battlefield.

280

The hunter Sylvius bolted up from his chair when he heard a cry of pain outside his window. He reached out with his mind to investigate and quickly recoiled in amazement. There was an unbelievably strong essence reader entering the building. He was on the second floor and decided to go down and meet this reader when a serving woman ran at him with a knife. He barely blocked her clumsy stab and upon touching her he felt her mind and discovered she was being controlled by the reader. He heard a commotion and cries coming from downstairs and realized that the reader was controlling all the servants against the hunters.

He quickly killed the servant woman and absorbed her essence for extra strength. He grabbed a sword and his bow and rushed downstairs to a scene of chaos. The few hunters were outnumbered three to one by servants and watchers that attacked without fear. Already several of his brothers were dead or dying. The enemy reader was standing near the door simply controlling the carnage with his mind. He watched one of his brothers fall to a watcher's blade and the intruder pulled his bright essence towards him. Sylvius expected him to drop dead when he absorbed it but instead he appeared to get stronger.

Before he could wonder how that was possible he felt the reader attack. The power on his mind was overwhelming and he realized he only had a few seconds before he was as good as dead. He quickly notched an arrow in his bow and fired from across the room. The reader dropped to the ground and Sylvius fell to his knees as the pressure against his mind stopped. He hadn't realized just how close he had been to losing control. He saw the reader stir and knew that he might continue his mental assault any second. He reached for another arrow but found the quiver empty. He looked about frantically for something to throw but couldn't find anything appropriate. It was then that he saw the essence leaving one of his fellow hunters. In a split second he decided that his only chance to match the strength of the intruder was to duplicate his actions. Sylvius pulled the bright essence towards him just as the enemy reader sat up.

The power flowing through him was unlike anything he had ever experienced, he couldn't understand what was happening around him and by the time he was lucid again, the enemy reader was staggering out the door. The few remaining watchers stood completely dumfounded and Sylvius realized he was the only hunter left in the building. He picked himself up intent on killing the one who did this, but realized he needed more power to do so. A great hunger overcame him and he had every surviving person in the area kill themselves. He took in their souls but it wasn't enough to satisfy him, he needed more.

He strode out into the daylight and saw the enemy reader riding out of the compound gate. He quickly headed for the stable to get his own horse, when a pair of his fellow hunters, along with a handful of watchers, came up from the field.

"Brother Sylvius we heard shouts, is everything ok? Who was that reader that left in such a hurry?" one of the hunters asked aloud. Sylvius cared little for what his comrade was saying and took control of the watchers surrounding the two hunters. He had them kill each one quickly with their blades and then made them kill each other. He took all of their souls and gathered them to himself. Now he could kill the reader, he thought, and he wouldn't even need a weapon. But why stop there? Nightgrove had over one-hundred people living in it; he could use them as well to increase his power. He grinned as he mounted his horse, he could give the reader a slight head start. After all, he reminded himself, sometimes the longest hunts were the best ones. He rode up into the town laughing.

Lily and the Northerners riding with her had come out of the trees yesterday. They were riding through the low foot hills of Trost still following her instincts. She didn't understand this bond she had with Tevarian but she knew that she was leading the others in the right direction. They had been riding for five days now, and she never once questioned that they were still on his trail.

She stopped at the top of a small rise to look out over the landscape in front of her. Small copses of trees could be seen here and there but mainly she saw grassland, as far as the eye could see. The two essendai that rode beside her also stopped, looking at her for direction. She knew that though they followed her as their guide, they would be the ones who decided Tevarian's fate, not her. That Katya didn't trust her to kill him was obvious, and despite Eurik's instructions to try and bring him back alive Lily knew that Edyth, the other essarai with them, had probably been told to take his life. Why else would another essarai have come along? In fact, Lily suspected that everyone with her had been told to kill Tevarian, including the five warriors that had come with them as protection from the predators that lived in the forest.

Some feeling inside her kept her sitting on the hill, watching. Suddenly she saw a horse come out of a grove of trees just a hundred yards ahead. A man wearing the black robes of a reader was bent over the horse's neck, heading straight toward them. The horse was moving erratically, the reins dangling loose and as she watched, the rider slowly slid off and landed on the ground. She knew immediately that it was Tevarian although she couldn't see his face. As she started to urge her horse forward, one of the essendai near her told her to wait. He pointed at the same grove of trees and she saw that another man on horseback was following him. He also was wearing the black robe of the readers.

The reader had drawn his sword and was now riding straight for Tevarian as he lay on the ground. Lily, heedless of her own safety, shouted "No!" and rode straight toward them. She could hear the others riding behind her and saw that the reader had also heard them. He had stopped before reaching Tevarian and was staring at the group of men behind her. She heard the horses neighing and the men shouting and when she looked around she could hardly believe her eyes. The Northmen were fighting each other, one of the essendai lay dead on the ground and the other was fighting off three of the warriors. As she watched he lost the fight and slid bleeding from his horse, an axe in his chest. The warriors now started battling each other and within minutes they all lay dead or dying on the ground.

Lily stared horrified at the scene that played out before her. Edyth had stayed off to the side during the conflict and now rode quickly over to Lily. "We must both ride toward him, you distract him and I'll kill him." She took off quickly as Lily kicked her horse to follow. As they drew nearer she saw what neither of them had seen before. The reader had drawn a bow and was aiming at Edyth, who was in the lead. As Lily shouted a warning Edyth swerved her horse and the arrow missed her. The reader had already set another arrow to his bow before they could reach him, though, and this one struck Edyth directly in the chest. Lily was so close now that she did the first thing she could think of and simply grabbed the man, knocking them both off their horses. She landed on top of him, and they were both stunned for a moment. She grabbed for his neck, putting her hands on his bare skin. He looked into her eyes, startled, as if he recognized her and hissed, "You." She knew she had only seconds before he would overpower her so she grabbed at his essence hard and fast. The power that filled her was overwhelming, like nothing she had ever experienced before, not even when she had taken Tevarian's powers. She held on, tightening her grip, refusing to let go even when she was certain that he must be dead. It was nothing like the feeling she got when she gently took someone's essence to replenish her own. That was almost a warm feeling as it settled into your own body. This was like falling off a cliff, the air rushing at you at incredible speeds, the power filling her so quickly that she thought she might explode with it. If she hadn't already been sitting on the ground, she would have fallen.

When she finally removed her hand from the reader, she looked around her at the carnage that he had caused. Edyth's body was not far from her, an arrow protruding from her heart, and she could see the bodies of all the Northlander's tumbled together on the low hill they had ridden down. So many had died today. She looked down at the reader and the realization hit her that she had just killed a man. Her hands started to shake as she dropped her head to her knees and wept.

Chapter 31

Gavrus took a few calming breaths and enjoyed a brief moment of privacy. There was always uneasiness before a battle, but this time was different. This time there was more at stake, but even worse than that was his lack of confidence in the men under him. Nearly two thirds of his army was nothing more than rabble which left his legions facing two to one odds. He heard the flap of the tent lift and turned to see Titus enter.

"They're here General." Gavrus grabbed his sword and belted it around his waist. Titus helped him put on his breast plate and he strapped on his helmet. Battles are not always won by the numbers he reminded himself and followed Titus out into the crisp dawn air. His tent was surrounded by tall trees that blocked the morning sun but it was still light enough for him to see his legionnaires concealed in the nearby forest. They had scraped the red paint from their shields and dirtied their red leather as best they could so that the slaves could distinguish friendly legionnaires from enemy ones.

Decmitius and Luscar were waiting for him and after Titus brought his horse they began to ride out of the woods accompanied only by his personal guard. For a while they rode in silence but eventually Decmitius spoke.

"I give us one chance in three."

"You haven't seen our foes yet," Luscar pointed out. "How can you make predictions?"

"Our enemy's force is comprised entirely of legionnaires, compared with only one third of our forces. Therefore our chances of victory, is one in three," Decmitius explained. Luscar was going to respond but Gavrus held up his hand.

"The plan will work," he said, wishing he felt as confident as he sounded. "I'm more concerned about what happens after our victory. Both of you will need to have the legions ready in case the slaves decide to betray us." Both men nodded and they continued the ride in silence. After a few moments they came out of the woods into a vast clearing. The slaves stood nervously amongst a few tents and wagons. Their leader, Smith, along with Gavin and Katya, approached him. Katya was scowling at him and Gavrus awaited some cynical comment that had become typical from her over the last two days, but it was Smith who spoke first.

"They're coming just as you said they would." Gavrus noticed that Smith's voice was slightly edgy and he hoped he could rely on a man who had never been in a large scale battle before. Gavrus quickly surveyed the field he had chosen for the battle. The Empire's legions were approaching from the south on a gradual incline; giving his forces a slight advantage while not being so inconvenient as to make the Empire reconsider its attack. They were coming as he expected they would; six of the enemy's ten legions were approaching in a wide line while four stayed in reserve. The slaves were positioned with their backs against a forest that allowed him to keep his legions hidden from the enemy's view.

"Is everything prepared?" he asked Smith, who nodded.

"Just be sure your legions don't take too long," Katya said coldly. Gavrus bit back a comment of his own but Gavin interjected on his behalf.

"The plan is sound, we've been preparing for two days Katya, everything will work." Her expression of distrust didn't change.

"I still don't understand why we don't retreat until my people arrive," she said.

"We don't have the supplies, and there isn't exactly an abundance of farms to the north of us," Gavrus said shaking his head; he swore it was the tenth time he had told her that since they had devised the plan.

Katya snorted and rode off to join the few essendai and essarai with her. Gavrus knew they would have a hard role to play countering any enemy readers from the Empire. He looked at the enemy forces, trying to gauge when they would arrive and turned to his two generals.

"Get the legions up and ready, keep them out of sight until you receive my signal." Both men nodded and rode back into the woods.

Everything was ready and Gavrus waited anxiously with the others as the legions slowly approached. He watched the slaves around him and saw a few standing with grim determination but most had fear in their eyes. It infuriated him that the lives of his soldiers depended on the slaves' will to stay and fight. He wondered how many had truly wanted their freedom, and how many were just following along. Today they were facing a tiger he realized, just as he had, and if they won they would earn their freedom.

The enemy was getting close now and Gavrus could hear the sound of the legion flutes playing on the light breeze. He gave Smith a nod and the slaves' leader rode off towards the right side of the front line. Orders were given and groups of women quickly circled around the many tents that were intermixed with the slave crowd.

"Archers!" came the cry and what few bowmen there were in the force quickly moved towards the front. Anyone who had seen the Empire fight knew that bows were not a very effective weapon against a well trained legion. Each of the six enemy legions quickly huddled into a tight formation and lifted their large rectangular shields over their heads. Their shields overlapped one another forming a protective roof resistant to arrows but that was exactly what Gavrus was waiting for. He nodded to one his guards behind him and the man blew a long note on a cattle horn.

All through the slave army the women circling the tents began to tear them down with tenacious speed. Underneath each cloth was a crudely constructed catapult. Over the last two days Gavrus had had many of the slaves and legionnaires building as many of these machines as he could. It had taken every cord of rope they had and started more than a few fights between legionnaires and slaves but in the end they built nearly four hundred of them. Had they had the resources, he could have had them lob clay pots filled with burning oil but as it was they had to make do with rocks picked from the field. They were only slightly bigger than his head but that was big enough.

Gavrus watched grimly as four hundred stones flew through the air and crashed into the tightly compacted legions. Shields cracked with the impact and men cried out as their comrades were crushed. Some of the rocks landed short but bounced forward breaking shins and ankles. Gavrus turned to the right where the slope was steepest to see Smith and his best men push forward a couple dozen boulders about waist height. They had spent the last two days trying to chip them into a spherical shape so they would roll properly. They started slow but had built up enough speed by the time they reached the rightmost legion. The effect was devastating, legionnaires tried to dodge the rolling boulders only to crash into their own comrades. Gavrus nodded to his guard with the horn and the man blew another long blast.

The slaves gave a great roar and charged, clearly heartened by seeing the legions battered by the artillery fire. Gavrus had told Smith to put his best warriors on the right, in hopes of collapsing the enemy line from one side. The legion there was completely out of formation due to the boulders, when Smith and his men hit them. The legions' weapons were designed for formation combat but their big shields and short swords were awkward in single combat. Gavrus could tell that Smith and his men were having the best of the fighting, but the rest of the battle line was not nearly as fortunate. Within minutes the other five legions began to push the slaves back despite the sloped ground and the catapult barrage. Gavin, who was still next to him, gave him a look of worry and impatience.

"Not yet," Gavrus said but Gavin still looked worried. After a few more minutes Gavrus judged that the time was right. He turned around and waved his hand to the trees, instantly legionnaires began pouring out. They quickly formed into their five groups and Gavrus dismounted to join them.

"Decmitius you and the fifty-fourth take the left," he shouted giving his best soldiers the toughest of the fighting. "Luscar take your legion to the right, we need to break their line quickly. The rest of you with me in the center of the line." He turned and started forward and the legions quickly followed. Titus and his personal guard formed around him and he left Gavin sitting on his horse with a nod.

Gavrus felt the familiar stomach sickness he always got before he faced death and did his best to quell it. The slaves were trying to make gaps so his legions could get through but they weren't trained soldiers and it took a while for him to get to the fighting.

It was strange to see red legionnaire shields and have them be his enemies but he wasted no time in charging at them. He kept his shield in front of him and threw all his weight behind it. To his right and left hundreds of his legionnaires did the same thing so both sides began a pushing war with their large square shields. Gavrus jabbed out with his short sword wounding the soldier in front of him and then pushed forward and knocked him to the ground. He was trampled on as his legions pressed forward.

As time passed he grew exhausted, his sword arm grew tired and it was a struggle to use his sword. He struck out clumsily and a legionnaire to his right slashed at his exposed side. He deflected the blow but the sword fell across his wrist cutting through his arm guard. He cried out in pain and was yanked back from behind before the legionnaire could strike at him again. It was Titus who had grabbed him.

"Sir you're wounded, fall back, you're no good to the army dead!" he shouted. Gavrus cursed in pain and anger but fell back through the ranks. One of his men quickly bandaged his arm and brought him his horse. Once he was up and mounted he could see how the battle was fairing. His legions were turning the tide, they had height advantage and with the slaves behind them they had the weight in numbers. The flanks were particularly strong, both Decmitius on the left and Luscar on the right were pressing hard. The slaves supported his legions with short range weapons where they could but most threw stones and javelins from behind his lines into the enemy's ranks. He hoped that none were hitting his own men.

What worried him most were the four enemy legions still in reserve. They had made no move to come aid their comrades in battle and Gavrus knew that they would still be fresh when they came to the front. They were also stopping him from using his last strategic move and he looked back worriedly at Gavin sitting alone on his horse. He needed to warn him to be careful but just then the rout began. It happened on the already weakened right side of the enemy line. Enemy legionnaires began to turn and run, and slowly the infection spread to the center and left of the battle line.

Gavrus quickly waved to Gavin who whistled loudly and began riding forward. Out of the forest a few hundred horsemen followed him. They were comprised of volunteer legionnaires and slaves and the few enormous Northmen. Gavrus had originally wanted one his men to lead the cavalry group but Smith would have nothing of it since most of the horses were from the escaped slaves. Gavin had been the compromised commander they could both agree upon and now Gavrus hoped he had enough common sense to not kill all of their horses.

Gavin and the cavalry wrapped around to the left of the battle and cut back quickly to hit the retreating enemy from the side. There was only three or four hundred yards that the Empire's soldiers had to traverse to reach the reserve legions but it proved to be a difficult crossing. The legionnaires became scattered individuals as they ran and made easy targets for the swift cavalry. Gavrus wished he could have given Gavin more horses but his few hundred mounted men still managed to trample, maim, or kill over a thousand of the enemy with little to no loss of men.

As this was happening, however, the slaves saw the enemy retreat and they charged forward in pursuit of the enemy legionnaires. Gavrus immediately recognized the danger they were putting themselves in. "Hold the line!" he shouted. His legions responded and formed into square formations but only some of the slaves heard him. Where was Smith, he wondered and tried desperately to get the slaves to turn around before it was too late.

The four enemy legions in reserve made gaps in their formations to allow their comrades to retreat behind them and then began to march forward. Gavin's cavalry pursued the enemy all the way to the enemy line and then using the speed of their horses quickly turned away from the advancing legions. Unfortunately they turned straight into the mass of slaves who were still trying to pursue the enemy. Pandemonium ensued as the retreating horses ran into their charging allies, knocking men to the ground and stopping both forces in their tracks. It was then that the four enemy legions charged into the confused masses inflicting heavy casualties. Gavrus could see Gavin frantically trying to get the slaves to retreat in good order but it was quickly becoming a rout.

"Damn it!" He analyzed the situation and realized that the slaves would come retreating straight back into his men. He had his legions space out widely, leaving large gaps in between each unit so that the slaves could retreat behind his line. He had his men advance and fortunately the slaves began retreating through his lines without incident. He spotted Gavin riding through and waved him over.

"Where the hell is Smith?" he demanded.

"I was going to ask you the same thing," Gavin shouted back.

"Fine, you're in charge of this rabble then," he said pointing to the slaves pouring through his legionnaires. "I want them split into two equal groups and sent to our flanks as soon as possible, understand?" Gavin nodded and quickly rode off. Gavrus turned to see his legions engage the approaching enemy. His men were more experienced but they were also tired from fighting and he knew victory wouldn't be easy unless something changed. He waited impatiently for the slaves to return to the battle and noticed that the enemy legions that had fled were turning now as well and coming back to the battlefield. Gavin had finally managed to rally the slaves and they returned to the battle line just as the enemy legionnaires did. Gavrus feared that they would break again once they got into the fray but Gavin had had them pick up shields and weapons from the fallen legionnaires so they were better equipped to stand and fight. Gavrus made a mental note that Gavin was a reliable man, worthy of command if he survived the day.

Both sides now had all of their soldiers in the wide battle line and Gavrus's mind raced for some possible option that could grant him a quick victory but he could think of nothing. Even with his wounded arm he felt the need to join his men in battle but before he could Katya rode up to him.

"We killed two readers but it seems the rest have fled. I think they know our victory is inevitable."

"Victory," he scoffed, "this is no victory; just a useless waste of life." She looked at him sharply.

"Can't you see we're winning, we have more spirit than they do." He had noticed that the Empire's soldiers were slowly losing ground but he knew it wasn't fast enough.

"When they finally break it will be too late," he said sadly. "There won't be enough of us to continue."

"My Northlanders will come," she said but he thought she sounded uncertain.

"I don't know how many barbarians you have hidden up in that frozen waste, but there are at least three more armies this size in the Empire," he said. Katya was silent and he knew whatever forces she had were not substantial enough to overcome such strength. "In the grand scheme, this is nothing more than a little spit on the Emperor's boots."

"Is there nothing else we can do?' she asked.

He shook his head, "Stalemates are like virgins; they're tight, move slowly, and there's blood everywhere." He laughed at the look of pure disgust she gave him. He drew his sword and began to advance to fight with his men.

"Wait!" Katya cried out, "look!" He looked to where she was pointing and saw a large group of soldiers coming over the side of the hill not but half a mile behind the enemy lines. In a few moments he could make out the red shields of Empire legionnaires. There were at least three legions of them approaching at a jog; he suspected they would reach the battle in less than five minutes. The enemy could see the legions as well and were greatly heartened by the coming reinforcements. They began to fight with new vigor and his men began to give ground. His mind went numb as he saw his certain defeat, he had never lost a battle before and the idea gave him a bad taste in his mouth. Where had the additional legions come from he wondered?

He turned to see Gavin ride up. "Should we retreat?" Gavin asked

"Where to?" he answered derisively.

"We could go north and meet with my warriors," Katya offered.

"Forget it. We only have rations for two days and your armies couldn't feed us. Besides we move too slowly to escape anyway. No, we'll make our stand here." With that he rode forward to the battle line.

He was about to dismount when a sudden suspicion overcame him. Three legions, the exact number he had left with Jacobo on Camar. Was it possible that he had gotten his letter and could have already made it here? He looked for the man carrying his standard and took it from him. He held it as high as he could from atop his horse and waved it about. It took a few moments but a single horseman rode before the three jogging legions and waved a banner in return. Gavrus could just make out the dark skin on the man's face. "It's Jacobo!" he shouted for all to hear, "the legions are ours!" He was elated and his mood quickly spread to his men. They began to chant 'Jacobo' and once again the tide turned in favor of his soldiers. The slaves joined in and the enemy slowly began to understand that the legions behind them were not their allies.

Jacobo's legions were still a full minute away when the Empire's soldiers began to turn and flee. His exhausted soldiers gave a great cry and pursued them as far as they could but it was Jacobo's troops that did the most damage as the Empire's soldiers tried to flee around them. Gavrus couldn't believe his luck, perhaps there was hope for this rebellion after all, he thought.

Hours later the wounded were still being carried to the women who hadn't participated in the battle. Katya and her healers were busy and Gavrus sat at a fire with his generals. His men were exhausted and lay about the field and though food was running short Gavrus didn't have the heart to send out hunting parties.

"Took your time getting here," he said to Jacobo through a mouthful of dry bread.

"Actually I didn't even want to come; it was the soldiers' idea."

"Is that so?"

"Yeah, I only tagged along when I heard you had women marching with your army," he said eyeing some of the slave women who were passing out rations. Everyone laughed, except Decmitius who remained as serious as ever.

"I don't know why you're laughing; things could have been a lot worse today if your legions hadn't shown up," Decmitius said but for some reason this only made them laugh all the harder. Jacobo eventually grew somber and spoke seriously.

"They brought a reader from the Empire, they tried to use me to control the men, but we managed to spread the word of your rebellion before he arrived. My men swarmed the reader and rescued me. We started for Trost as soon as we could but a storm held us from crossing the channel for a day."

"That storm had impeccable timing then," Gavrus said. "Had you arrived a day before, enemy legions may not have engaged us and we may have fought a very different battle." He turned to Luscar, "How many men have we lost?" Luscar had been wounded by a blade to the ribs and he sat very still as he spoke.

"Too soon to tell, but I would venture almost ten thousand of our own men and probably twice that of the slaves." All was silent as they digested this and Gavrus was startled when he saw Smith and Gavin approach. Smith's bald head was covered in dry blood and Gavrus suspected that one of Katya's healers had tended to him since he saw no bandages covering a wound.

"So, what now?" Smith asked bluntly.

"Now we go south to Nazbar. It's the only viable option for finding the supplies I need to keep my army intact." Gavrus waited for Smith to speak but it was Decmitius who spoke up next.

"And what of the slaves?" he asked rudely, acting as if Smith and Gavin didn't even exist. Both Gavrus and Smith knew that his legions had the strength to defeat the slave force but Gavrus also knew that he needed every man he could get, so he chose his next words very carefully.

"Smith's people fought for their freedom today and they earned it. They are no longer slaves and I would gladly welcome their support as I march south." He held his breath as he waited for Smith to respond. He wanted the extra man power but Smith had to follow his orders if this rebellion was going to work.

Smith looked him in the eyes before he spoke. "To Nazbar then," he said simply and walked away.

Chapter 32

Lily only gave herself a moment to grieve before she wiped her eyes quickly and realized that she should check to see if anyone had survived. She silently chastised herself for even waiting this long and hurried over to the warriors. She went among them but it quickly became obvious that she alone was alive. She almost gave in to despair when suddenly she remembered Tevarian. He had fallen from his horse a short distance away from where the fighting had occurred and with everything happening so quickly she'd forgotten him. She hurried over to find him flat on his face in the long grass, an arrow protruding from his side. She gently turned him over, expecting the worse, and was amazed to see that he still breathed.

The arrow had broken when he fell from his horse making it easy for Lily to pull it out. Sliding her hand under his shirt she quickly placed it over the wound and healed him. He moaned and tried to move but she pushed her hand against his chest to hold him still, looking him over carefully for more wounds. She brushed his hair back from his forehead, quietly telling him to lie still. As she moved his hair she saw the tattoo, a triangle with a book in its center. A black book. Joan's words suddenly came to mind. *"You will find what you are seeking to the north; you must follow the black book."* Could this be the black book she meant? True, she had found her mother in the north but she had also found Tevarian. Was she supposed to follow him?

She still had her hand in Tevarian's hair and was staring at the tattoo when he opened his eyes. He blinked, looking surprised to find Lily with him. "What happened?" he asked her weakly.

"We've been searching for you. You were being chased by that reader," she said and pointed to the reader's body lying nearby. "He took control of everyone with me and had them kill each other." She swallowed, trying not to cry again, before she could continue, "then he shot Edyth with his bow." Her voice broke and she was barely able to whisper, "I killed him; I drained him of all his power." She wrapped her arms about herself and shuddered.

Tevarian hadn't moved as she told him the story. He lay still, the tattoo showing clearly against his pale forehead. Lily stared at the black book. "What does the tattoo on your forehead mean?" she asked him.

Her question appeared to catch him off guard but he answered her without hesitation. "The book represents the book of essence which contains the rules a reader is supposed to live by. The three points of the triangle represent the Emperor, his hierarchy and the readers. The Emperor, of course, stands at the apex of the triangle." He stopped speaking, a look of surprise appearing on his face. "The apex, of course, the apex of the triangle." Now he gave a small unwelcome laugh. "That must be what she meant," he muttered quietly.

Lily saw that Tevarian was trying to sit up and reached out to help him. He looked slightly uncomfortable as she took his hand, but let her help him to sit. "Where were you going?" she asked him.

"I didn't know, but I do now." He stood and then after a moment's hesitation he reached out his hand to help Lily up. He walked to where his horse stood cropping the grass. Grabbing the reins he led the horse back to where Lily was standing. "I'm going to Roh Vec," he said abruptly. He checked the tightness of the saddle and grabbed the pommel in readiness to mount, then hesitated as he looked at Lily, "At least that's what I want to do but now that you're here, what are you going to do with me?"

She answered him with the truth, surprised that he had asked. "I'm supposed to either kill you or bring you back to the Northlands."

"Which will you do?"

Lily honestly had no idea how to answer him and was surprised that he took what she told him so calmly. "I think right now that we need to burn the bodies of the dead. I'm not sure after that. Will you help me?"

"Do you really think we need to? I'm sure the wild animals will take care of them eventually," he said callously.

Lily felt a little sick at the thought of that. "No, we need to burn them and I need your help to do it."

Tevarian shrugged but helped her. It took them most of the morning to find enough dry wood to make a bonfire and move all the bodies on it. Lily didn't want to include the body of the reader with the Northerners but also didn't like the thought of leaving him to be eaten by animals. In the end they put him on the bonfire too.

While they worked Tevarian asked Lily how they had found him. "It was the bond we share," she said. "They call it the Drasana, it only happens between essendai and essarai. Apparently it formed when you attacked me and I took your power. When I thought of you, I knew which direction to go. It led me straight here."

He stared at her a moment but said no more about it, leaving Lily wondering what he thought about the bond and her.

It was late afternoon by the time the fire had burned down enough that they felt it was safe to leave it. Lily had watched the bodies burn and said a silent prayer to the Maker. She had spent much of the afternoon trying to figure out what she should do next. She knew Eurik should be told what had happened but she didn't like the thought of traveling the five days back to Jorval alone and even if he would come with her, Tevarian couldn't return or she was sure they would kill him. Gavin was gone and she had no idea where to find him. And then there was Joan's prophecy about following the black book. Was she supposed to follow Tevarian to Roh Vec?

They had gathered the few horses that hadn't run off and each mounted one and Lily still hadn't decided what to do. When Tevarian turned his horse to the southeast, she rode behind him without a word spoken. He seemed to accept her presence as if she belonged there or maybe, she thought, he hadn't even noticed that she was with him. He seemed lost in his own world, preoccupied with something.

She urged her horse forward until she rode beside him. Tevarian looked over at her as she came alongside and said simply, "Thank you."

"For what?" she asked him, puzzled by his words.

"For saving my life."

She accepted his thanks without comment. She didn't know if it was his words, their bond, or Joan's prophecy, but suddenly she knew what she was going to do. If, however, she was going to ride all the way to Roh Vec with him it was time she got some answers. "What are we going to do in Roh Vec, Tevarian?"

He seemed to accept her choice of the word *we* without a problem as he looked at her and said, "The only thing we can do. We're going to kill the Emperor."

Here ends Book one of the Drasana series. Book two, entitled Essendai, finds Lily and Tevarian traveling to Roh Vec in search of the Emperor and Gavrus continuing his fight against the Empire with the help of Gavin and the Northlanders.

To find out more about the authors and their books, check out their website at fuchsd5.wix.com/headsortales.

Made in the USA
Middletown, DE
29 June 2015